X-VENTURE XPLORERS™
KINGDOM OF ANIMALS

LION KING

PAPERCUTZ™

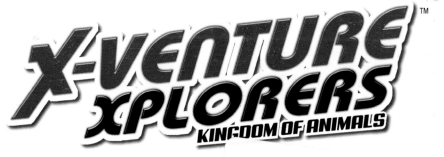

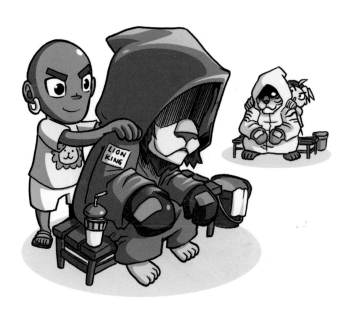

X-VENTURE XPLORERS™
KINGDOM OF ANIMALS

#1 RAGE OF THE KINGS

SLAIUM / MENG — Story
BLACK INK TEAM — Art
BLACK INK TEAM — Cover Illustration
KOK CHUN / PUPPETEER — Illustrator
EVA / MAX / YUUZU / FUNFUN / KC / SIEW — Coloring
KIAT — Translator

KENNY CHUA — Creative Director
KIAONG — Art Director
BEAN — Original Graphic & Layout

MARK McNABB — Editor & Production
NIUH JIT ENG / ROSS BAUER — Original Editor
JEFF WHITMAN — Managing Editor
ERIC STORMS — Editorial Intern
JIM SALICRUP
Editor-in-Chief

Papercutz books may be purchased for business or promotional use.
For information on bulk purchase please contact Macmillan
Corporate and Premium Sales Department at (800) 221-7945 x5442.

ISBN HC: 978-1-5458-0549-7
ISBN PB: 978-1-5458-0550-3

Printed in Malaysia by Ultimate Print Sdn. Bhd.
October 2020

Distributed by Macmillan
First Papercutz Printing

X-VENTURE XPLORERS™

KINGDOM OF ANIMALS

#1 RAGE OF THE KINGS

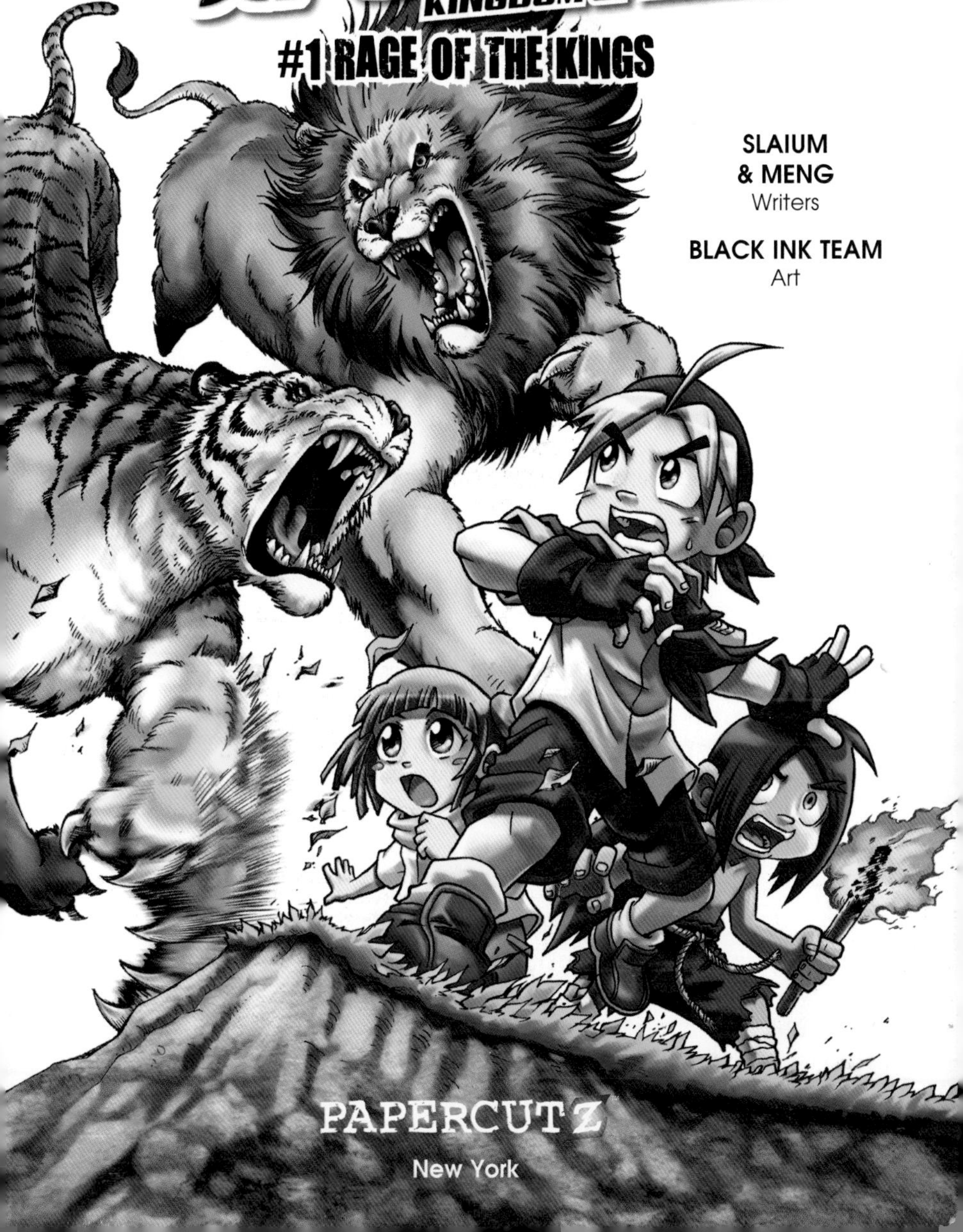

SLAIUM & MENG
Writers

BLACK INK TEAM
Art

PAPERCUTZ
New York

FOREWORD

As a result of their entry into the educational sphere in recent years, the perception of comics as frivolous and fantastical fiction has slowly been changing. For students, the partnership of words and pictures has been reported to enhance information retention, and consequently comics are having an increasingly important role in the learning process. Educational comics have become a source of extra-curricular knowledge; harnessing young learners' enthusiasm for well-visualized and creative stories which simultaneously convey comprehensible information.

X-VENTURE XPLORERS pits animal antagonists against each other. Battles between beasts of similar strength such as Lion Vs. Tiger, Elephant Vs. Rhinoceros, Boa Vs. Crocodile and so forth not only offer young readers the joy of books, but also a starting point to enjoy learning about the natural world.

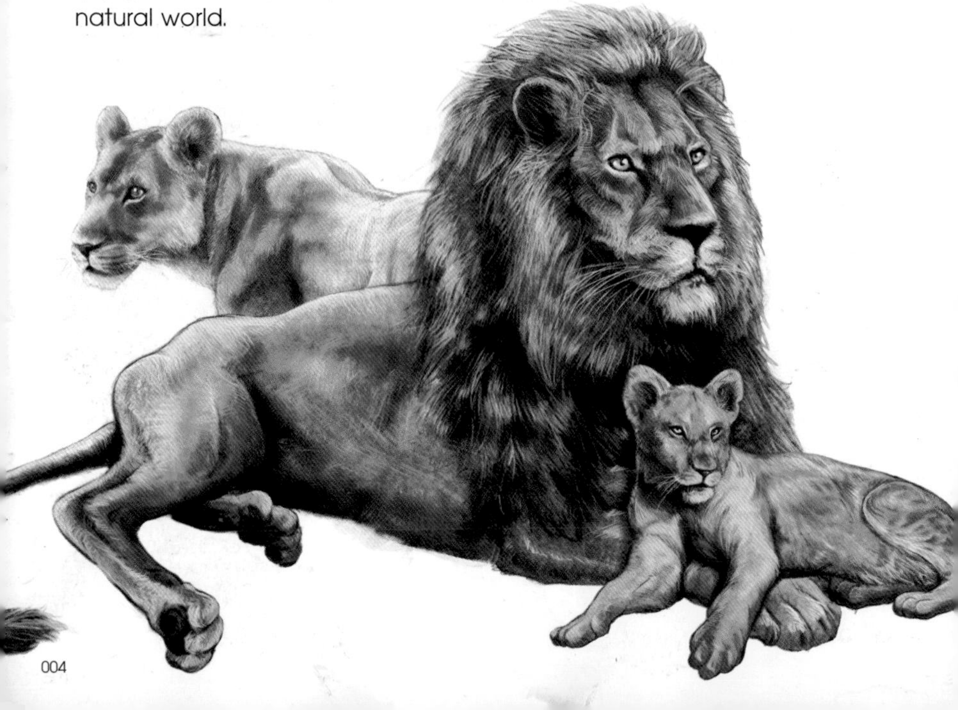

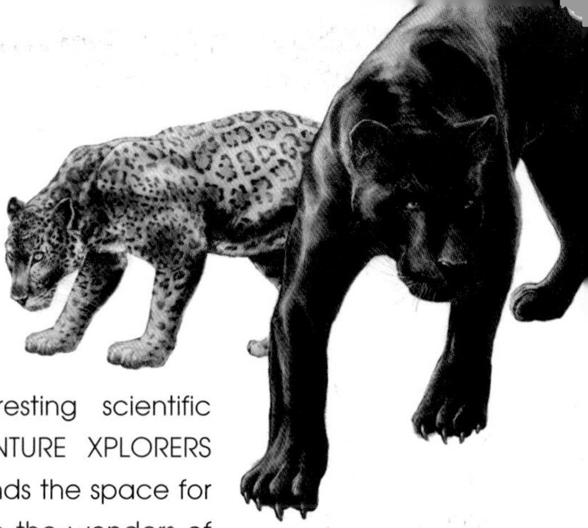

Upholding the principle of interesting scientific knowledge central to any X-VENTURE XPLORERS comic series, we provide young minds the space for imagination and help them explore the wonders of natural science. As an educational comic, this series prioritizes the moral values of love and friendship, courage and the joy of learning so as to help nurture the right values in our readers.

Incisive information alongside vivid visuals, interspersing story chapters provide readers with ample and accessible knowledge of wildlife and their world. Additionally, to gauge what they have learned, they can test their wits by answering a short quiz on what they have read. With equal emphasis on entertainment and education, it ought to be clear that X-VENTURE XPLORERS power represents financial value, fun and furnishes a fecund factual future for our formative friends!

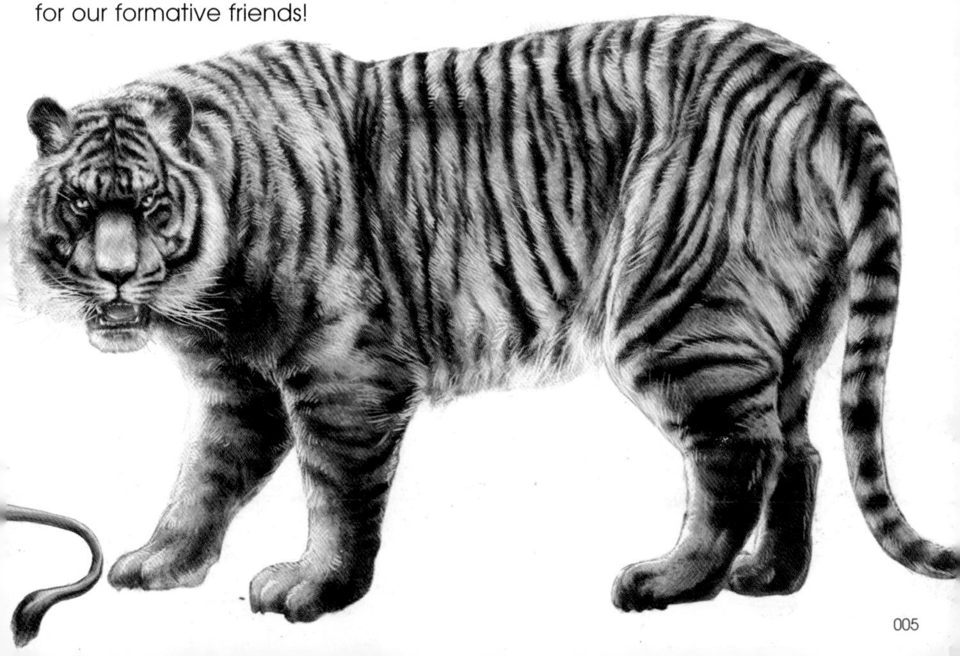

CAST

SHERRY

Hardworking and a keen learner, she wishes to become a veterinarian. She assumes the role of peacemaker, especially between Jake and Louis who argue constantly.

JAKE

Brave and passionate, he enjoys the company of animals and is proud of being a boy scout. He is often careless, however, causing trouble for himself and his friends.

TAZEN

A little native with a huge appetite who grew up in the Sumatran rainforest, raised by orangutans. Has the ability to communicate with animals, but finds humans a harder prospect.

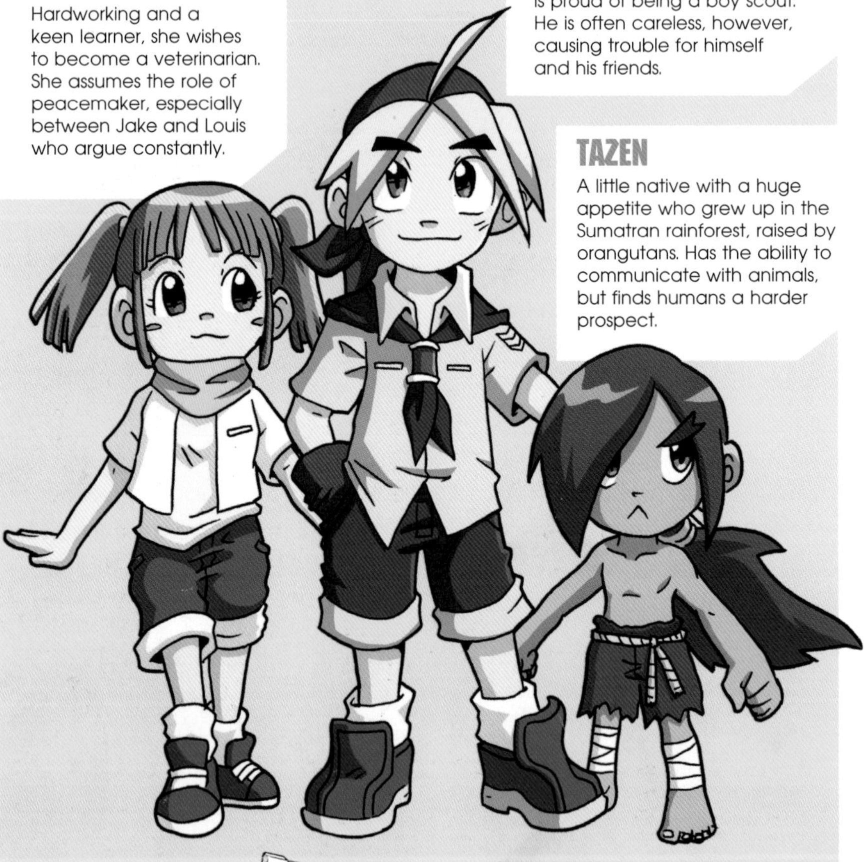

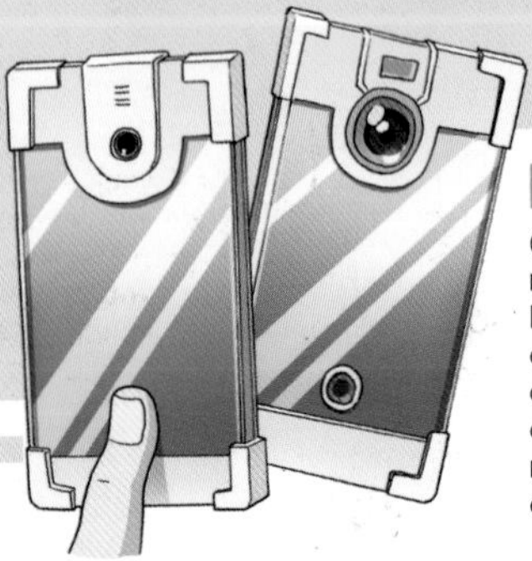

NLIZR

(Natural Life Zoographic Resource, more commonly known as "the analyzer") Dr. Darwin's e-evolution in evidence; able to record, analyze, extrapolate details pertaining to localized ecology, climate, lifeform identification and much more via an instant uplink to the lab database.

LOUIS

Despite being loud, lazy, and constantly antagonizing Jake, he never accepts failure and is a very reliable partner during a crisis.

KWAME

A member of the Bushmen tribe of South Africa, he knows the wild like the back of his hand, constantly on the alert for potential threats, both animal and otherwise.

BEAN

Shy and quiet, and short in stature, makes up in extraordinary wealth of knowledge what he lacks in physical size.

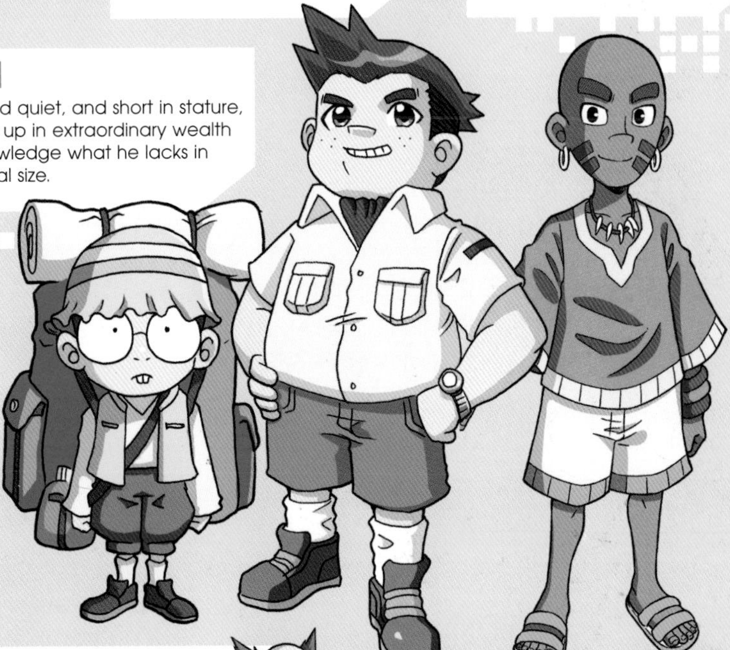

DR. DARWIN

A renowned authority in the fields of biology and zoology, who remains in impeccable physical shape, despite his age, with a flair for the dramatic. Harsh but generous, he demands focus and discipline from the X-Venture team at all times, or else!

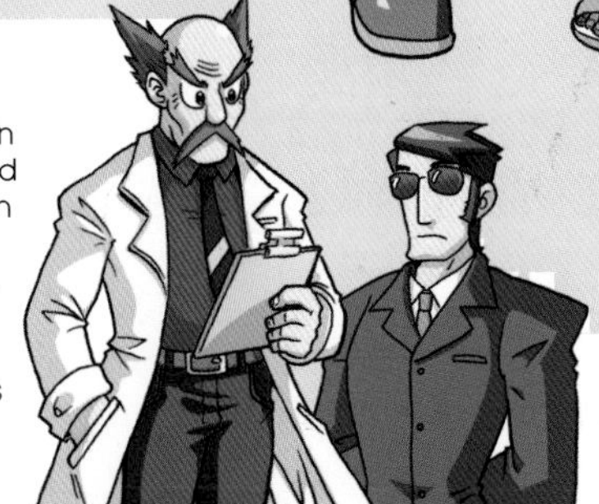

SMITH

Dr. Darwin's faithful assistant's dedicated diligence to his duties does him no favors when facing the ripping rages of his buff boss!

CONTENTS

*Some animal sizes have been altered to make the comics as visually dramatic and exciting as possible

CHAPTER 1

SEEKING THE KING!

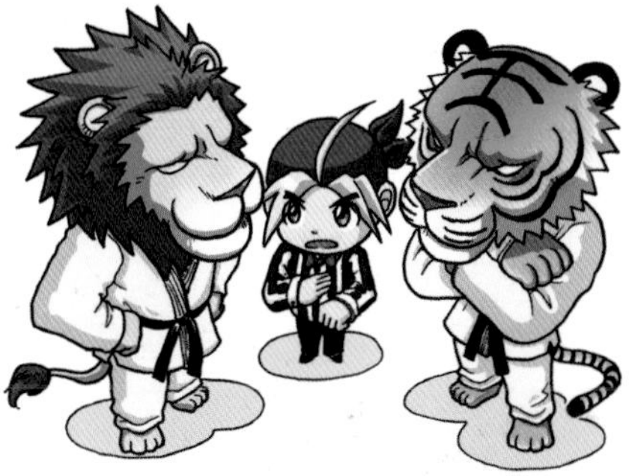

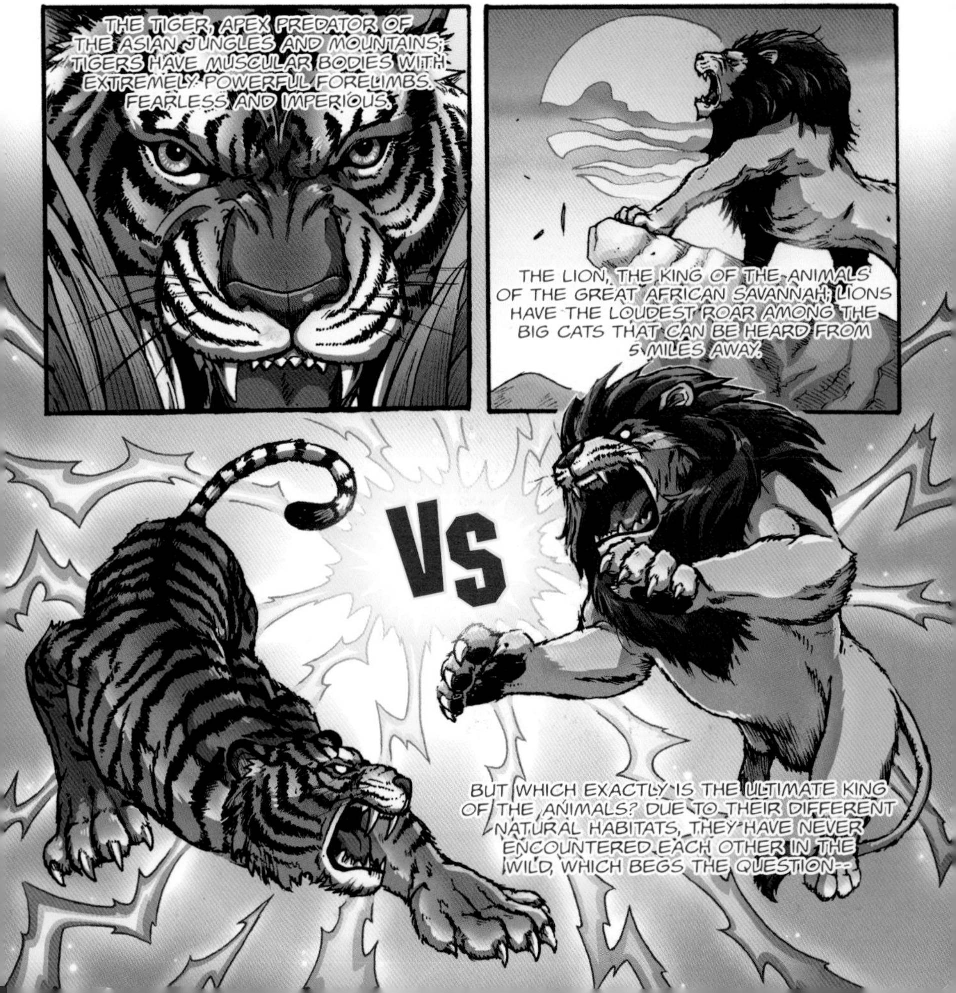
THE TIGER, APEX PREDATOR OF THE ASIAN JUNGLES AND MOUNTAINS; TIGERS HAVE MUSCULAR BODIES WITH EXTREMELY POWERFUL FORELIMBS. FEARLESS AND IMPERIOUS.
THE LION, THE KING OF THE ANIMALS OF THE GREAT AFRICAN SAVANNAH; LIONS HAVE THE LOUDEST ROAR AMONG THE BIG CATS THAT CAN BE HEARD FROM 5 MILES AWAY.
VS
BUT WHICH EXACTLY IS THE ULTIMATE KING OF THE ANIMALS? DUE TO THEIR DIFFERENT NATURAL HABITATS, THEY HAVE NEVER ENCOUNTERED EACH OTHER IN THE WILD, WHICH BEGS THE QUESTION--

THE PHYSICAL AND MENTAL STRENGTH OF THE TIGER IS INDISPUTABLE!

THE LION IS NOTHING COMPARED TO IT!

THE TIGER IS KING OF THE ANIMALS! TIGERS RULE!

OH--

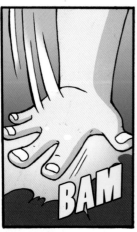

BAM

JAKE, DO YOU EVEN REALIZE THE NONSENSE, YOU'RE SPEWING?

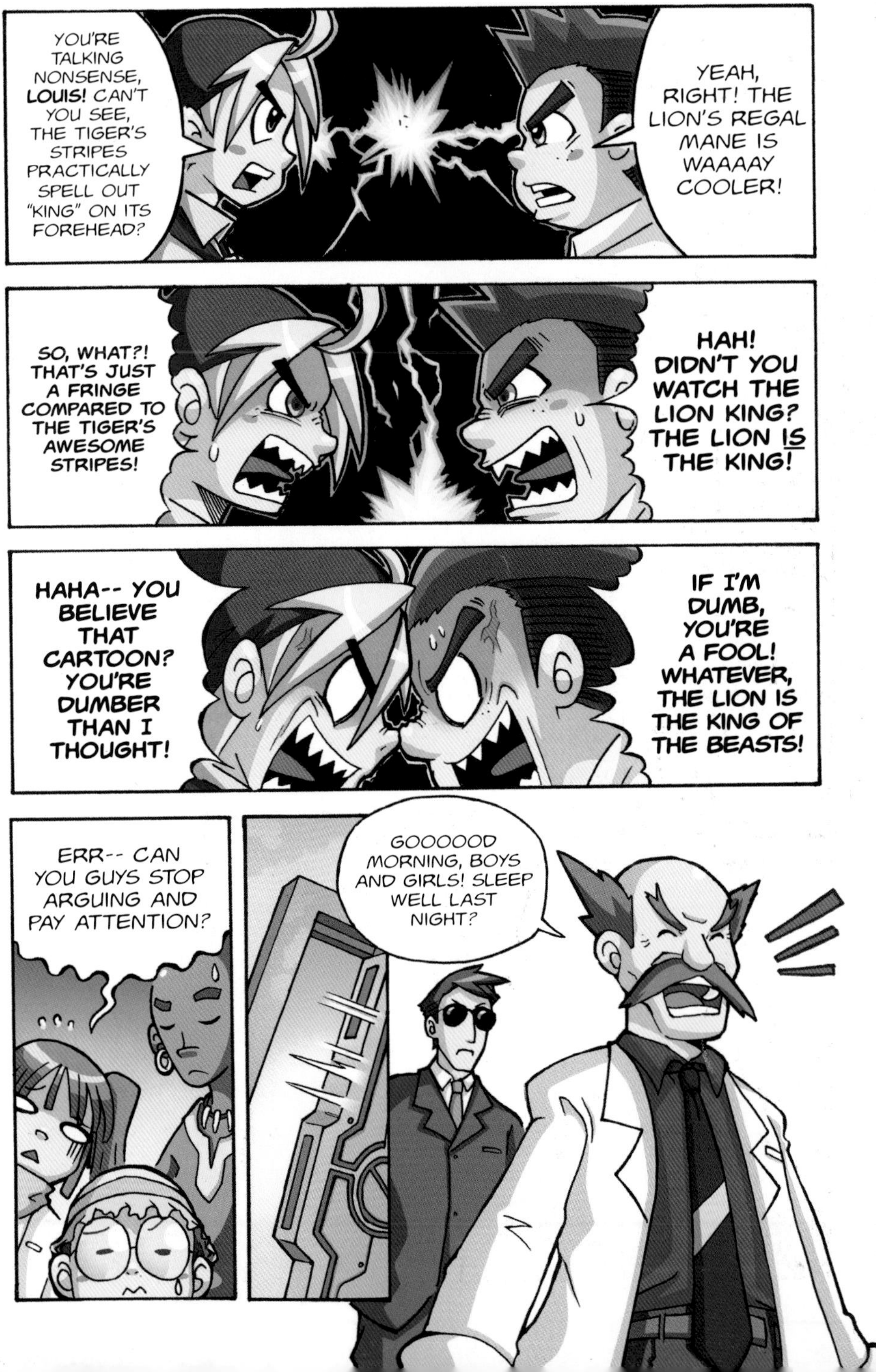
YOU'RE TALKING NONSENSE, LOUIS! CAN'T YOU SEE, THE TIGER'S STRIPES PRACTICALLY SPELL OUT "KING" ON ITS FOREHEAD?
YEAH, RIGHT! THE LION'S REGAL MANE IS WAAAAY COOLER!
SO, WHAT?! THAT'S JUST A FRINGE COMPARED TO THE TIGER'S AWESOME STRIPES!
HAH! DIDN'T YOU WATCH THE LION KING? THE LION IS THE KING!
HAHA-- YOU BELIEVE THAT CARTOON? YOU'RE DUMBER THAN I THOUGHT!
IF I'M DUMB, YOU'RE A FOOL! WHATEVER, THE LION IS THE KING OF THE BEASTS!
ERR-- CAN YOU GUYS STOP ARGUING AND PAY ATTENTION?
GOOOOOD MORNING, BOYS AND GIRLS! SLEEP WELL LAST NIGHT?

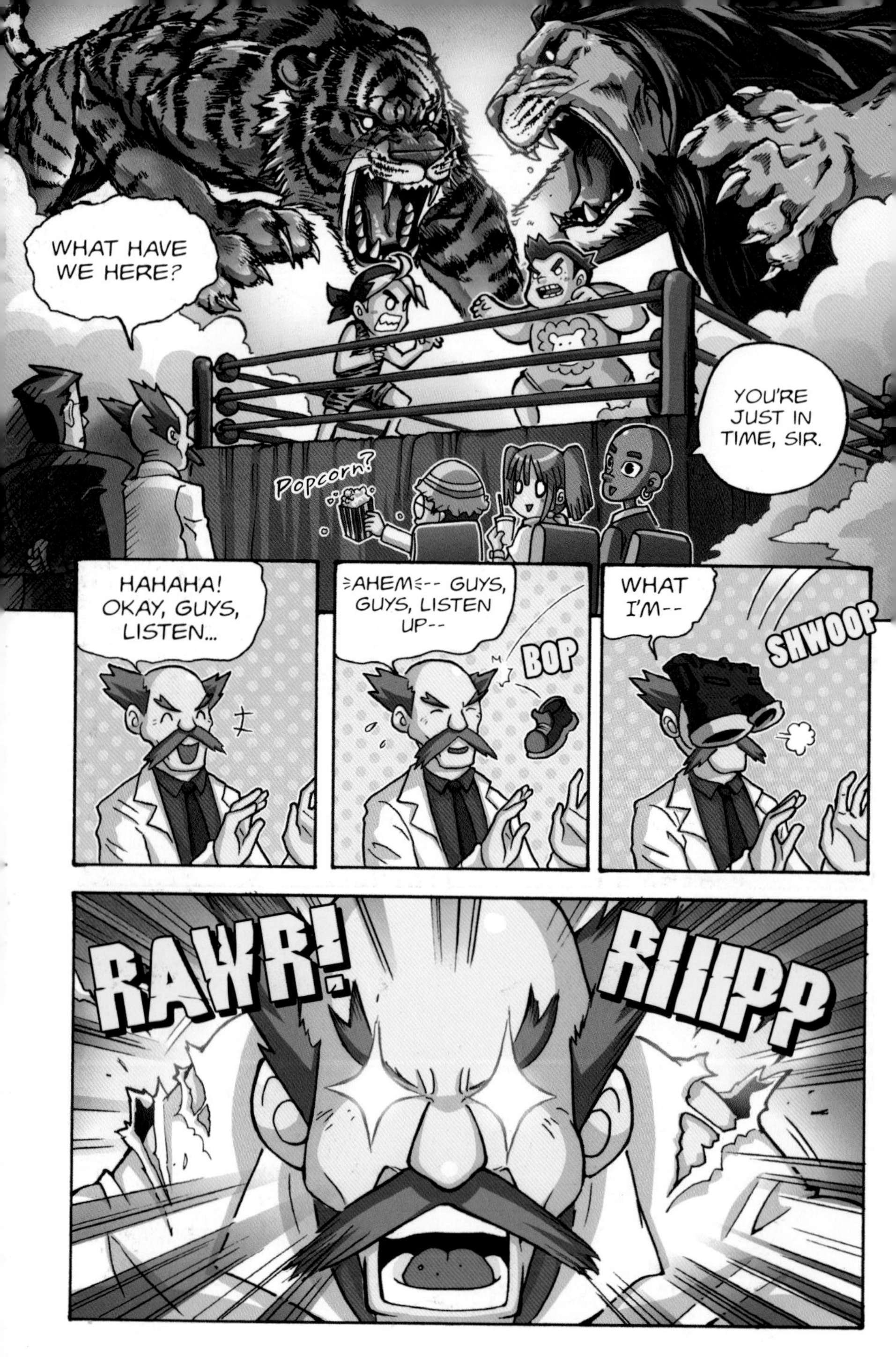
WHAT HAVE WE HERE?
YOU'RE JUST IN TIME, SIR.
Popcorn?
HAHAHA! OKAY, GUYS, LISTEN...
AHEM-- GUYS, GUYS, LISTEN UP--
BOP
WHAT I'M--
SHWOOP
RAWR!
RIIIPP

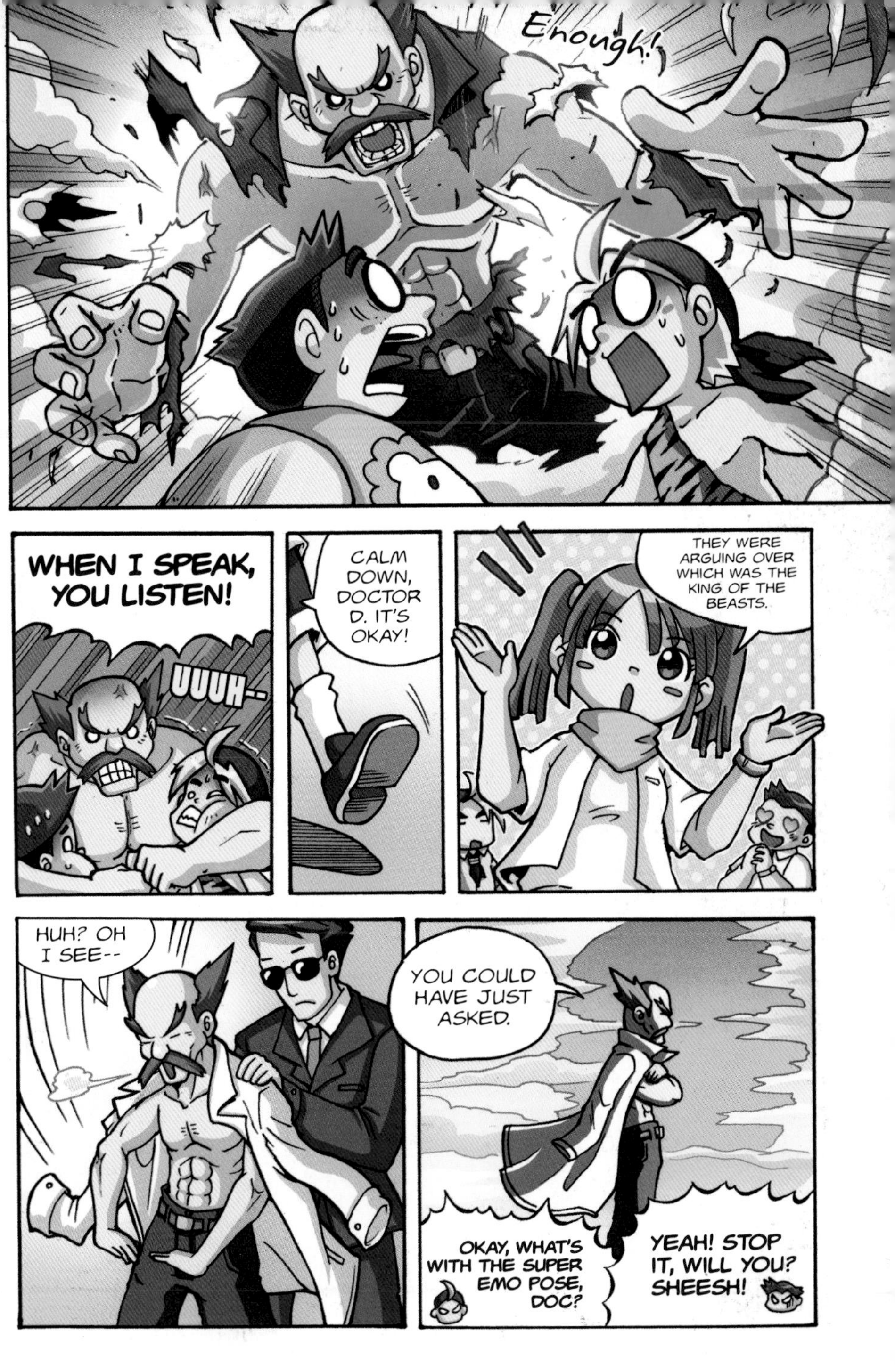
Enough!
WHEN I SPEAK, YOU LISTEN!
UUUH-
CALM DOWN, DOCTOR D. IT'S OKAY!
THEY WERE ARGUING OVER WHICH WAS THE KING OF THE BEASTS.
HUH? OH I SEE--
YOU COULD HAVE JUST ASKED.
OKAY, WHAT'S WITH THE SUPER EMO POSE, DOC?
YEAH! STOP IT, WILL YOU? SHEESH!

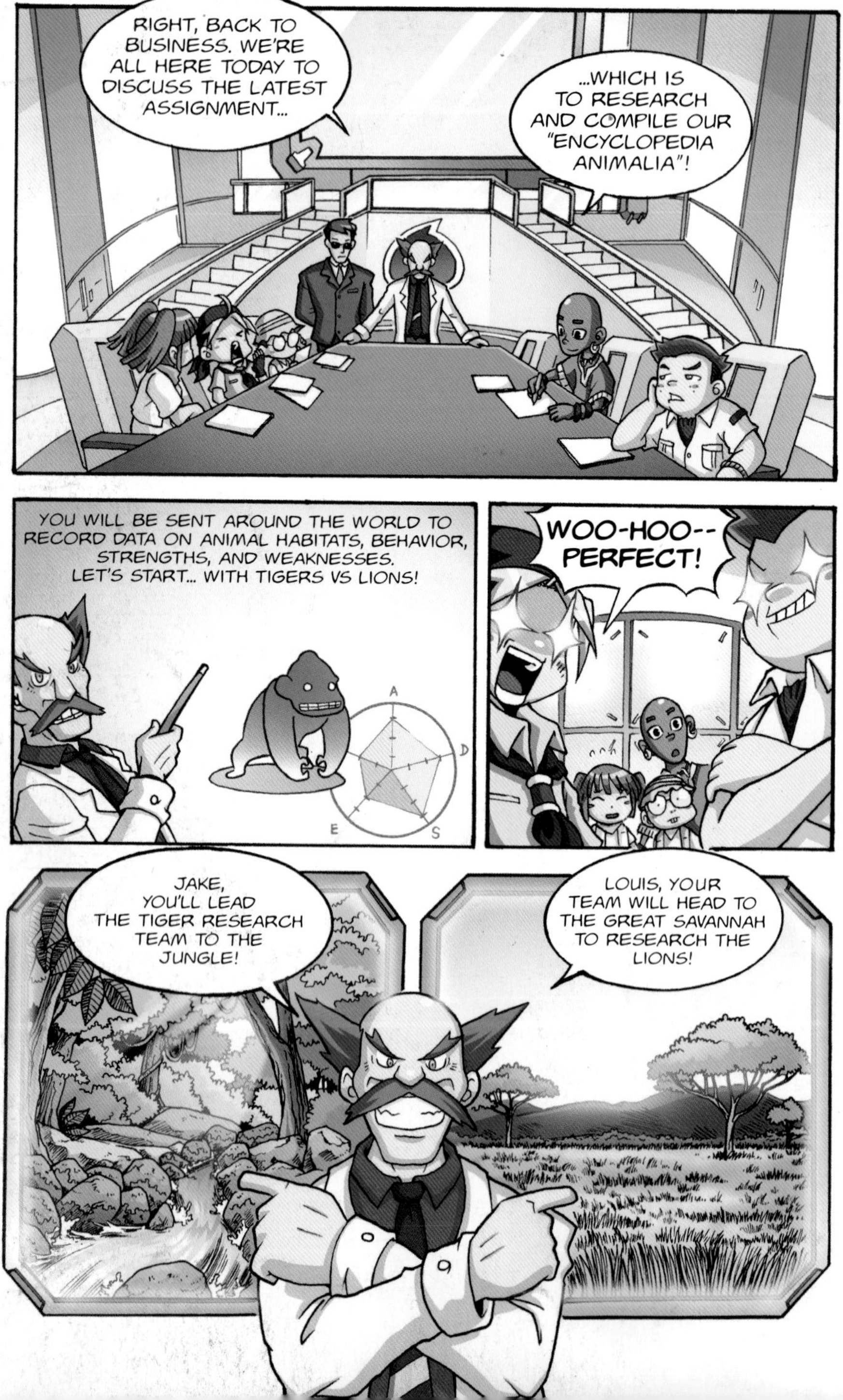
RIGHT, BACK TO BUSINESS. WE'RE ALL HERE TODAY TO DISCUSS THE LATEST ASSIGNMENT...
...WHICH IS TO RESEARCH AND COMPILE OUR "ENCYCLOPEDIA ANIMALIA"!
YOU WILL BE SENT AROUND THE WORLD TO RECORD DATA ON ANIMAL HABITATS, BEHAVIOR, STRENGTHS, AND WEAKNESSES. LET'S START... WITH TIGERS VS LIONS!
A
D
S
E
WOO-HOO-- PERFECT!
JAKE, YOU'LL LEAD THE TIGER RESEARCH TEAM TO THE JUNGLE!
LOUIS, YOUR TEAM WILL HEAD TO THE GREAT SAVANNAH TO RESEARCH THE LIONS!

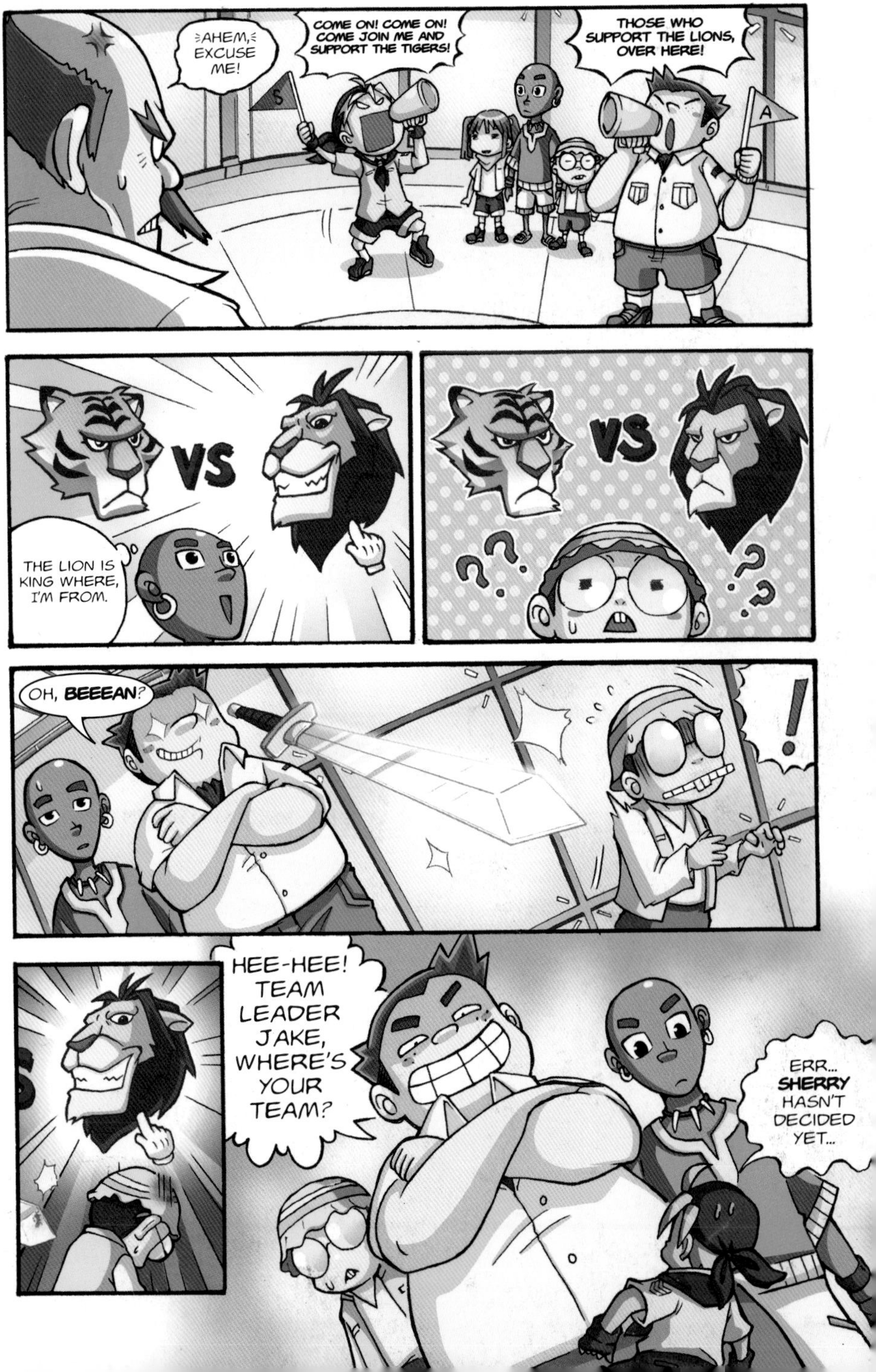
AHEM, EXCUSE ME!
COME ON! COME ON! COME JOIN ME AND SUPPORT THE TIGERS!
THOSE WHO SUPPORT THE LIONS, OVER HERE!
S
A
VS
THE LION IS KING WHERE, I'M FROM.
VS
OH, BEEEAN?
HEE-HEE! TEAM LEADER JAKE, WHERE'S YOUR TEAM?
ERR... SHERRY HASN'T DECIDED YET...

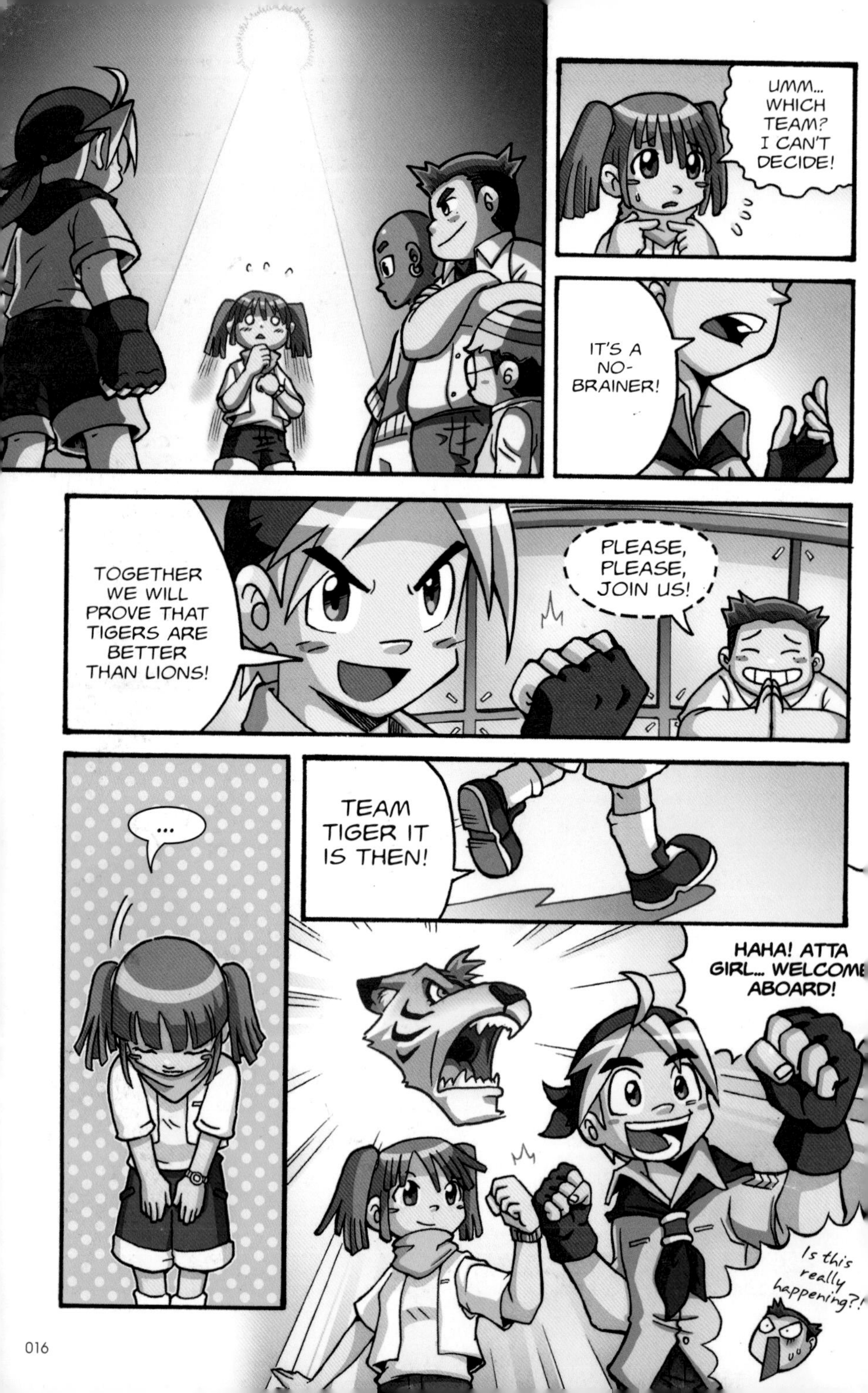
UMM... WHICH TEAM? I CAN'T DECIDE!
IT'S A NO-BRAINER!
TOGETHER WE WILL PROVE THAT TIGERS ARE BETTER THAN LIONS!
PLEASE, PLEASE, JOIN US!
...
TEAM TIGER IT IS THEN!
HAHA! ATTA GIRL... WELCOME ABOARD!
Is this really happening?!

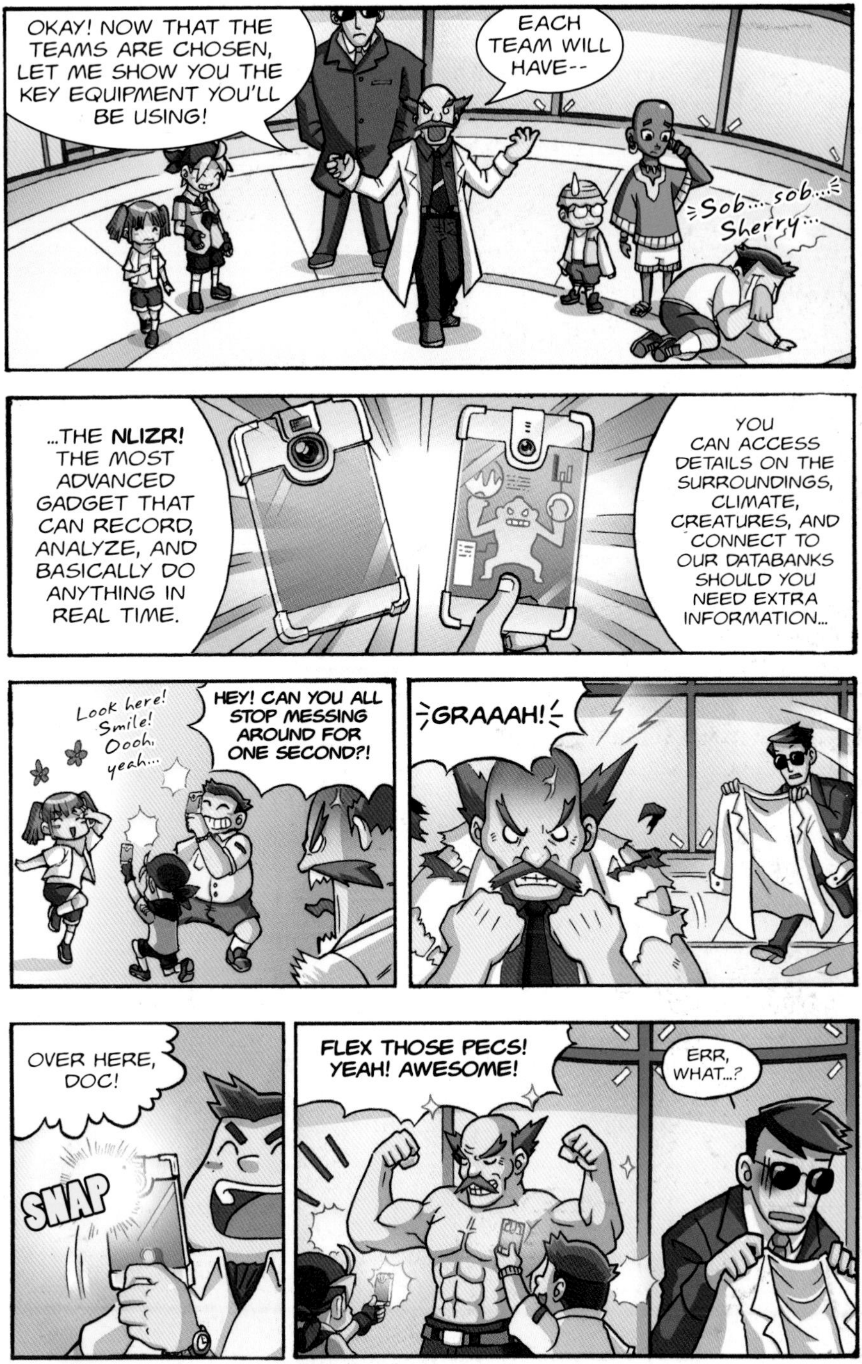
OKAY! NOW THAT THE TEAMS ARE CHOSEN, LET ME SHOW YOU THE KEY EQUIPMENT YOU'LL BE USING!
EACH TEAM WILL HAVE--
Sob... sob... Sherry...
...THE NLIZR! THE MOST ADVANCED GADGET THAT CAN RECORD, ANALYZE, AND BASICALLY DO ANYTHING IN REAL TIME.
YOU CAN ACCESS DETAILS ON THE SURROUNDINGS, CLIMATE, CREATURES, AND CONNECT TO OUR DATABANKS SHOULD YOU NEED EXTRA INFORMATION...
Look here! Smile! Oooh, yeah...
HEY! CAN YOU ALL STOP MESSING AROUND FOR ONE SECOND?!
GRAAAH!
OVER HERE, DOC!
SNAP
FLEX THOSE PECS! YEAH! AWESOME!
ERR, WHAT...?

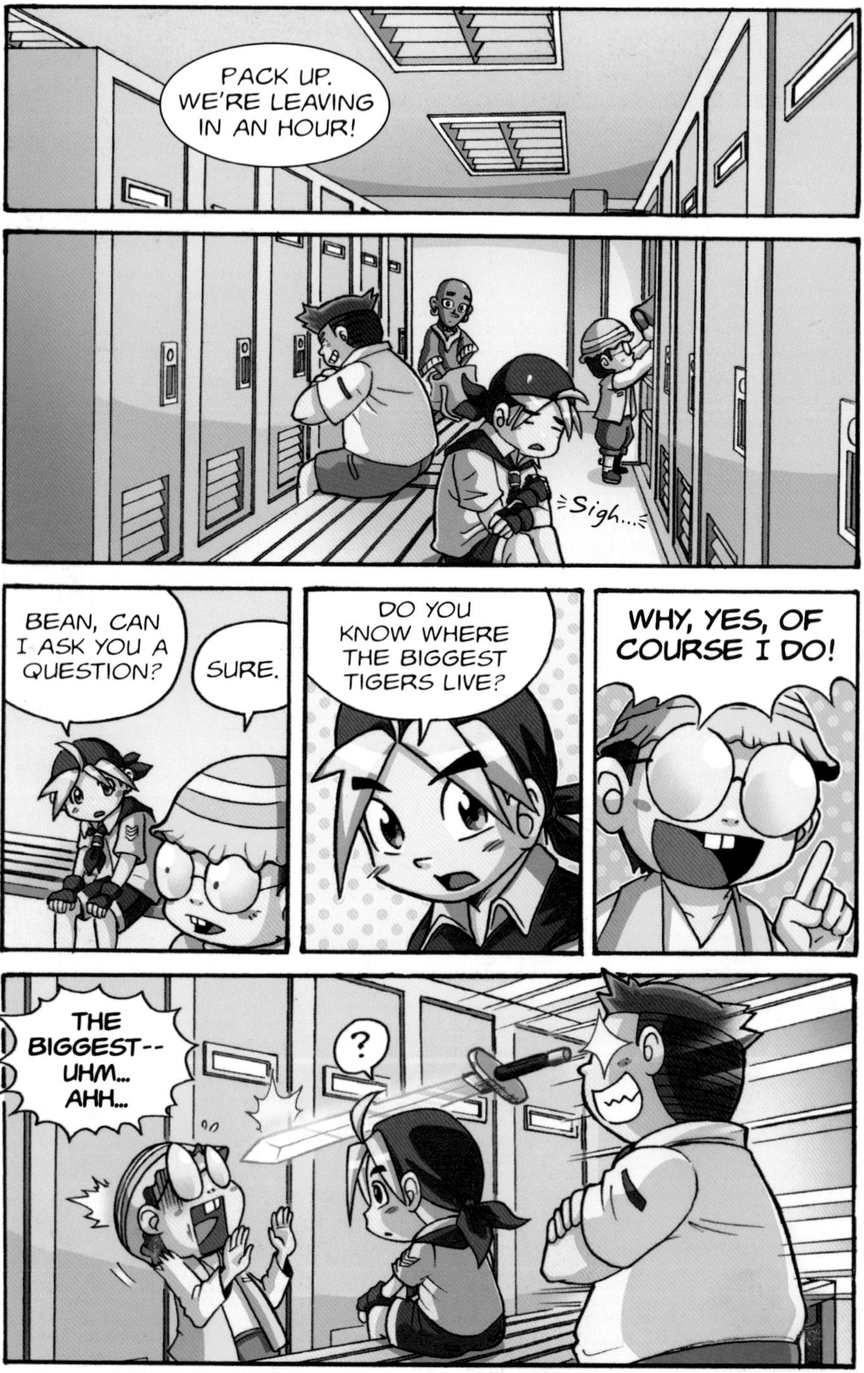
PACK UP. WE'RE LEAVING IN AN HOUR!
Sigh...
BEAN, CAN I ASK YOU A QUESTION?
SURE.
DO YOU KNOW WHERE THE BIGGEST TIGERS LIVE?
WHY, YES, OF COURSE I DO!
THE BIGGEST-- UHM... AHH...
?

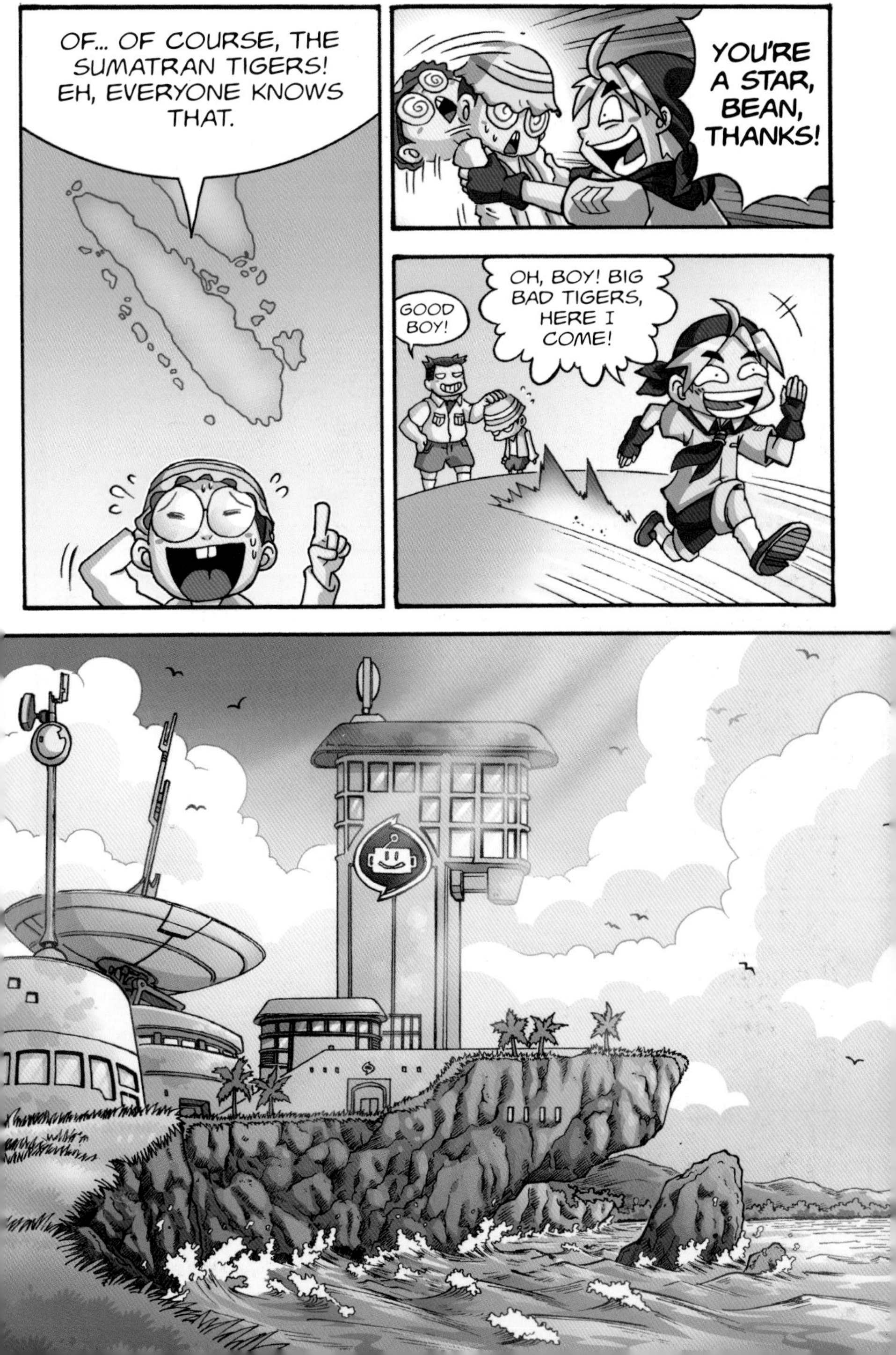
OF... OF COURSE, THE SUMATRAN TIGERS! EH, EVERYONE KNOWS THAT.
YOU'RE A STAR, BEAN, THANKS!
GOOD BOY!
OH, BOY! BIG BAD TIGERS, HERE I COME!

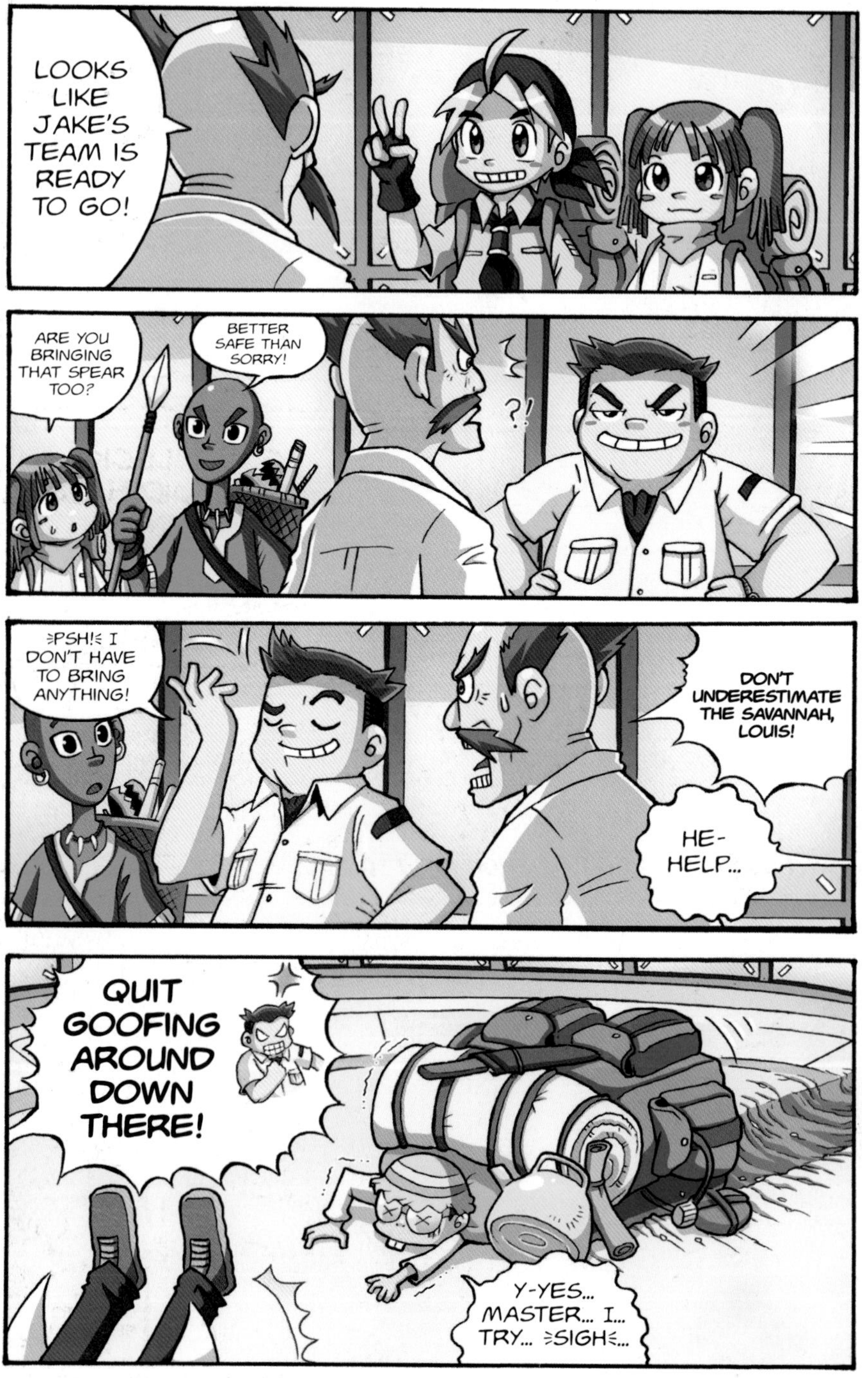
LOOKS LIKE JAKE'S TEAM IS READY TO GO!
ARE YOU BRINGING THAT SPEAR TOO?
BETTER SAFE THAN SORRY!
?!
≥PSH!≤ I DON'T HAVE TO BRING ANYTHING!
DON'T UNDERESTIMATE THE SAVANNAH, LOUIS!
HE-HELP...
QUIT GOOFING AROUND DOWN THERE!
Y-YES... MASTER... I... TRY... ≥SIGH≤...

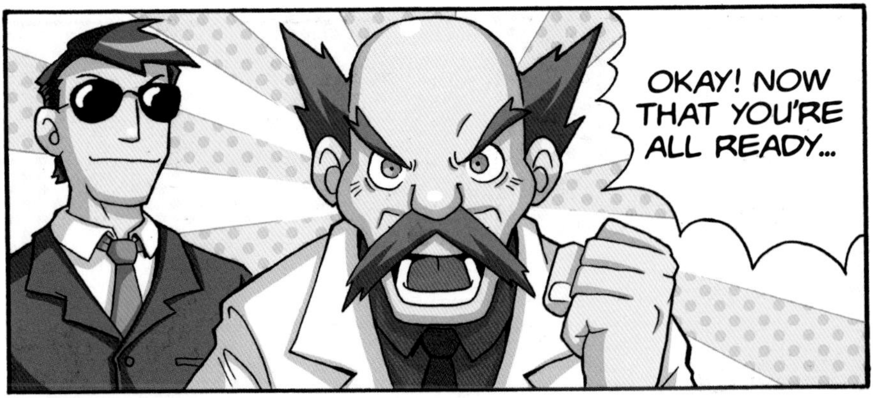
OKAY! NOW THAT YOU'RE ALL READY...

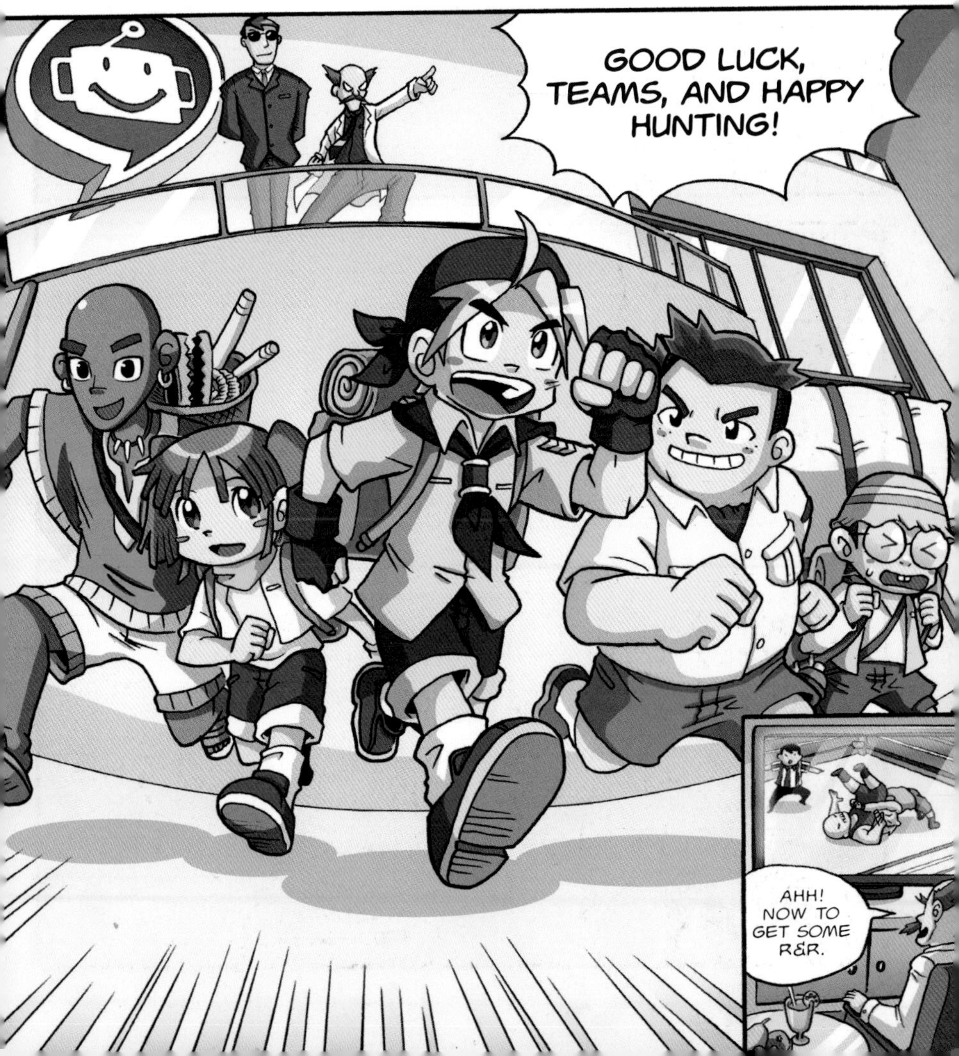
GOOD LUCK, TEAMS, AND HAPPY HUNTING!
AHH! NOW TO GET SOME R&R.

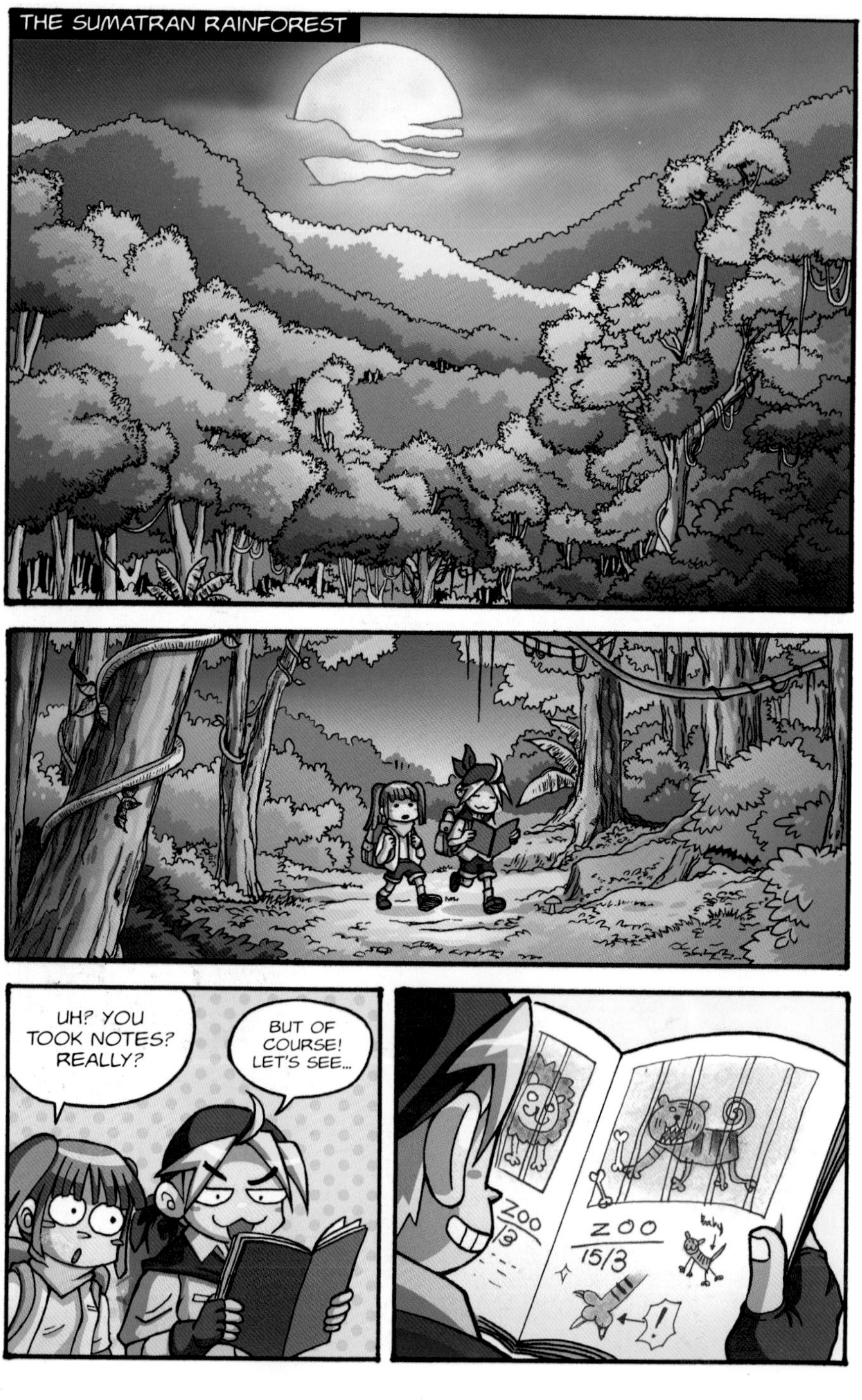
THE SUMATRAN RAINFOREST
UH? YOU TOOK NOTES? REALLY?
BUT OF COURSE! LET'S SEE...
ZOO
15/3
Baby
!

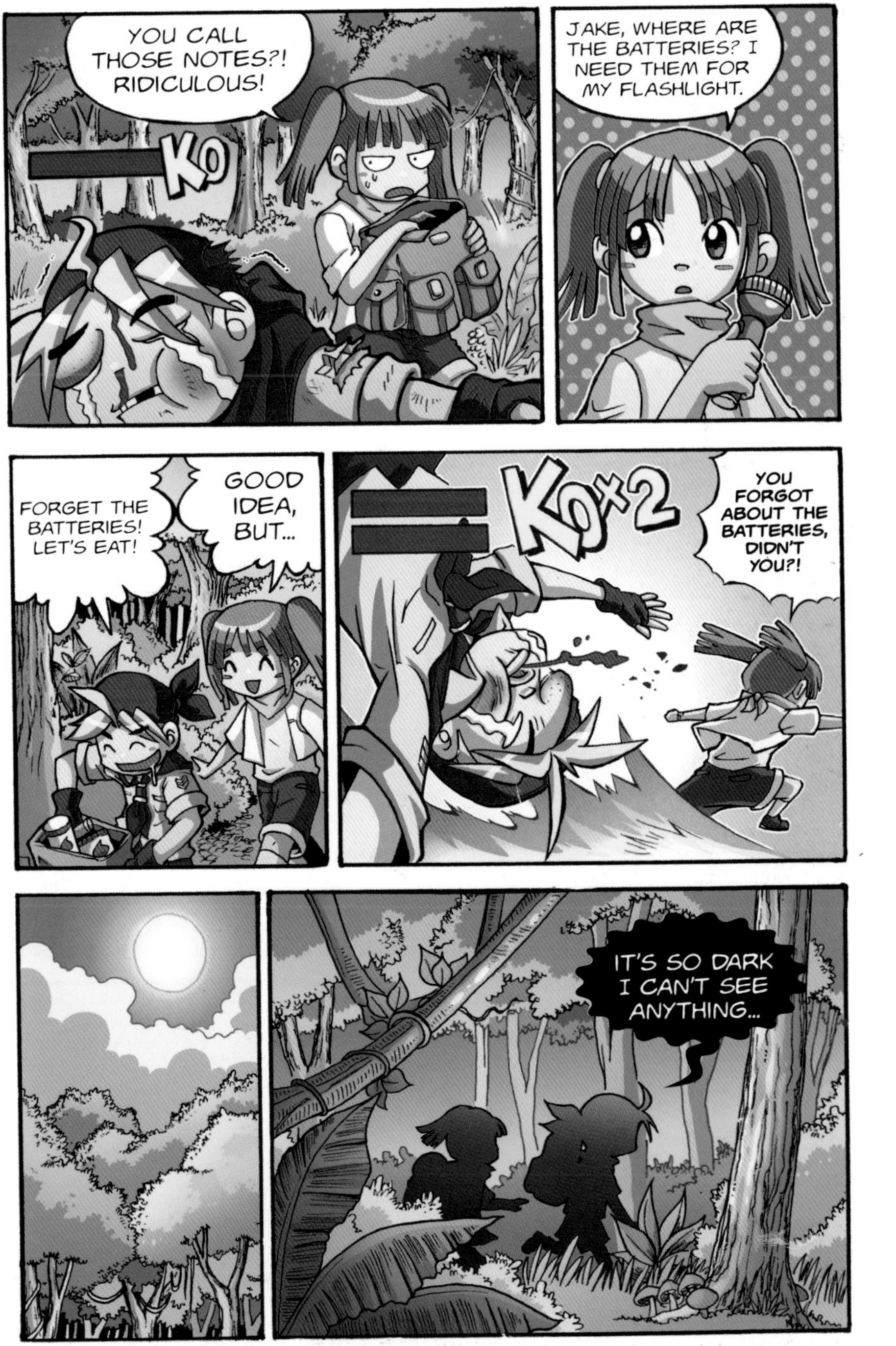
YOU CALL THOSE NOTES?! RIDICULOUS!
KO
JAKE, WHERE ARE THE BATTERIES? I NEED THEM FOR MY FLASHLIGHT.
FORGET THE BATTERIES! LET'S EAT!
GOOD IDEA, BUT...
KO×2
YOU FORGOT ABOUT THE BATTERIES, DIDN'T YOU?!
IT'S SO DARK I CAN'T SEE ANYTHING...

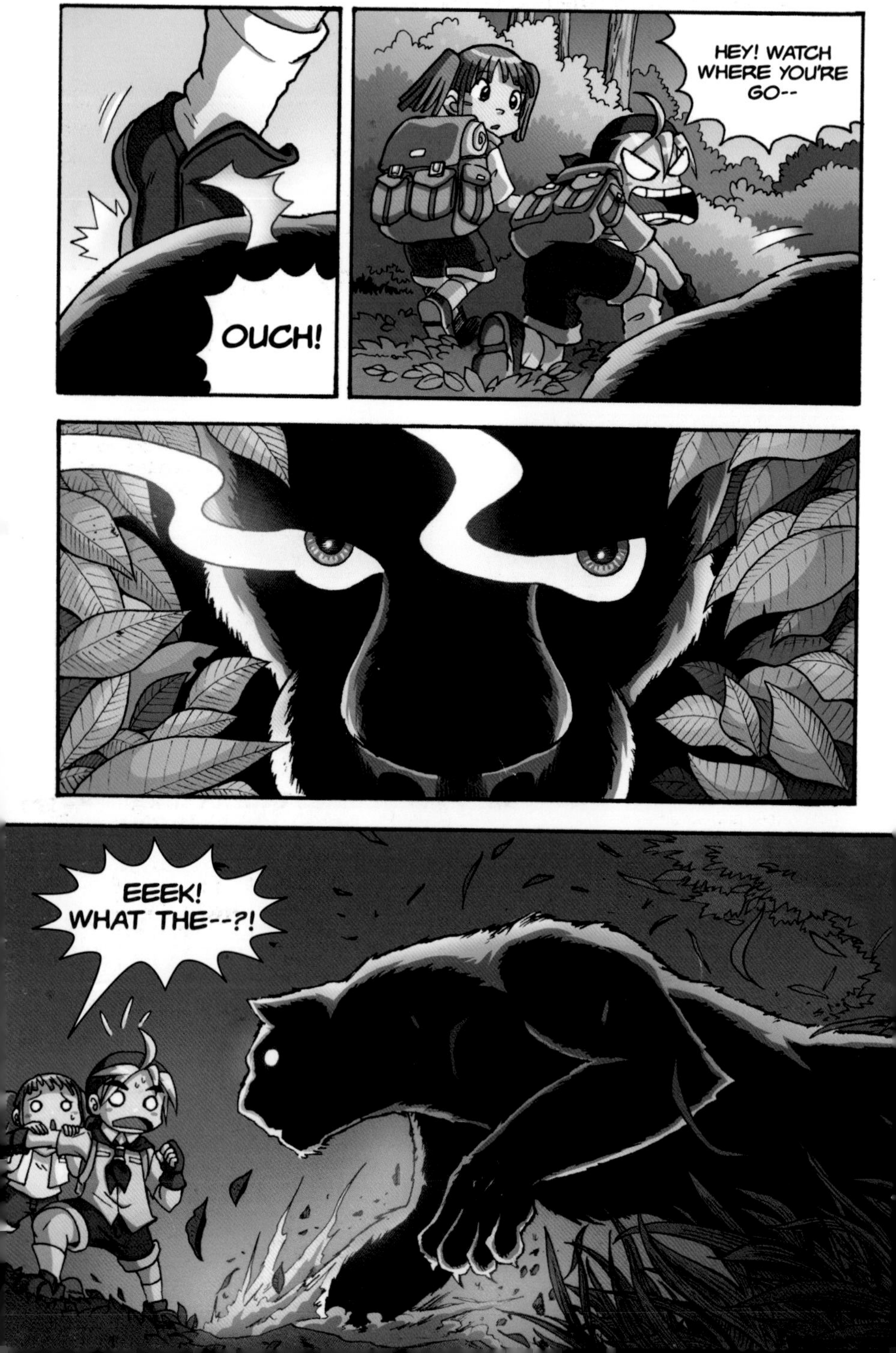
OUCH!
HEY! WATCH WHERE YOU'RE GO--
EEEK! WHAT THE--?!

FELIDAE

What is felidae?

Felidae is the biological classification for the family of cats, members of which are known as felids; the most familiar felid is the domestic cat, which first became associated with humans about 10,000 years ago; but the family includes all other wild cats, including the big cats.

Family Felidae

The felids of family Felidae include the big cats such as the lion, tiger, leopard, jaguar, and cheetah, as well as the felinae — the small to medium-sized cats such as the puma, lynx, caracal, and bobcat. All cats are efficient hunters and are known as apex predators (animals at the top of the food chain who prey on other animals).

FELID ANATOMY

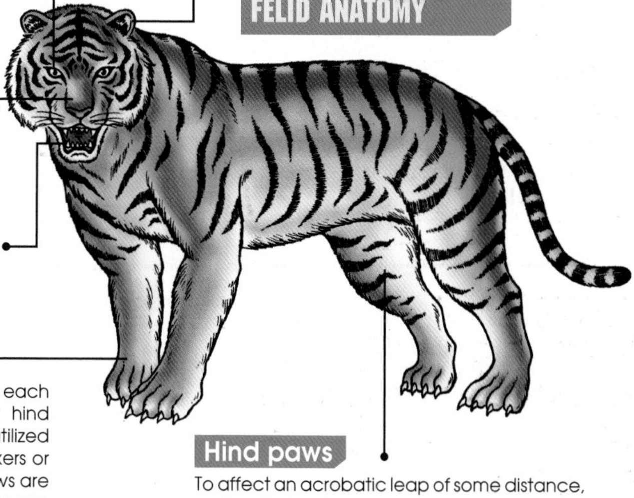

Eyes

Cats see extremely well due to a unique layer of mirror-like cells called the tapetum lucidum behind the retina, which grants them extremely acute vision even in near darkness. Like humans, cats cannot see in complete darkness.

Ears

With a sense of hearing nearly 5 times stronger than humans, felids are able to detect high frequency sounds made by other animals. This is especially crucial in locating prey when hunting.

Nose

All felids have very sensitive olfactory senses to detect prey, danger, as well as the right time to mate.

Teeth

The four paired upper and lower canines are used to bite and tear into prey, targeting the neck area.

Forepaws

Felids have five claws on each forepaw and four on each hind paw. The forepaws are mostly utilized defensively, to stave off attackers or to incapacitate prey. Felid claws are retractable, meaning that they can be sheathed while walking or at rest, unleashing them when attacking or climbing. This explains why family Felidae are stealth experts.

Hind paws

To affect an acrobatic leap of some distance, or the darting lunge, felids require powerful back limbs that generate great leverage off the ground. This enables, the killing strike, lashing out to capture its oblivious prey.

Tongue

Comprising rows of thorny projections called papillae, the tongue is used not only to taste food (mostly salty, bitter, and sour) but also for grooming and scraping meat remnants from bone.

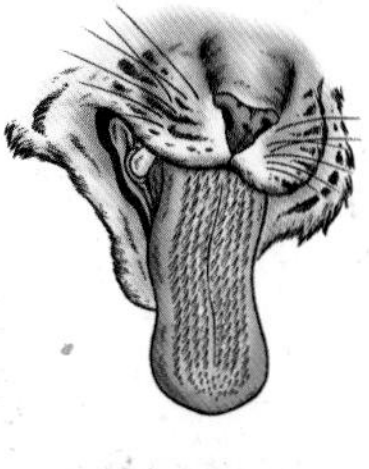

FELIDAE EVOLUTION

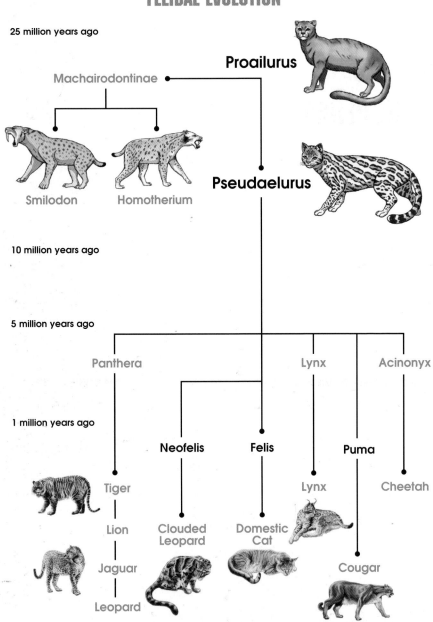

25 million years ago

Proailurus

Machairodontinae

Smilodon

Homotherium

Pseudaelurus

10 million years ago

5 million years ago

Panthera

Lynx

Acinonyx

1 million years ago

Neofelis

Felis

Puma

Tiger

Lynx

Cheetah

Lion

Clouded Leopard

Domestic Cat

Jaguar

Cougar

Leopard

CHAPTER 2

THE BEAST WHISPERER

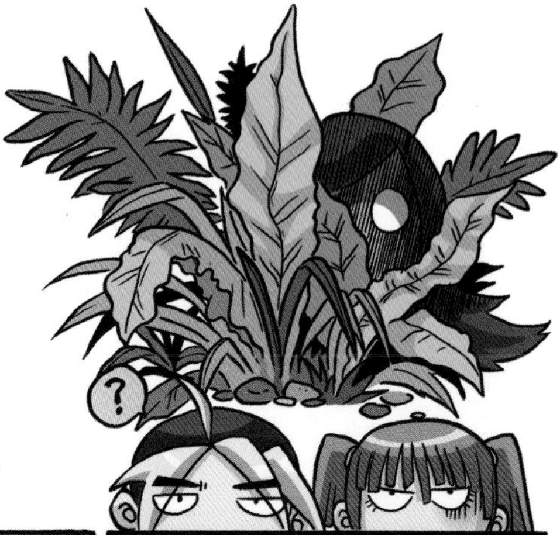

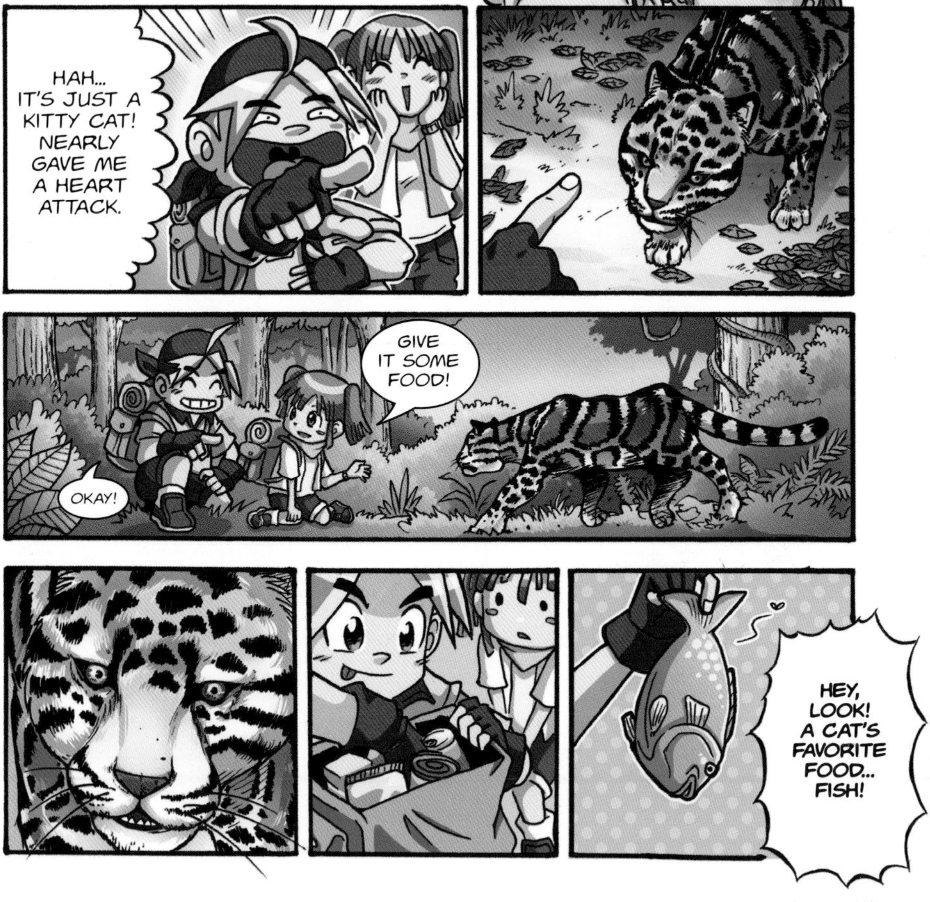
HAH... IT'S JUST A KITTY CAT! NEARLY GAVE ME A HEART ATTACK.
GIVE IT SOME FOOD!
OKAY!
HEY, LOOK! A CAT'S FAVORITE FOOD... FISH!

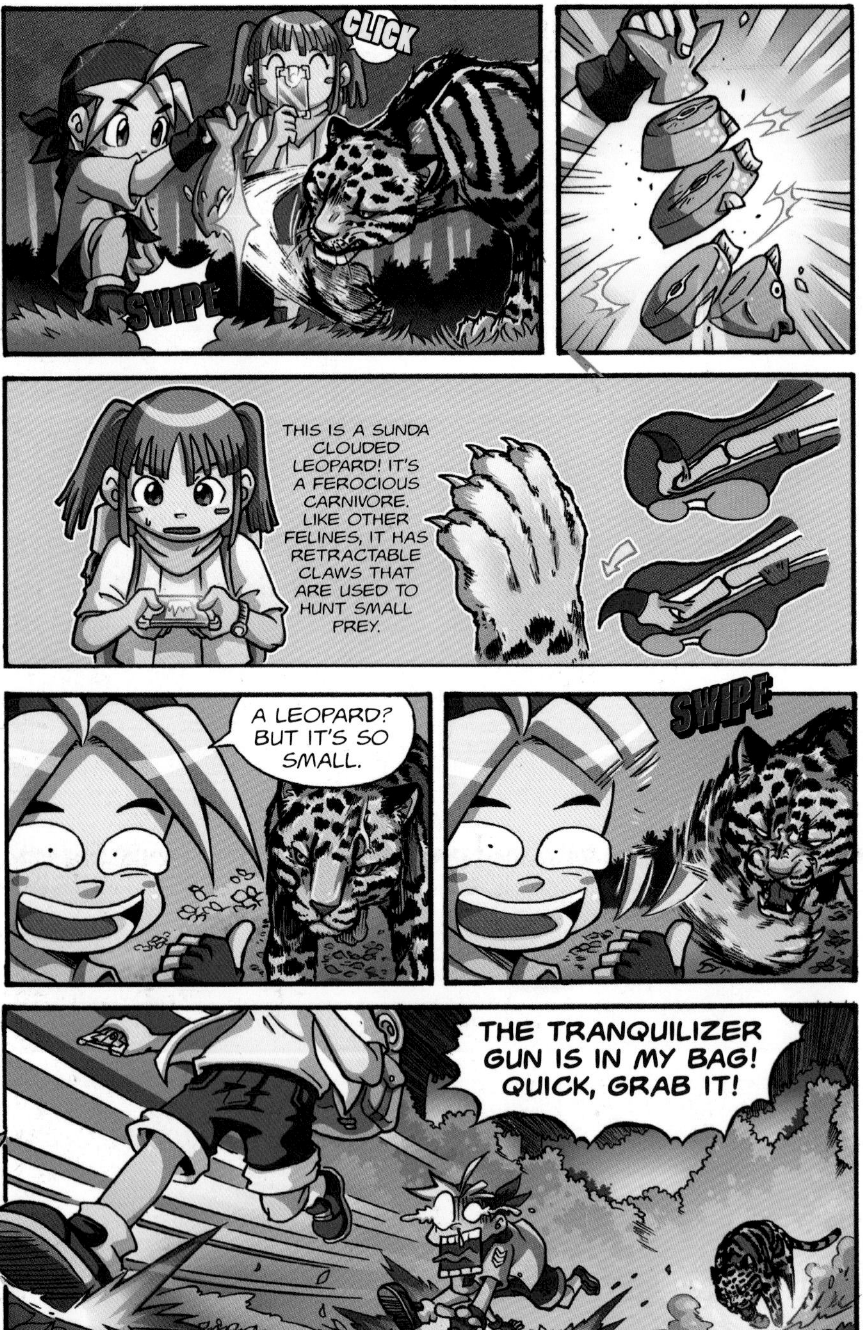
CLICK
SWIPE
THIS IS A SUNDA CLOUDED LEOPARD! IT'S A FEROCIOUS CARNIVORE. LIKE OTHER FELINES, IT HAS RETRACTABLE CLAWS THAT ARE USED TO HUNT SMALL PREY.
A LEOPARD? BUT IT'S SO SMALL.
SWIPE
THE TRANQUILIZER GUN IS IN MY BAG! QUICK, GRAB IT!

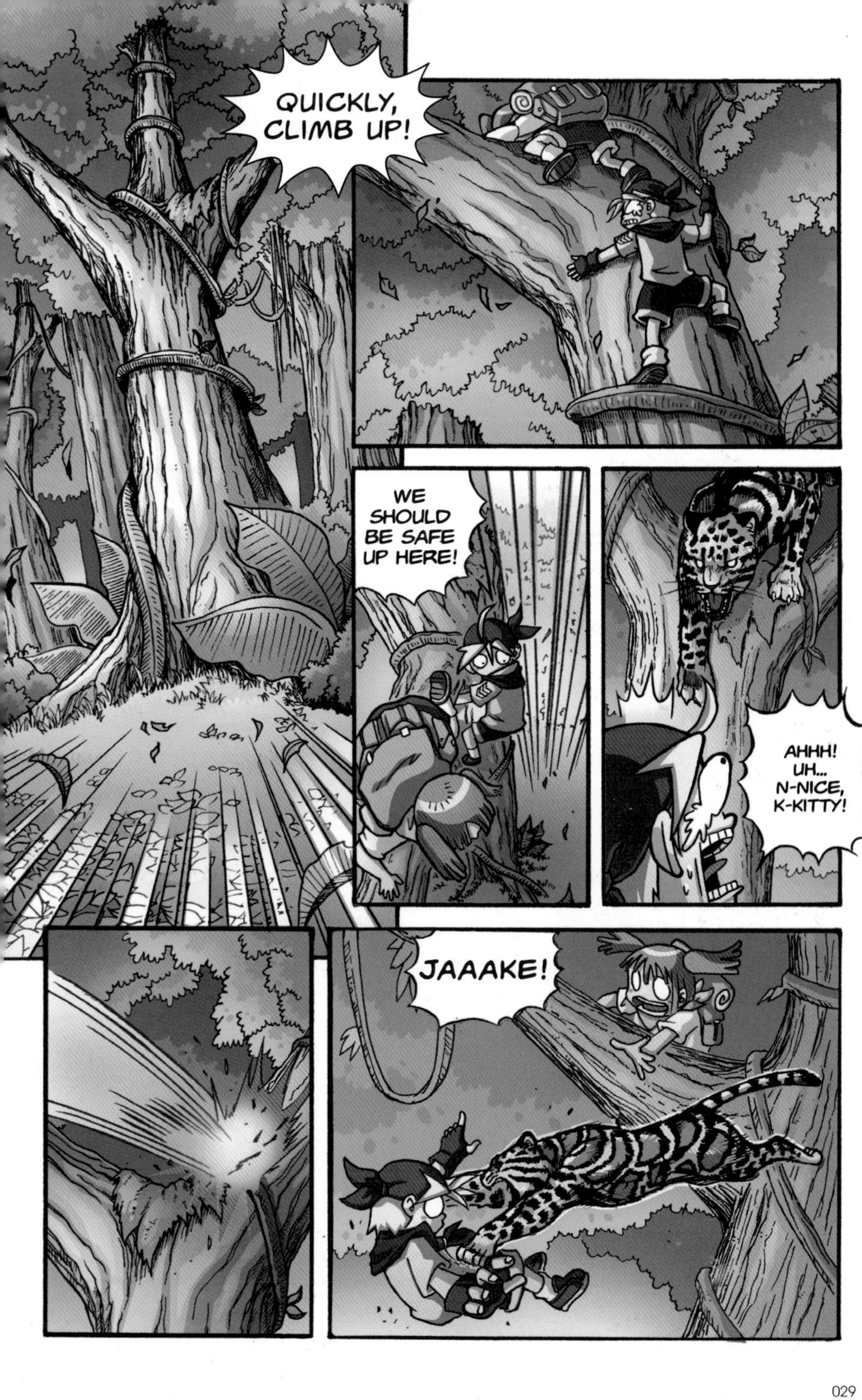
QUICKLY, CLIMB UP!
WE SHOULD BE SAFE UP HERE!
AHHH! UH... N-NICE, K-KITTY!
JAAAKE!

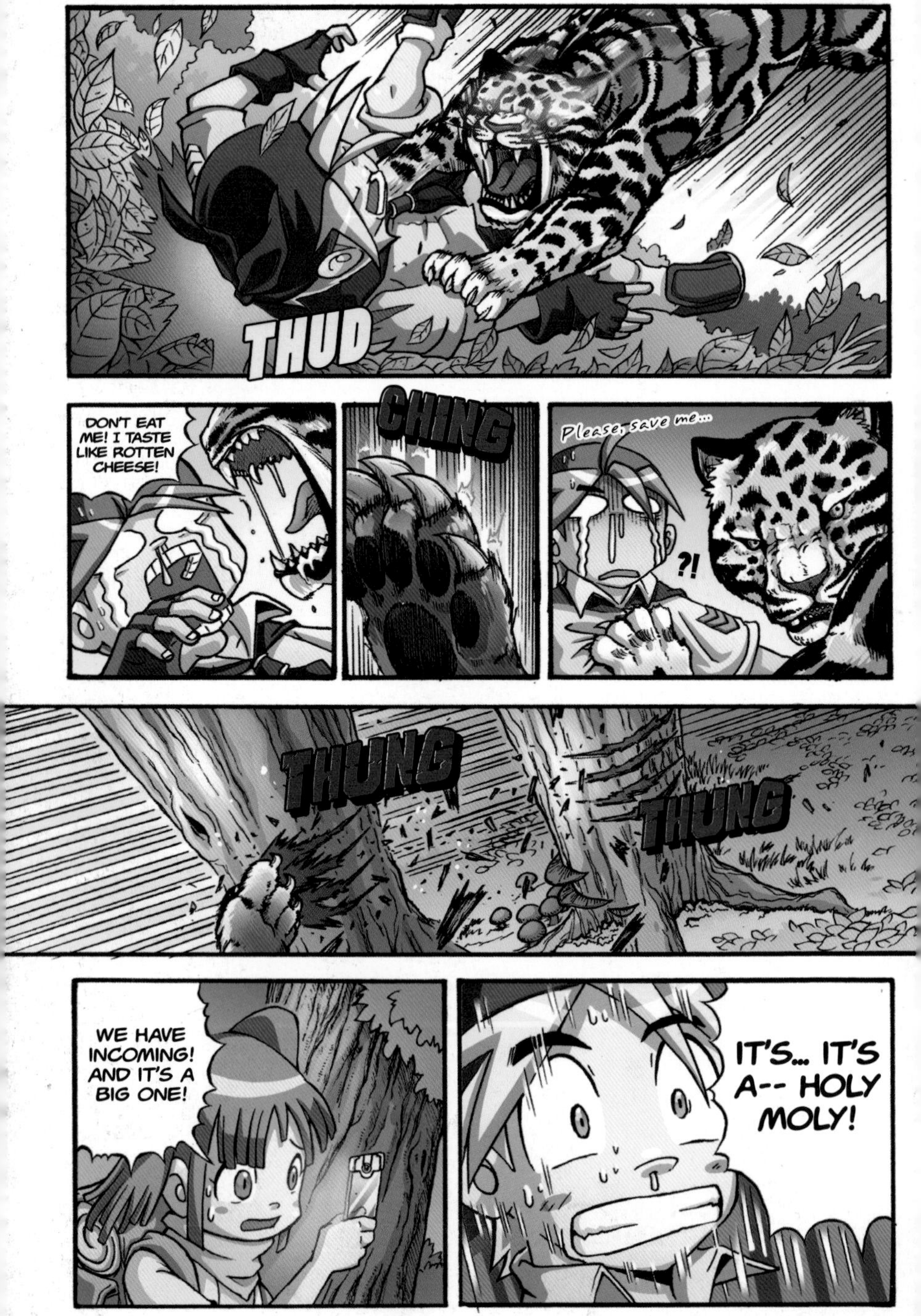
THUD
DON'T EAT ME! I TASTE LIKE ROTTEN CHEESE!
CHING
Please, save me...
?!
THUNG
THUNG
WE HAVE INCOMING! AND IT'S A BIG ONE!
IT'S... IT'S A-- HOLY MOLY!

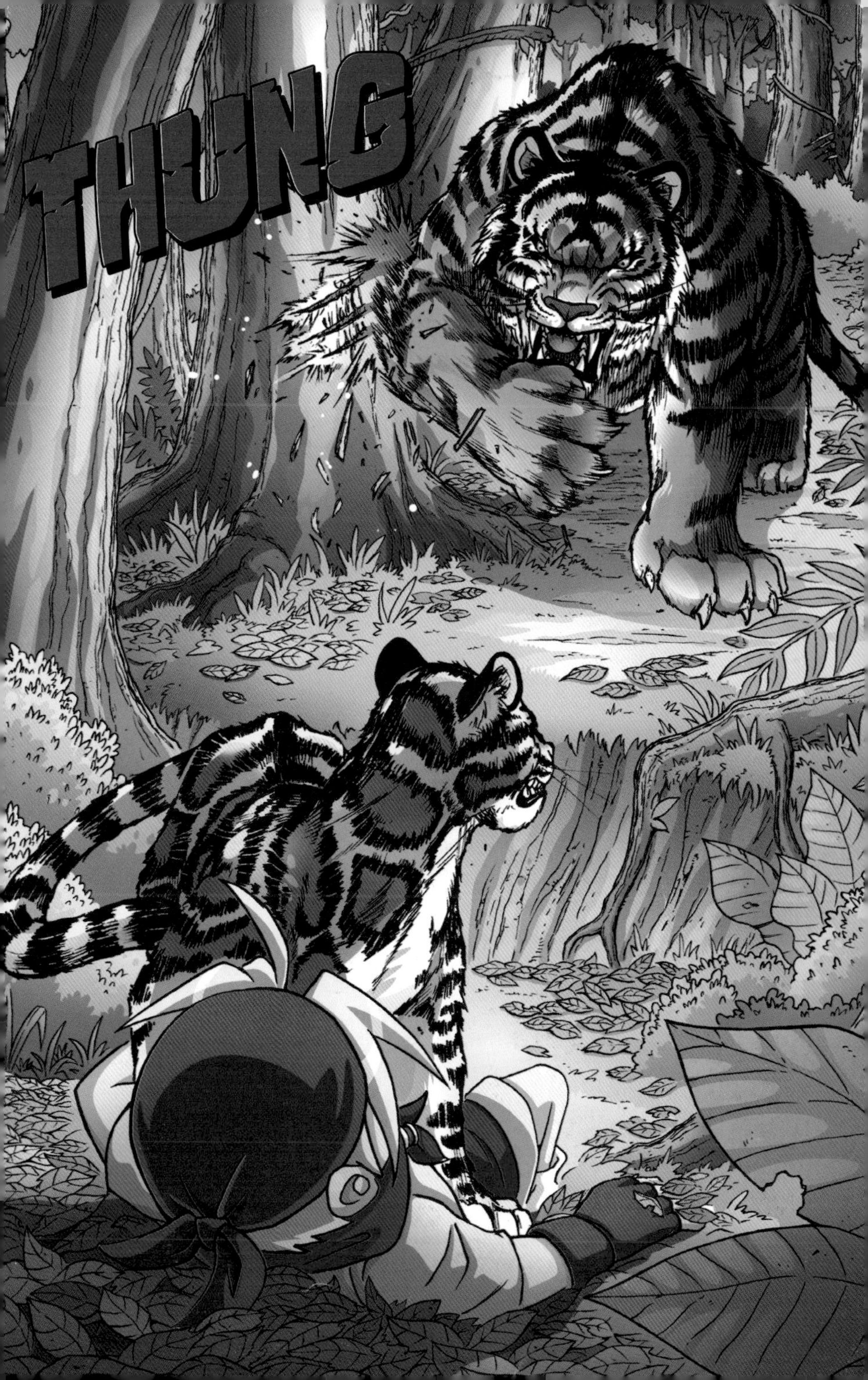
THUNG

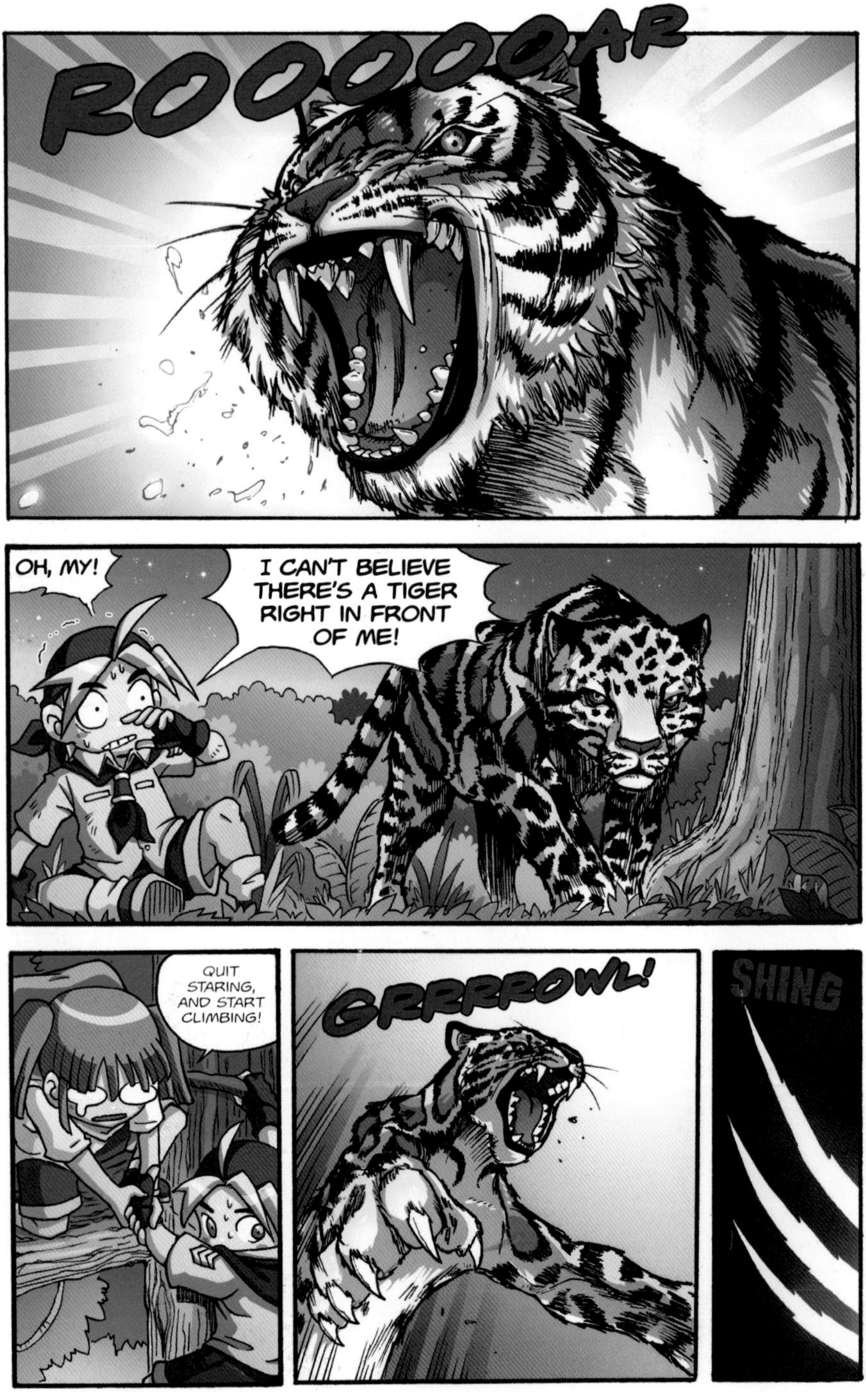
ROOOOOAR
OH, MY!
I CAN'T BELIEVE THERE'S A TIGER RIGHT IN FRONT OF ME!
QUIT STARING, AND START CLIMBING!
GRRRROWL!
SHING

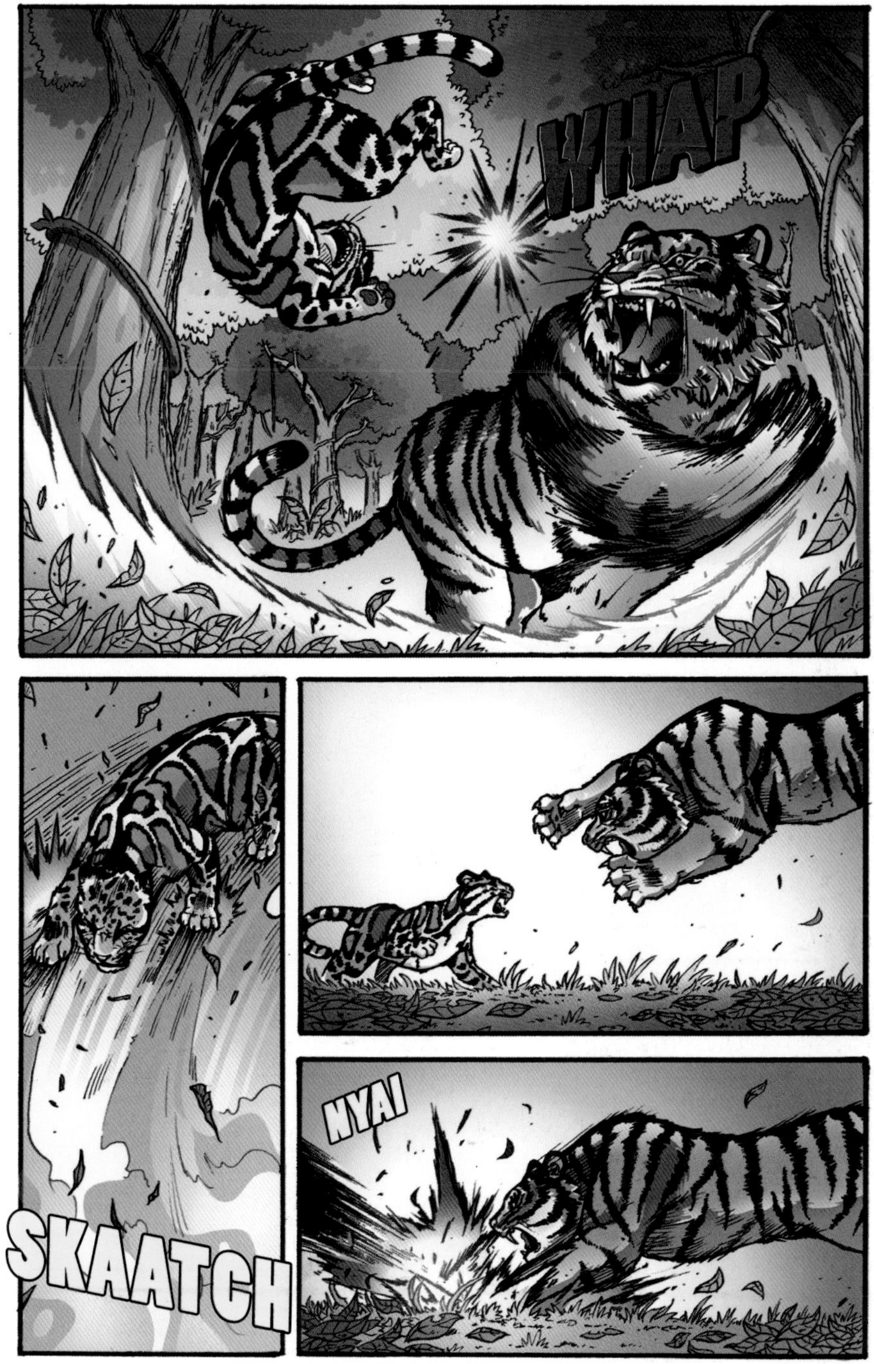
WHAP
SKAATCH
NYAI

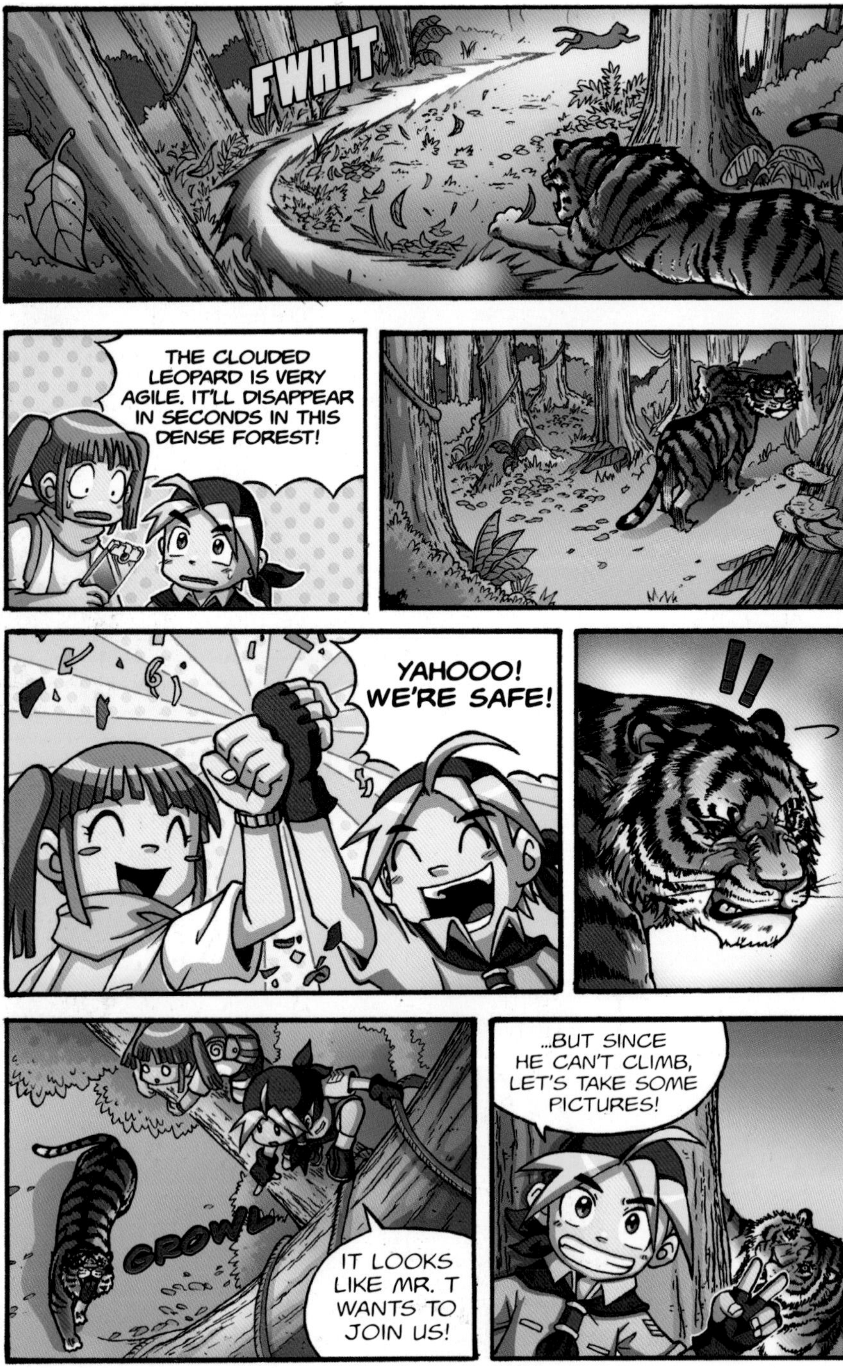
FWHIT
THE CLOUDED LEOPARD IS VERY AGILE. IT'LL DISAPPEAR IN SECONDS IN THIS DENSE FOREST!
YAHOOO! WE'RE SAFE!
!!
GROWL
IT LOOKS LIKE MR. T WANTS TO JOIN US!
...BUT SINCE HE CAN'T CLIMB, LET'S TAKE SOME PICTURES!

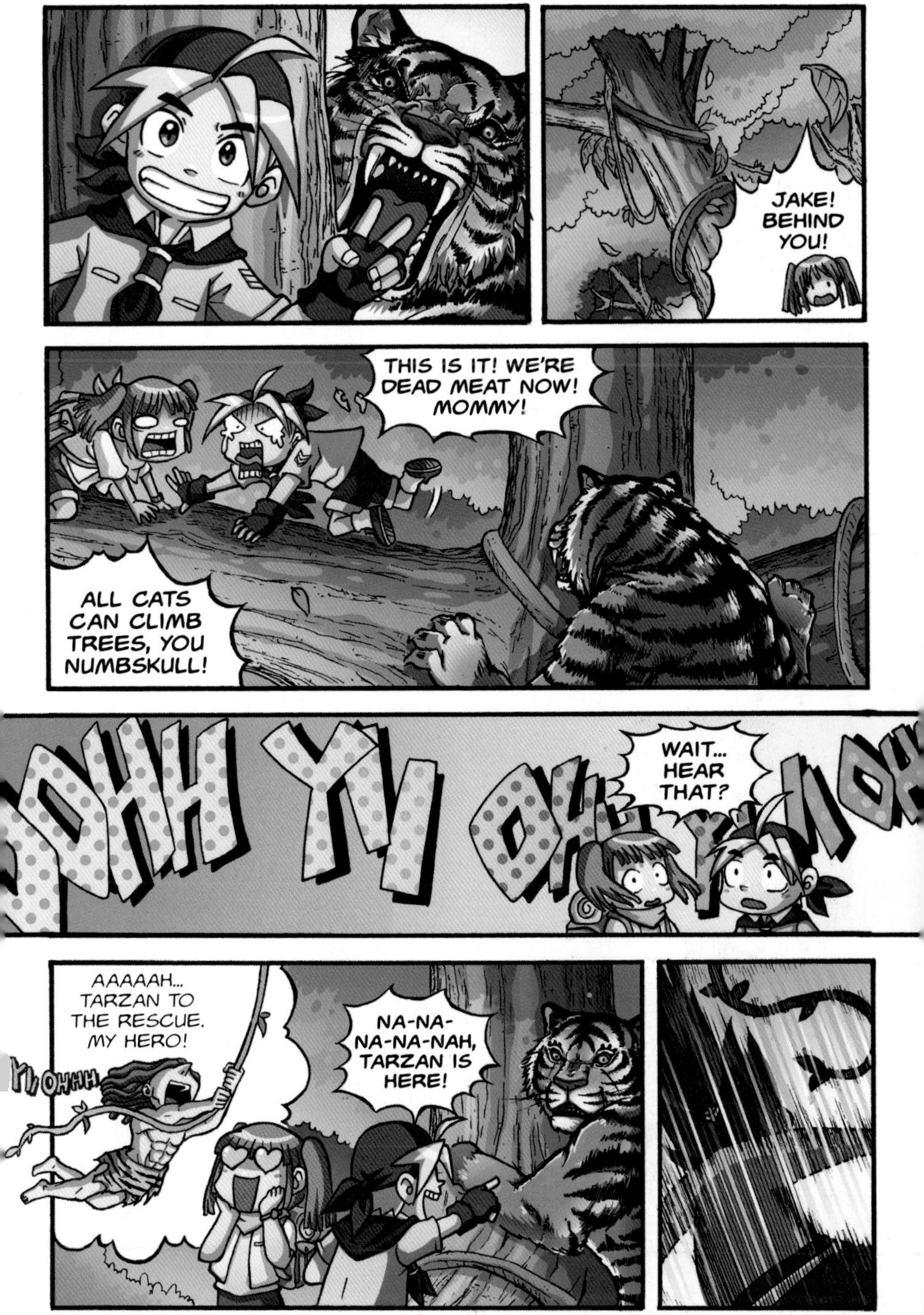
JAKE! BEHIND YOU!
THIS IS IT! WE'RE DEAD MEAT NOW! MOMMY!
ALL CATS CAN CLIMB TREES, YOU NUMBSKULL!
OHH YI OH
WAIT... HEAR THAT?
AAAAAH... TARZAN TO THE RESCUE. MY HERO!
YI OHHH
NA-NA-NA-NA-NAH, TARZAN IS HERE!

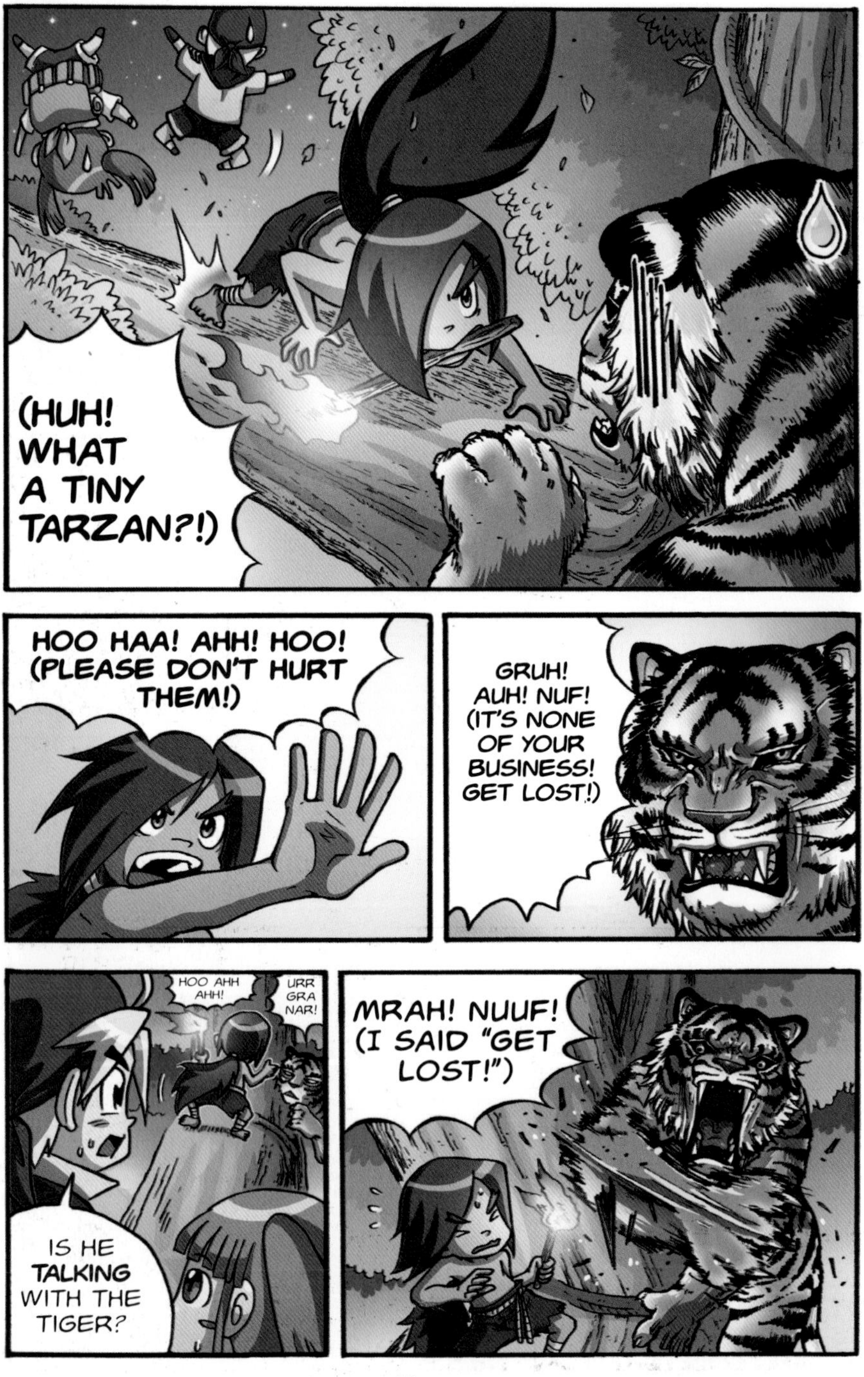
(HUH! WHAT A TINY TARZAN?!)
HOO HAA! AHH! HOO! (PLEASE DON'T HURT THEM!)
GRUH! AUH! NUF! (IT'S NONE OF YOUR BUSINESS! GET LOST!)
HOO AHH AHH!
URR GRA NAR!
IS HE TALKING WITH THE TIGER?
MRAH! NUUF! (I SAID "GET LOST!")

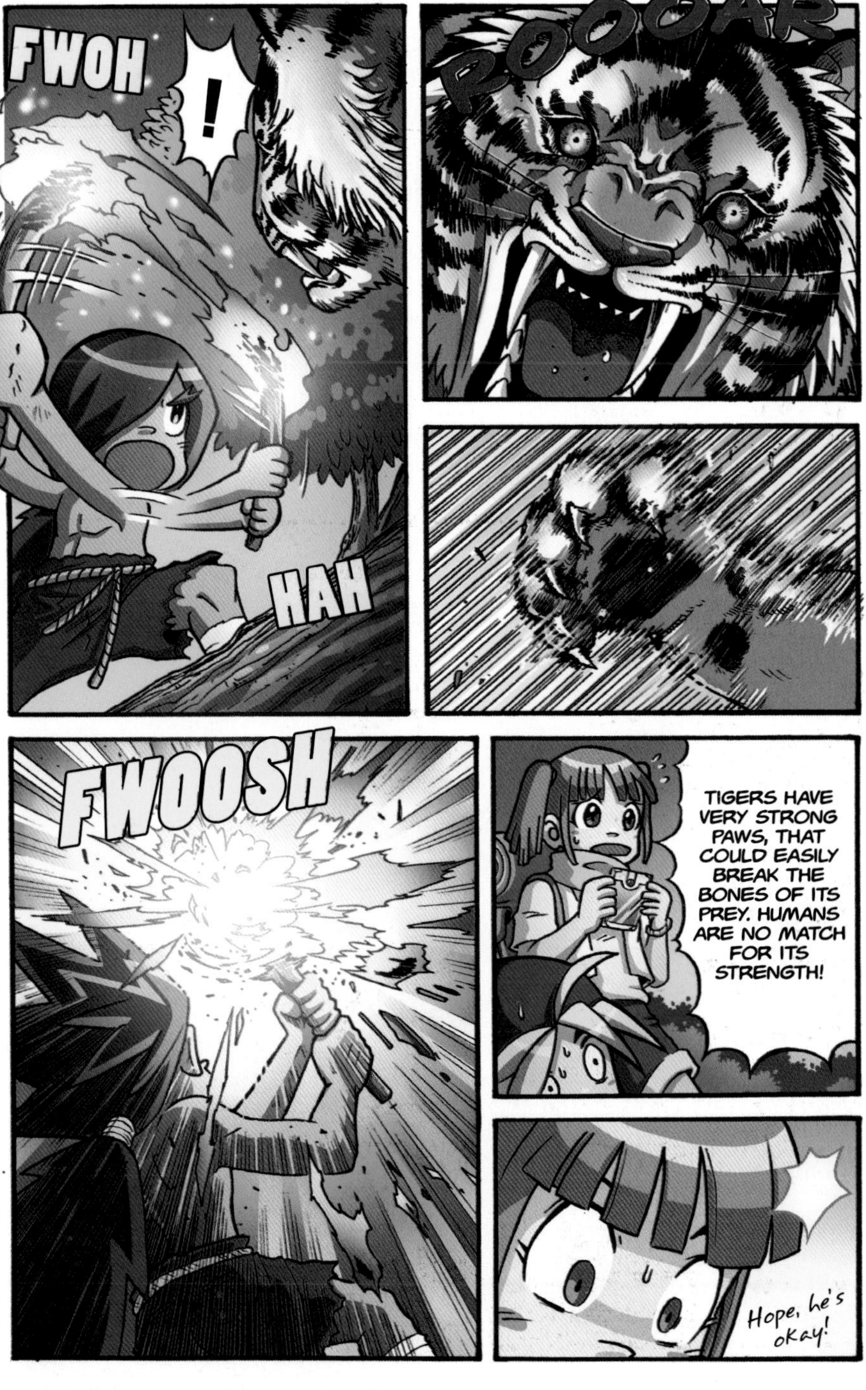
FWOH
!
HAH
ROOOOAR
FWOOSH
TIGERS HAVE VERY STRONG PAWS, THAT COULD EASILY BREAK THE BONES OF ITS PREY. HUMANS ARE NO MATCH FOR ITS STRENGTH!
Hope, he's okay!

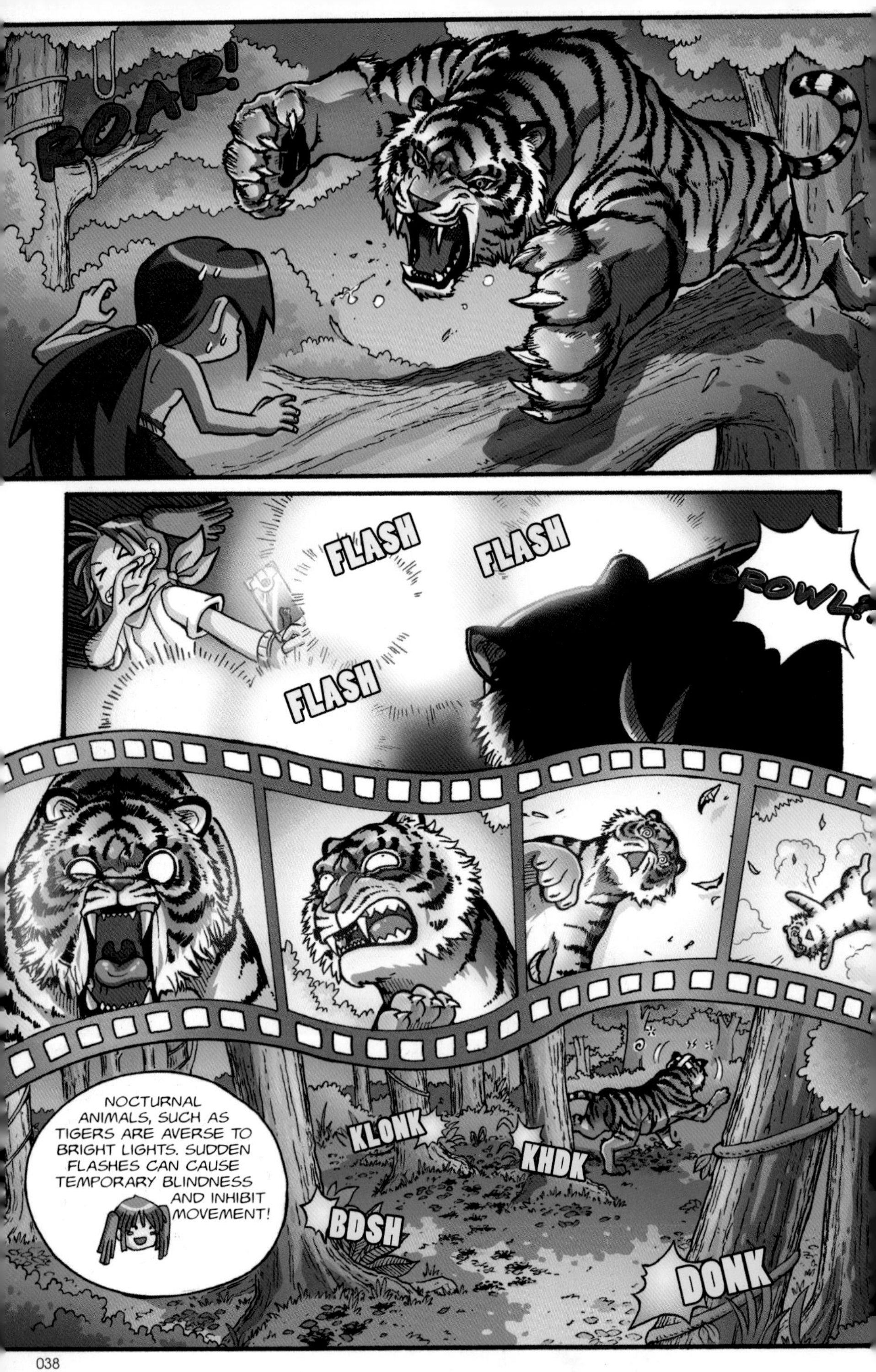
ROAR!
FLASH
FLASH
FLASH
GROWL?!
NOCTURNAL ANIMALS, SUCH AS TIGERS ARE AVERSE TO BRIGHT LIGHTS. SUDDEN FLASHES CAN CAUSE TEMPORARY BLINDNESS AND INHIBIT MOVEMENT!
KLONK
KHDK
BDSH
DONK

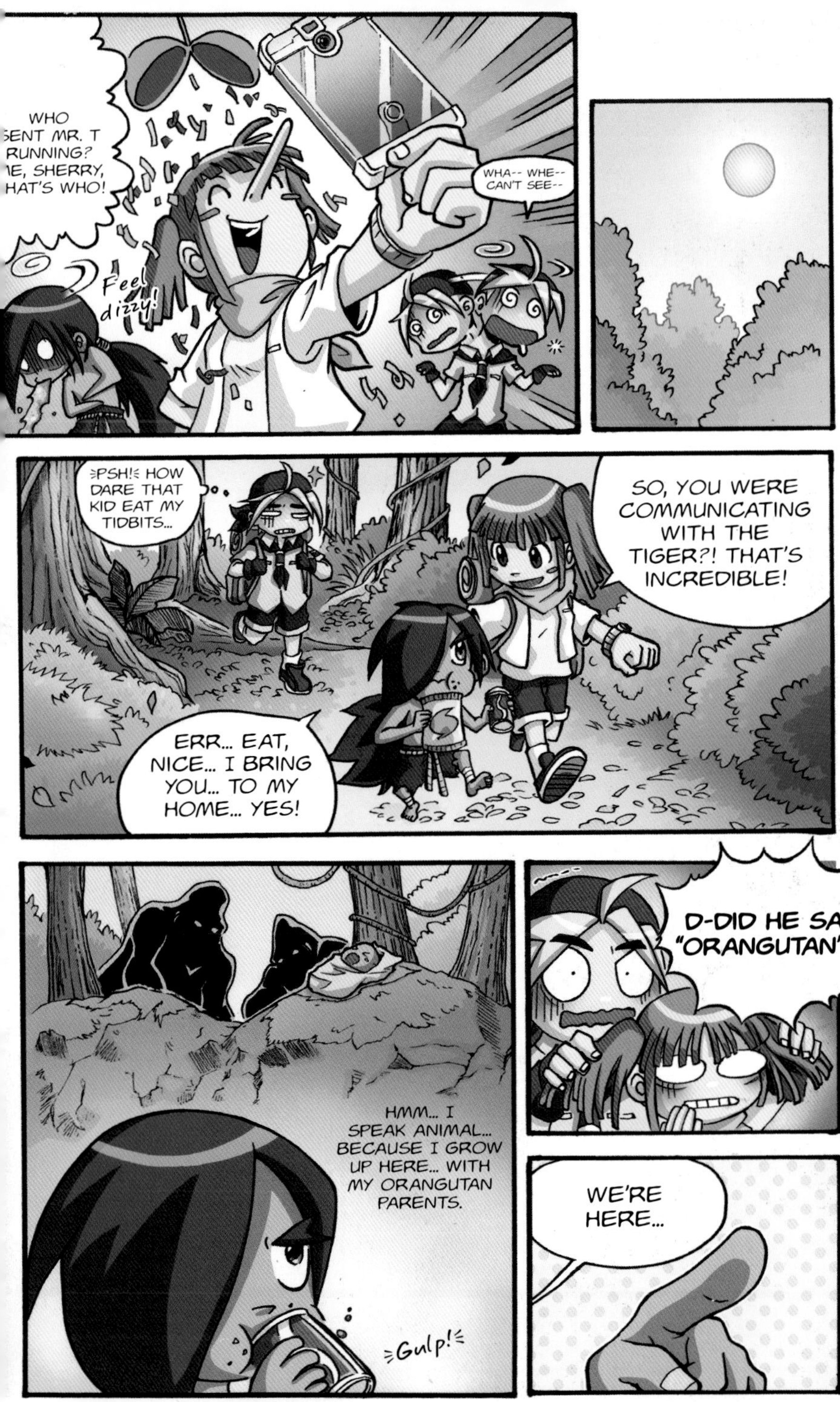
WHO
SENT MR. T
RUNNING?
ME, SHERRY,
THAT'S WHO!
Feel dizzy!
WHA-- WHE--
CAN'T SEE--
PSH! HOW DARE THAT KID EAT MY TIDBITS...
SO, YOU WERE COMMUNICATING WITH THE TIGER?! THAT'S INCREDIBLE!
ERR... EAT, NICE... I BRING YOU... TO MY HOME... YES!
HMM... I SPEAK ANIMAL... BECAUSE I GROW UP HERE... WITH MY ORANGUTAN PARENTS.
Gulp!
D-DID HE SAY "ORANGUTAN"?!
WE'RE HERE...

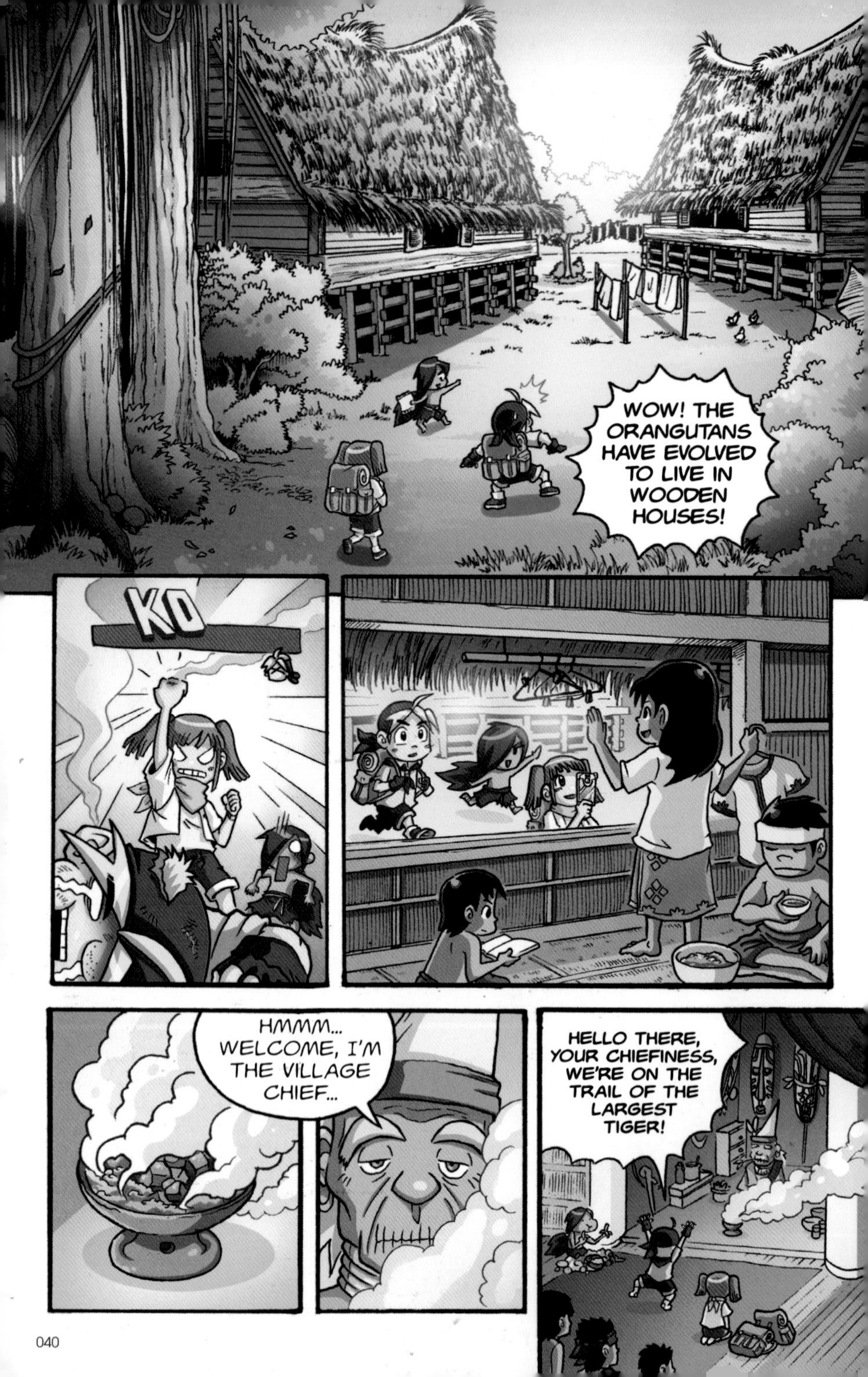
WOW! THE ORANGUTANS HAVE EVOLVED TO LIVE IN WOODEN HOUSES!
KO
HMMM... WELCOME, I'M THE VILLAGE CHIEF...
HELLO THERE, YOUR CHIEFINESS, WE'RE ON THE TRAIL OF THE LARGEST TIGER!

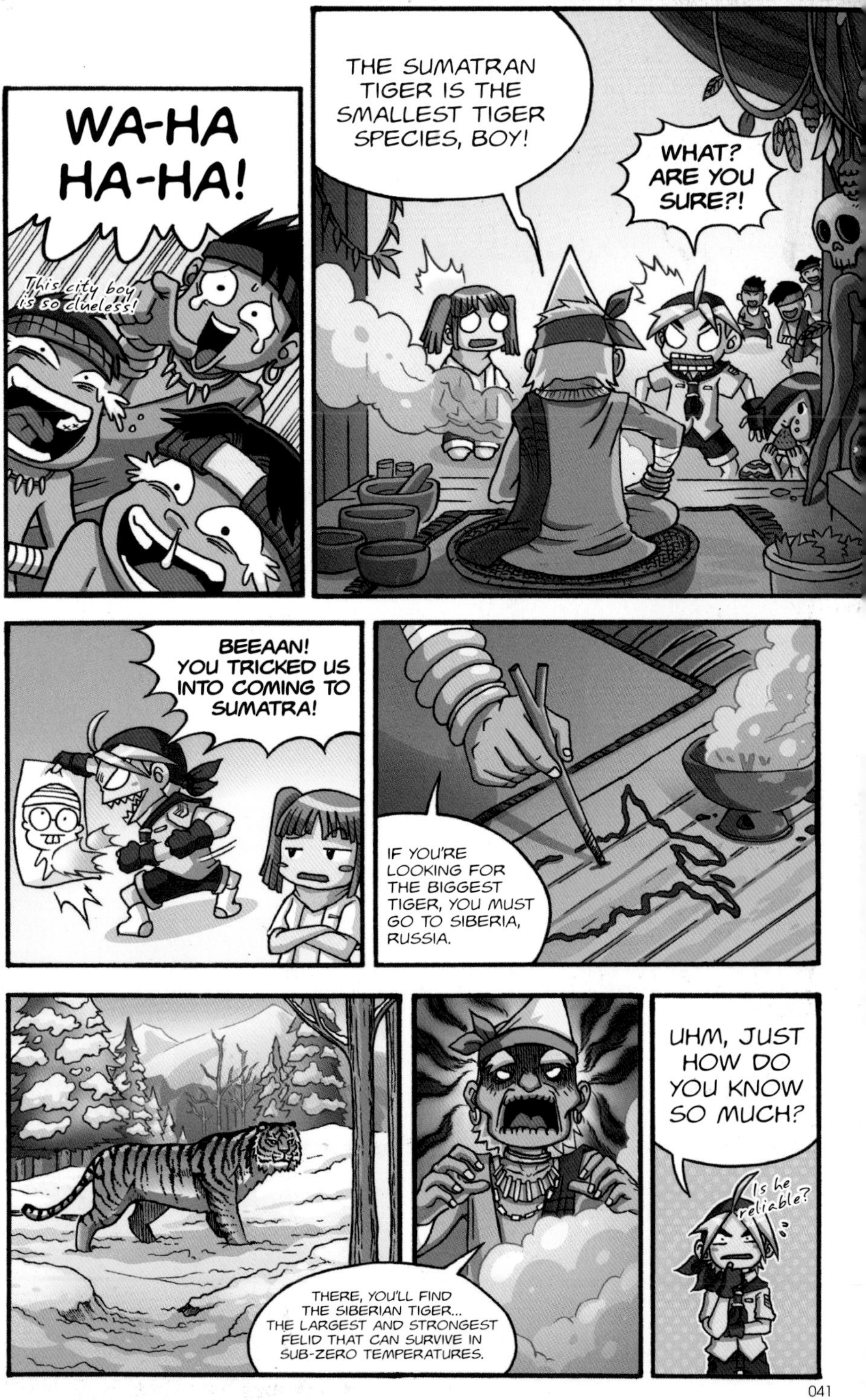
WA-HA HA-HA!
This city boy is so clueless!
THE SUMATRAN TIGER IS THE SMALLEST TIGER SPECIES, BOY!
WHAT? ARE YOU SURE?!
BEEAAN! YOU TRICKED US INTO COMING TO SUMATRA!
IF YOU'RE LOOKING FOR THE BIGGEST TIGER, YOU MUST GO TO SIBERIA, RUSSIA.
THERE, YOU'LL FIND THE SIBERIAN TIGER... THE LARGEST AND STRONGEST FELID THAT CAN SURVIVE IN SUB-ZERO TEMPERATURES.
UHM, JUST HOW DO YOU KNOW SO MUCH?
Is he reliable?

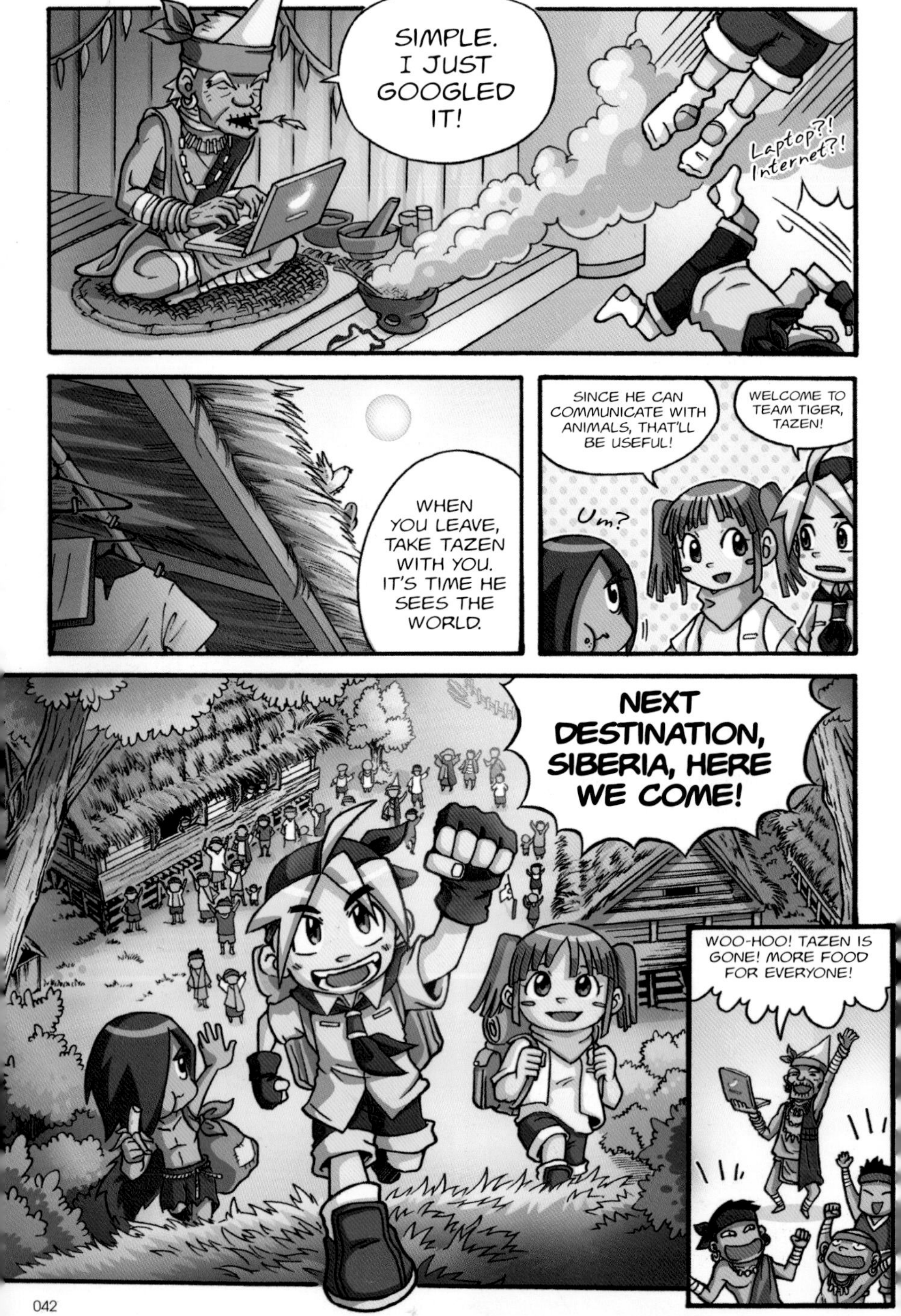
SIMPLE. I JUST GOOGLED IT!
Laptop?! Internet?!
WHEN YOU LEAVE, TAKE TAZEN WITH YOU. IT'S TIME HE SEES THE WORLD.
SINCE HE CAN COMMUNICATE WITH ANIMALS, THAT'LL BE USEFUL!
WELCOME TO TEAM TIGER, TAZEN!
Um?
NEXT DESTINATION, SIBERIA, HERE WE COME!
WOO-HOO! TAZEN IS GONE! MORE FOOD FOR EVERYONE!

Conservation Status

Extinct	Extinct in the Wild	Critically Endangered	Endangered	Vulnerable	Near Threatened	Least Concern
EX	EW	CR	EN	VU	NT	LC

Species: Neofelis nebulosa
Length (including tail): 4.25 to 6.5 feet
Weight: 24 to 50 pounds
Common prey: Forest deer and birds
Distribution: Himalayan foothills to mainland Southeast Asia
Habitats: Open or closed tropical forests

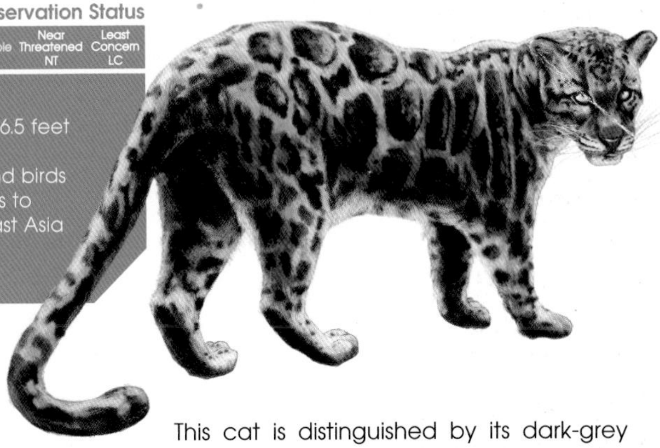

CLOUDED LEOPARD

Strength
Intelligence
Attack
Defense
Speed

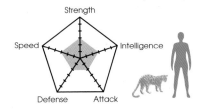

This cat is distinguished by its dark-grey blotches bordered by curved or looped stripe markings. An excellent climber, it uses its long tail for balance and stability. Generally solitary, it becomes active around dawn or dusk. The female breeds once a year, giving birth to around 3 cubs that are blind till they are 10 days old.

Conservation Status

Extinct	Extinct in the Wild	Critically Endangered	Endangered	Vulnerable	Near Threatened	Least Concern
EX	EW	CR	EN	VU	NT	LC

Species: Neofelis diardi
Length (including tail): 6 to 6.5 feet
Weight: 26 to 55 pounds
Common prey: From deer to wild boar
Distribution: Sumatra and Borneo
Habitats: Tropical forest

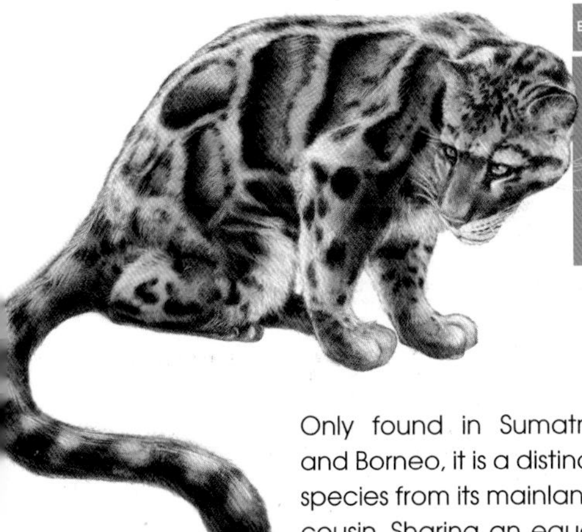

SUNDA CLOUDED LEOPARD

Only found in Sumatra and Borneo, it is a distinct species from its mainland cousin. Sharing an equal affinity for climbing, the Sunda clouded leopard is distinguished by two clear black stripes on the neck, it is more abundant in Borneo, where the absence of tigers means it is the apex rainforest predator.

Strength
Intelligence
Attack
Defense
Speed

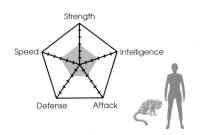

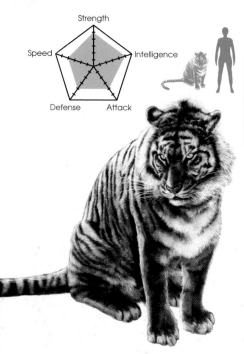

Strength

Speed — Intelligence

Defense — Attack

Conservation Status

Extinct EX	Extinct in the Wild EW	Critically Endangered CR	Endangered EN	Vulnerable VU	Near Threatened NT	Least Concern LC

Species: Panthera tigris sumatrae
Length (excluding tail): 7 to 10 feet
Weight: 165 to 309 pounds
Common prey: From deer to wild pigs
and livestock
Distribution: Sumatra
Habitat: Tropical forest

SUMATRAN TIGER

Found exclusively in Sumatra, it is one of the smallest tiger subspecies. Due to massive habitat destruction, its population has dwindled to less than 700 worldwide. More closely striped than other tigers, it lives in lowland, sub-mountainous regions and near mangrove forests. It preys primarily upon deer and wild pigs, its excellent swimming prowess, allowing it to sometimes catch fish.

LITTLE AND LARGE; SUMATRAN VS. SIBERIAN TIGER

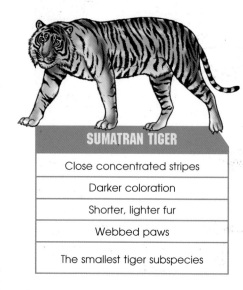

SUMATRAN TIGER	SIBERIAN TIGER
Close concentrated stripes	Loosely arranged stripes
Darker coloration	Paler coloration
Shorter, lighter fur	Longer, thicker fur
Webbed paws	Thick padded paws
The smallest tiger subspecies	The largest tiger subspecies (able to grow to twice the size of Sumatran tigers)

CHAPTER 3

LYING LOW WITH LIONS

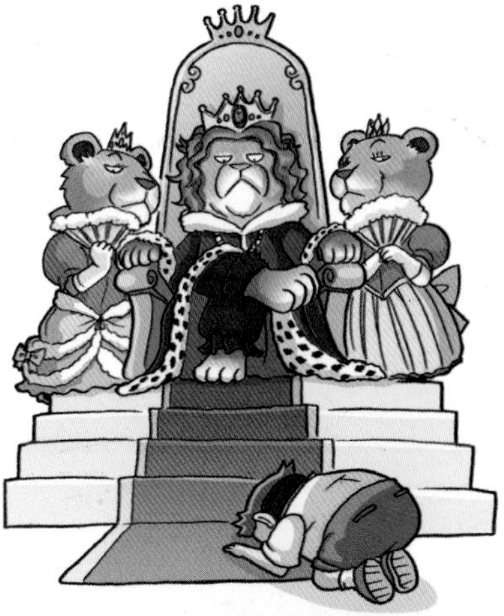

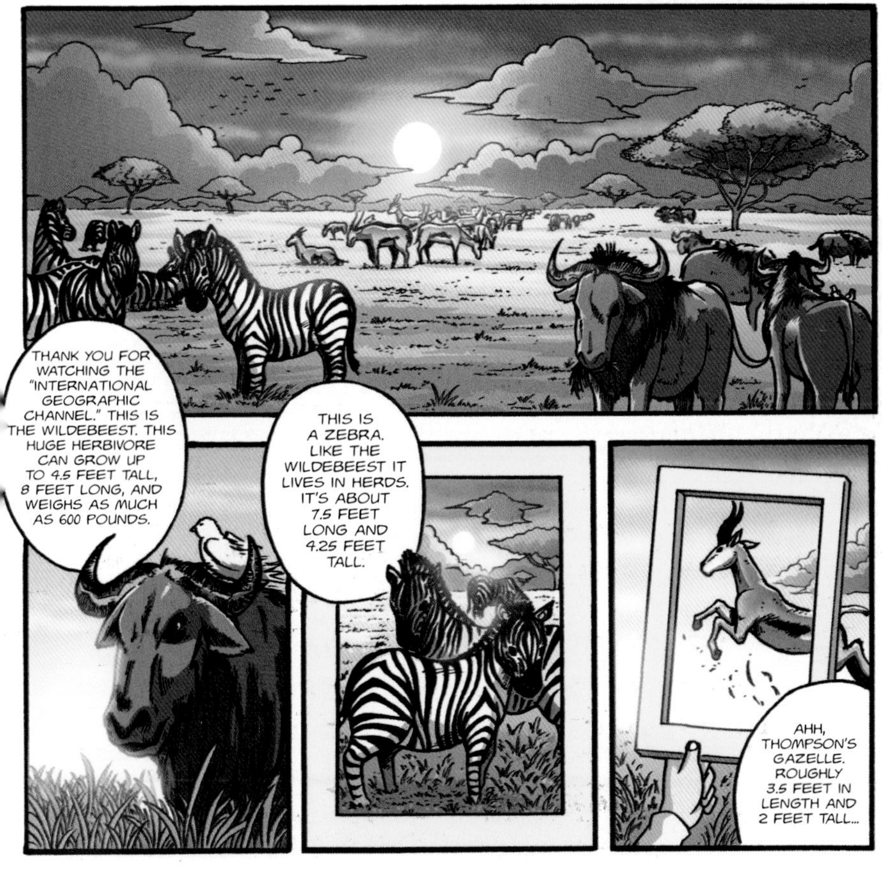

THANK YOU FOR WATCHING THE "INTERNATIONAL GEOGRAPHIC CHANNEL." THIS IS THE WILDEBEEST. THIS HUGE HERBIVORE CAN GROW UP TO 4.5 FEET TALL, 8 FEET LONG, AND WEIGHS AS MUCH AS 600 POUNDS.
THIS IS A ZEBRA. LIKE THE WILDEBEEST IT LIVES IN HERDS. IT'S ABOUT 7.5 FEET LONG AND 4.25 FEET TALL.
AHH, THOMPSON'S GAZELLE. ROUGHLY 3.5 FEET IN LENGTH AND 2 FEET TALL...

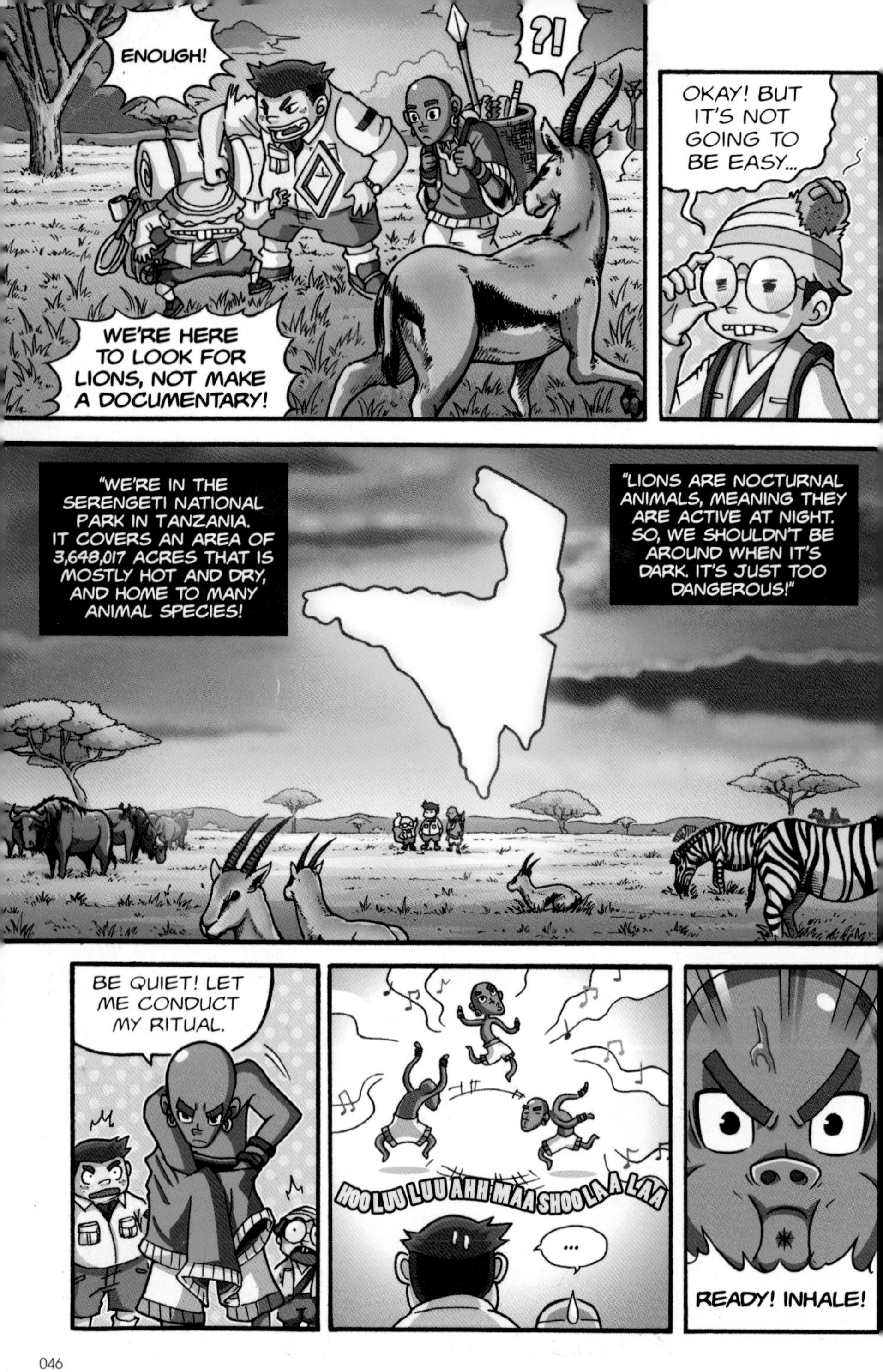
ENOUGH!
?!
WE'RE HERE TO LOOK FOR LIONS, NOT MAKE A DOCUMENTARY!
OKAY! BUT IT'S NOT GOING TO BE EASY...
"WE'RE IN THE SERENGETI NATIONAL PARK IN TANZANIA. IT COVERS AN AREA OF 3,648,017 ACRES THAT IS MOSTLY HOT AND DRY, AND HOME TO MANY ANIMAL SPECIES!
"LIONS ARE NOCTURNAL ANIMALS, MEANING THEY ARE ACTIVE AT NIGHT. SO, WE SHOULDN'T BE AROUND WHEN IT'S DARK. IT'S JUST TOO DANGEROUS!"
BE QUIET! LET ME CONDUCT MY RITUAL.
HOO LUU LUU AHH MAA SHOO LA A LAA
...
READY! INHALE!

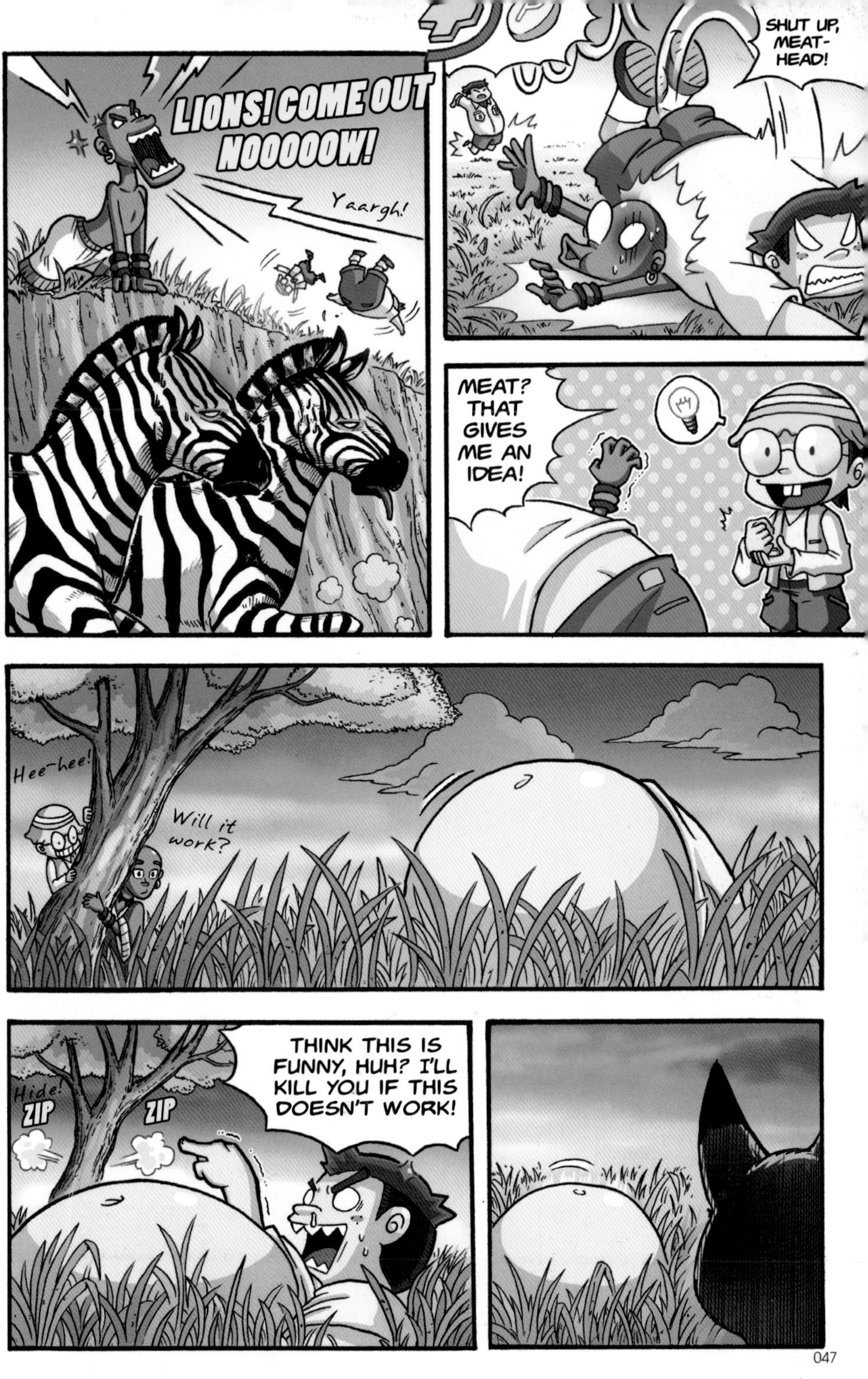
LIONS! COME OUT NOOOOOW!
Yaargh!
SHUT UP, MEAT-HEAD!
MEAT? THAT GIVES ME AN IDEA!
Hee-hee!
Will it work?
Hide!
ZIP
ZIP
THINK THIS IS FUNNY, HUH? I'LL KILL YOU IF THIS DOESN'T WORK!

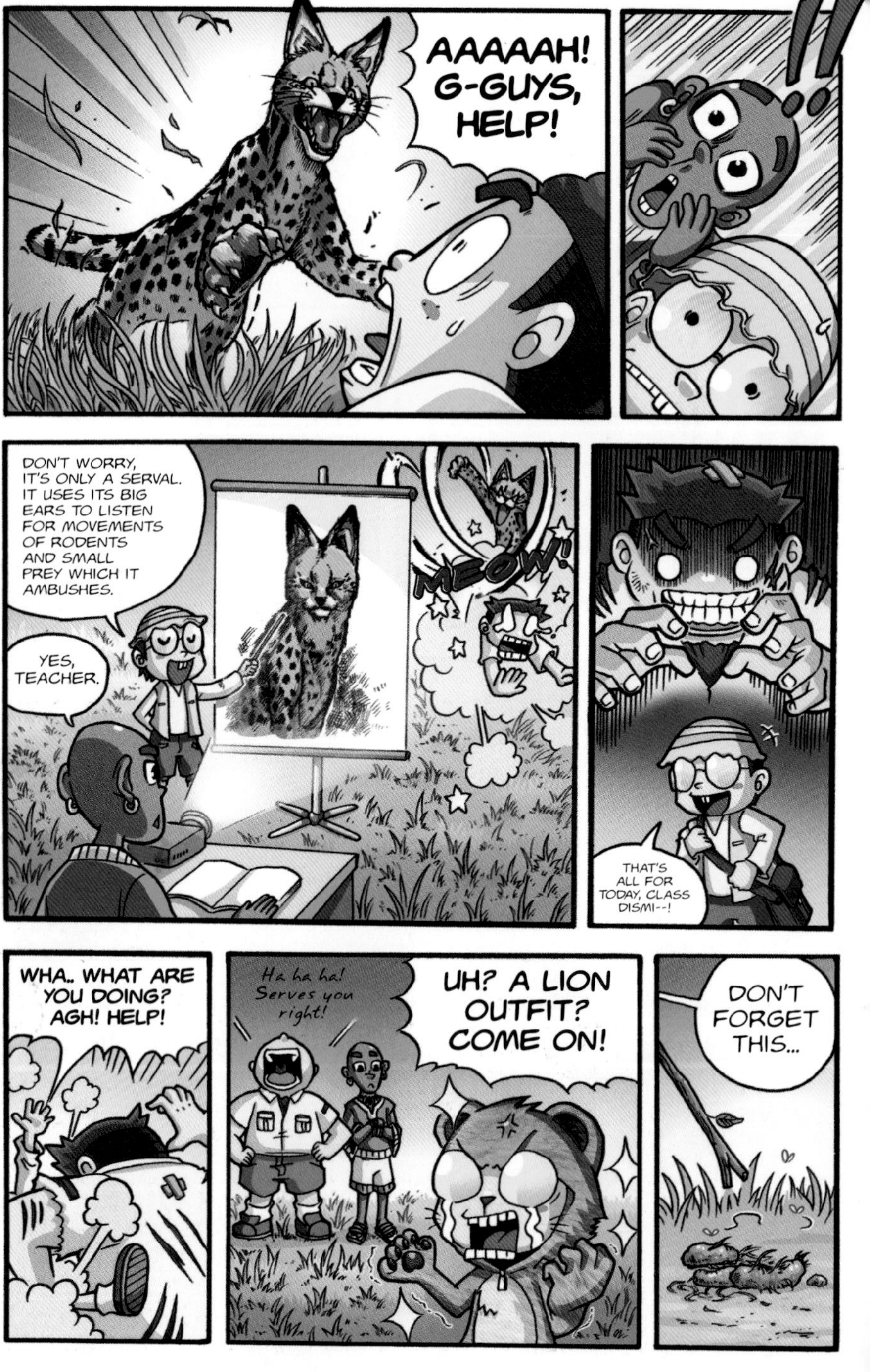

AAAAAH! G-GUYS, HELP!
DON'T WORRY, IT'S ONLY A SERVAL. IT USES ITS BIG EARS TO LISTEN FOR MOVEMENTS OF RODENTS AND SMALL PREY WHICH IT AMBUSHES.
YES, TEACHER.
MEOW!
THAT'S ALL FOR TODAY, CLASS DISMI--!
WHA.. WHAT ARE YOU DOING? AGH! HELP!
Ha ha ha! Serves you right!
UH? A LION OUTFIT? COME ON!
DON'T FORGET THIS...

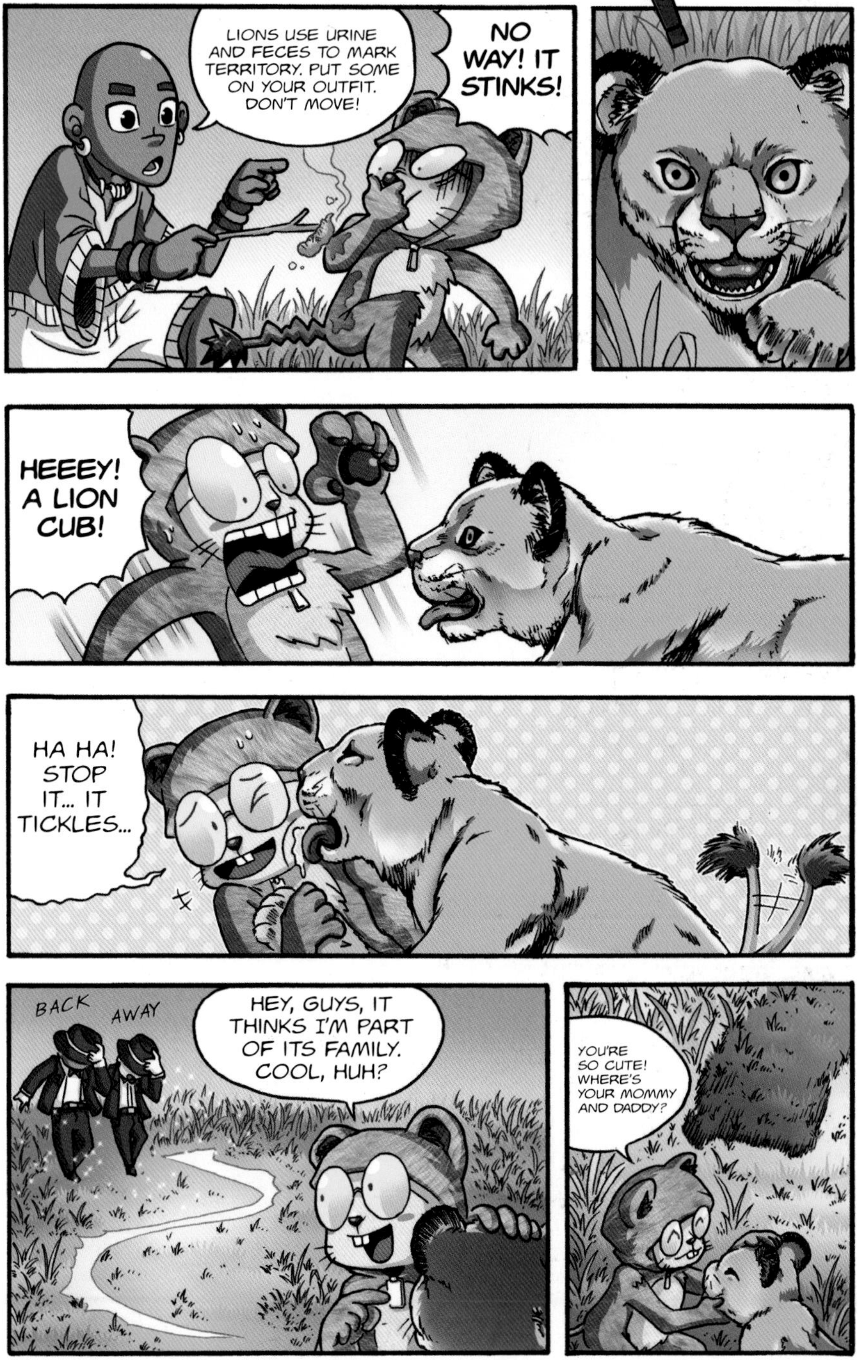
LIONS USE URINE AND FECES TO MARK TERRITORY. PUT SOME ON YOUR OUTFIT. DON'T MOVE!
NO WAY! IT STINKS!
HEEEY! A LION CUB!
HA HA! STOP IT... IT TICKLES...
BACK
AWAY
HEY, GUYS, IT THINKS I'M PART OF ITS FAMILY. COOL, HUH?
YOU'RE SO CUTE! WHERE'S YOUR MOMMY AND DADDY?

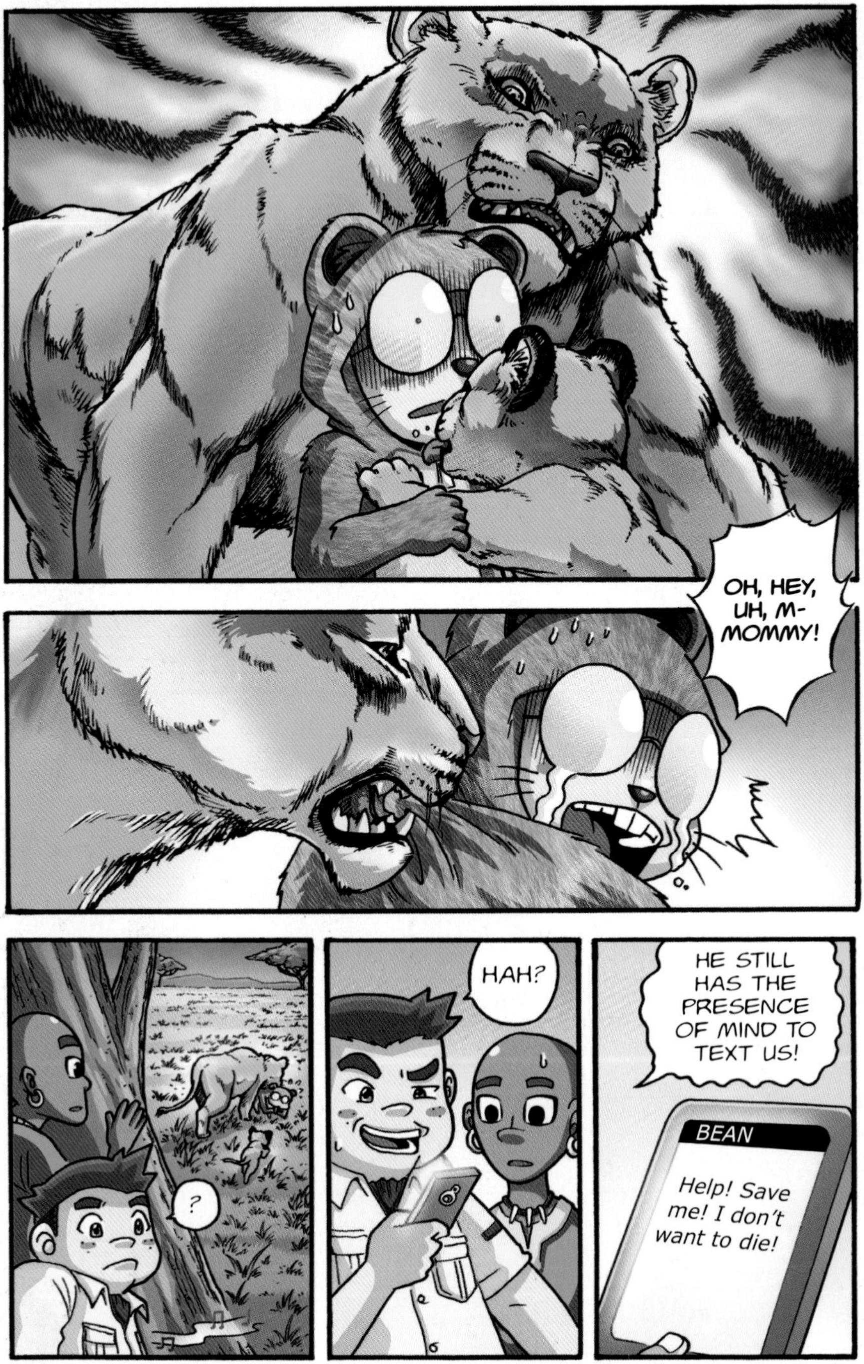
OH, HEY, UH, M-MOMMY!
?
HAH?
HE STILL HAS THE PRESENCE OF MIND TO TEXT US!
BEAN
Help! Save me! I don't want to die!

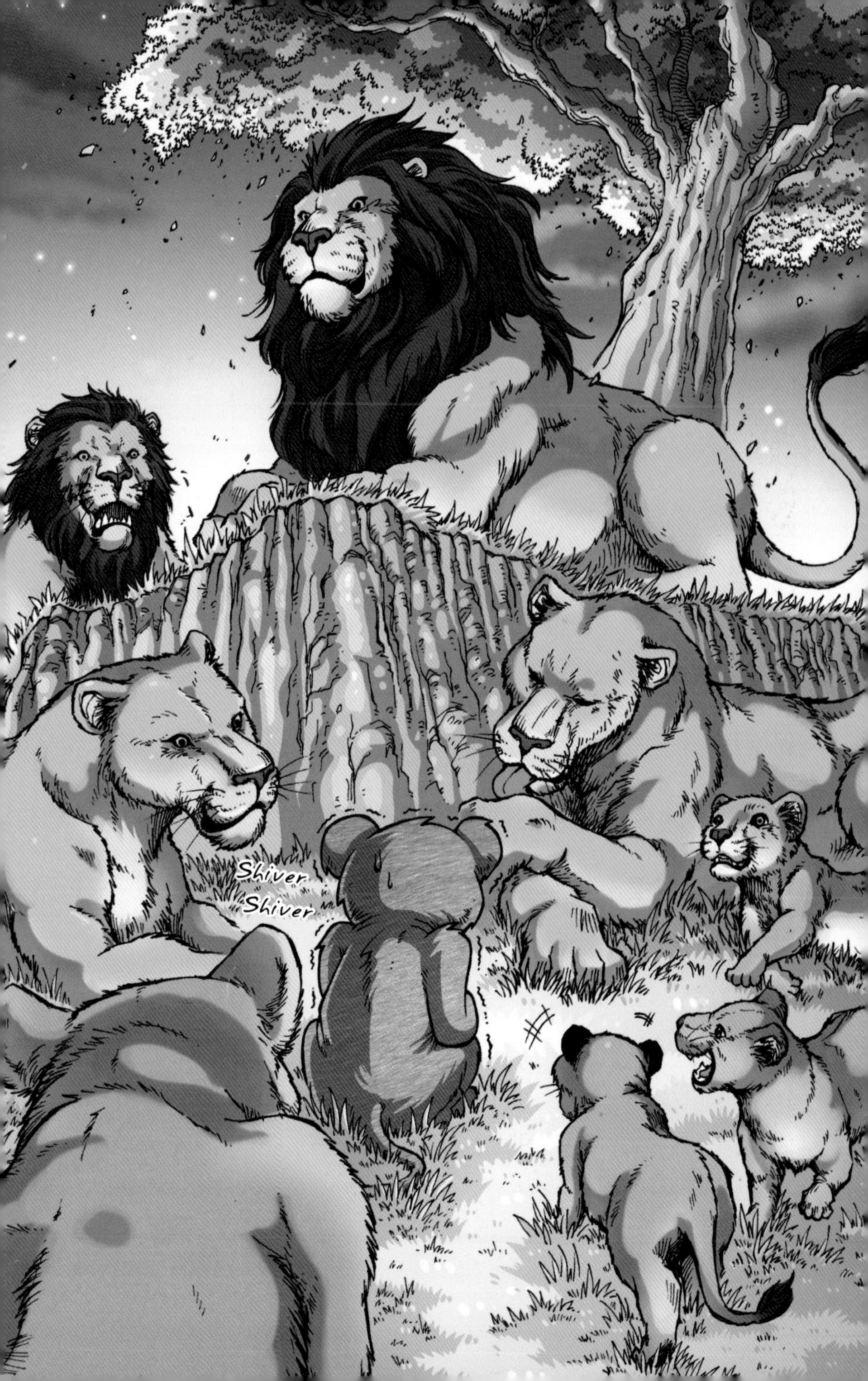
Shiver
Shiver

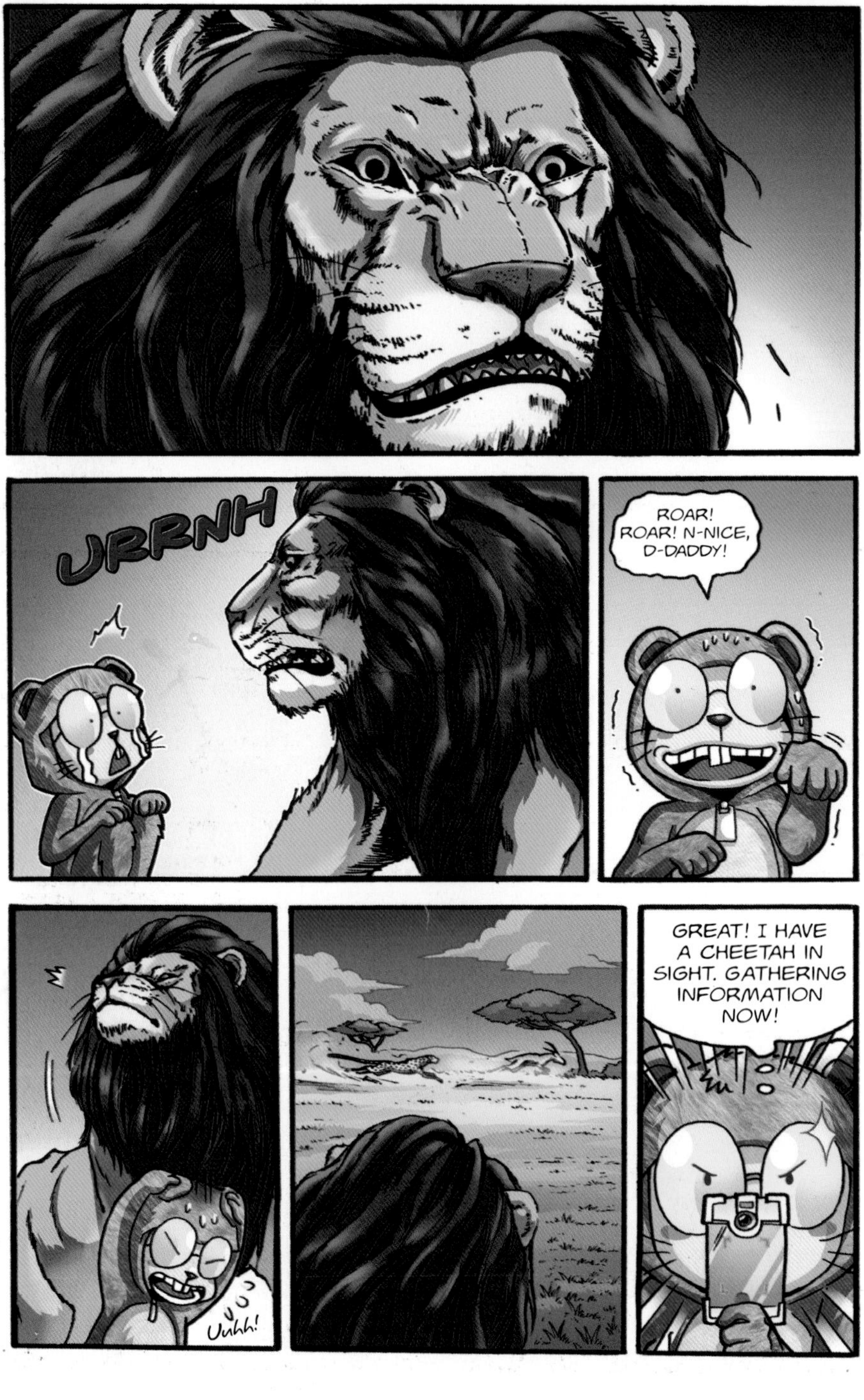
URRNH
ROAR! ROAR! N-NICE, D-DADDY!
Uuhh!
GREAT! I HAVE A CHEETAH IN SIGHT. GATHERING INFORMATION NOW!

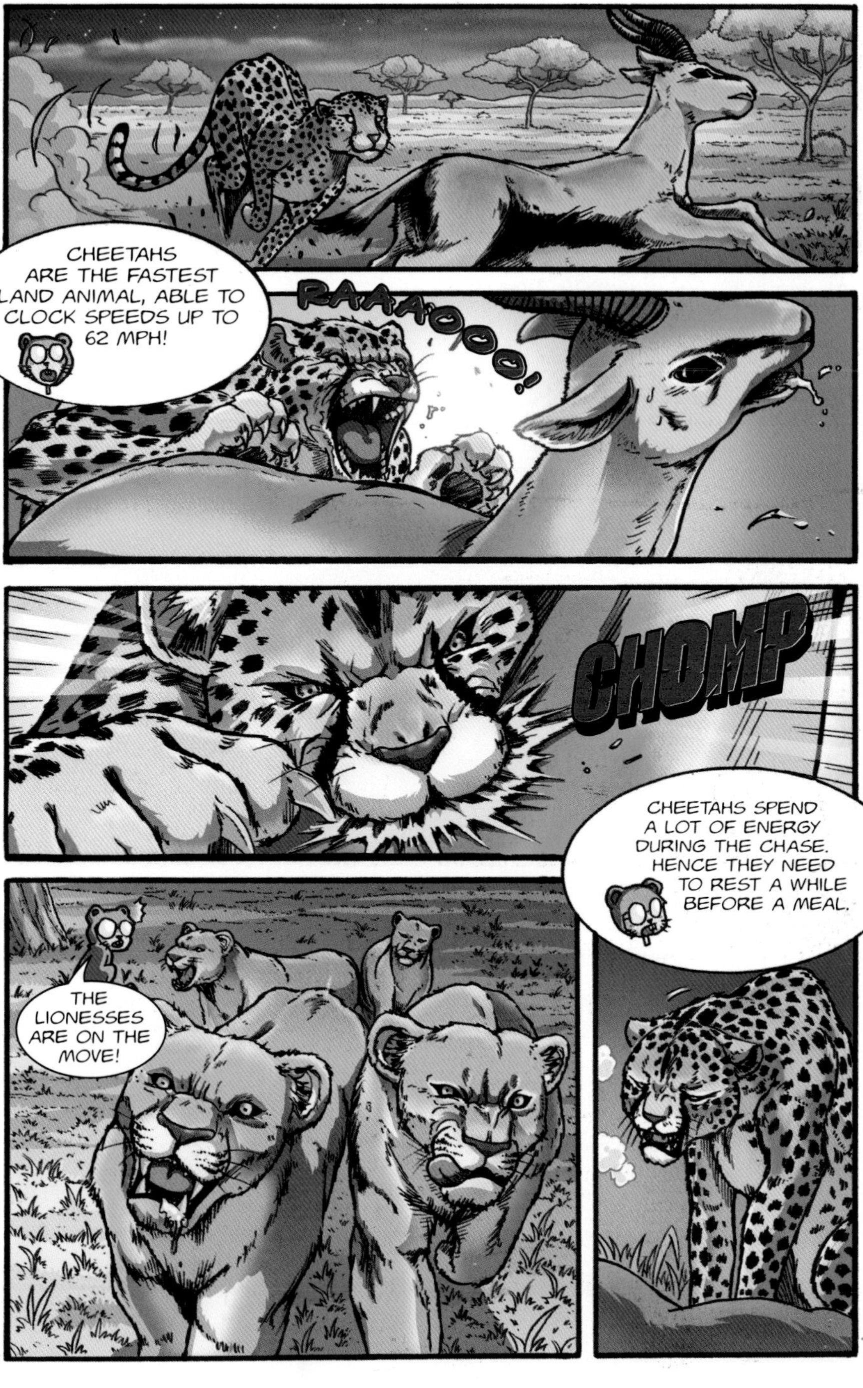
CHEETAHS ARE THE FASTEST LAND ANIMAL, ABLE TO CLOCK SPEEDS UP TO 62 MPH!
RAAAOOOO!
CHOMP
CHEETAHS SPEND A LOT OF ENERGY DURING THE CHASE. HENCE THEY NEED TO REST A WHILE BEFORE A MEAL.
THE LIONESSES ARE ON THE MOVE!

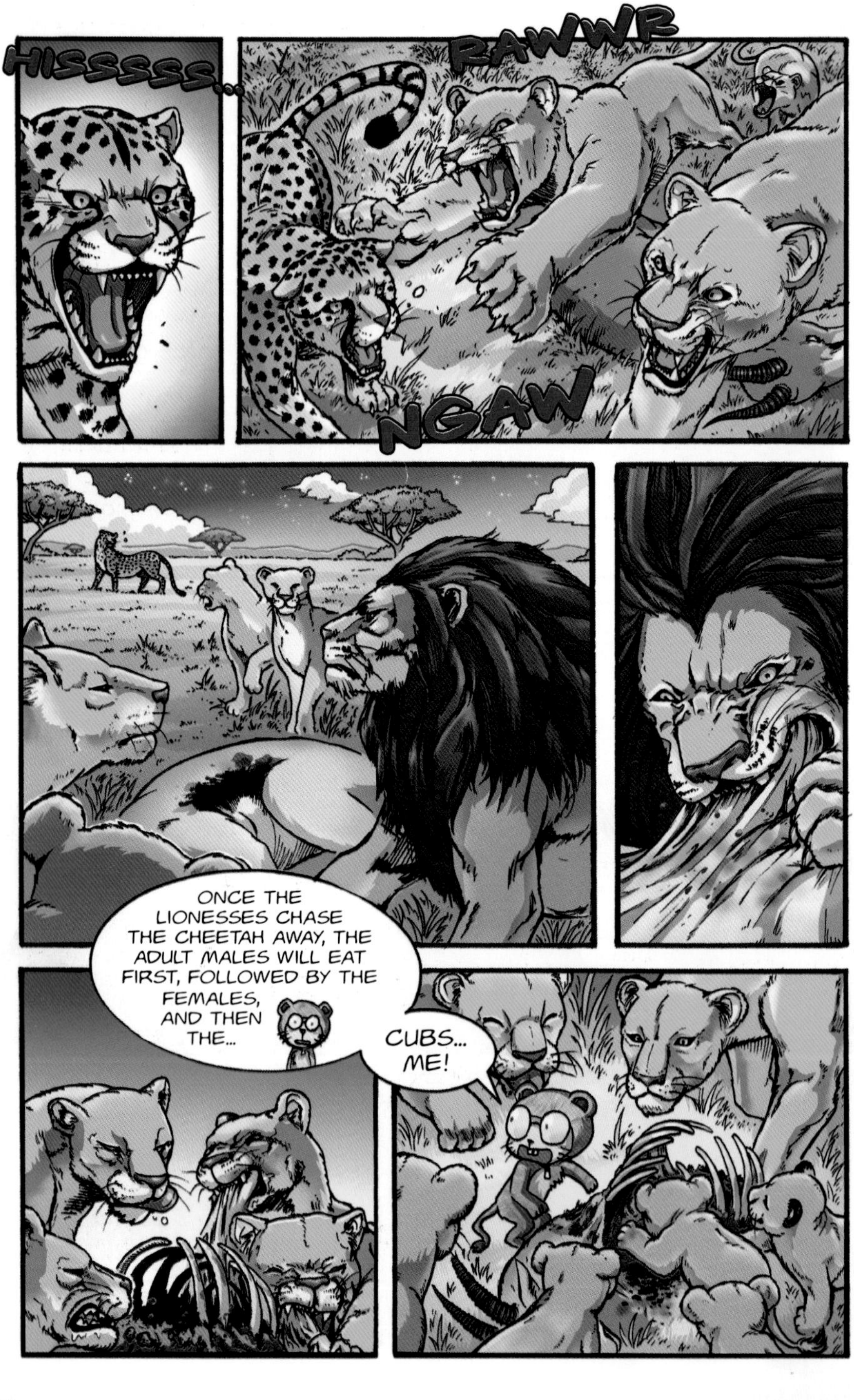

HISSSSS...
RAWWR
NGAW
ONCE THE LIONESSES CHASE THE CHEETAH AWAY, THE ADULT MALES WILL EAT FIRST, FOLLOWED BY THE FEMALES, AND THEN THE...
CUBS... ME!

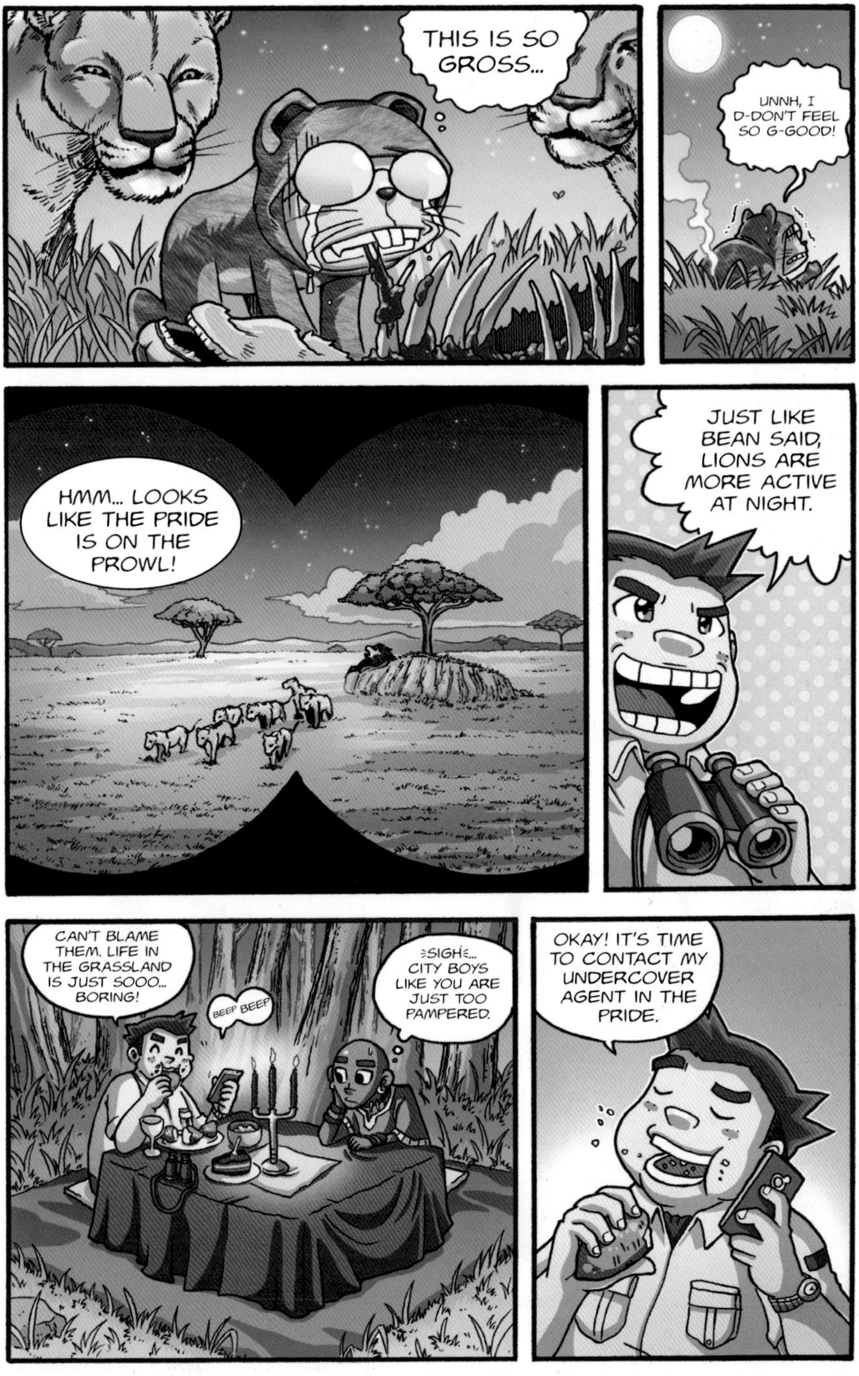
THIS IS SO GROSS...
UNNH, I D-DON'T FEEL SO G-GOOD!
HMM... LOOKS LIKE THE PRIDE IS ON THE PROWL!
JUST LIKE BEAN SAID, LIONS ARE MORE ACTIVE AT NIGHT.
CAN'T BLAME THEM. LIFE IN THE GRASSLAND IS JUST SOOO... BORING!
BEEP BEEP
≶SIGH≷... CITY BOYS LIKE YOU ARE JUST TOO PAMPERED.
OKAY! IT'S TIME TO CONTACT MY UNDERCOVER AGENT IN THE PRIDE.

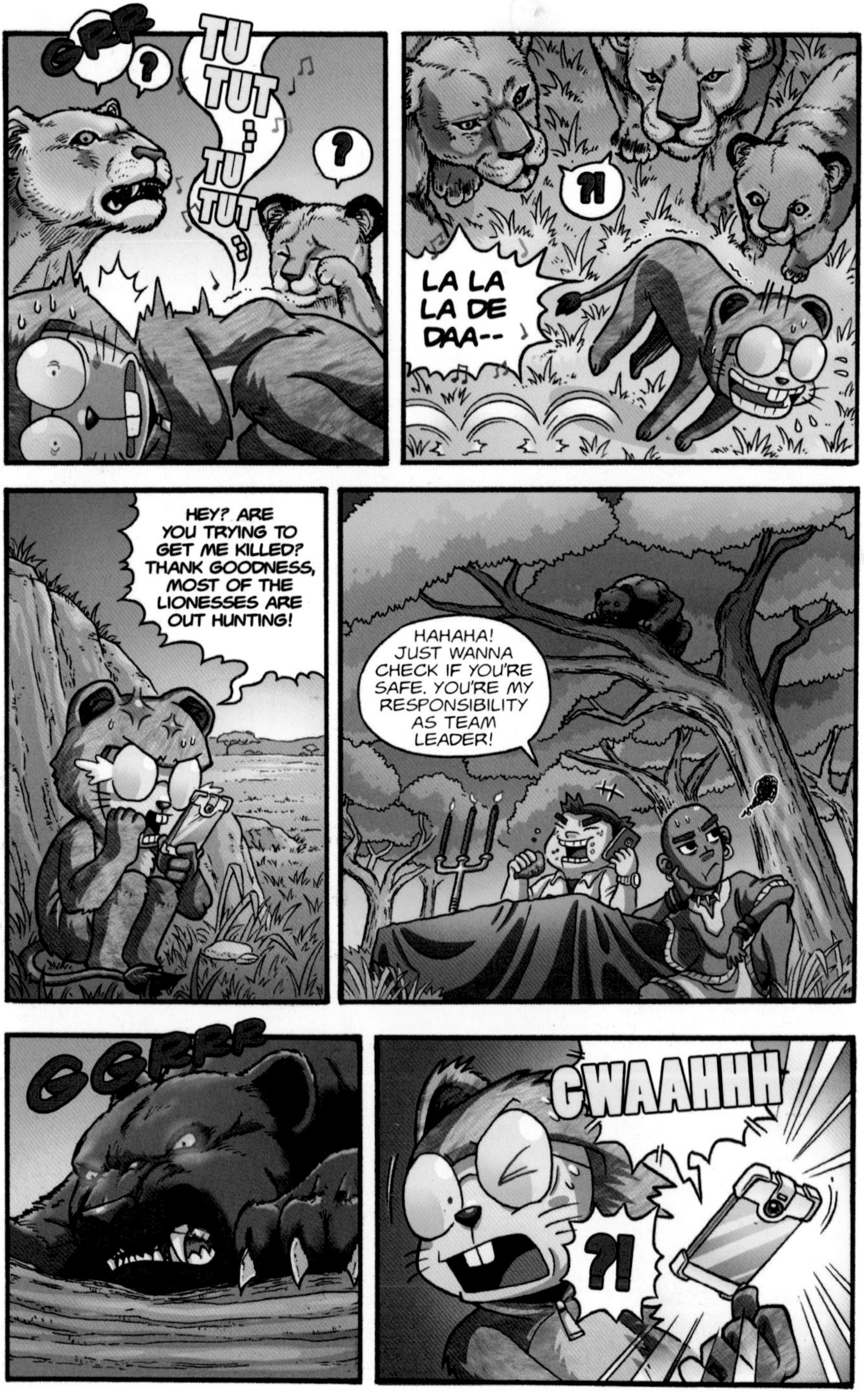
GRR
?
TU TUT .. TU TUT ..
?
?!
LA LA LA DE DAA--
HEY? ARE YOU TRYING TO GET ME KILLED? THANK GOODNESS, MOST OF THE LIONESSES ARE OUT HUNTING!
HAHAHA! JUST WANNA CHECK IF YOU'RE SAFE. YOU'RE MY RESPONSIBILITY AS TEAM LEADER!
GGRRR
CWAAHHH
?!

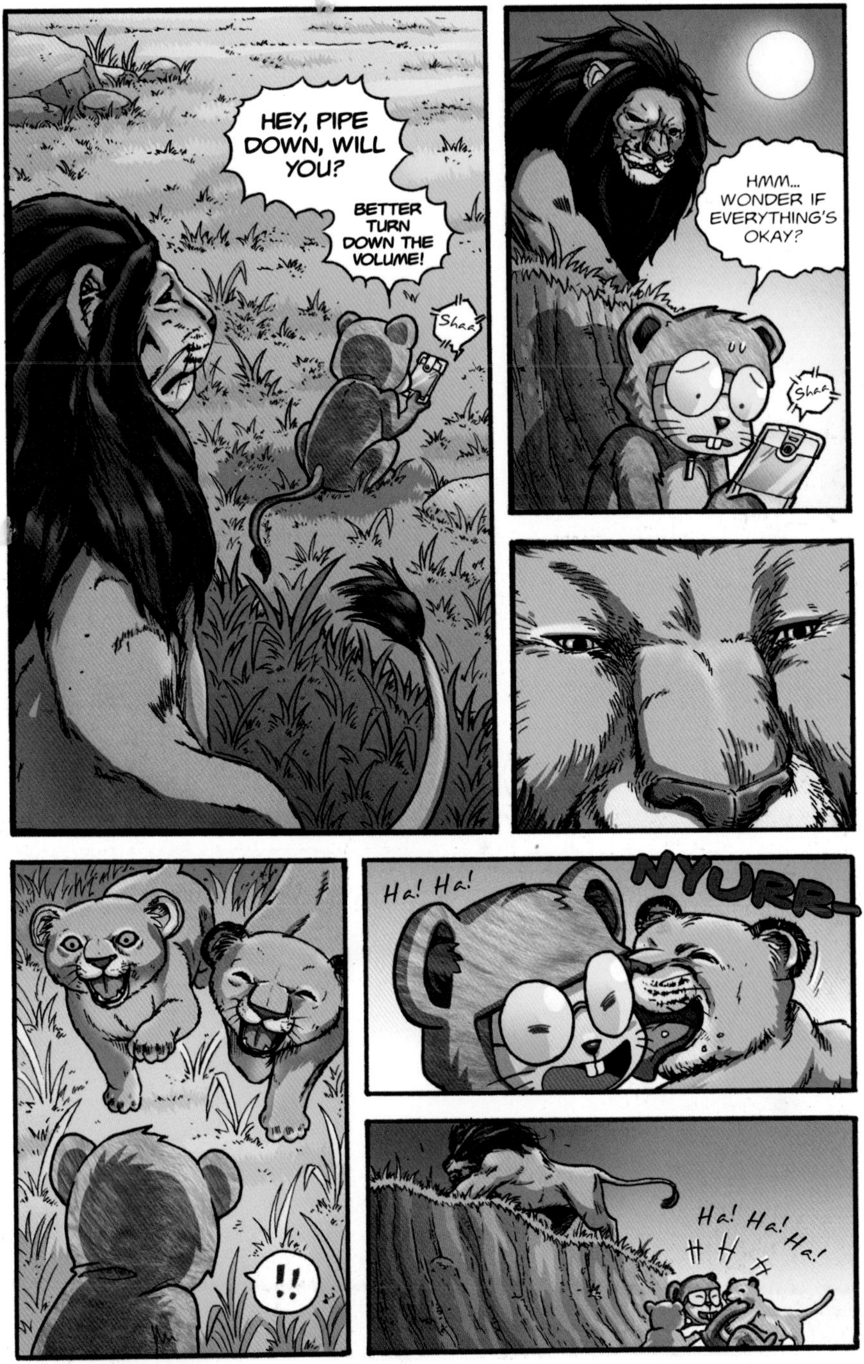
HEY, PIPE DOWN, WILL YOU?
BETTER TURN DOWN THE VOLUME!
Shaa
HMM... WONDER IF EVERYTHING'S OKAY?
Shaa
!!
Ha! Ha!
NYURR-
Ha! Ha! Ha!

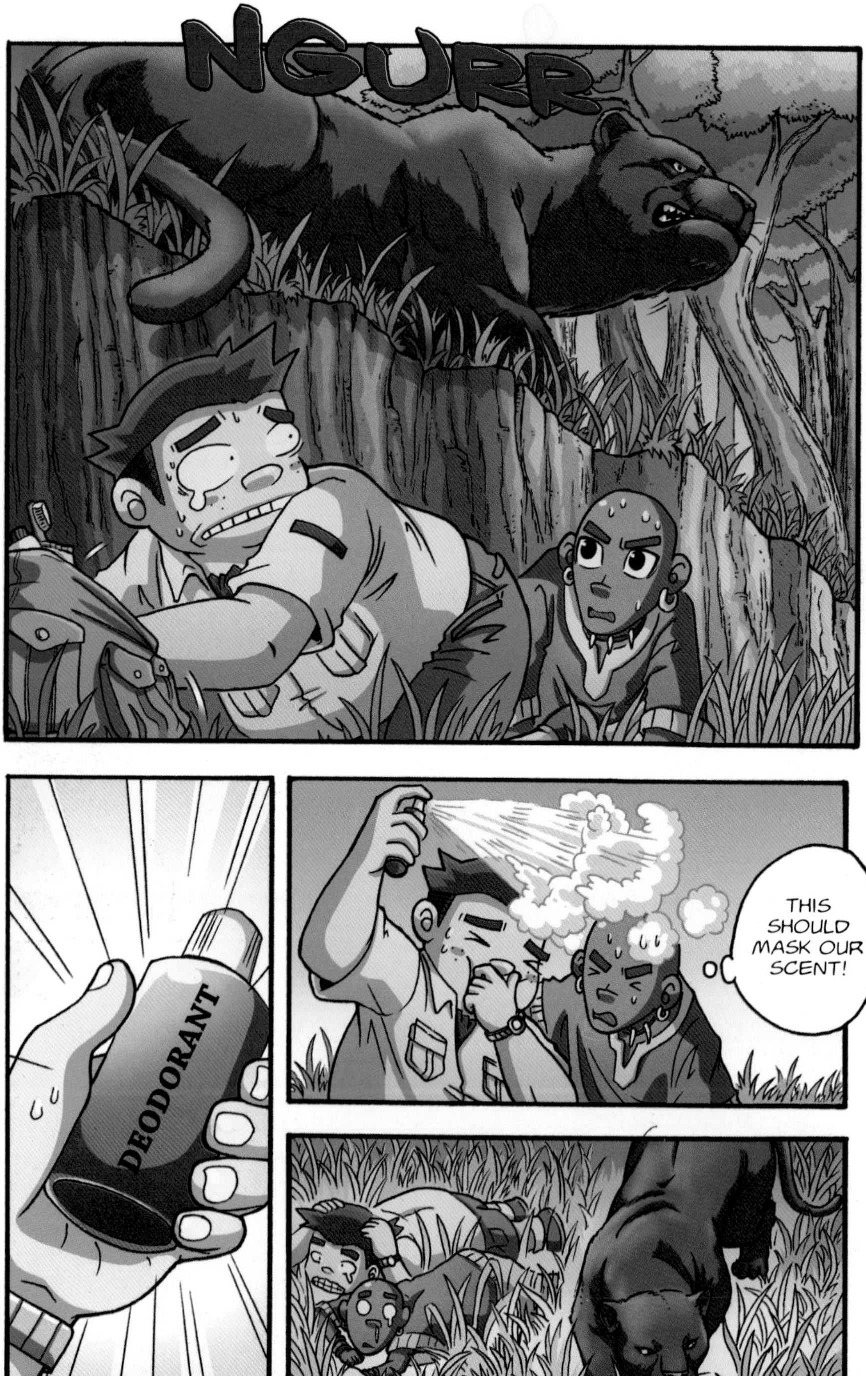
NGURR
DEODORANT
THIS SHOULD MASK OUR SCENT!

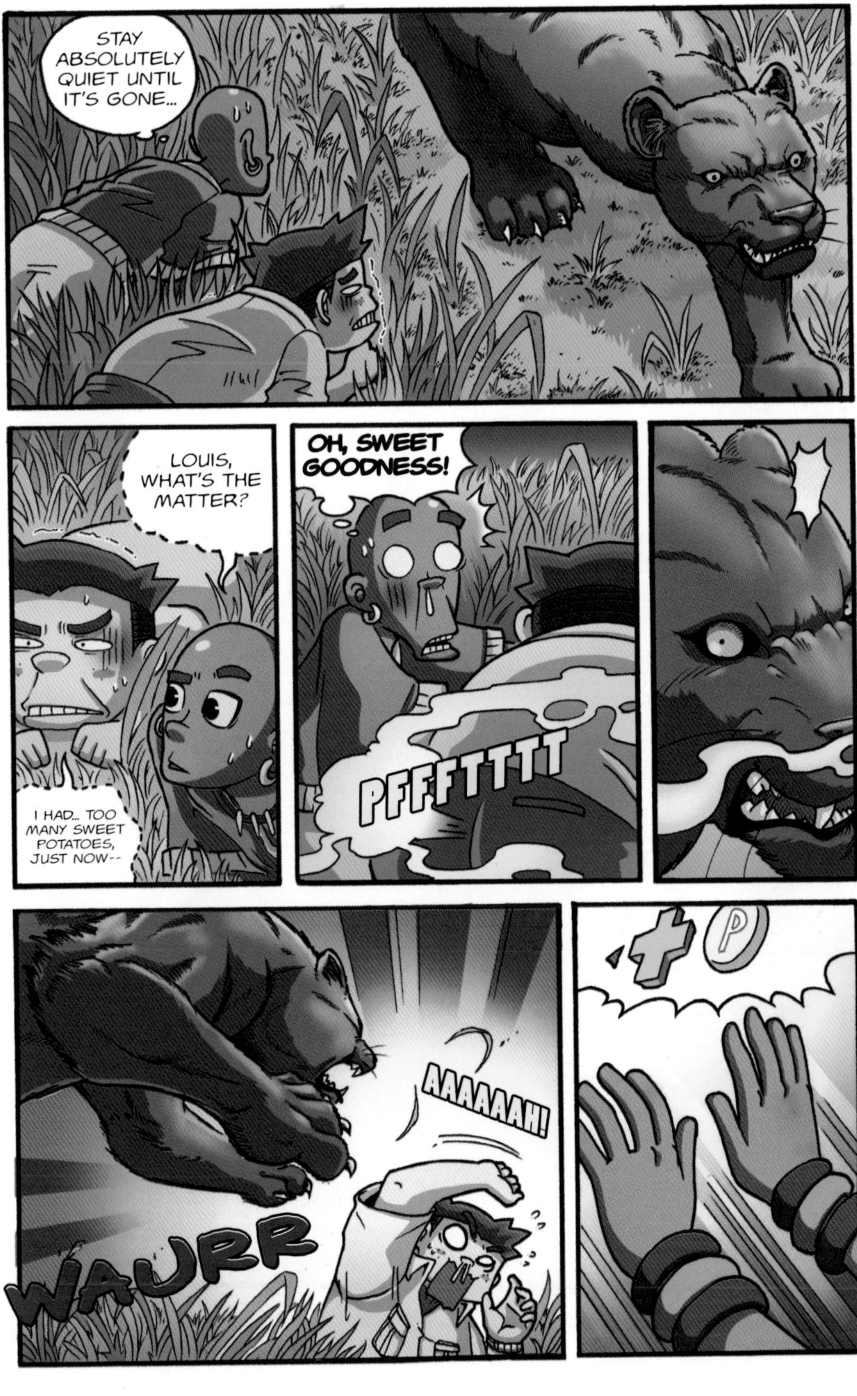

STAY ABSOLUTELY QUIET UNTIL IT'S GONE...
LOUIS, WHAT'S THE MATTER?
I HAD... TOO MANY SWEET POTATOES, JUST NOW--
OH, SWEET GOODNESS!
PFFFTTTT
AAAAAAH!
WAURR

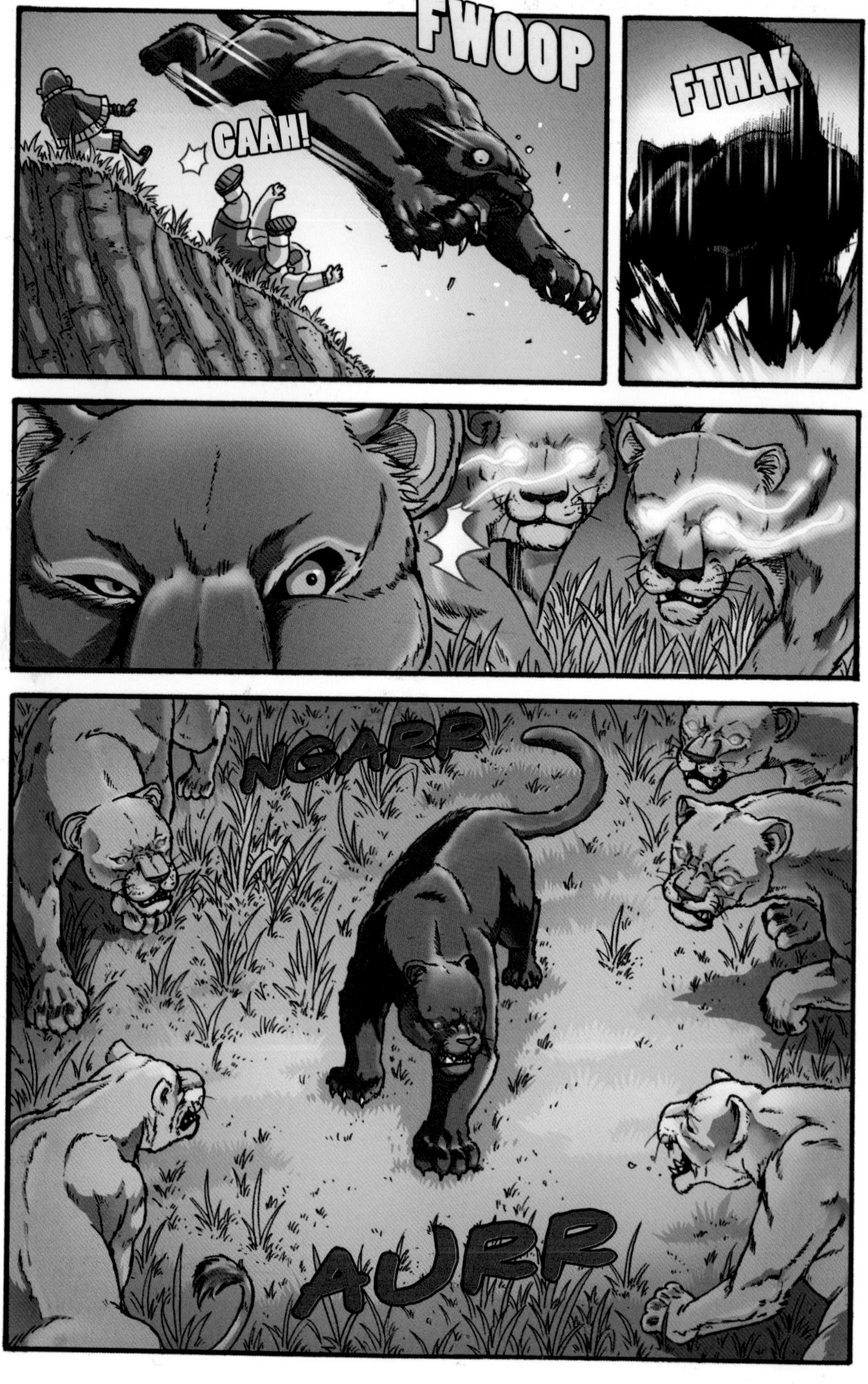
FWOOP
CAAH!
FTHAK
NGARR
AURR

Strength
Speed
Intelligence
Defense
Attack

Conservation Status

Extinct EX	Extinct in the Wild EW	Critically Endangered CR	Endangered EN	Vulnerable VU	Near Threatened NT	Least Concern LC

Species: Prionailurus viverrinus
Length (including tail): 2.60 ft to 4 ft
Weight: 11 to 35 pounds
Common prey: From insects to fish and small rodents
Distribution: West and Southeast Asia (From Pakistan to India and Java)
Habitat: Swamps, marshy riverine areas

FISHING CAT

About twice the size of a domestic cat, the fishing cat is an expert swimmer. Swimming great distances, sometimes underwater to catch fish, this feline supplements its diet with rodents, birds, and reptiles. Distinguishable by an elongated, flat-nosed head, short rounded ears, and dark horizontal markings, it is a solitary nocturnal hunter.

Conservation Status

Extinct EX	Extinct in the Wild EW	Critically Endangered CR	Endangered EN	Vulnerable VU	Near Threatened NT	Least Concern LC

Species: Prionailurus bengalensis
Length (including tail): 2.3 ft to little over 3 ft
Weight: 1 lb to 15 lb
Common prey: From insects to small rodents
Distribution: South and Southeast Asia (India to Korea to Sumatra)
Habitat: Tropical and sub-tropical forests, and near rivers

LEOPARD CAT

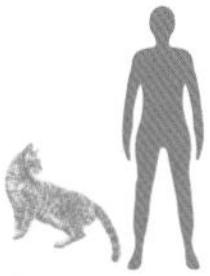

Strength
Speed
Intelligence
Defense
Attack

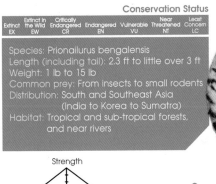

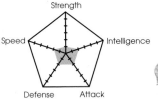

The leopard cat is the most widely found Asian small cat, with 12 subspecies spread across the continent. About the size of a domestic cat, it has longer legs and well-defined webbed feet with a short, narrow muzzle. Its body is marked by black spots of varying shade and size. Predominantly nocturnal, it is an agile climber, and can swim, though prefers to hunt in the trees.

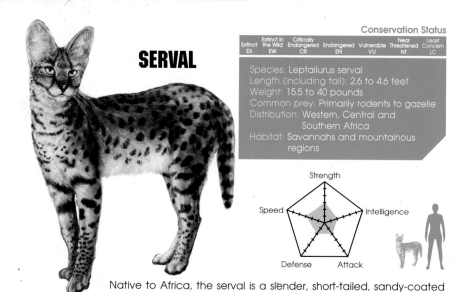

SERVAL

Conservation Status

Extinct	Extinct in the Wild	Critically Endangered	Endangered	Vulnerable	Near Threatened	Least Concern
EX	EW	CR	EN	VU	NT	LC

Species: Leptailurus serval
Length (including tail): 2.6 to 4.6 feet
Weight: 15.5 to 40 pounds
Common prey: Primarily rodents to gazelle
Distribution: Western, Central and Southern Africa
Habitat: Savannahs and mountainous regions

Strength
Speed
Intelligence
Defense
Attack

Native to Africa, the serval is a slender, short-tailed, sandy-coated spotted cat. It ranges from the grassland plains to mountainous areas which are 1.86 miles above sea level. Characterized by its long legs (longest in relation to its body among all felids) and slender frame, the serval uses its acute sense of hearing to locate prey underground, with an astonishing successful hunt percentage of 50% compared to 30% for lions.

Conservation Status

Extinct	Extinct in the Wild	Critically Endangered	Endangered	Vulnerable	Near Threatened	Least Concern
EX	EW	CR	EN	VU	NT	LC

Species: Felis margarita
Length (including tail): 2 to 2.62 feet
Weight: 3 to 7 pounds
Common prey: Small rodents to small reptiles
Distribution: Northern Africa, Central and Southwest Asia
Habitat: Sandy and stony desert

Strength
Speed
Intelligence
Defense
Attack

SAND CAT

A small, stocky cat with short legs and a relatively long tail. The sand cat fur is of a pale sandy color, usually without spots or stripes. Adapted to survive extremely dry conditions where temperatures range between 23°F to 126°F, it has pockets of fur between its toes for insulation against the hot sand, burrowing underground to avoid direct sunlight or cold winds. Usually solitary except during mating season, they inhabit abandoned burrows, seeking shelter in the day and warmth at night.

CHAPTER 4

TRAILED AND TRAPPED!

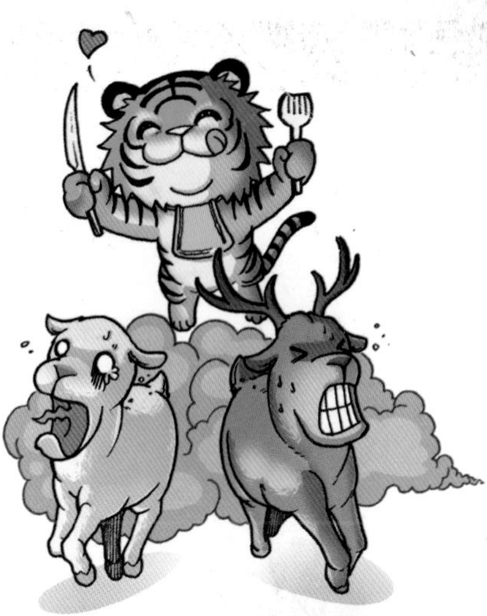

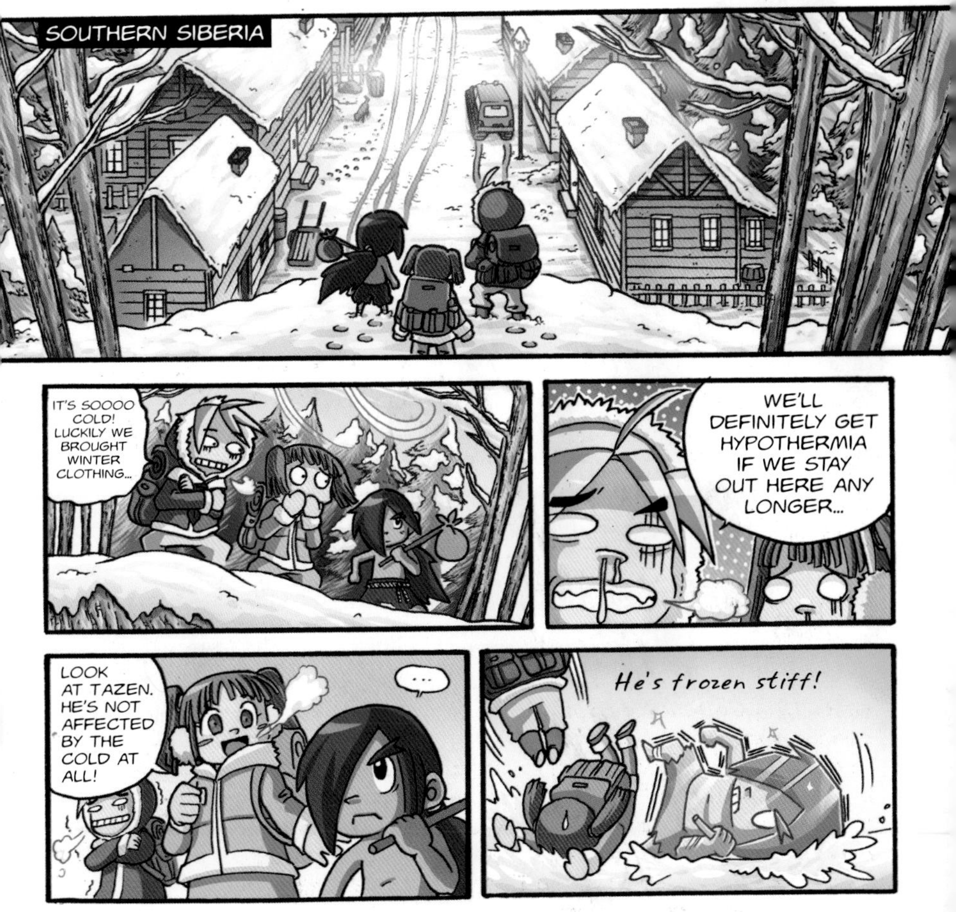
SOUTHERN SIBERIA
IT'S SOOOO COLD! LUCKILY WE BROUGHT WINTER CLOTHING...
WE'LL DEFINITELY GET HYPOTHERMIA IF WE STAY OUT HERE ANY LONGER...
LOOK AT TAZEN. HE'S NOT AFFECTED BY THE COLD AT ALL!
...
He's frozen stiff!

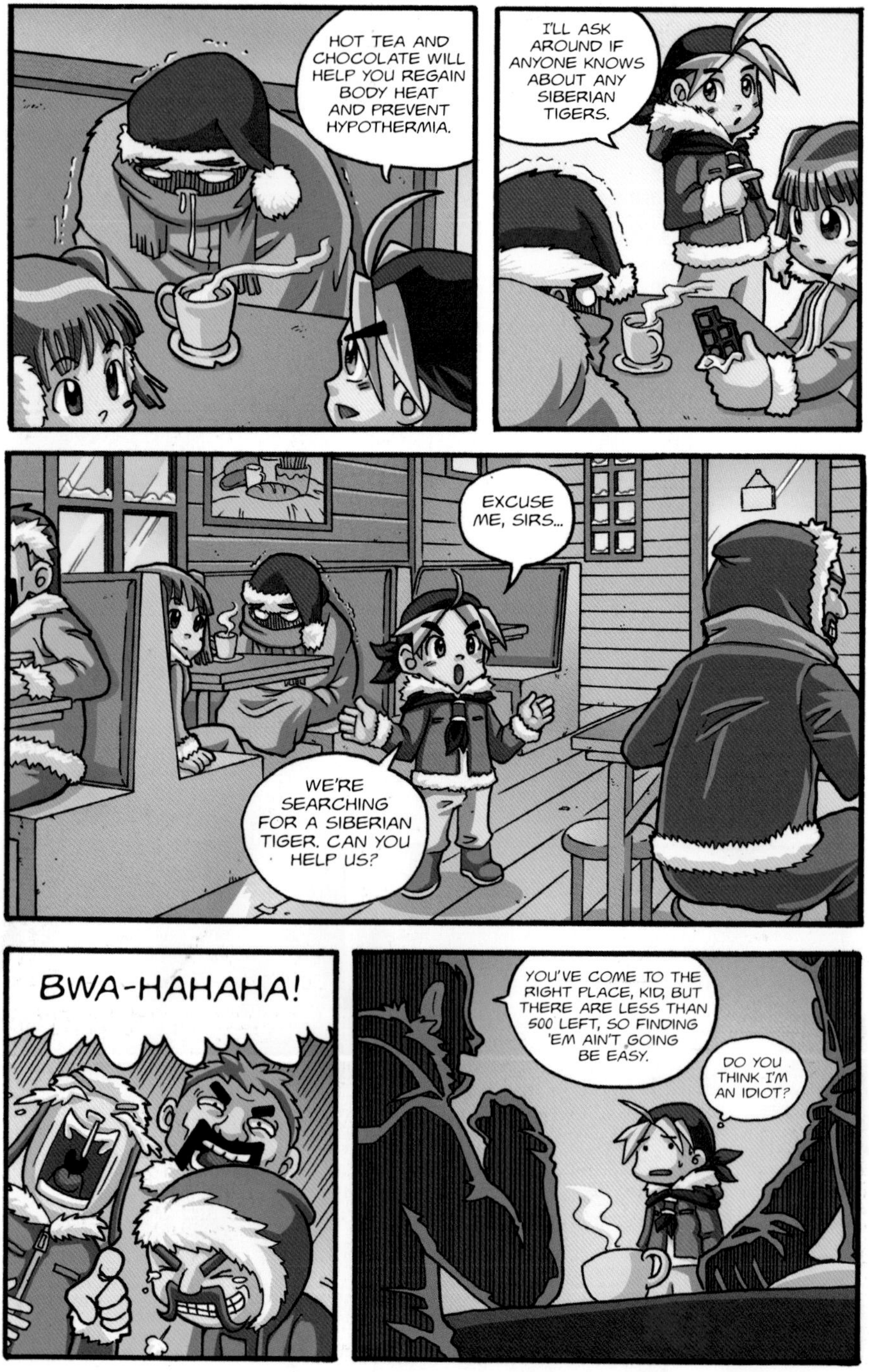
HOT TEA AND CHOCOLATE WILL HELP YOU REGAIN BODY HEAT AND PREVENT HYPOTHERMIA.
I'LL ASK AROUND IF ANYONE KNOWS ABOUT ANY SIBERIAN TIGERS.
EXCUSE ME, SIRS...
WE'RE SEARCHING FOR A SIBERIAN TIGER. CAN YOU HELP US?
BWA-HAHAHA!
YOU'VE COME TO THE RIGHT PLACE, KID, BUT THERE ARE LESS THAN 500 LEFT, SO FINDING 'EM AIN'T GOING BE EASY.
DO YOU THINK I'M AN IDIOT?

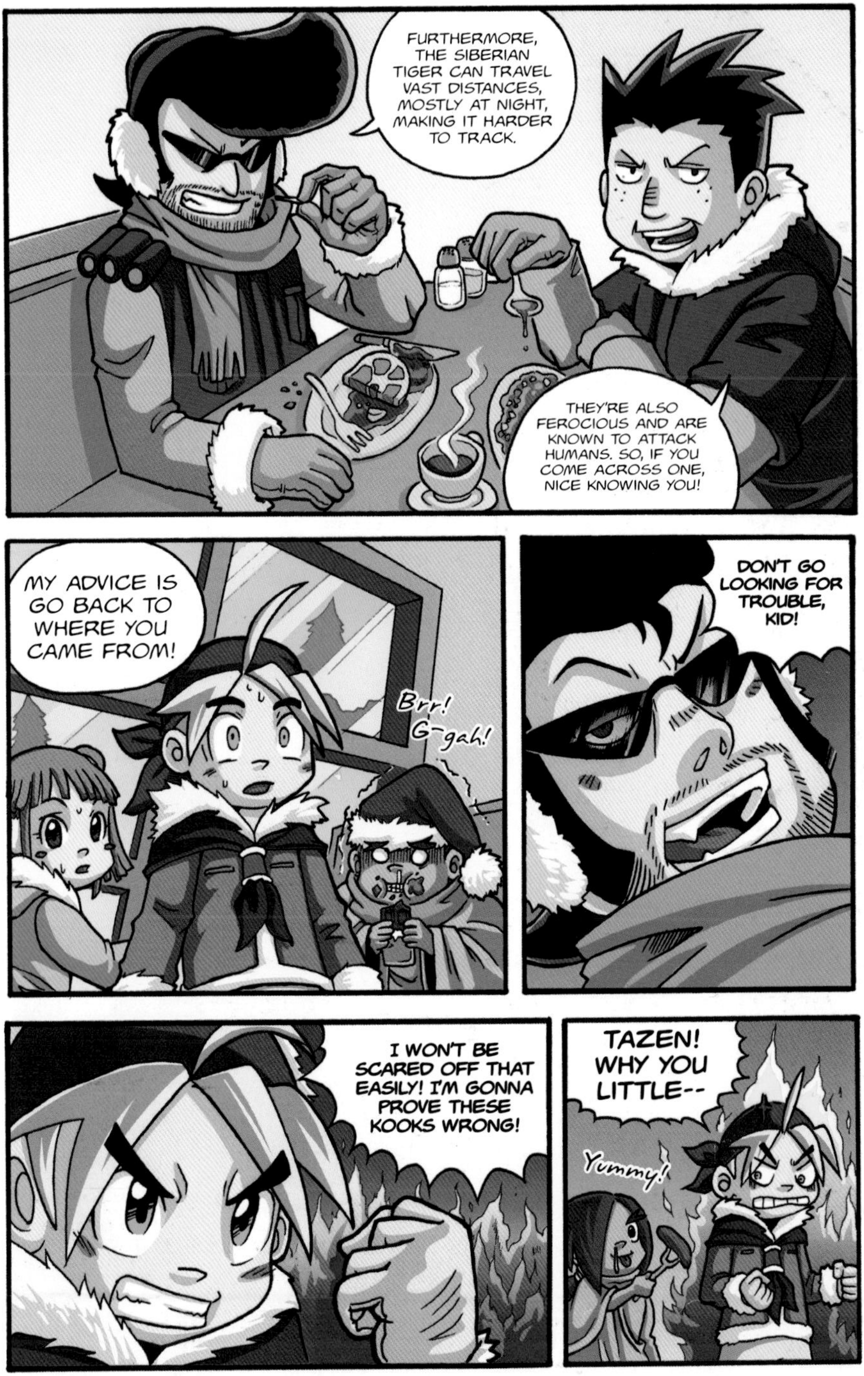
FURTHERMORE, THE SIBERIAN TIGER CAN TRAVEL VAST DISTANCES, MOSTLY AT NIGHT, MAKING IT HARDER TO TRACK.
THEY'RE ALSO FEROCIOUS AND ARE KNOWN TO ATTACK HUMANS. SO, IF YOU COME ACROSS ONE, NICE KNOWING YOU!
MY ADVICE IS GO BACK TO WHERE YOU CAME FROM!
Brr! G-gah!
DON'T GO LOOKING FOR TROUBLE, KID!
I WON'T BE SCARED OFF THAT EASILY! I'M GONNA PROVE THESE KOOKS WRONG!
TAZEN! WHY YOU LITTLE--
Yummy!

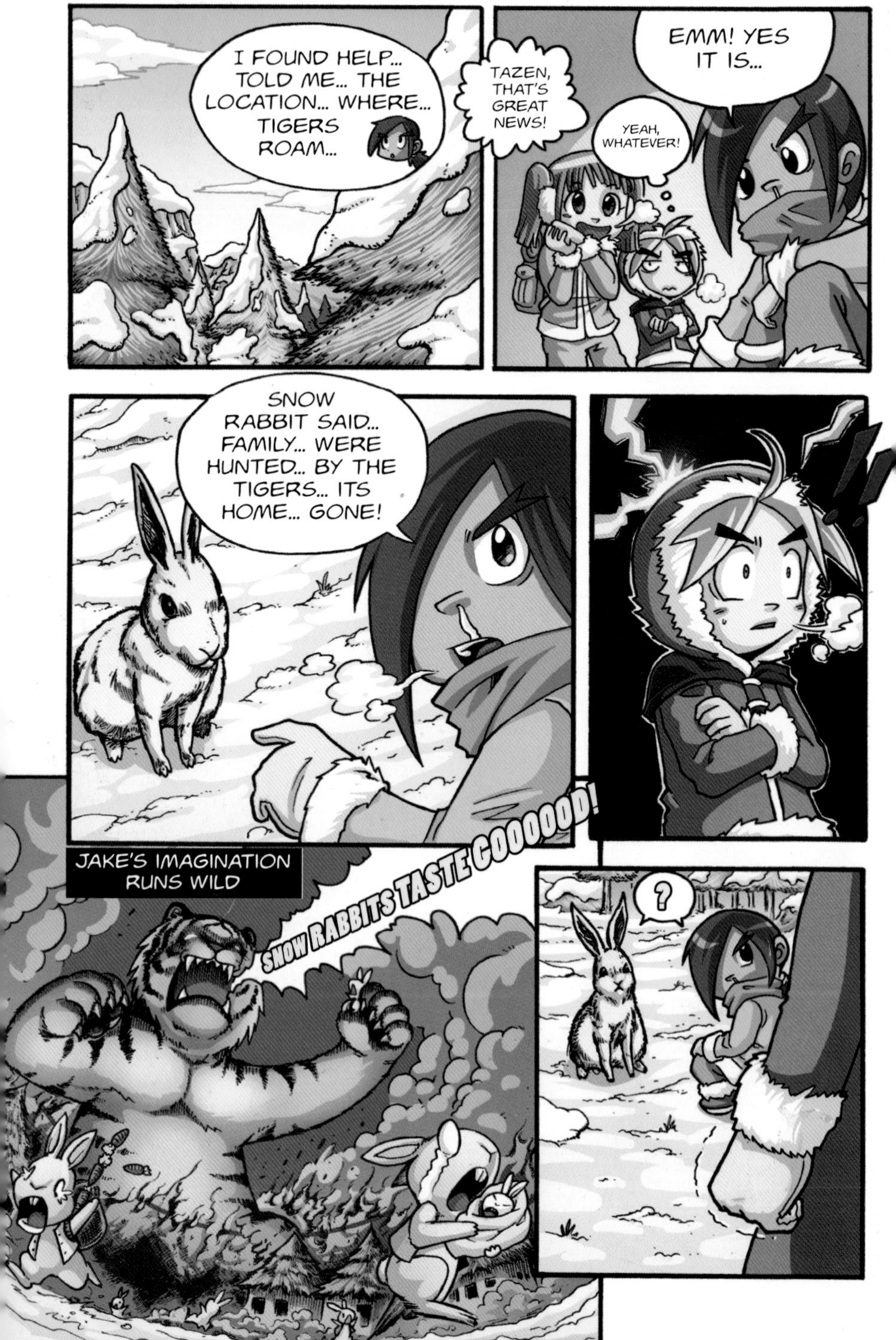
I FOUND HELP... TOLD ME... THE LOCATION... WHERE... TIGERS ROAM...
TAZEN, THAT'S GREAT NEWS!
EMM! YES IT IS...
YEAH, WHATEVER!
SNOW RABBIT SAID... FAMILY... WERE HUNTED... BY THE TIGERS... ITS HOME... GONE!
JAKE'S IMAGINATION RUNS WILD
SNOW RABBITS TASTE GOOOOOD!
?

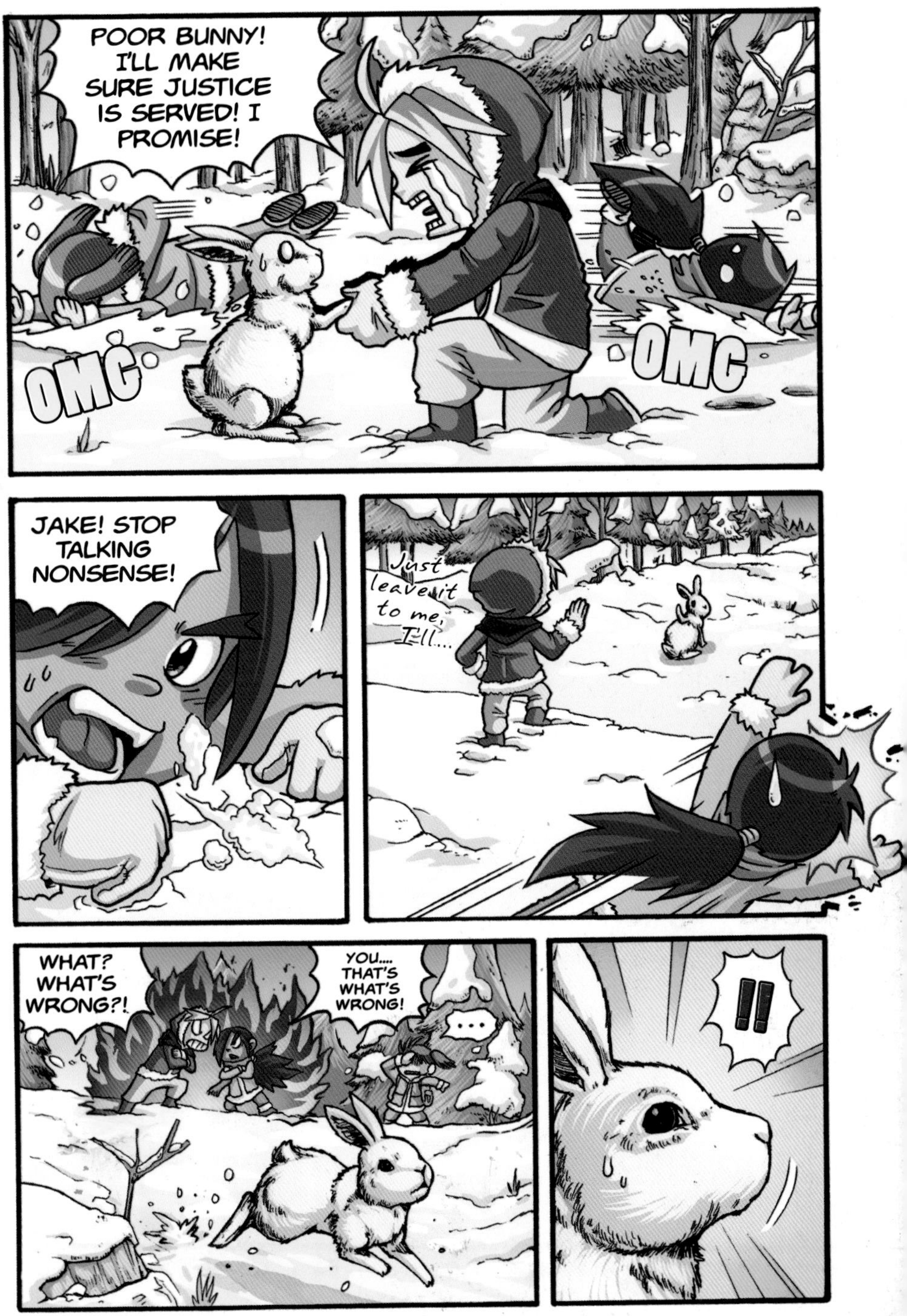
POOR BUNNY! I'LL MAKE SURE JUSTICE IS SERVED! I PROMISE!
OMG
OMG
JAKE! STOP TALKING NONSENSE!
Just leave it to me, I'll...
WHAT? WHAT'S WRONG?!
YOU.... THAT'S WHAT'S WRONG!
...
!!

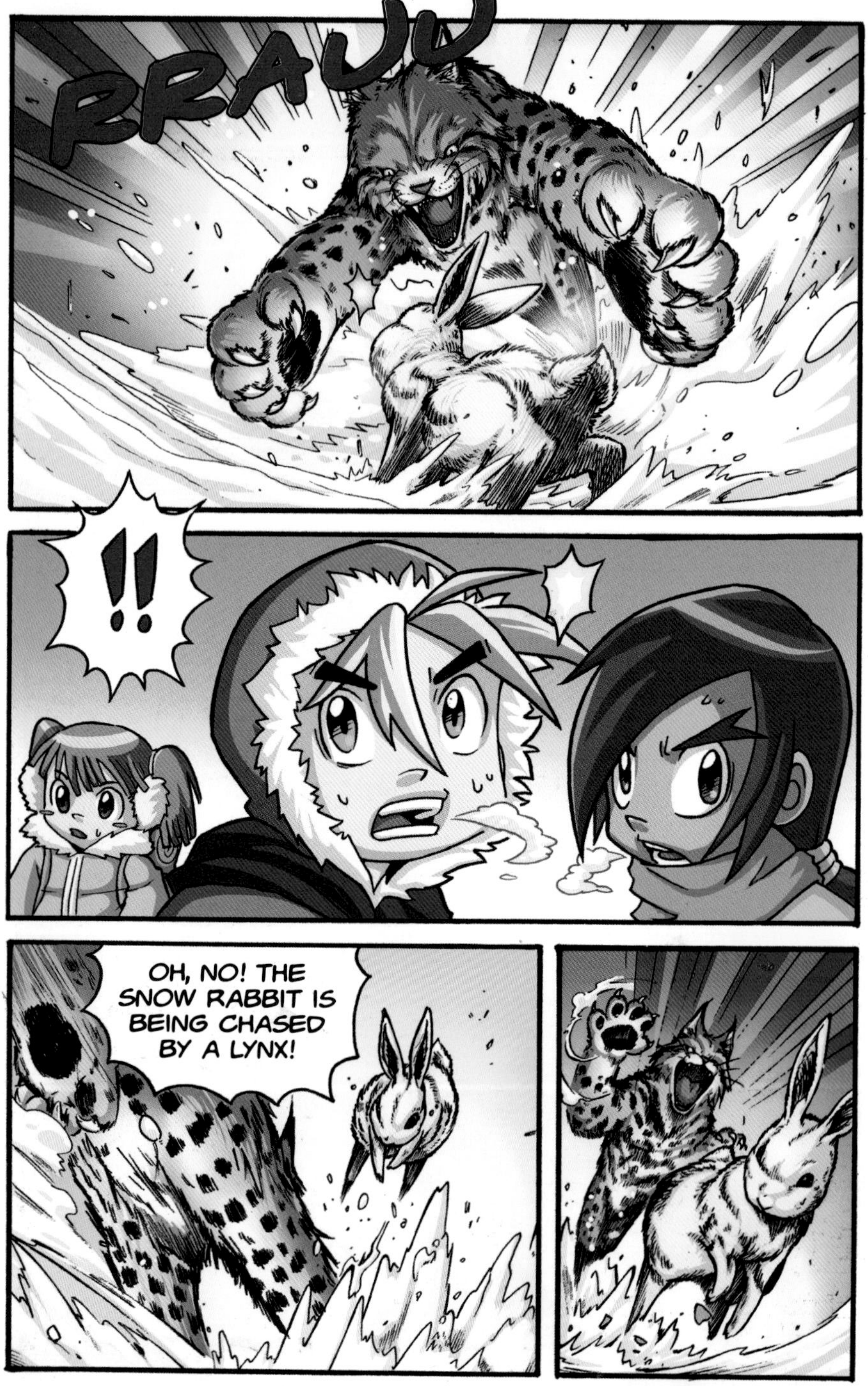
PRAWW
!!
OH, NO! THE SNOW RABBIT IS BEING CHASED BY A LYNX!

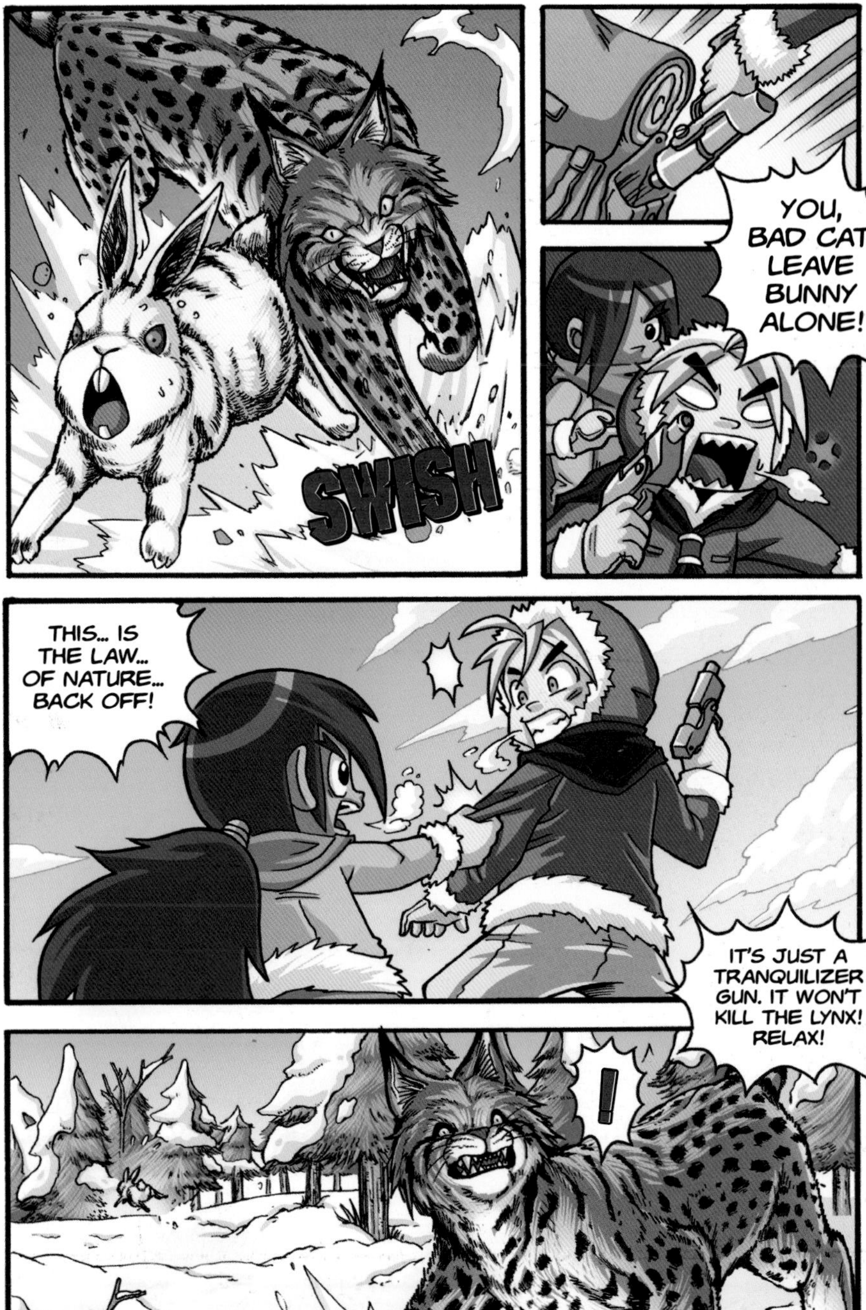
SWISH
YOU, BAD CAT, LEAVE BUNNY ALONE!
THIS... IS THE LAW... OF NATURE... BACK OFF!
IT'S JUST A TRANQUILIZER GUN. IT WON'T KILL THE LYNX! RELAX!
!

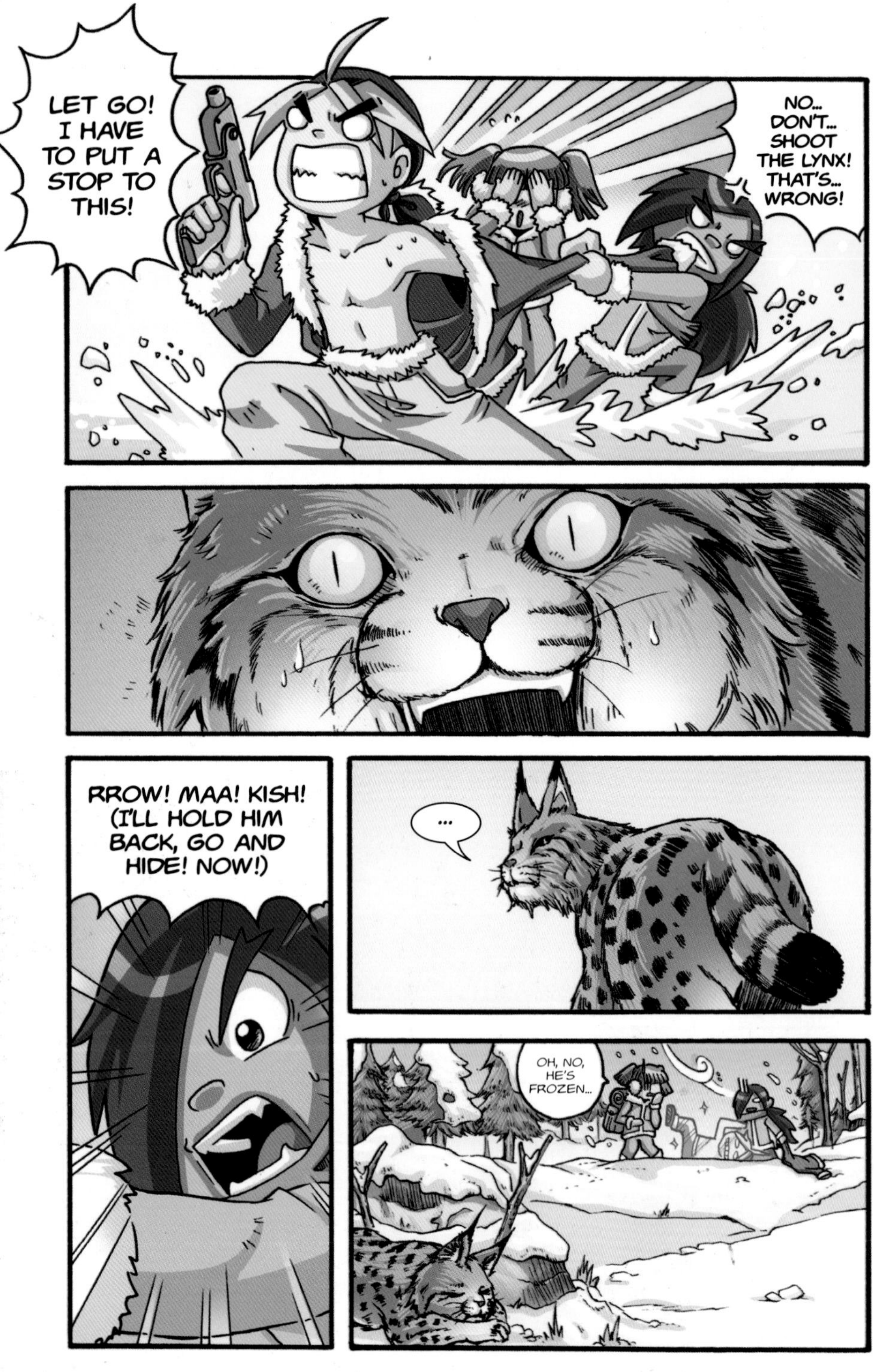
LET GO! I HAVE TO PUT A STOP TO THIS!
NO... DON'T... SHOOT THE LYNX! THAT'S... WRONG!
RROW! MAA! KISH! (I'LL HOLD HIM BACK, GO AND HIDE! NOW!)
...
OH, NO, HE'S FROZEN...

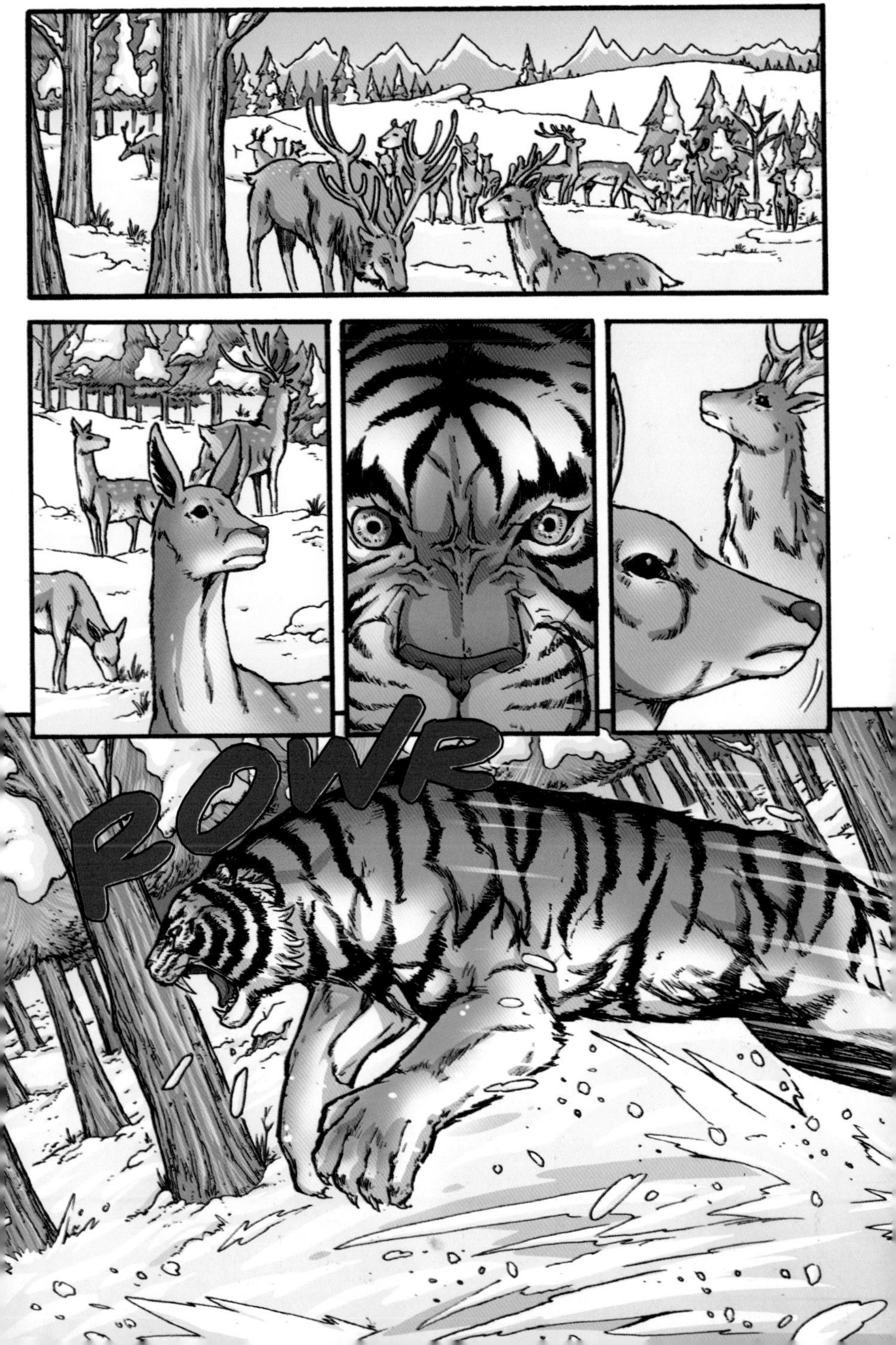
ROWR

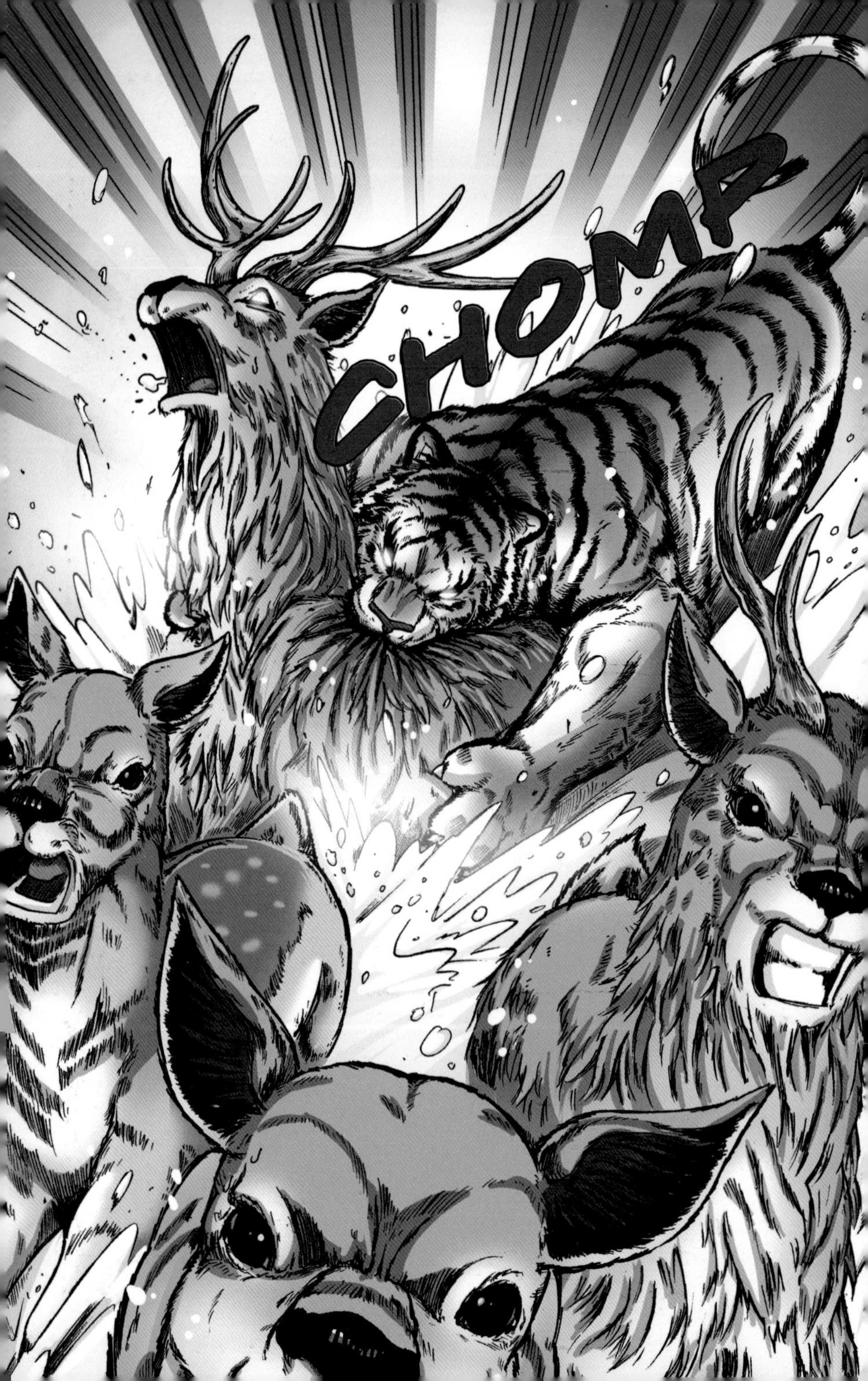
CHOMP

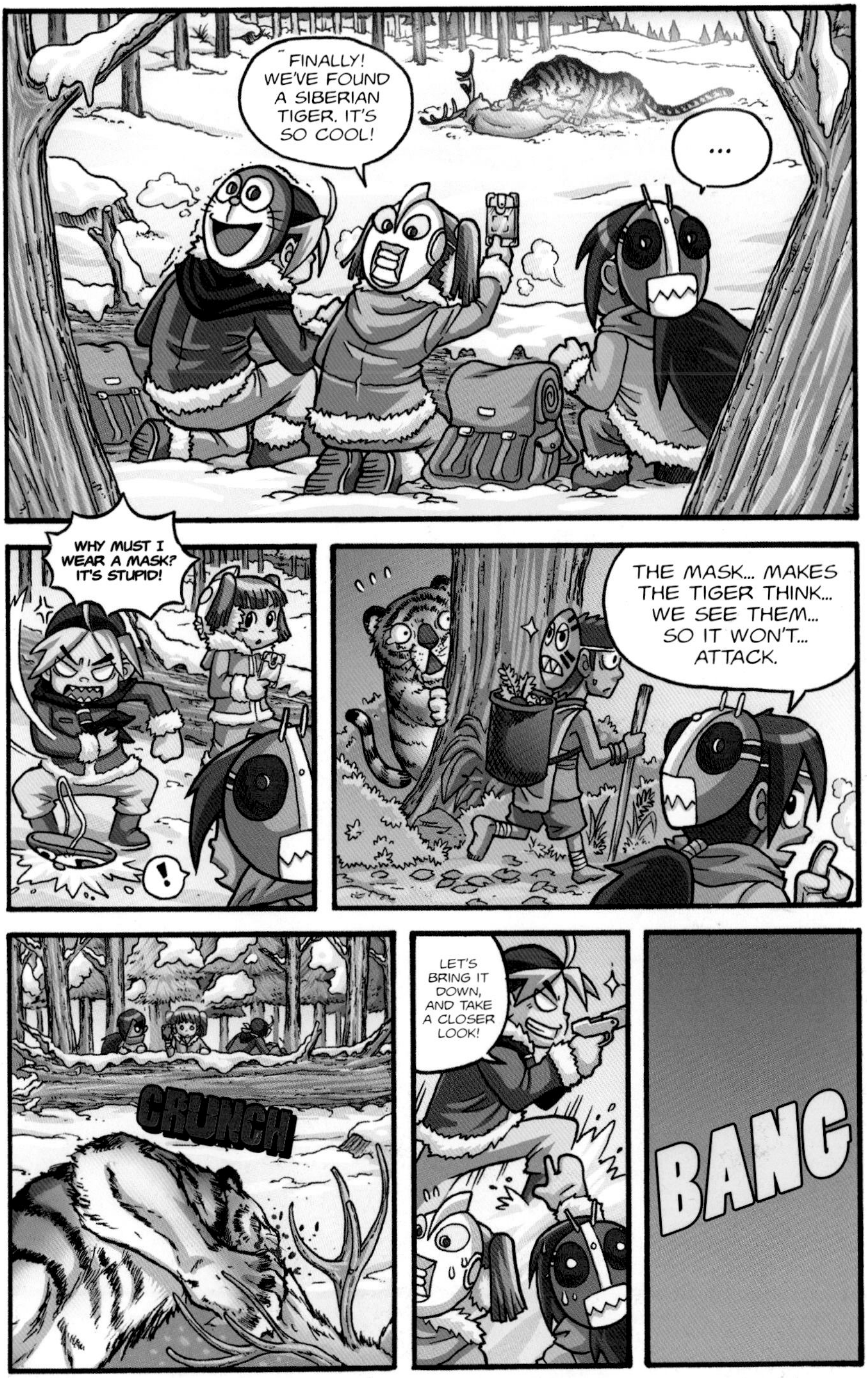
FINALLY! WE'VE FOUND A SIBERIAN TIGER. IT'S SO COOL!
...
WHY MUST I WEAR A MASK? IT'S STUPID!
!
THE MASK... MAKES THE TIGER THINK... WE SEE THEM... SO IT WON'T... ATTACK.
CRUNCH
LET'S BRING IT DOWN, AND TAKE A CLOSER LOOK!
BANG

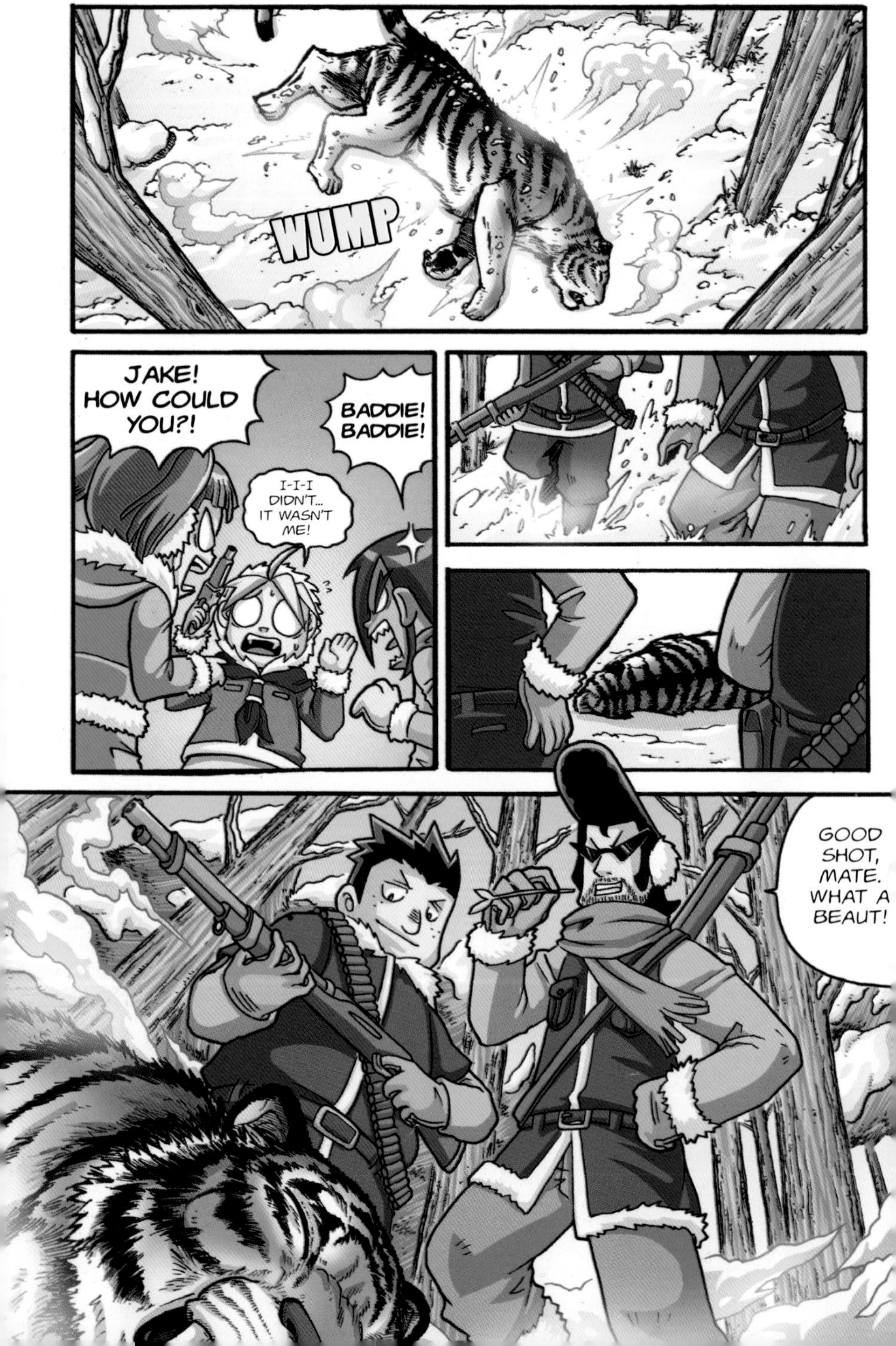
WUMP
JAKE! HOW COULD YOU?!
BADDIE! BADDIE!
I-I-I DIDN'T... IT WASN'T ME!
GOOD SHOT, MATE. WHAT A BEAUT!

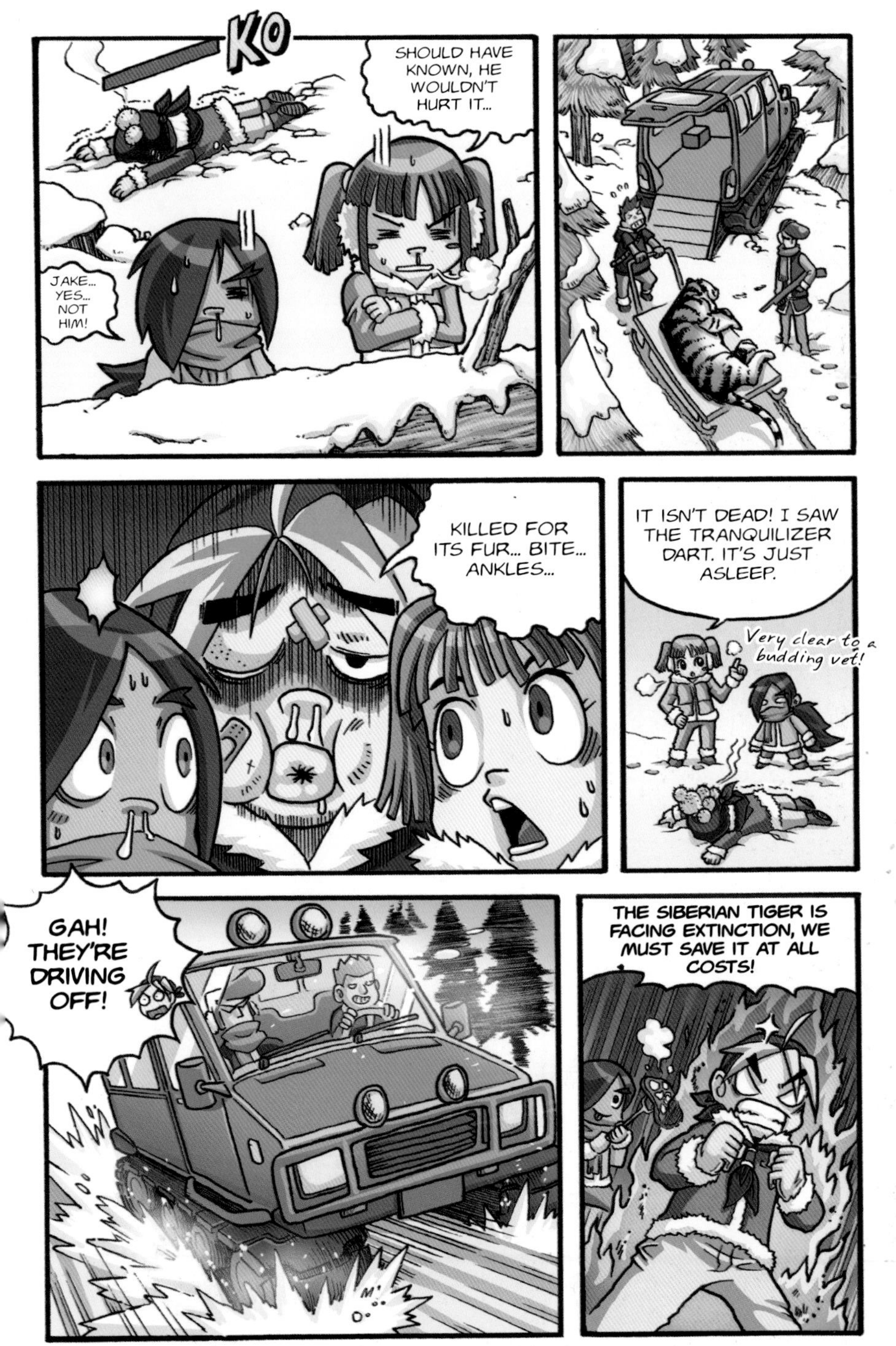
KO
SHOULD HAVE KNOWN, HE WOULDN'T HURT IT...
JAKE... YES... NOT HIM!
KILLED FOR ITS FUR... BITE... ANKLES...
IT ISN'T DEAD! I SAW THE TRANQUILIZER DART. IT'S JUST ASLEEP.
Very clear to a budding vet!
GAH! THEY'RE DRIVING OFF!
THE SIBERIAN TIGER IS FACING EXTINCTION, WE MUST SAVE IT AT ALL COSTS!

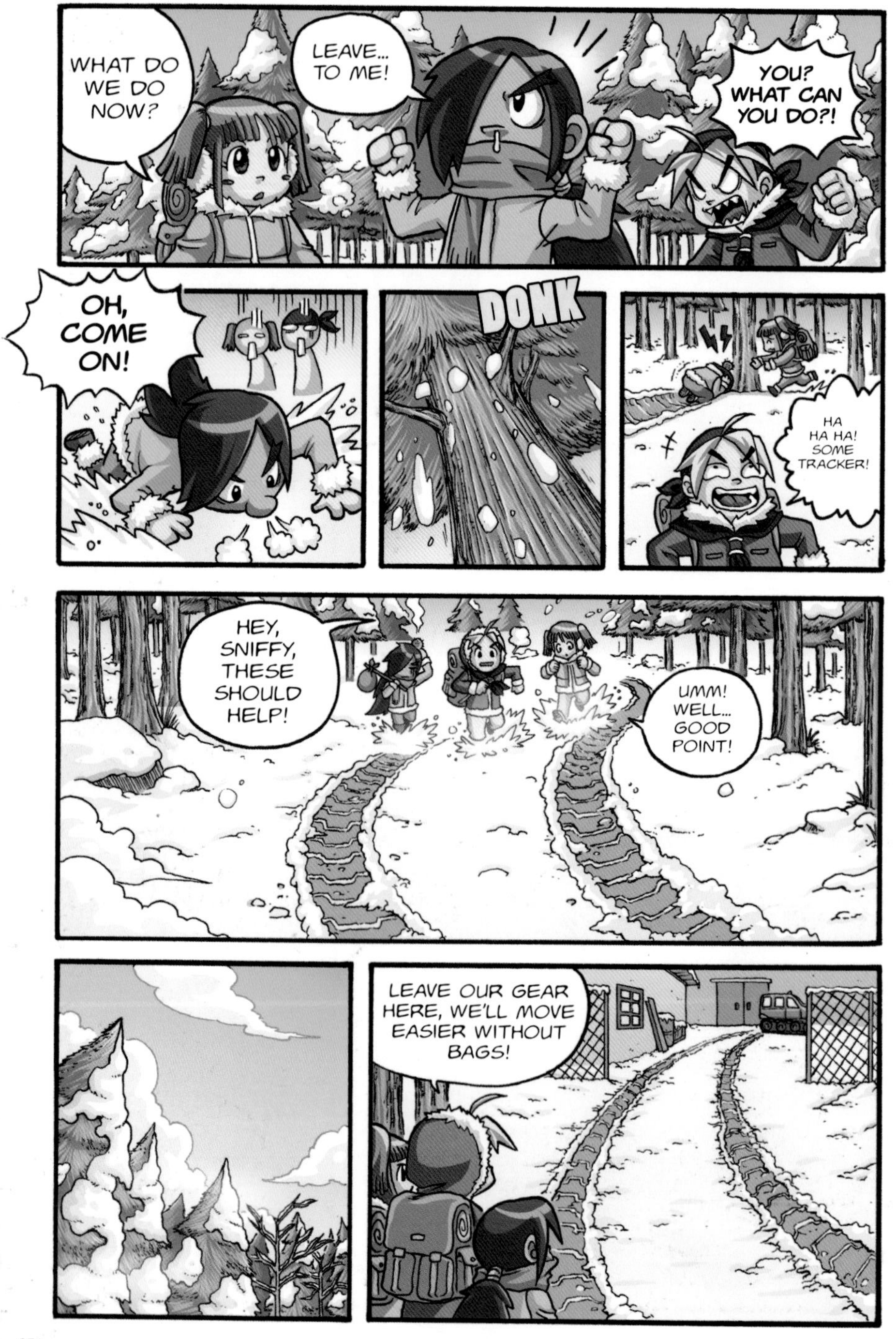
WHAT DO WE DO NOW?
LEAVE... TO ME!
YOU? WHAT CAN YOU DO?!
OH, COME ON!
DONK
HA HA HA! SOME TRACKER!
HEY, SNIFFY, THESE SHOULD HELP!
UMM! WELL... GOOD POINT!
LEAVE OUR GEAR HERE, WE'LL MOVE EASIER WITHOUT BAGS!

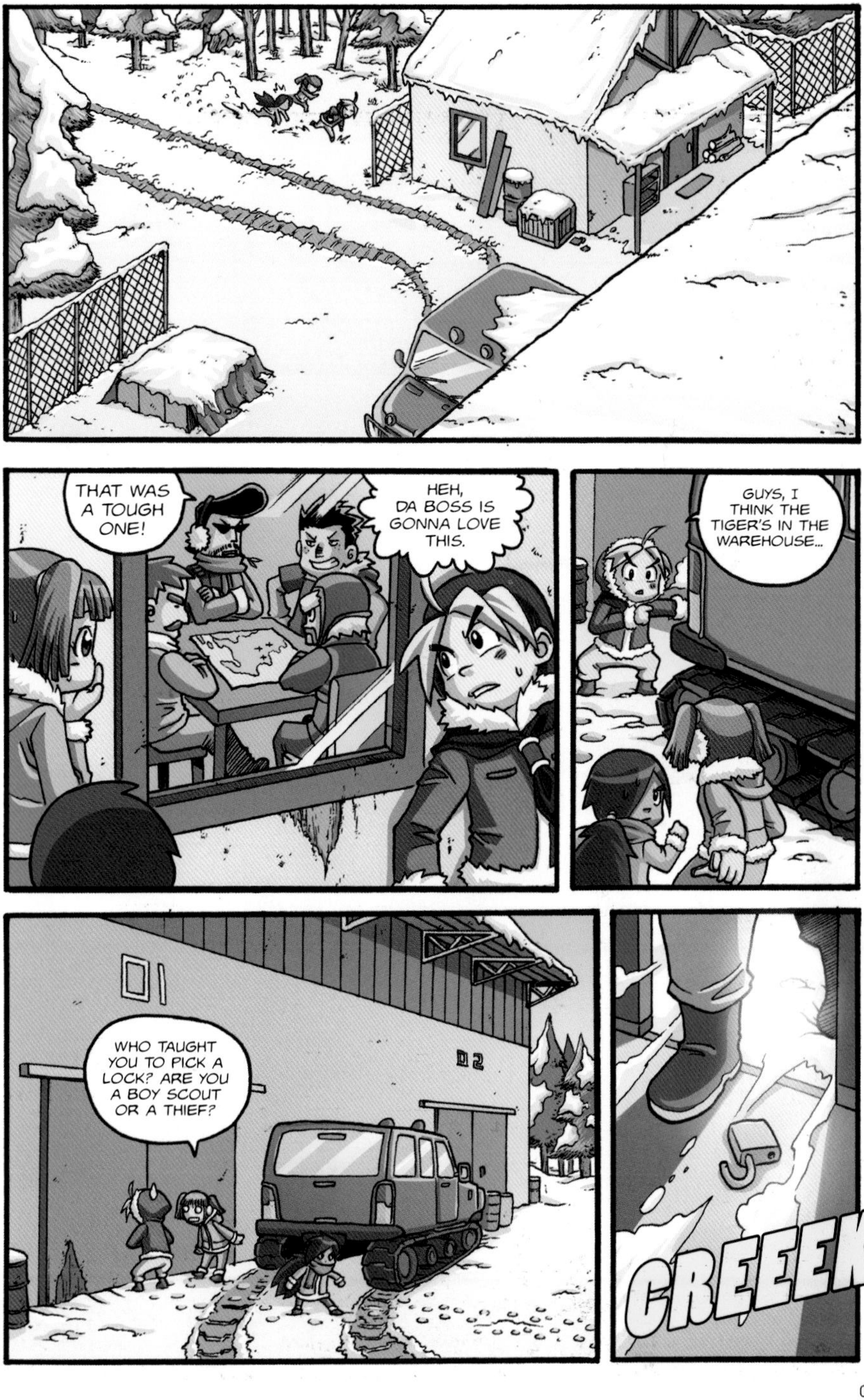
THAT WAS A TOUGH ONE!
HEH, DA BOSS IS GONNA LOVE THIS.
GUYS, I THINK THE TIGER'S IN THE WAREHOUSE...
01
02
WHO TAUGHT YOU TO PICK A LOCK? ARE YOU A BOY SCOUT OR A THIEF?
CREEEK

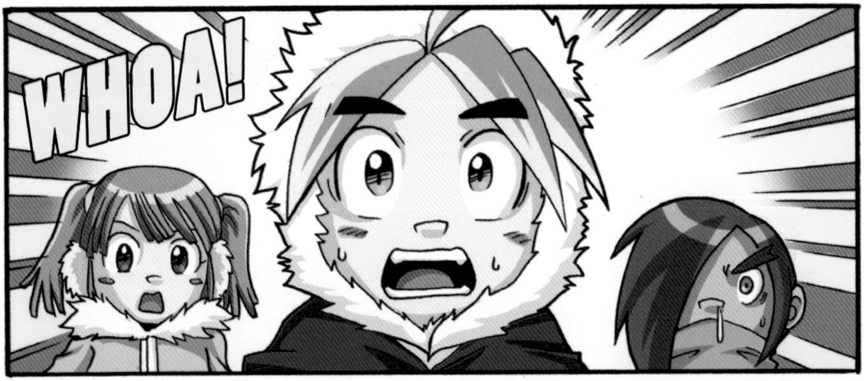
WHOA!

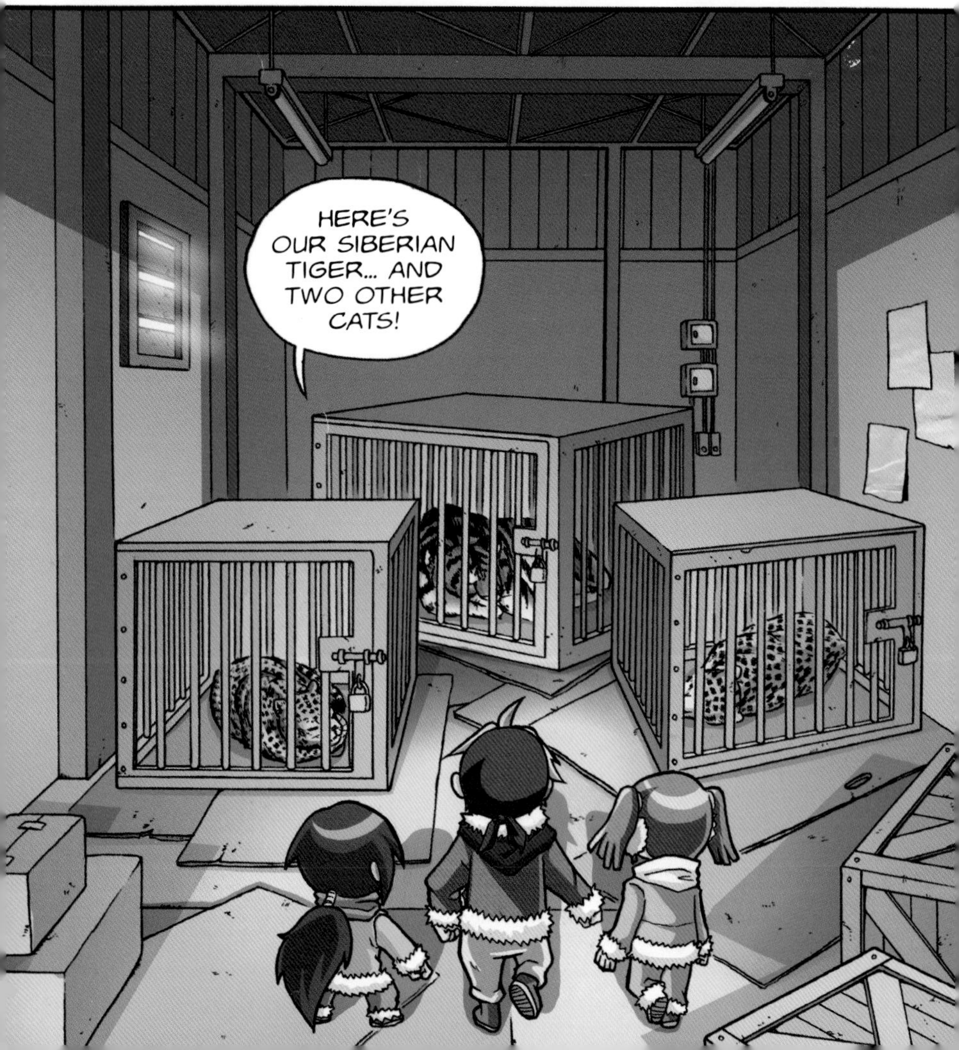
HERE'S OUR SIBERIAN TIGER... AND TWO OTHER CATS!

Conservation Status

Extinct	Extinct in the Wild	Critically Endangered	Endangered	Vulnerable	Near Threatened	Least Concern
EX	EW	CR	EN	VU	NT	LC

Species: Lynx
Length (including tail): 3.3 to 5.3 feet
Weight: 17.5 to 66 pounds
Common prey: Hares, deer, and rodents
Distribution: Northern Europe, Siberia, and Asia; Central to Southwestern China
Habitat: Arctic forests and highlands

EURASIAN LYNX

Strength
Intelligence
Attack
Defense
Speed

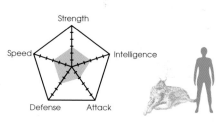

The largest of all lynx species, the eurasian lynx is a tenacious predator known to kill much larger prey than itself, such as deer. This cat is distinguishable by tufts of hair on the tip of each ear and a large body relative to a small head. Its thick fur and webbed paws, which it uses like snowshoes to negotiate snowy terrain with ease, all serves to adapt this bob-tailed cat to its Sub-Arctic habitat. Solitary and elusive, lynx are very quiet and seldom heard, remnants of prey or snowy tracks are usually observed long before the animal is.

The tufts of hair on its ear tips, serve more than a purely decorative purpose; actually accentuating the lynx's already excellent hearing, in order to detect prey muffled by thick snow. Like most cats, lynx have excellent vision, and can spot prey as far as 246 feet away. ▶

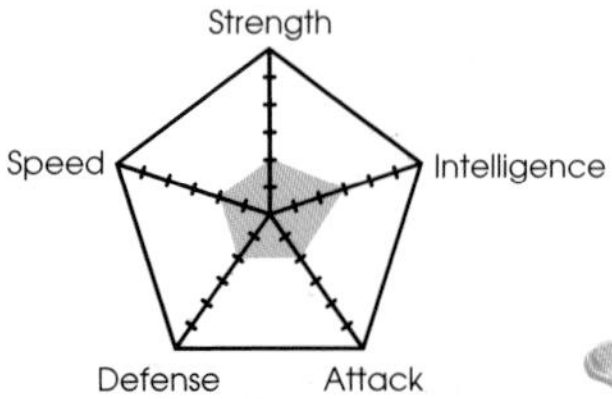
Strength
Intelligence
Attack
Defense
Speed

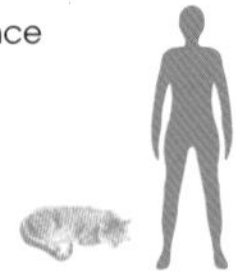

Conservation Status

Extinct EX	Extinct In the Wild EW	Critically Endangered CR	Endangered EN	Vulnerable VU	Near Threatened NT	Least Concern LC

Species: Felis silvestris
Length (including tail): 2 to 4.25 feet
Weight: 6.5 to 18 pounds
Common prey: Rodents, birds, poultry (if close by)
Distribution: Europe, Africa, and Central Asia
Habitat: Forests, grasslands, scrublands

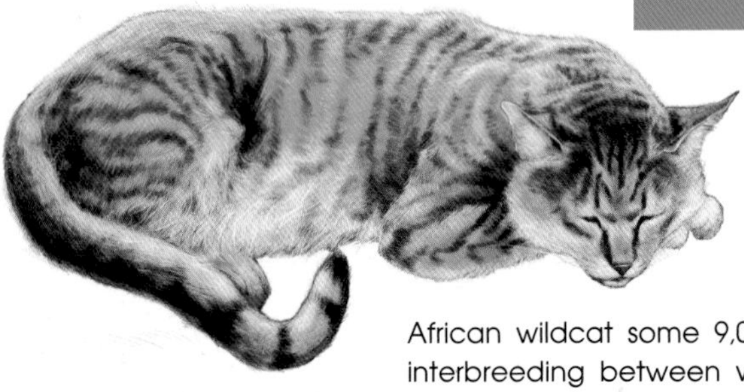

WILDCATS

Archaeological and genetic evidence has suggested that the house cat was genetically derived from a domesticated African wildcat some 9,000 to 10,000 years ago. Indeed interbreeding between wildcat and domestic feline has been extensive. Smaller than other Felinae, the wildcat is larger than the house cat, resembling a striped tabby, but with longer legs and a more robust build. It lives in diverse habitats from sub-Saharan to temperate environments and exhibits different coat patterns based on locality. Usually stalking or ambushing prey, wildcats have been observed prowling the branches in search of food.

Conservation Status

Extinct EX	Extinct In the Wild EW	Critically Endangered CR	Endangered EN	Vulnerable VU	Near Threatened NT	Least Concern LC

Species: Puma yagouaroundi
Length (including tail): 2.6 to 4.6 feet
Weight: 7.7 to 20 pounds
Common prey: Rodents, small reptiles, birds
Distribution: Central and South America
Habitat: Lowland bushland, grassy riverbanks

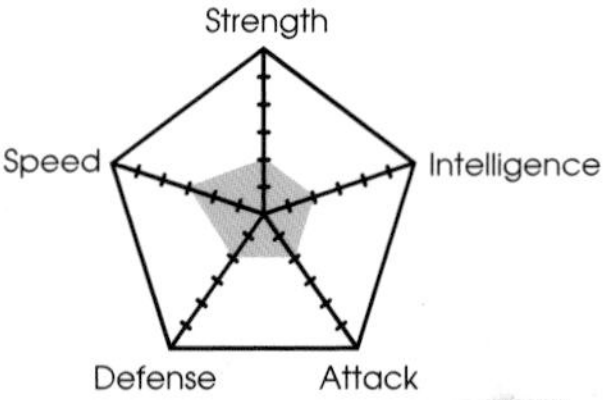
Strength
Intelligence
Attack
Defense
Speed

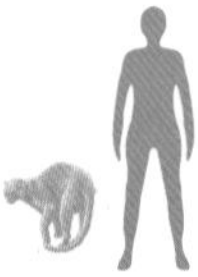

JAGUARUNDI

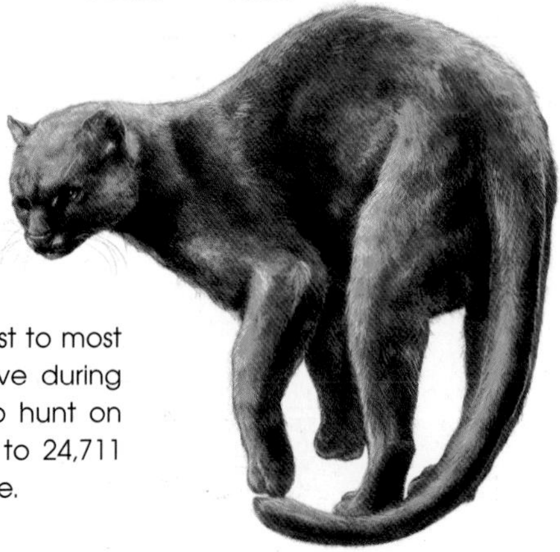

A small-sized wild cat, the jaguarundi is characterized by its short legs, short rounded ears and an elongated body with either a greyish or red coat. In contrast to most cats, this species is primarily diurnal (active during daytime). A talented climber, it prefers to hunt on the ground, and covers a territory of up to 24,711 acres, which like other felids, it prowls alone.

CHAPTER 5

THE ANIMALS STRIKE BACK!

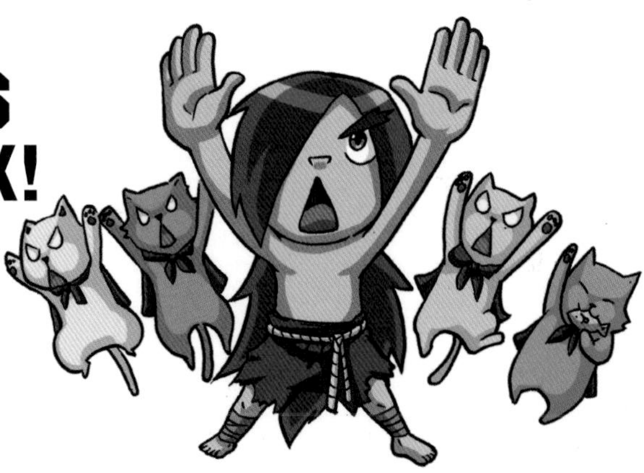

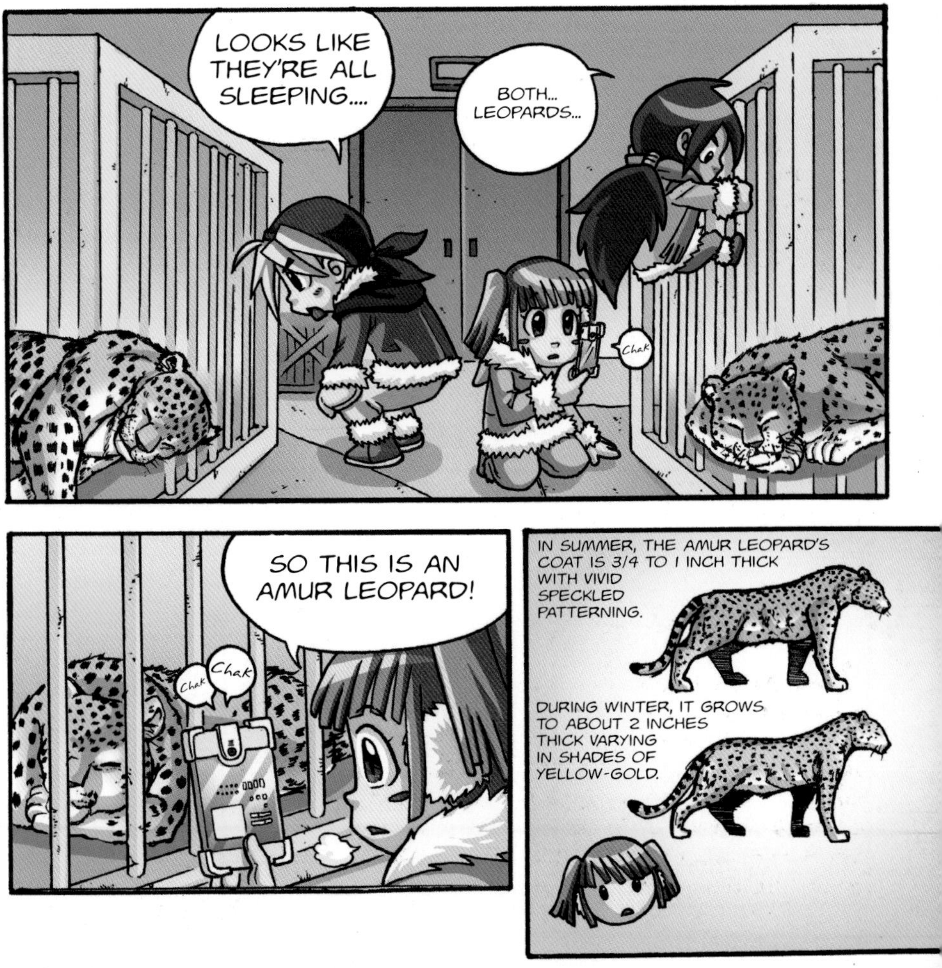
LOOKS LIKE THEY'RE ALL SLEEPING....
BOTH... LEOPARDS...
Chak
SO THIS IS AN AMUR LEOPARD!
Chak
Chak
IN SUMMER, THE AMUR LEOPARD'S COAT IS 3/4 TO 1 INCH THICK WITH VIVID SPECKLED PATTERNING.
DURING WINTER, IT GROWS TO ABOUT 2 INCHES THICK VARYING IN SHADES OF YELLOW-GOLD.

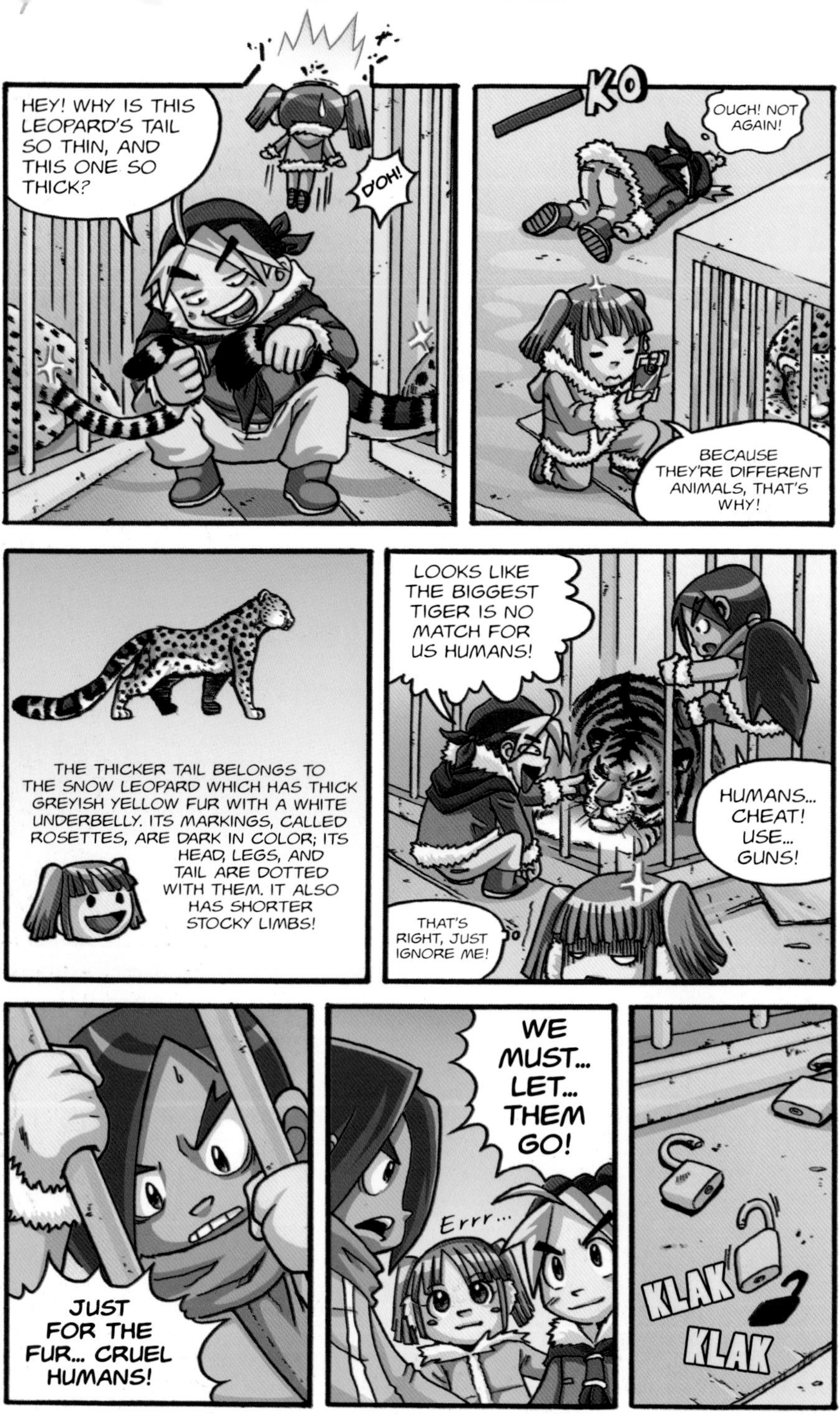
HEY! WHY IS THIS LEOPARD'S TAIL SO THIN, AND THIS ONE SO THICK?
D'OH!
KO
OUCH! NOT AGAIN!
BECAUSE THEY'RE DIFFERENT ANIMALS, THAT'S WHY!
THE THICKER TAIL BELONGS TO THE SNOW LEOPARD WHICH HAS THICK GREYISH YELLOW FUR WITH A WHITE UNDERBELLY. ITS MARKINGS, CALLED ROSETTES, ARE DARK IN COLOR; ITS HEAD, LEGS, AND TAIL ARE DOTTED WITH THEM. IT ALSO HAS SHORTER STOCKY LIMBS!
LOOKS LIKE THE BIGGEST TIGER IS NO MATCH FOR US HUMANS!
HUMANS... CHEAT! USE... GUNS!
THAT'S RIGHT, JUST IGNORE ME!
JUST FOR THE FUR... CRUEL HUMANS!
WE MUST... LET... THEM GO!
Errr...
KLAK
KLAK

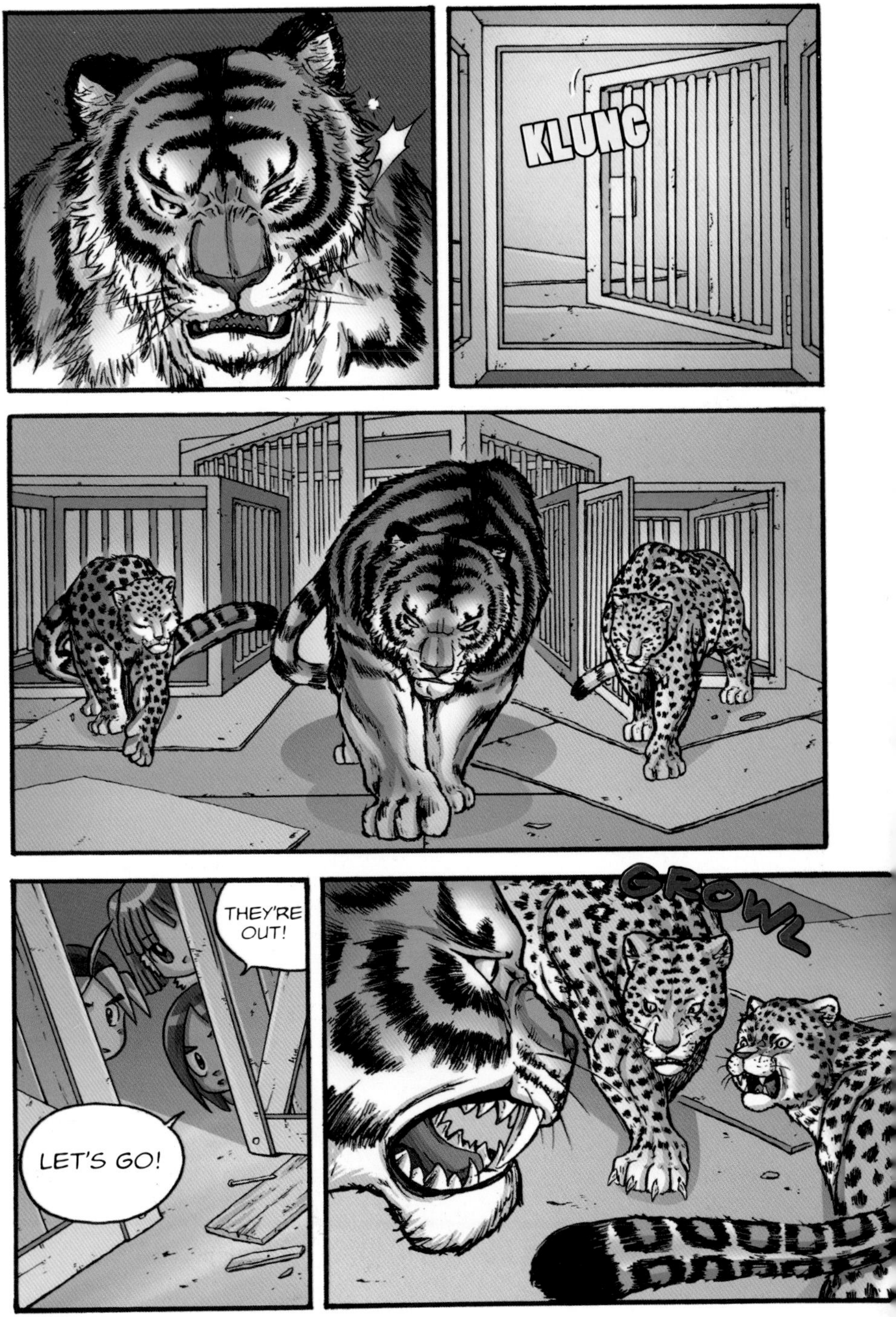
KLUNG
THEY'RE OUT!
LET'S GO!
GROWL

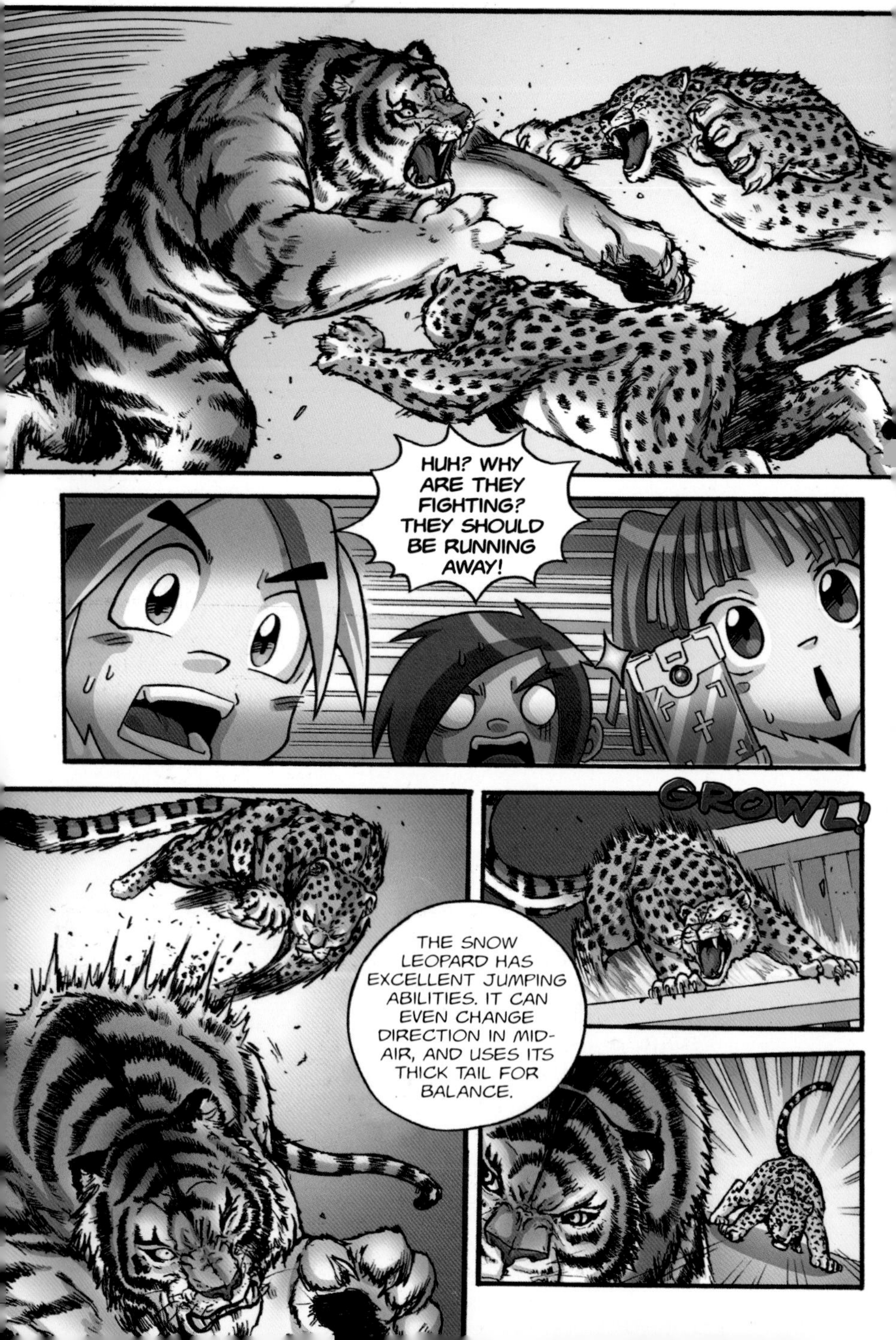
HUH? WHY ARE THEY FIGHTING? THEY SHOULD BE RUNNING AWAY!
GROWL!
THE SNOW LEOPARD HAS EXCELLENT JUMPING ABILITIES. IT CAN EVEN CHANGE DIRECTION IN MID-AIR, AND USES ITS THICK TAIL FOR BALANCE.

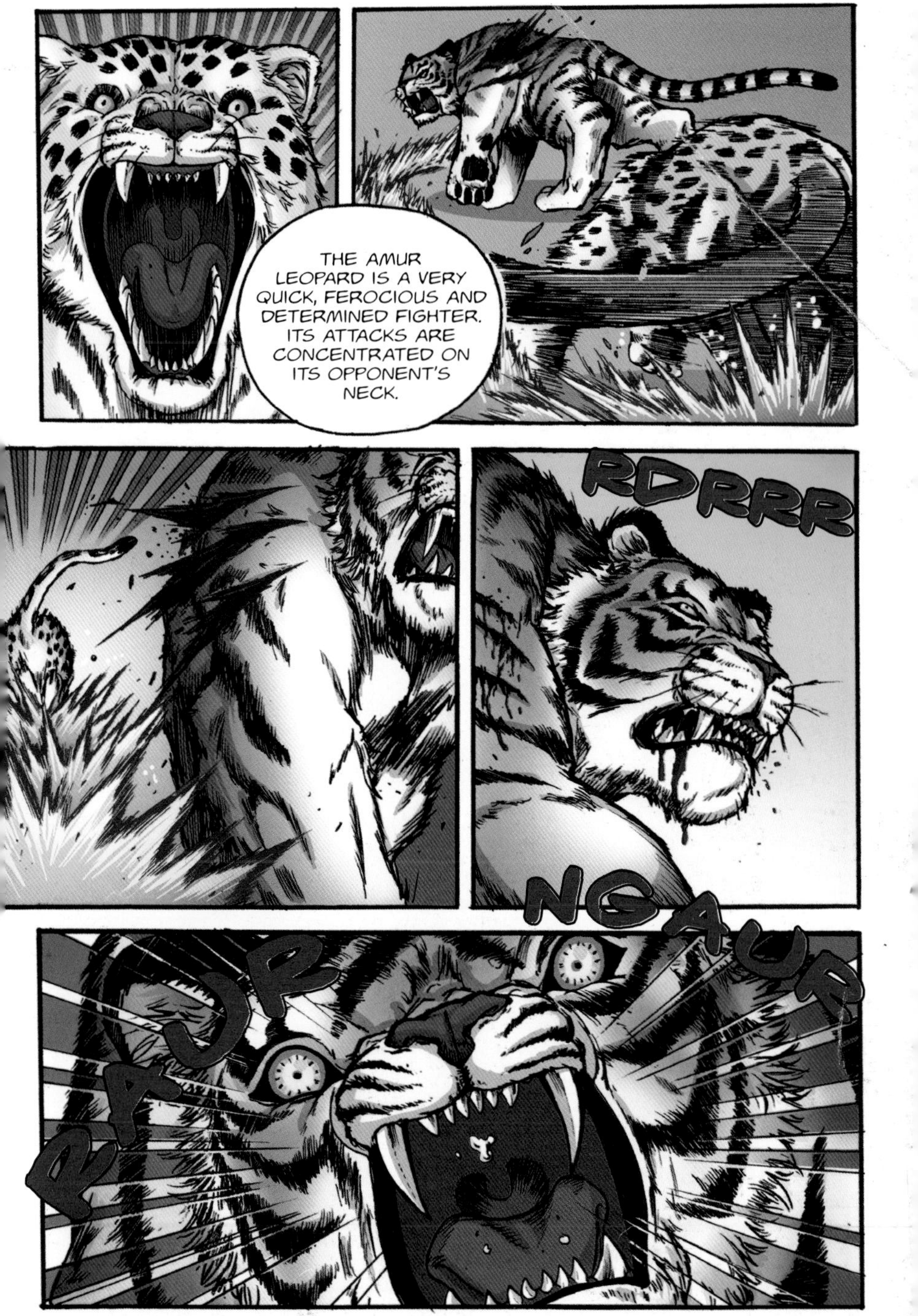
THE AMUR LEOPARD IS A VERY QUICK, FEROCIOUS AND DETERMINED FIGHTER. ITS ATTACKS ARE CONCENTRATED ON ITS OPPONENT'S NECK.
RDRRR
NGAUR
RAUR

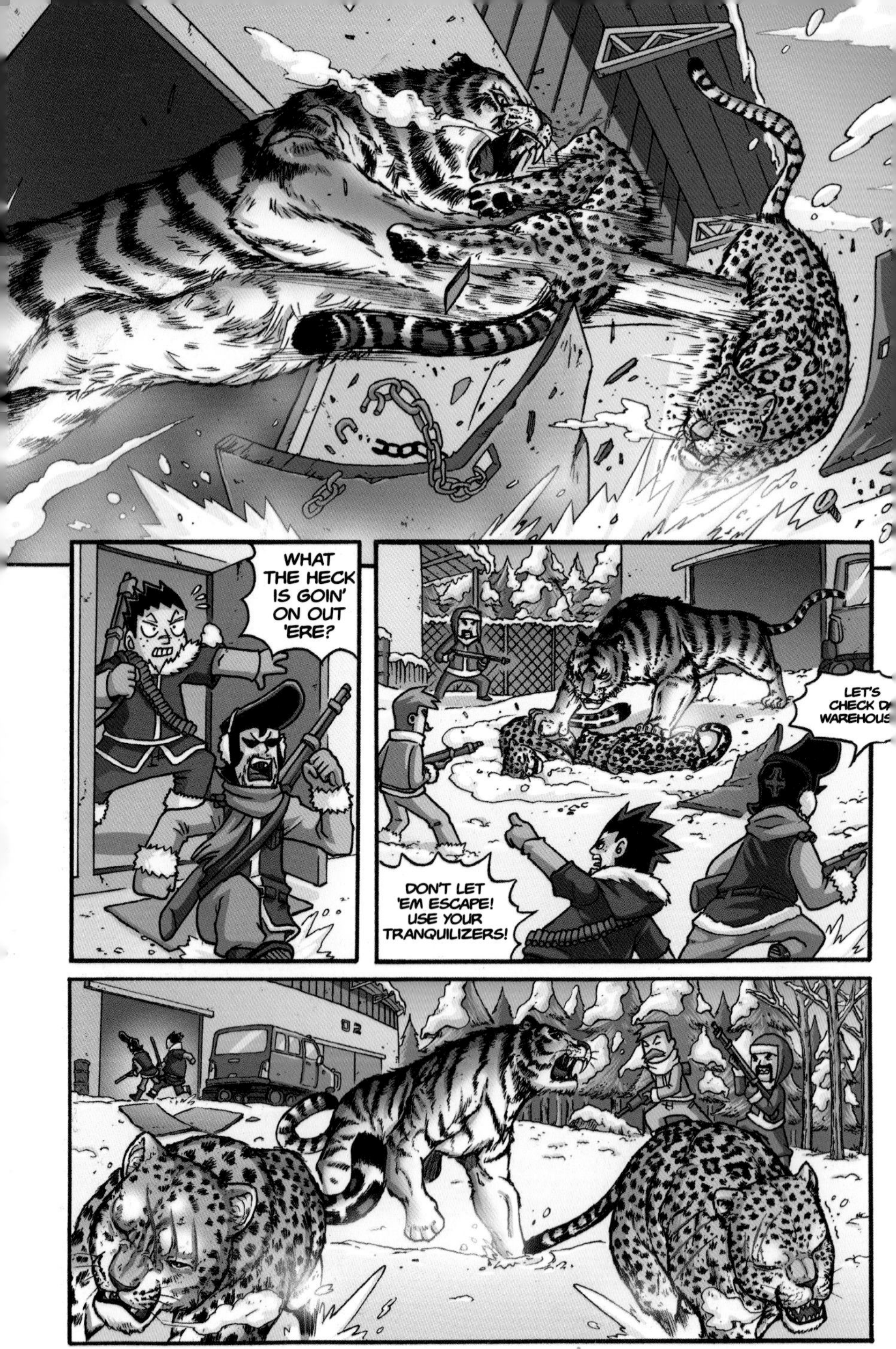
WHAT THE HECK IS GOIN' ON OUT 'ERE?
LET'S CHECK DA WAREHOUS
DON'T LET 'EM ESCAPE! USE YOUR TRANQUILIZERS!
02

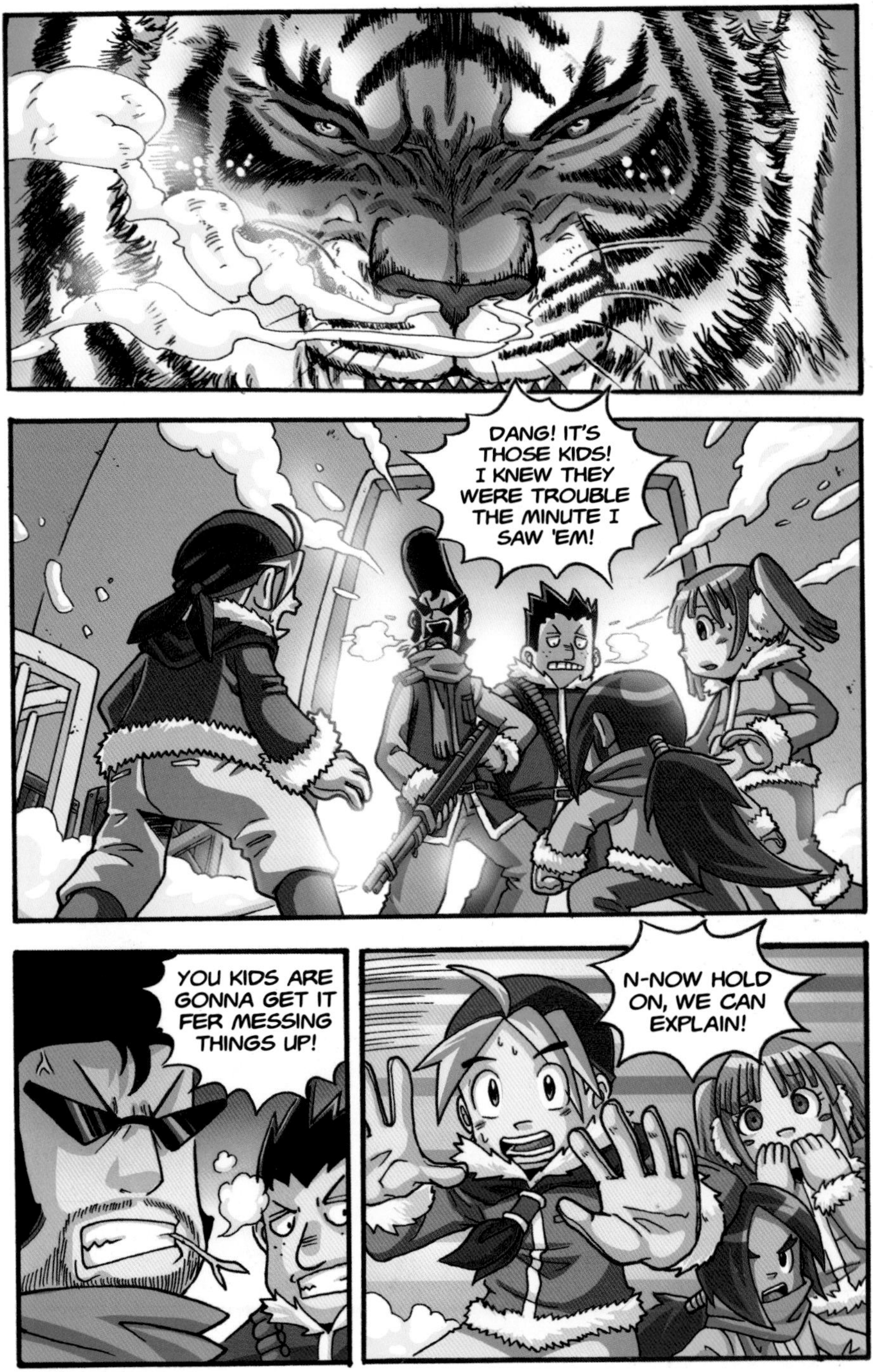
DANG! IT'S THOSE KIDS! I KNEW THEY WERE TROUBLE THE MINUTE I SAW 'EM!
YOU KIDS ARE GONNA GET IT FER MESSING THINGS UP!
N-NOW HOLD ON, WE CAN EXPLAIN!

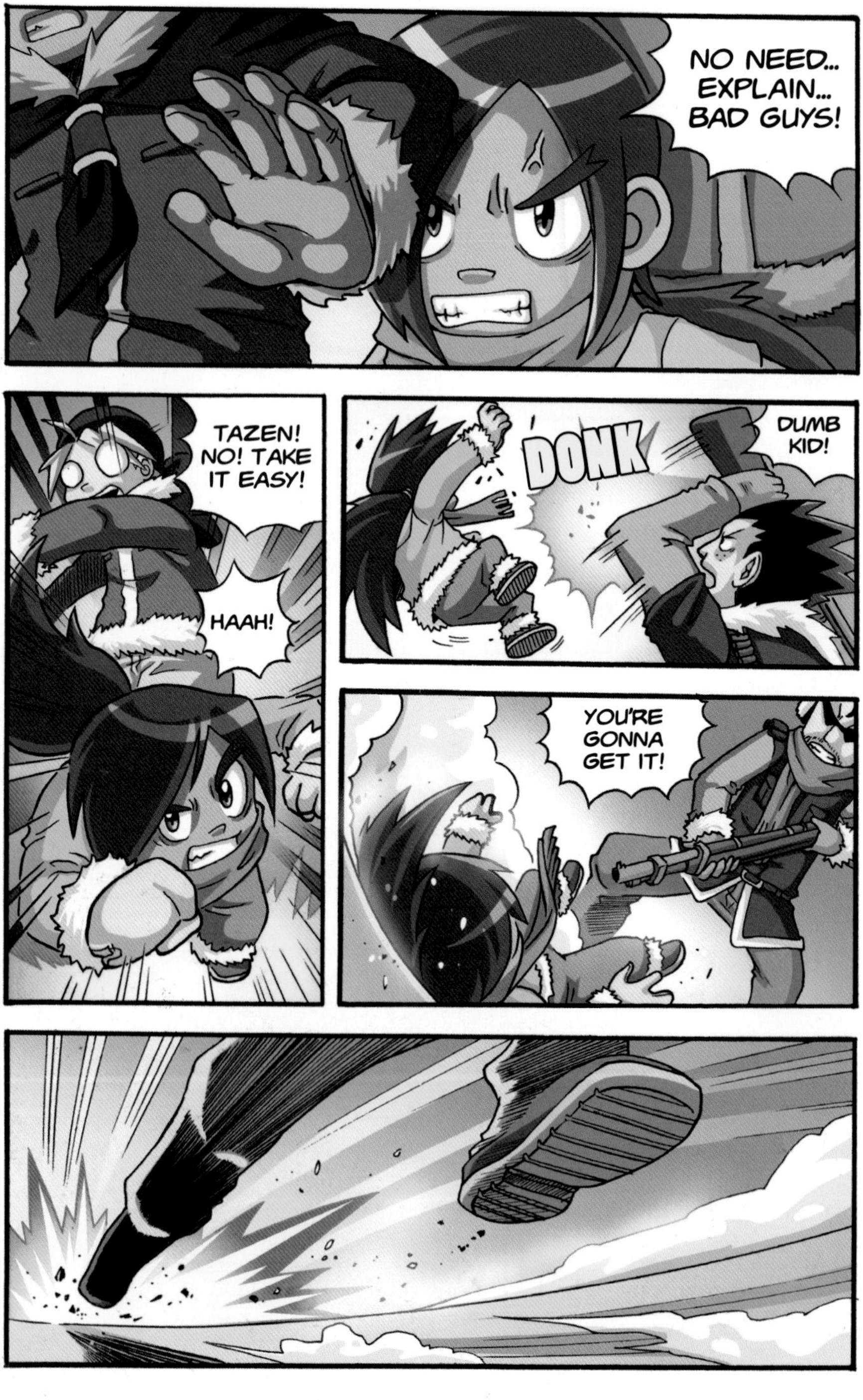
NO NEED... EXPLAIN... BAD GUYS!
TAZEN! NO! TAKE IT EASY!
HAAH!
DONK
DUMB KID!
YOU'RE GONNA GET IT!

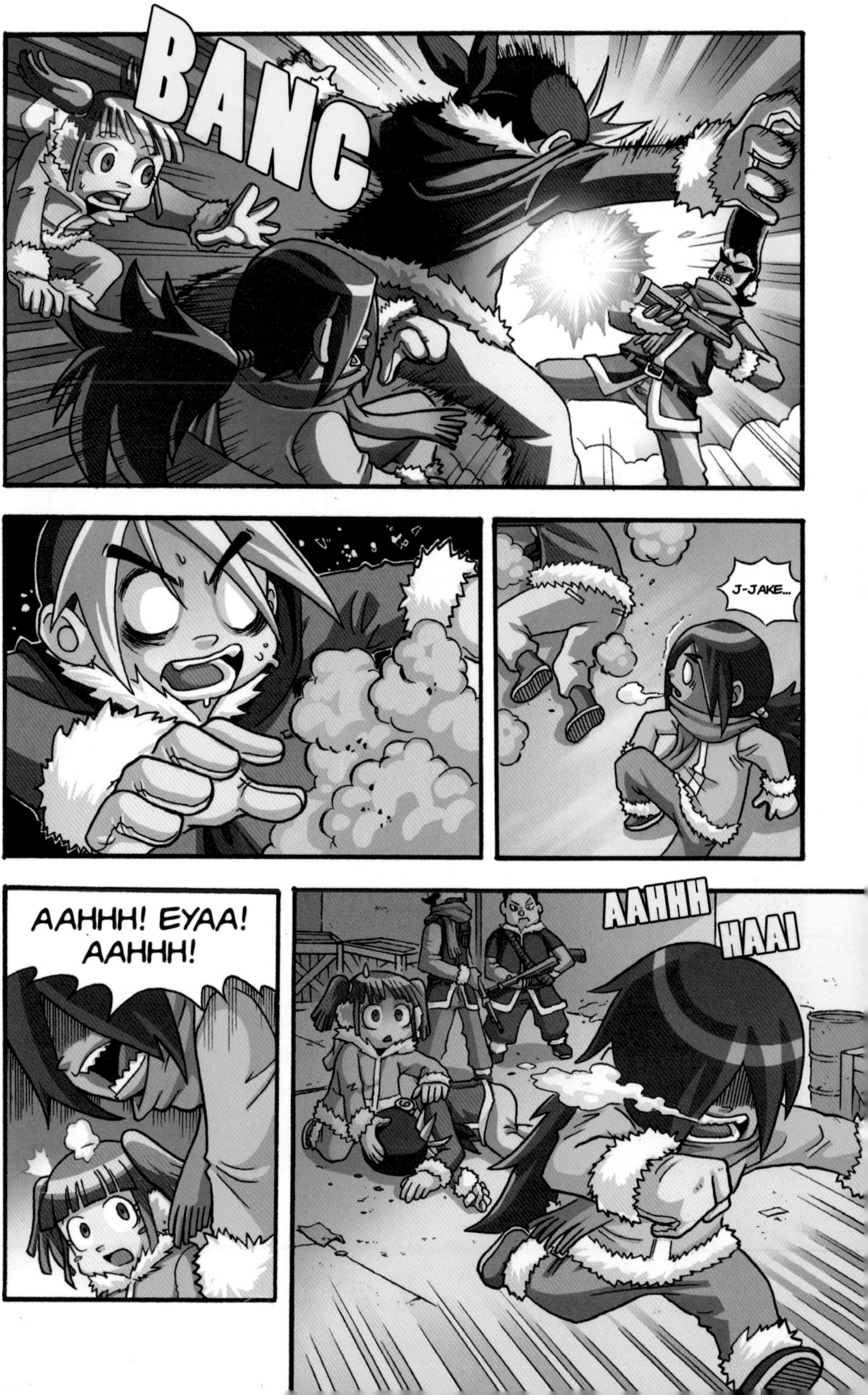
BANG
J-JAKE...
AAHHH! EYAA! AAHHH!
AAHHH
HAAI

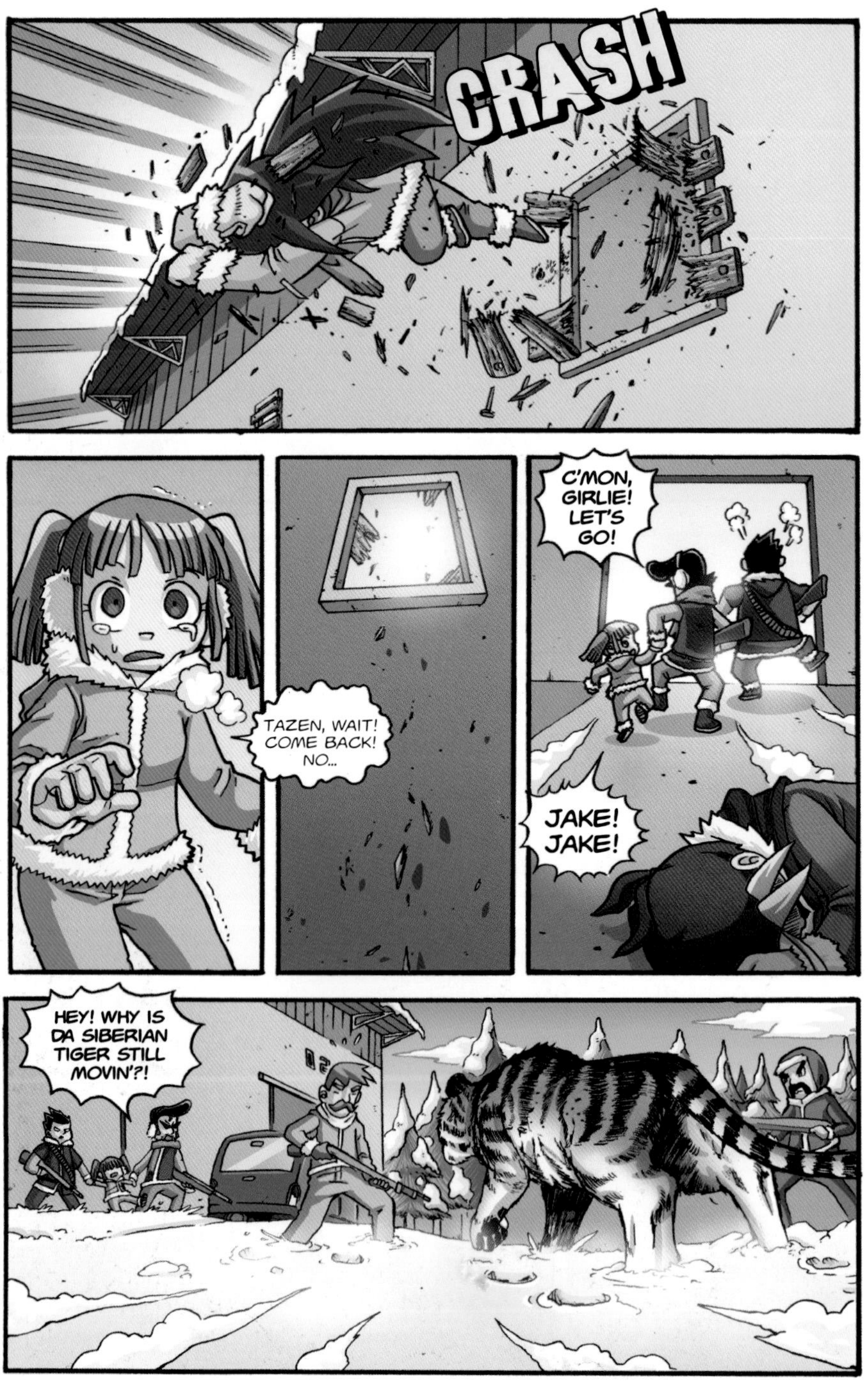
CRASH
TAZEN, WAIT! COME BACK! NO...
C'MON, GIRLIE! LET'S GO!
JAKE! JAKE!
HEY! WHY IS DA SIBERIAN TIGER STILL MOVIN'?!

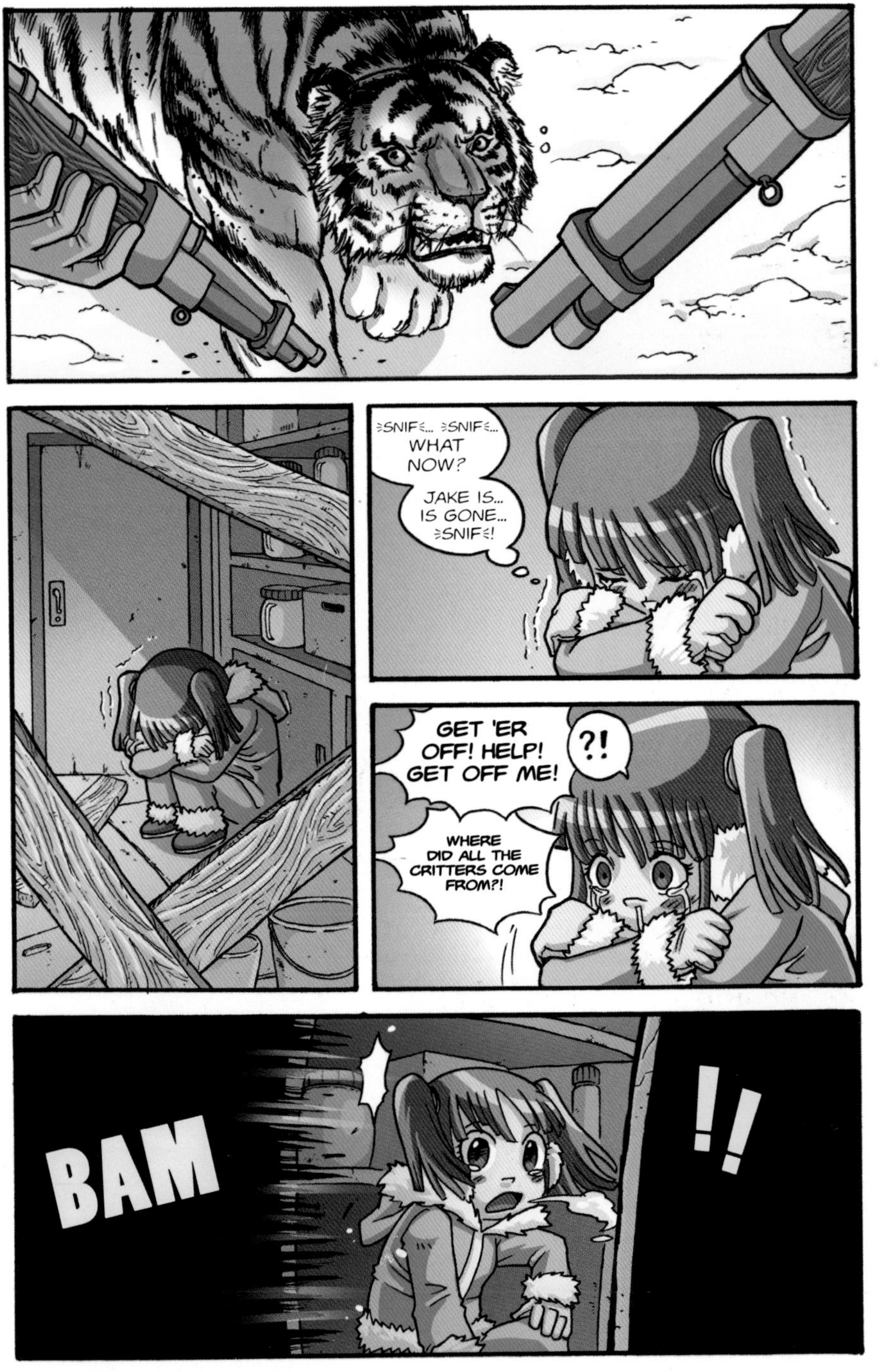

≈SNIF≈... ≈SNIF≈... WHAT NOW?
JAKE IS... IS GONE... ≈SNIF≈!
GET 'ER OFF! HELP! GET OFF ME!
?!
WHERE DID ALL THE CRITTERS COME FROM?!
BAM
!!

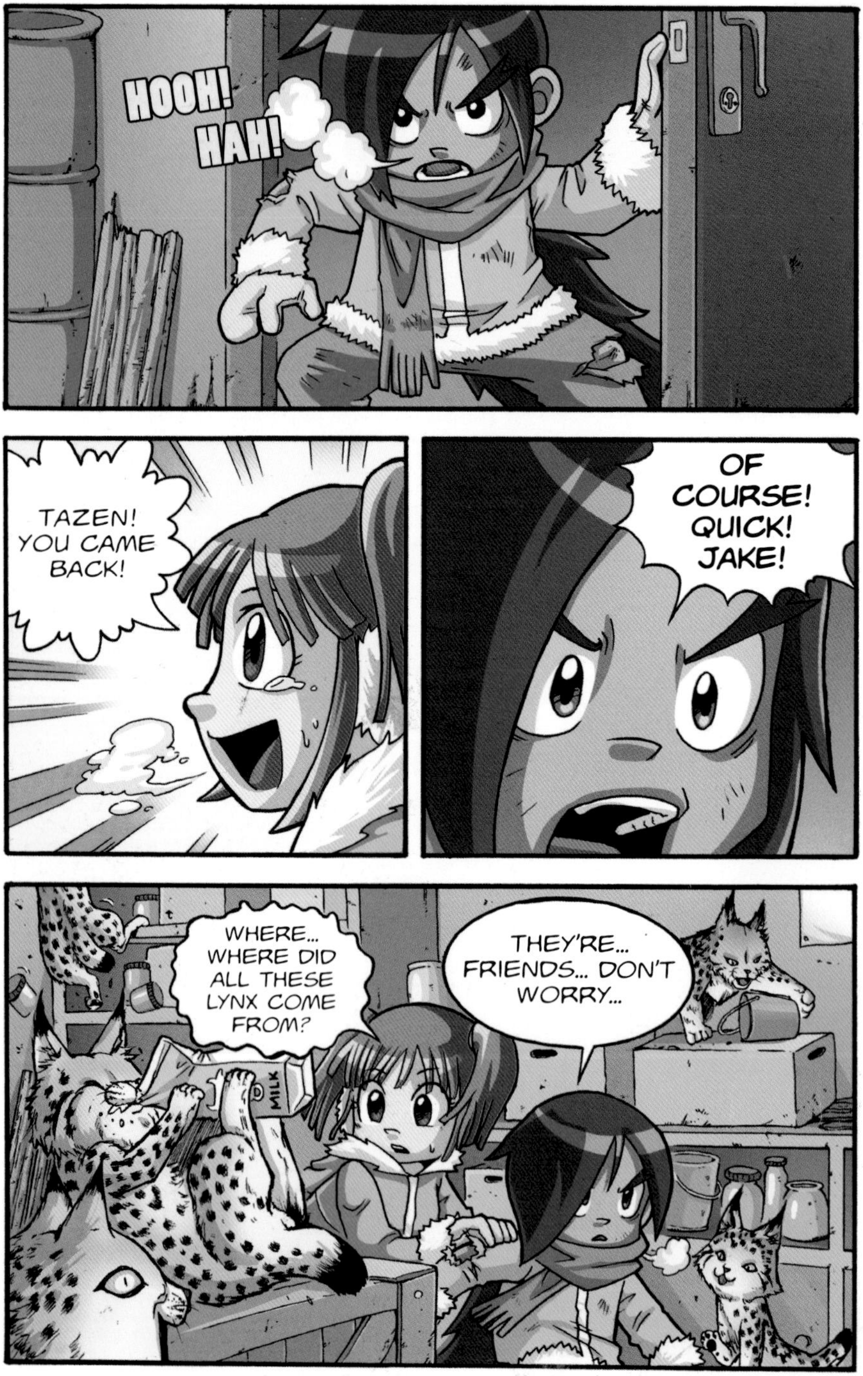
HOOH! HAH!
TAZEN! YOU CAME BACK!
OF COURSE! QUICK! JAKE!
WHERE... WHERE DID ALL THESE LYNX COME FROM?
THEY'RE... FRIENDS... DON'T WORRY...
MILK

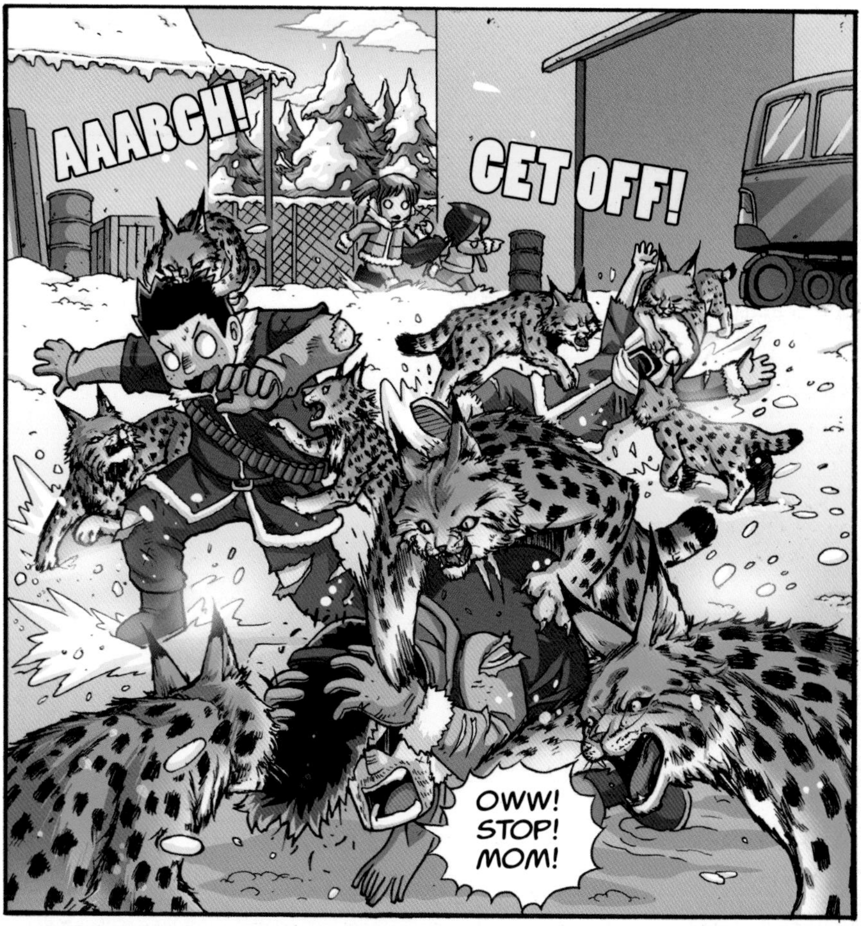
AAARCH!
GET OFF!
OWW!
STOP!
MOM!

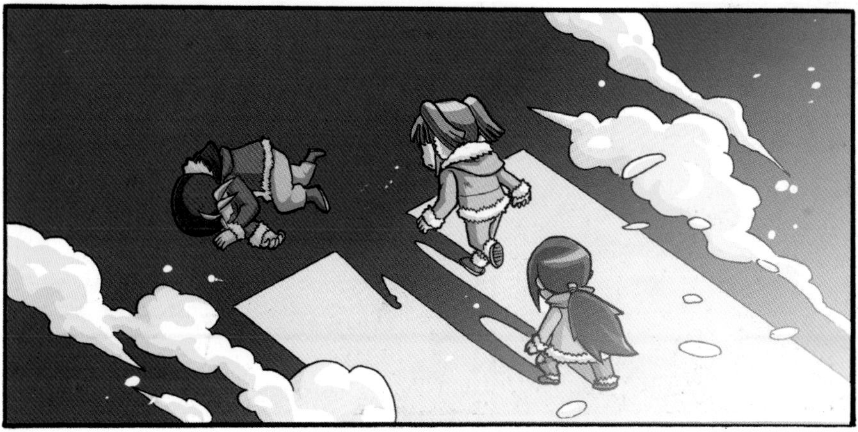

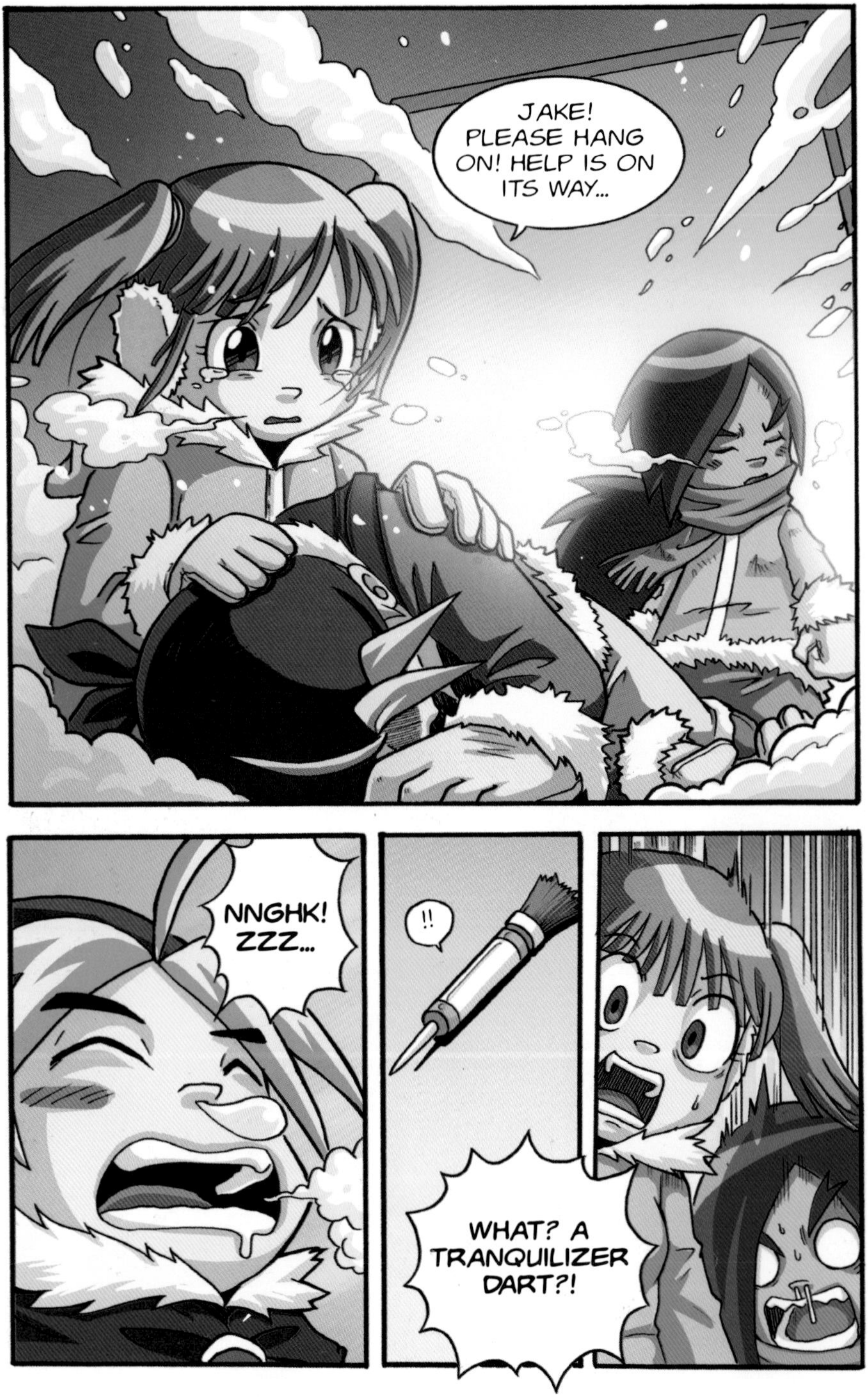
JAKE! PLEASE HANG ON! HELP IS ON ITS WAY...
NNGHK! ZZZ...
!!
WHAT? A TRANQUILIZER DART?!

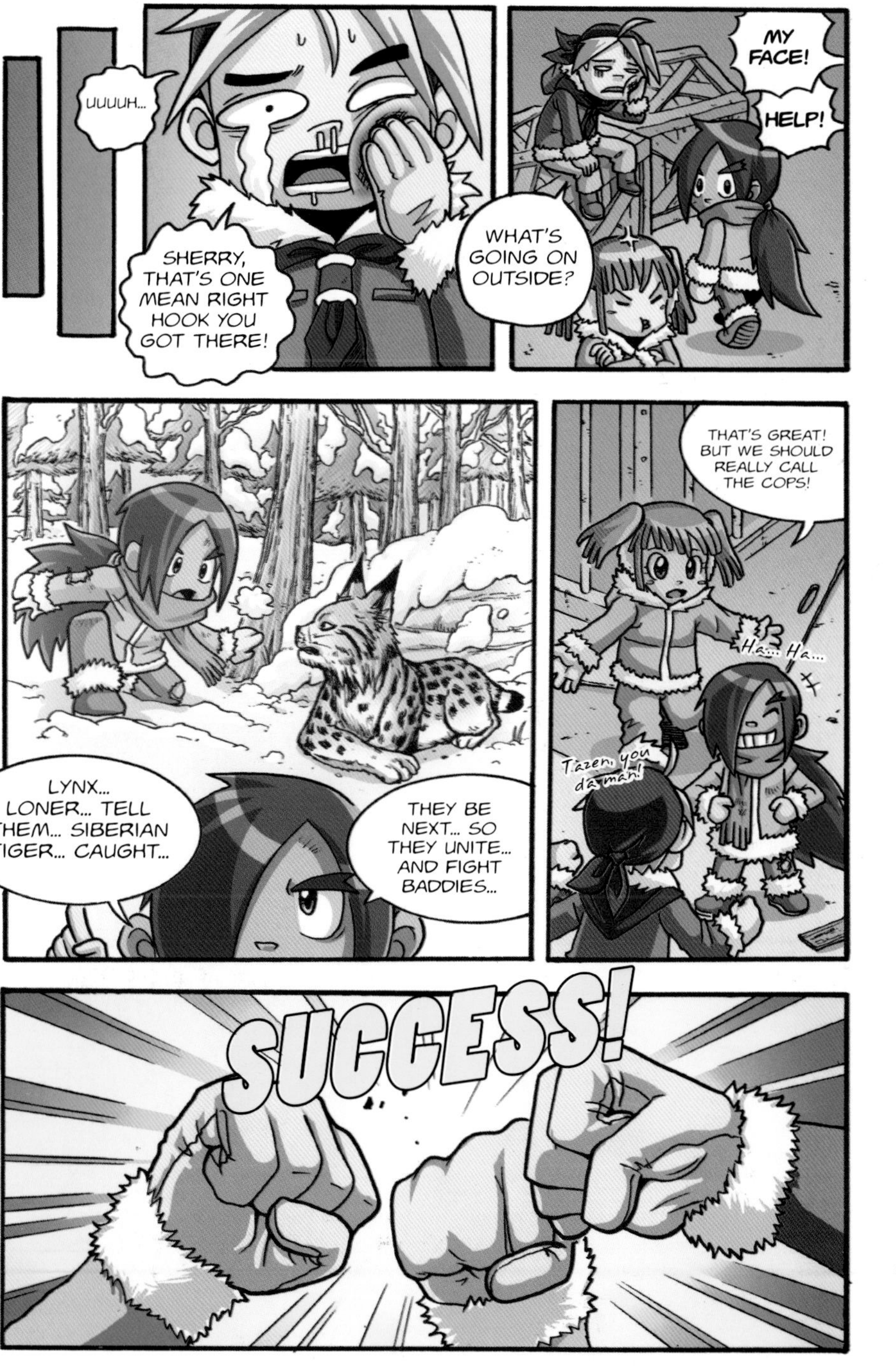
UUUUH...
SHERRY, THAT'S ONE MEAN RIGHT HOOK YOU GOT THERE!
MY FACE!
HELP!
WHAT'S GOING ON OUTSIDE?
LYNX... LONER... TELL THEM... SIBERIAN TIGER... CAUGHT...
THEY BE NEXT... SO THEY UNITE... AND FIGHT BADDIES...
THAT'S GREAT! BUT WE SHOULD REALLY CALL THE COPS!
Ha... Ha...
Tazen, you da man!
SUCCESS!

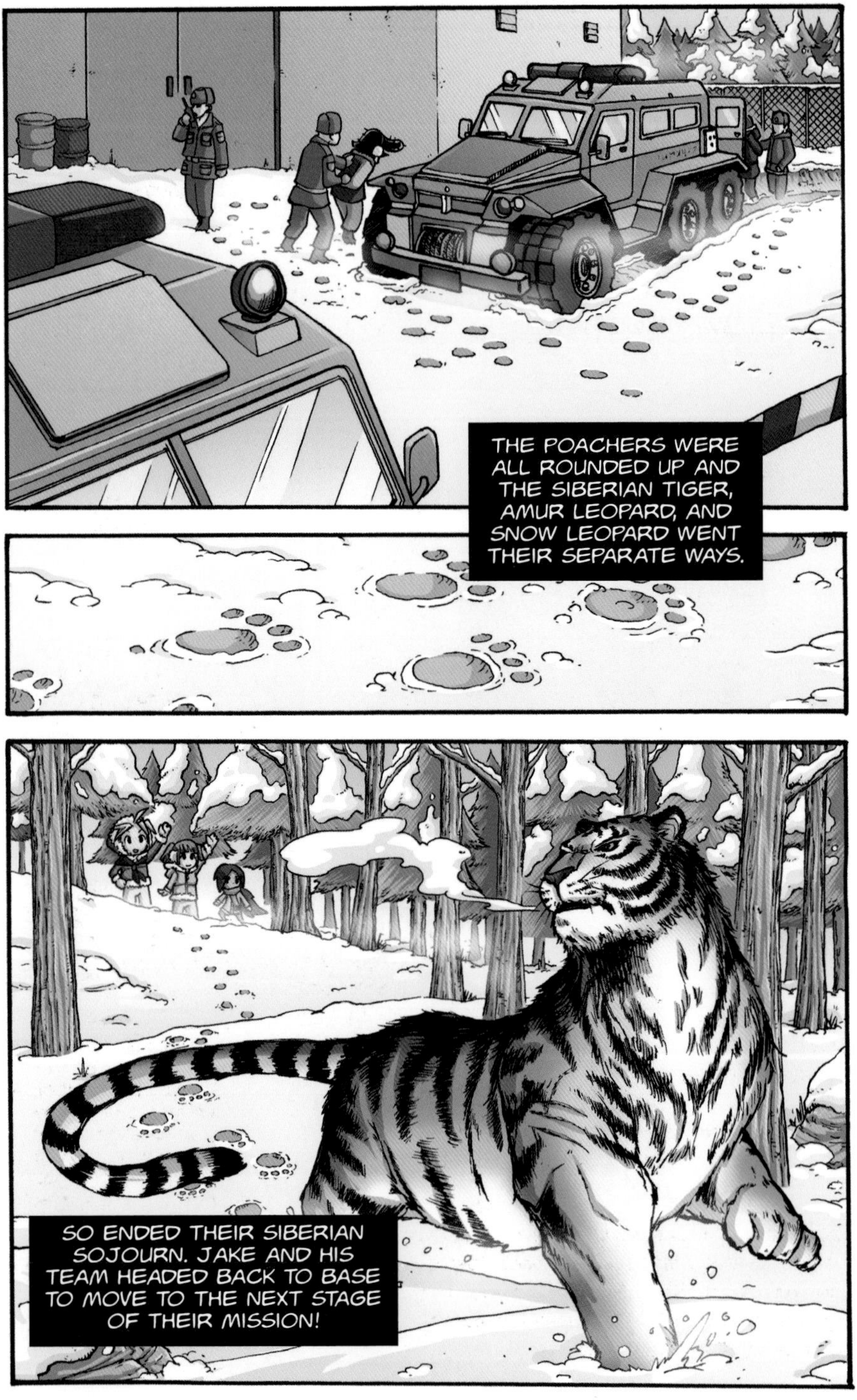
THE POACHERS WERE ALL ROUNDED UP AND THE SIBERIAN TIGER, AMUR LEOPARD, AND SNOW LEOPARD WENT THEIR SEPARATE WAYS.
SO ENDED THEIR SIBERIAN SOJOURN. JAKE AND HIS TEAM HEADED BACK TO BASE TO MOVE TO THE NEXT STAGE OF THEIR MISSION!

Conservation Status

Extinct EX	Extinct in the Wild EW	Critically Endangered CR	Endangered EN	Vulnerable VU	Near Threatened NT	Least Concern LC

Species: Panthera pardus
Length (including tail): 5 to 9 feet
Weight: 50 to 200 pounds
Common prey: From dung beetles to
    common eland (deer)
Distribution: Central to South Africa and
    southern Asia
Habitat: Ranges from rainforest
    to desert terrain

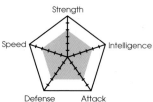

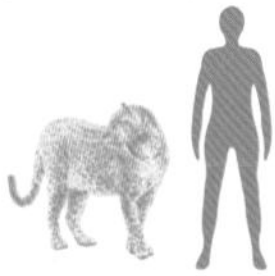

Strength

Speed

Intelligence

Defense

Attack

LEOPARD

Leopards are the smallest but most adaptable felid among the 4 "big cats" — the tiger, lion, and jaguar. It is distinguished by its short legs, elongated body and black or dark "rosette" markings. Leopards are opportunistic hunters that will eat non-typical prey such as beetles and even small crocodiles. Stealthy and aggressive, encounters between rival leopards can be potentially fatal, and they are also known to attack humans when food is scarce. Some leopard subspecies such as the Amur leopard are critically endangered due to habitat loss, poaching, and inbreeding. Rare melanistic individuals (an excess of the pigment melanin) are known as black panthers, or panthers.

The "rosette" pattern of spots endows it with significant camouflage, making the leopard, a byword for stealth. Smaller and lighter than the other "big cats," leopards can run at speeds of 36 miles per hour, capable of both stalking and chasing prey through the long grasses, or ambushing them from above.

▲ The leopard is a good swimmer, but is better known as a powerful climber; possessing incredible jaw strength that allows it to drag its kill, sometimes twice its weight, up a tree to keep it away from other predators such as hyenas and lions.

Strength
Speed
Intelligence
Defense
Attack

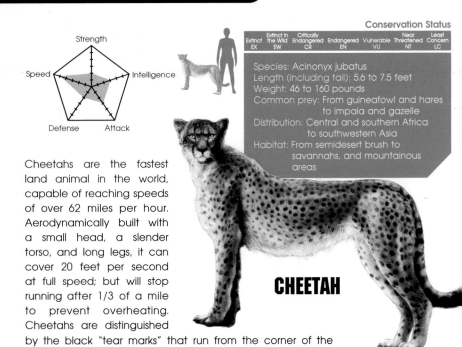

Conservation Status

Extinct EX	Extinct in the Wild EW	Critically Endangered CR	Endangered EN	Vulnerable VU	Near Threatened NT	Least Concern LC

Species: Acinonyx jubatus
Length (including tail): 5.6 to 7.5 feet
Weight: 46 to 160 pounds
Common prey: From guineafowl and hares to impala and gazelle
Distribution: Central and southern Africa to southwestern Asia
Habitat: From semidesert brush to savannahs, and mountainous areas

CHEETAH

Cheetahs are the fastest land animal in the world, capable of reaching speeds of over 62 miles per hour. Aerodynamically built with a small head, a slender torso, and long legs, it can cover 20 feet per second at full speed; but will stop running after 1/3 of a mile to prevent overheating. Cheetahs are distinguished by the black "tear marks" that run from the corner of the eyes to the mouth, which have been found to reduce glare, allowing them to utilize their excellent vision. Unlike other felids, cheetahs are diurnal and hunt using vision rather than scent; prey is stalked to within 33 to 99 feet, and then chased. The cheetah has an average hunting success rate of around 50%.

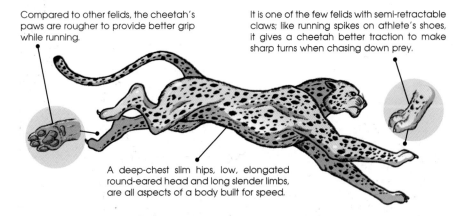

Compared to other felids, the cheetah's paws are rougher to provide better grip while running.

It is one of the few felids with semi-retractable claws; like running spikes on athlete's shoes, it gives a cheetah better traction to make sharp turns when chasing down prey.

A deep-chest slim hips, low, elongated round-eared head and long slender limbs, are all aspects of a body built for speed.

Cheetahs rely solely on speed for survival, but will abandon the chase after failing to secure a kill within a minute due to how much energy is expended.

CHAPTER 6

A MATTER OF PRIDE

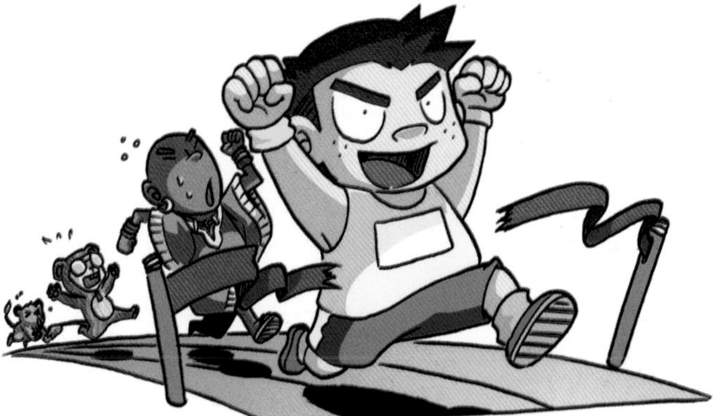

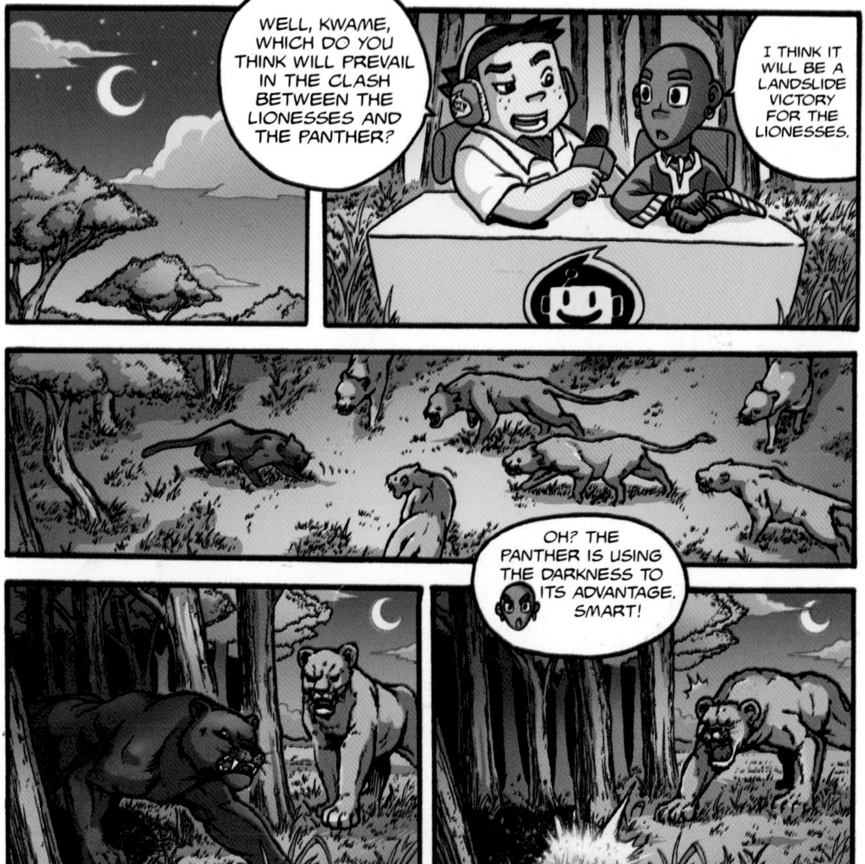
WELL, KWAME, WHICH DO YOU THINK WILL PREVAIL IN THE CLASH BETWEEN THE LIONESSES AND THE PANTHER?
I THINK IT WILL BE A LANDSLIDE VICTORY FOR THE LIONESSES.
OH? THE PANTHER IS USING THE DARKNESS TO ITS ADVANTAGE. SMART!

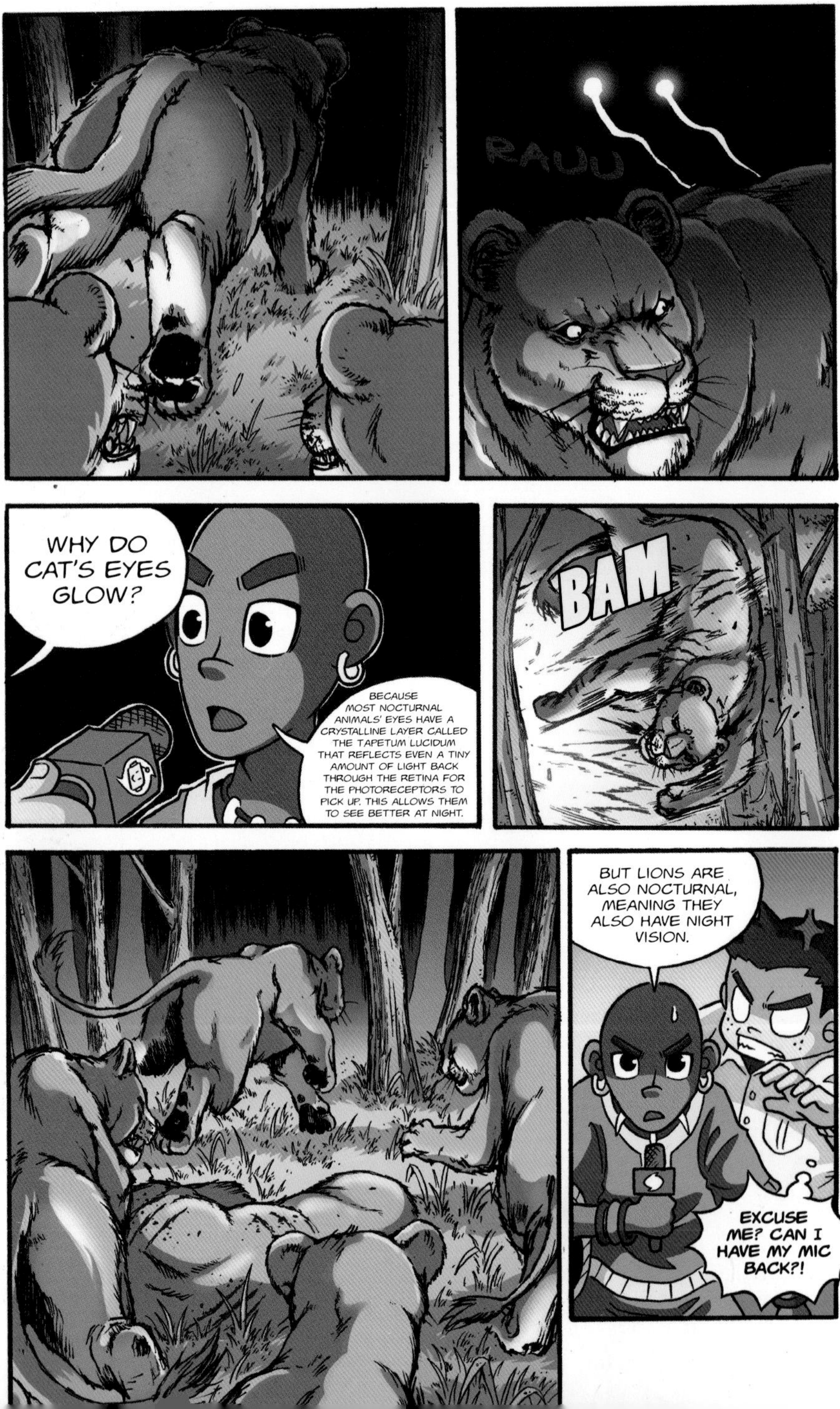
RAUU
WHY DO CAT'S EYES GLOW?
BECAUSE MOST NOCTURNAL ANIMALS' EYES HAVE A CRYSTALLINE LAYER CALLED THE TAPETUM LUCIDUM THAT REFLECTS EVEN A TINY AMOUNT OF LIGHT BACK THROUGH THE RETINA FOR THE PHOTORECEPTORS TO PICK UP. THIS ALLOWS THEM TO SEE BETTER AT NIGHT.
BAM
BUT LIONS ARE ALSO NOCTURNAL, MEANING THEY ALSO HAVE NIGHT VISION.
EXCUSE ME? CAN I HAVE MY MIC BACK?!

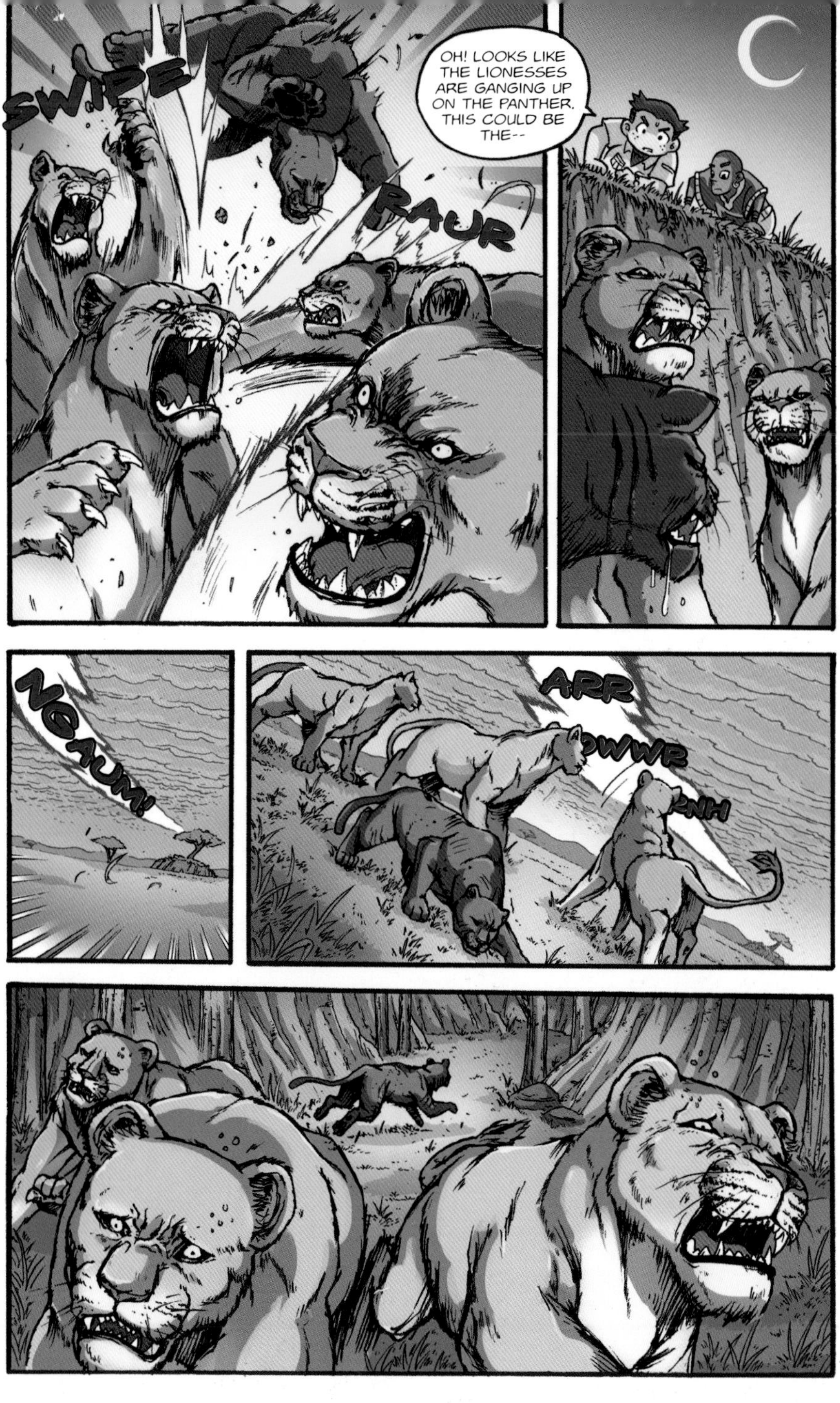
SWIPE
RAUR
OH! LOOKS LIKE THE LIONESSES ARE GANGING UP ON THE PANTHER. THIS COULD BE THE--
NGAUM!
ARR
OWWR
RNH

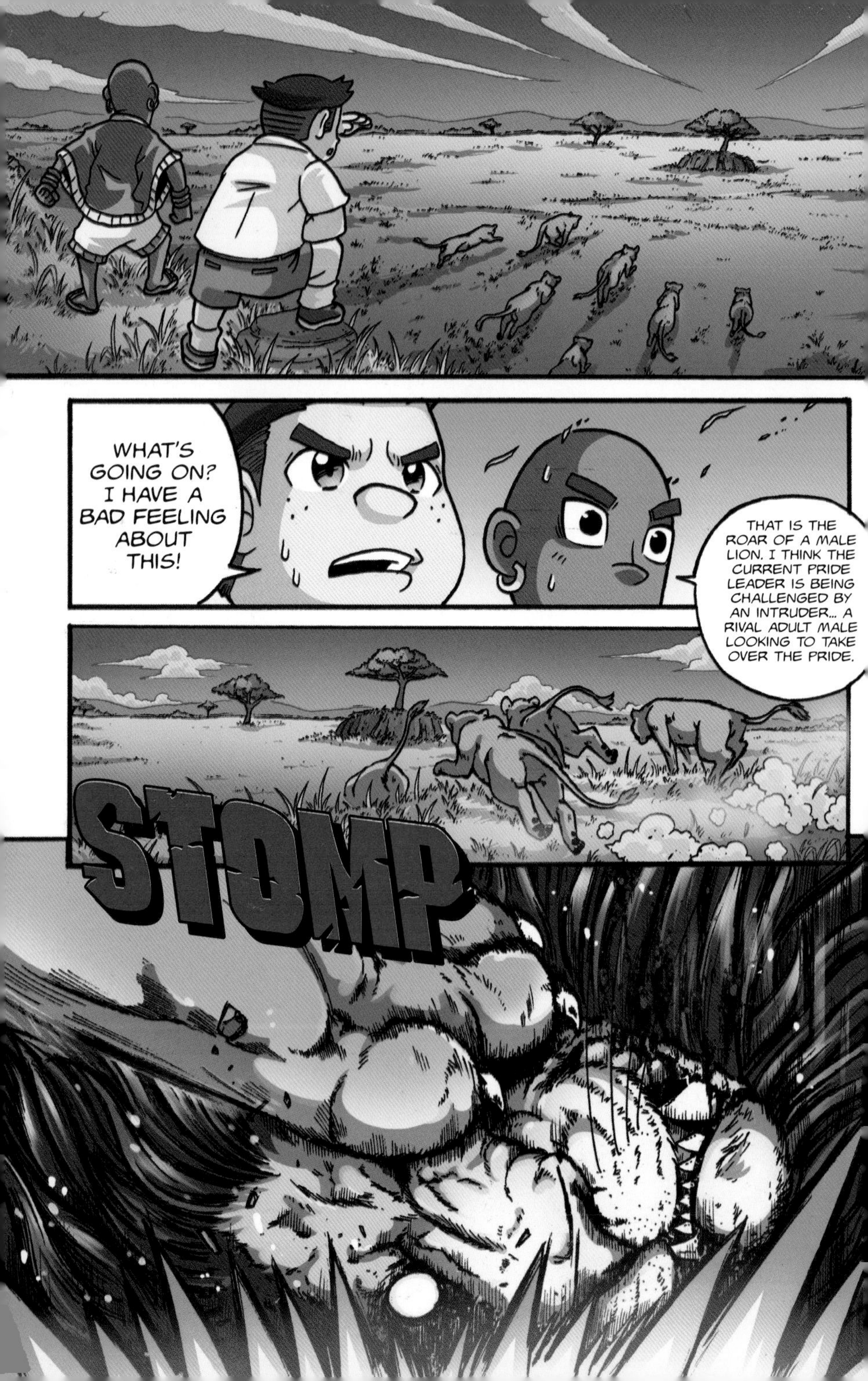
WHAT'S GOING ON? I HAVE A BAD FEELING ABOUT THIS!
THAT IS THE ROAR OF A MALE LION. I THINK THE CURRENT PRIDE LEADER IS BEING CHALLENGED BY AN INTRUDER... A RIVAL ADULT MALE LOOKING TO TAKE OVER THE PRIDE.
STOMP

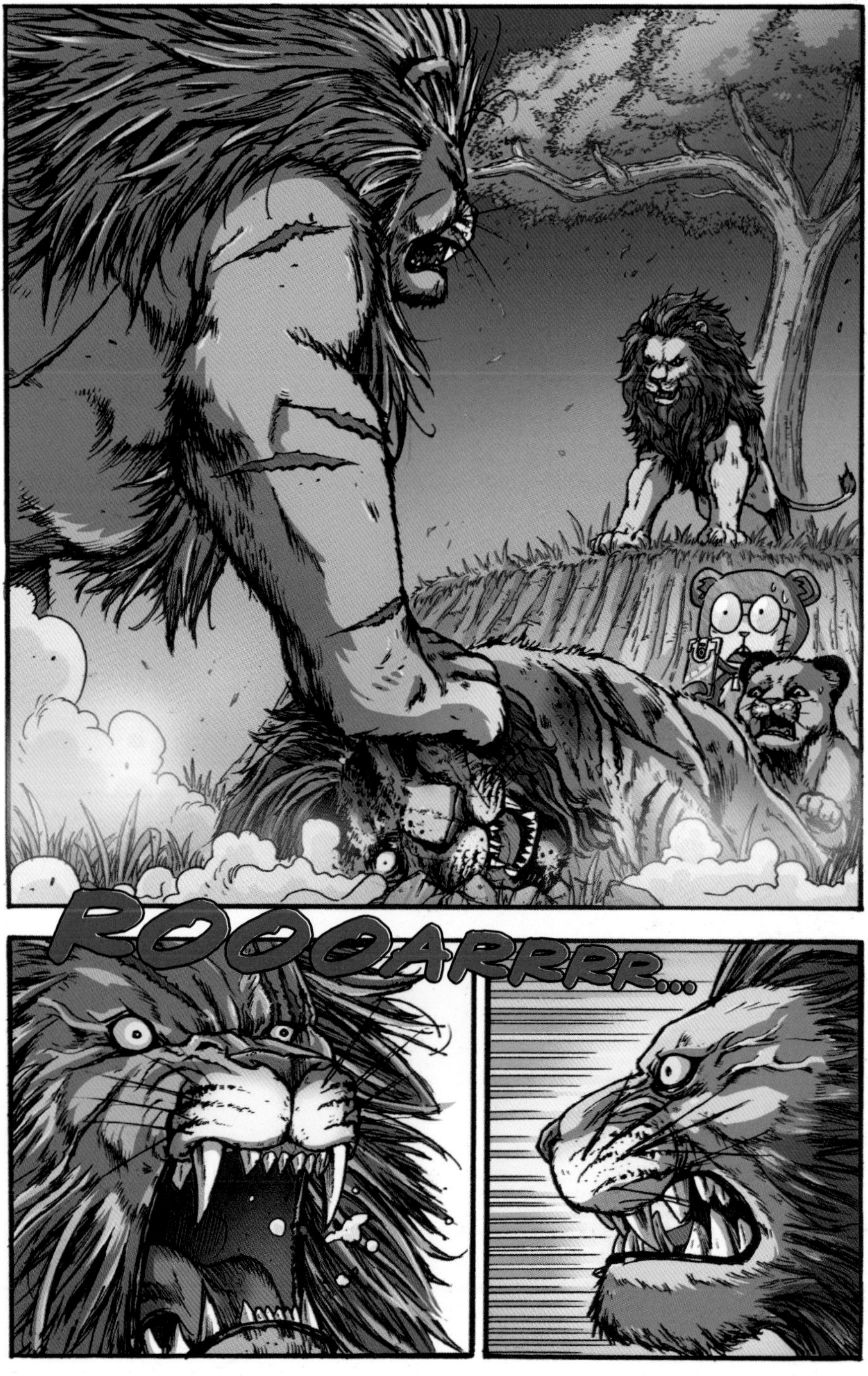
ROOOARRRR...

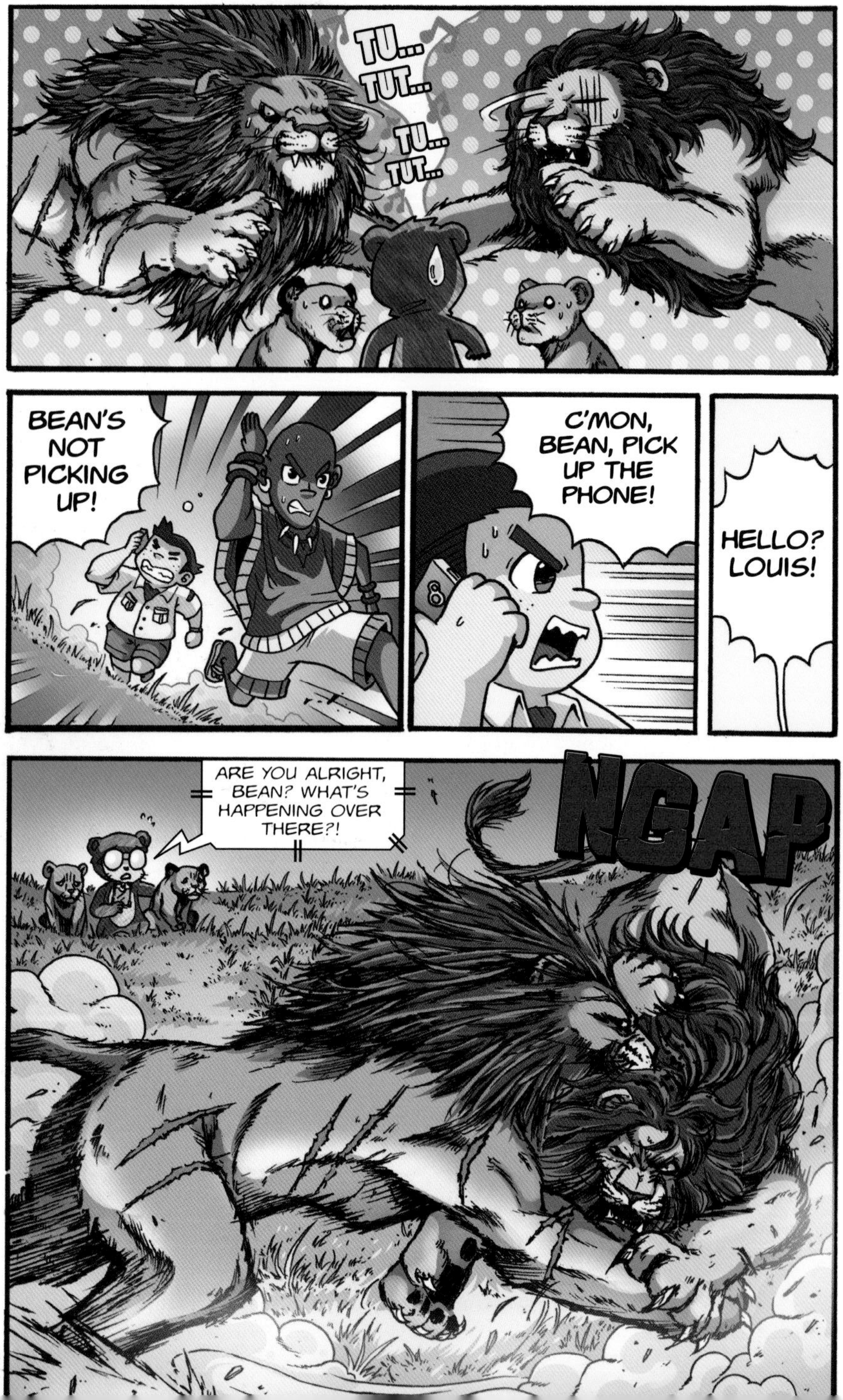
TU... TUT...
TU... TUT...
BEAN'S NOT PICKING UP!
C'MON, BEAN, PICK UP THE PHONE!
HELLO? LOUIS!
ARE YOU ALRIGHT, BEAN? WHAT'S HAPPENING OVER THERE?!
NGAP

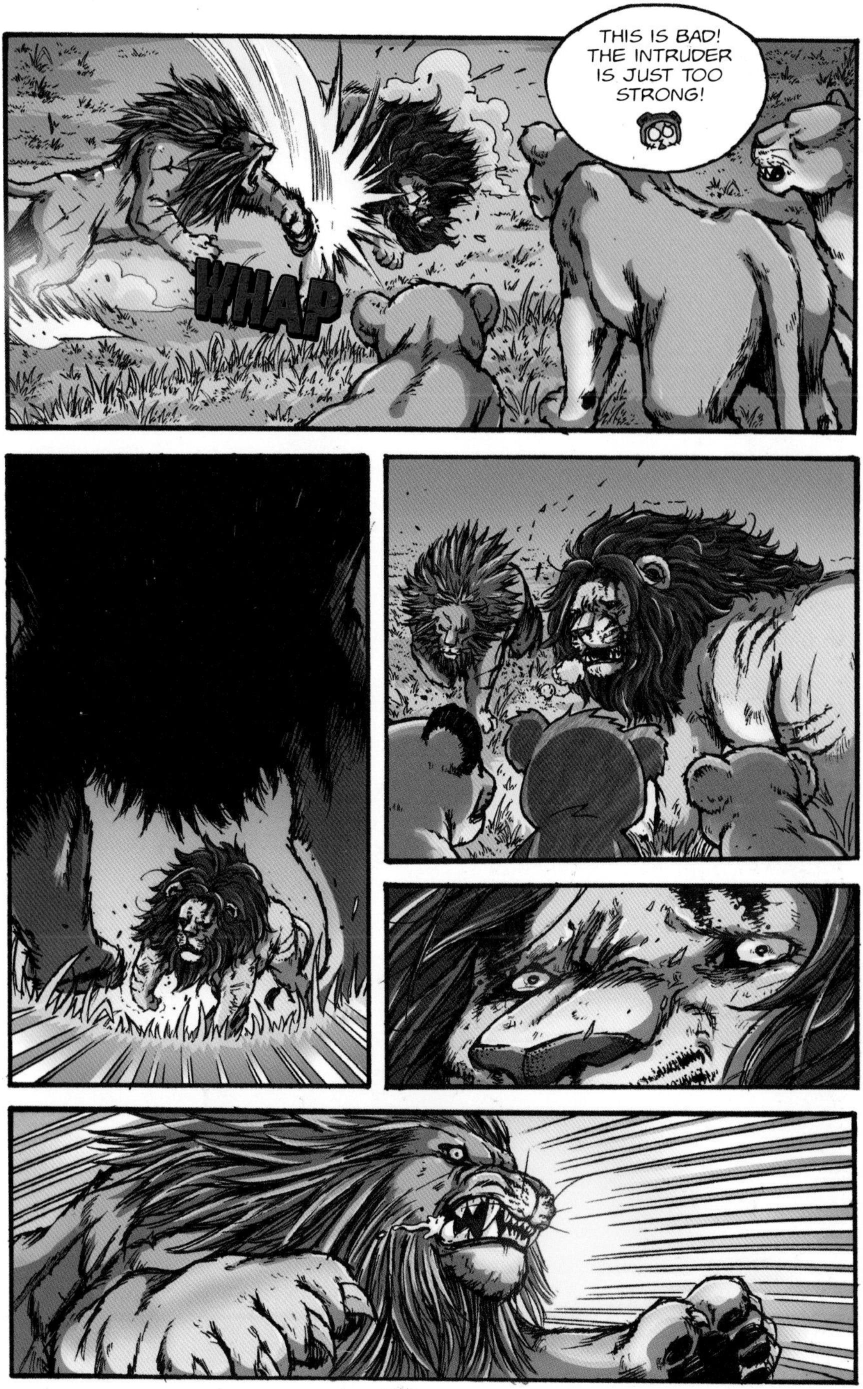
THIS IS BAD! THE INTRUDER IS JUST TOO STRONG!
WHAP

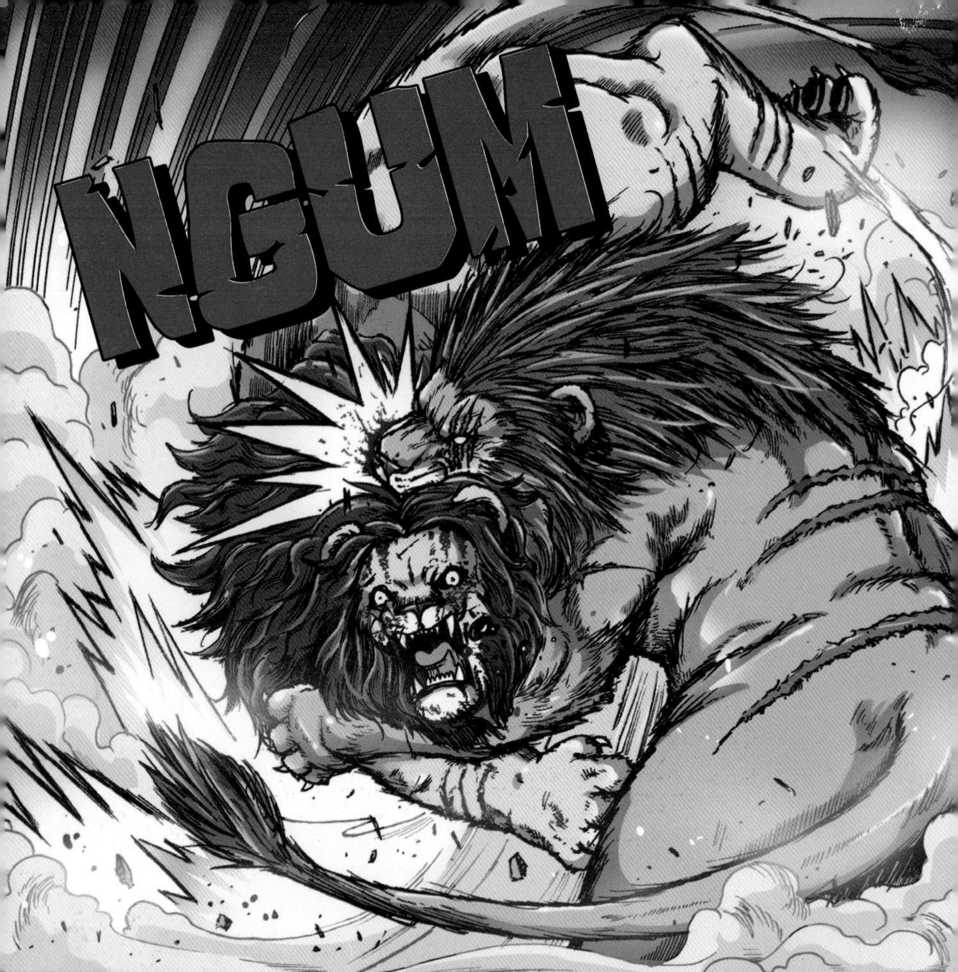
NGUM

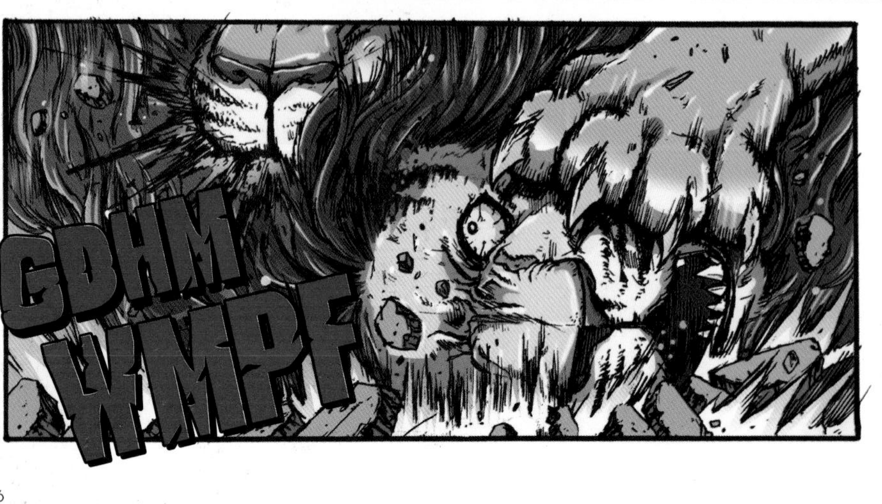
GDHM
WMPF

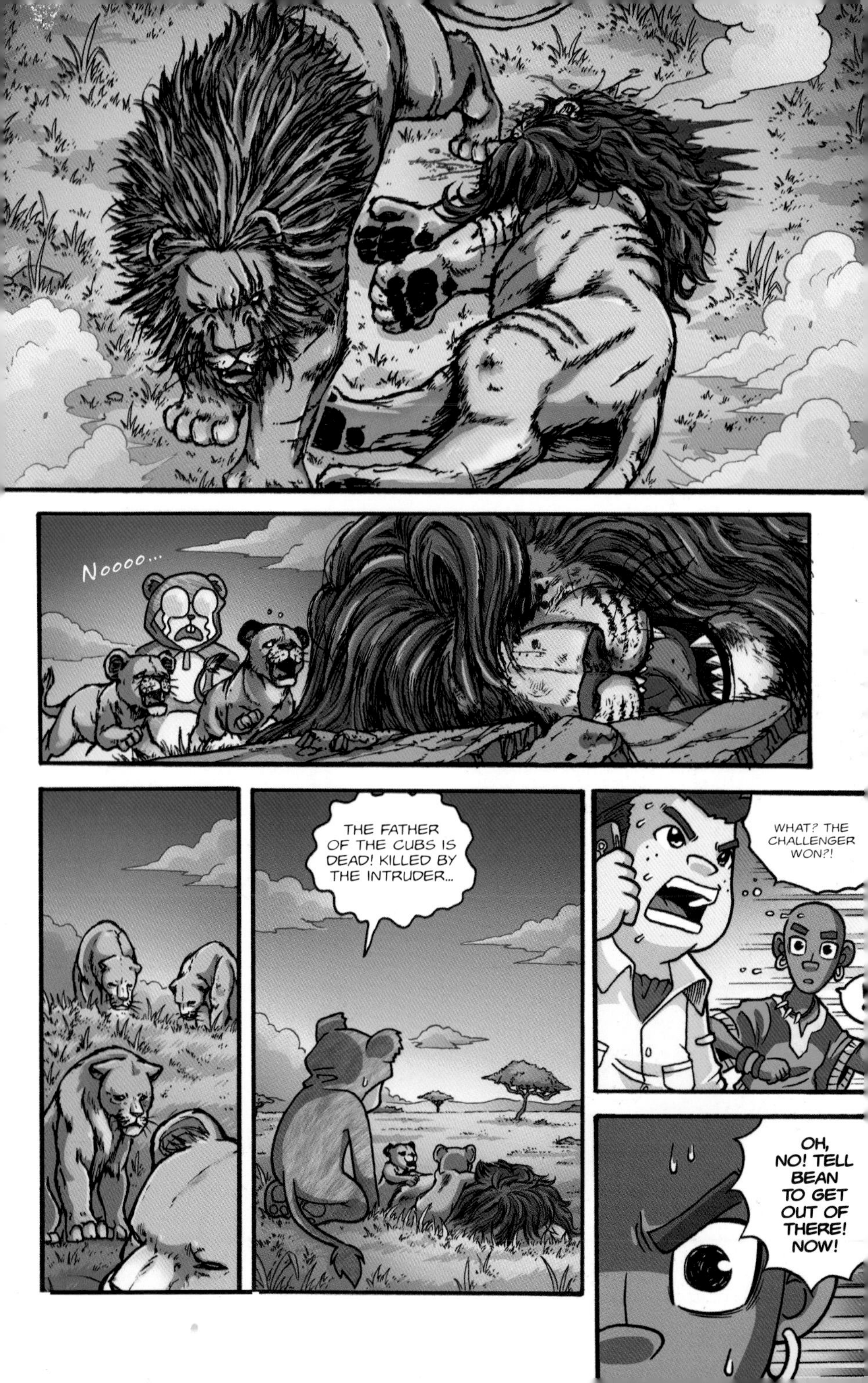
Noooo...
THE FATHER OF THE CUBS IS DEAD! KILLED BY THE INTRUDER...
WHAT? THE CHALLENGER WON?!
OH, NO! TELL BEAN TO GET OUT OF THERE! NOW!

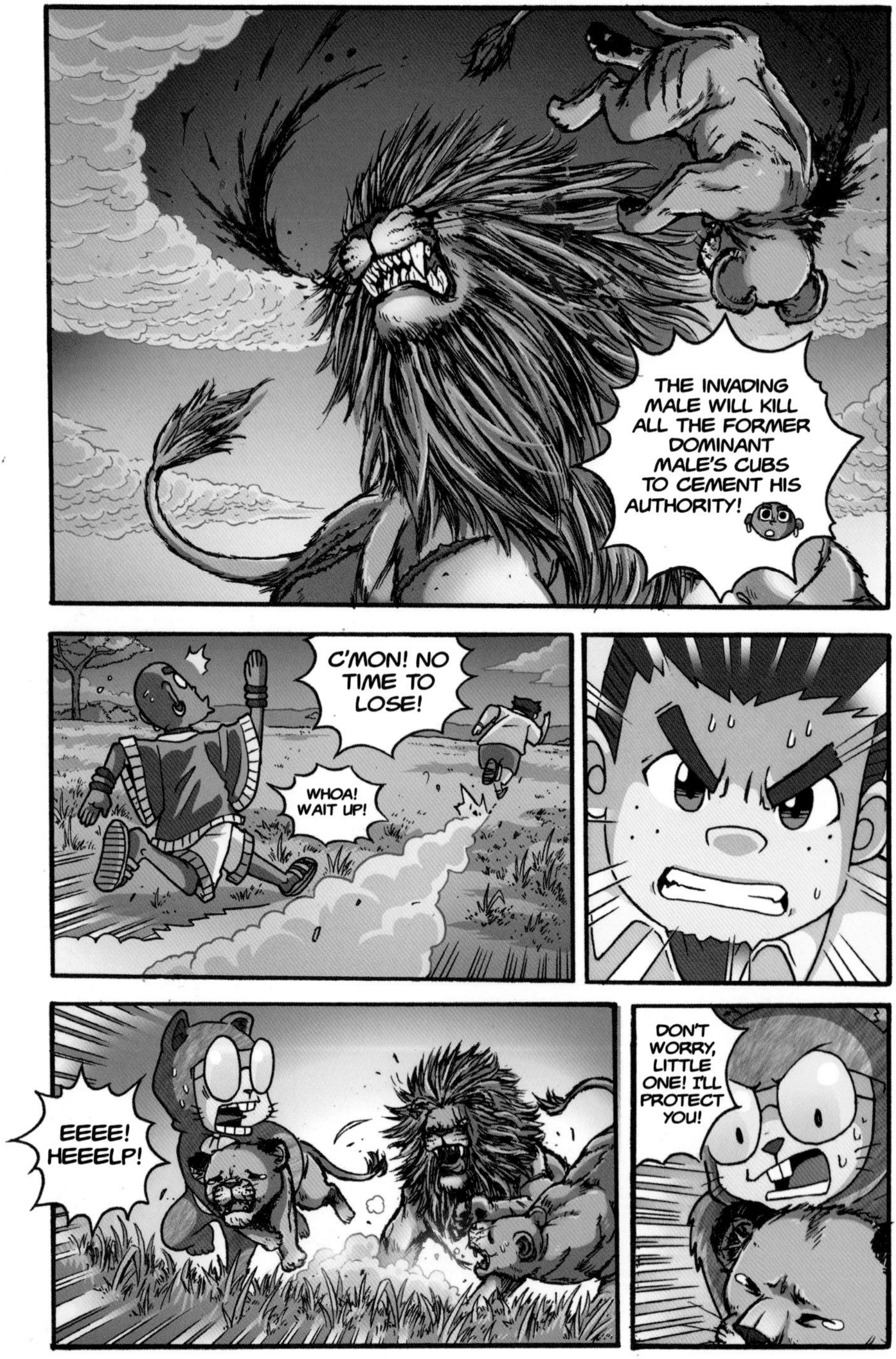
THE INVADING MALE WILL KILL ALL THE FORMER DOMINANT MALE'S CUBS TO CEMENT HIS AUTHORITY!
C'MON! NO TIME TO LOSE!
WHOA! WAIT UP!
EEEE! HEEELP!
DON'T WORRY, LITTLE ONE! I'LL PROTECT YOU!

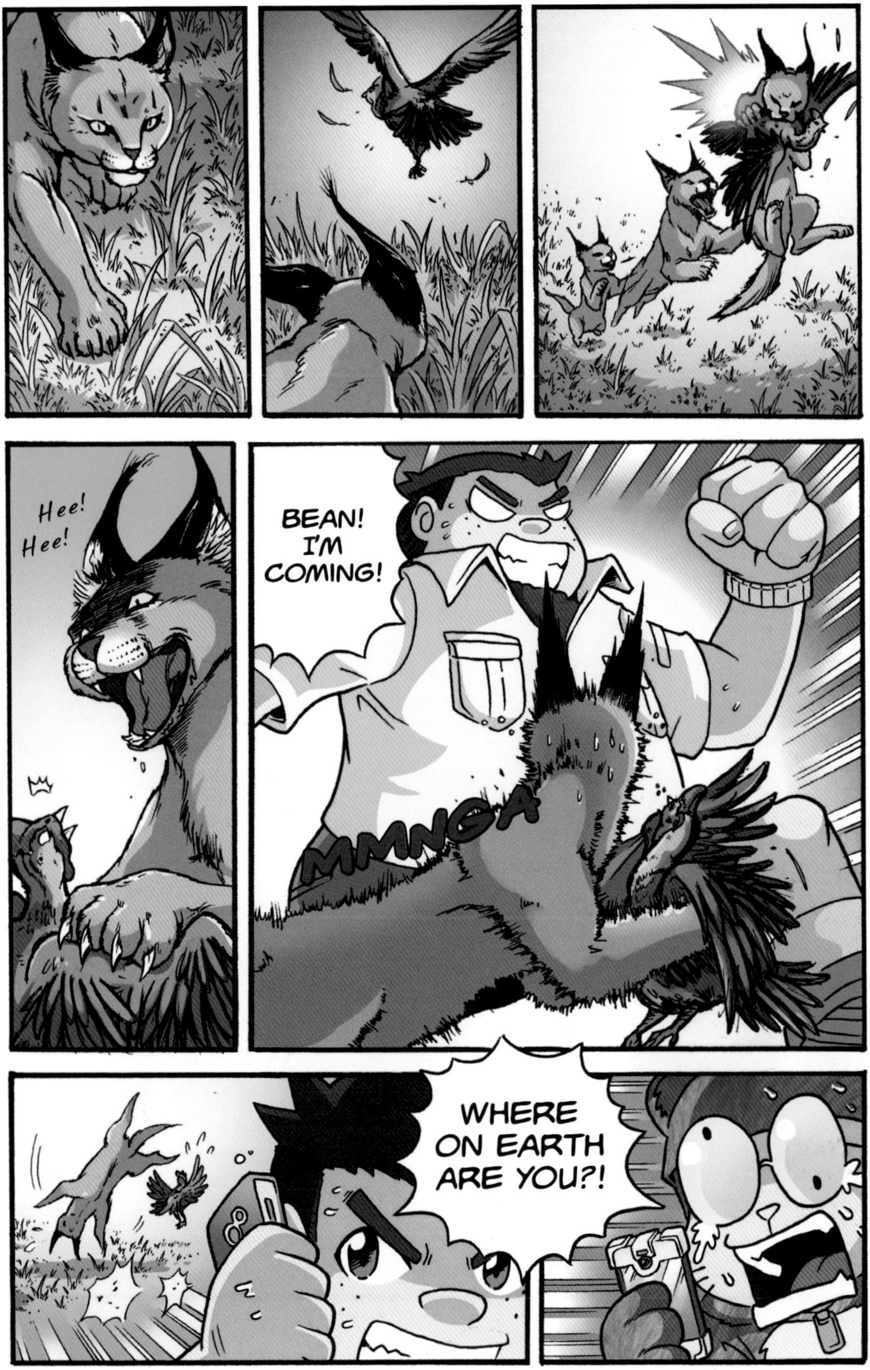
Hee!
Hee!
BEAN! I'M COMING!
MMNGA
WHERE ON EARTH ARE YOU?!

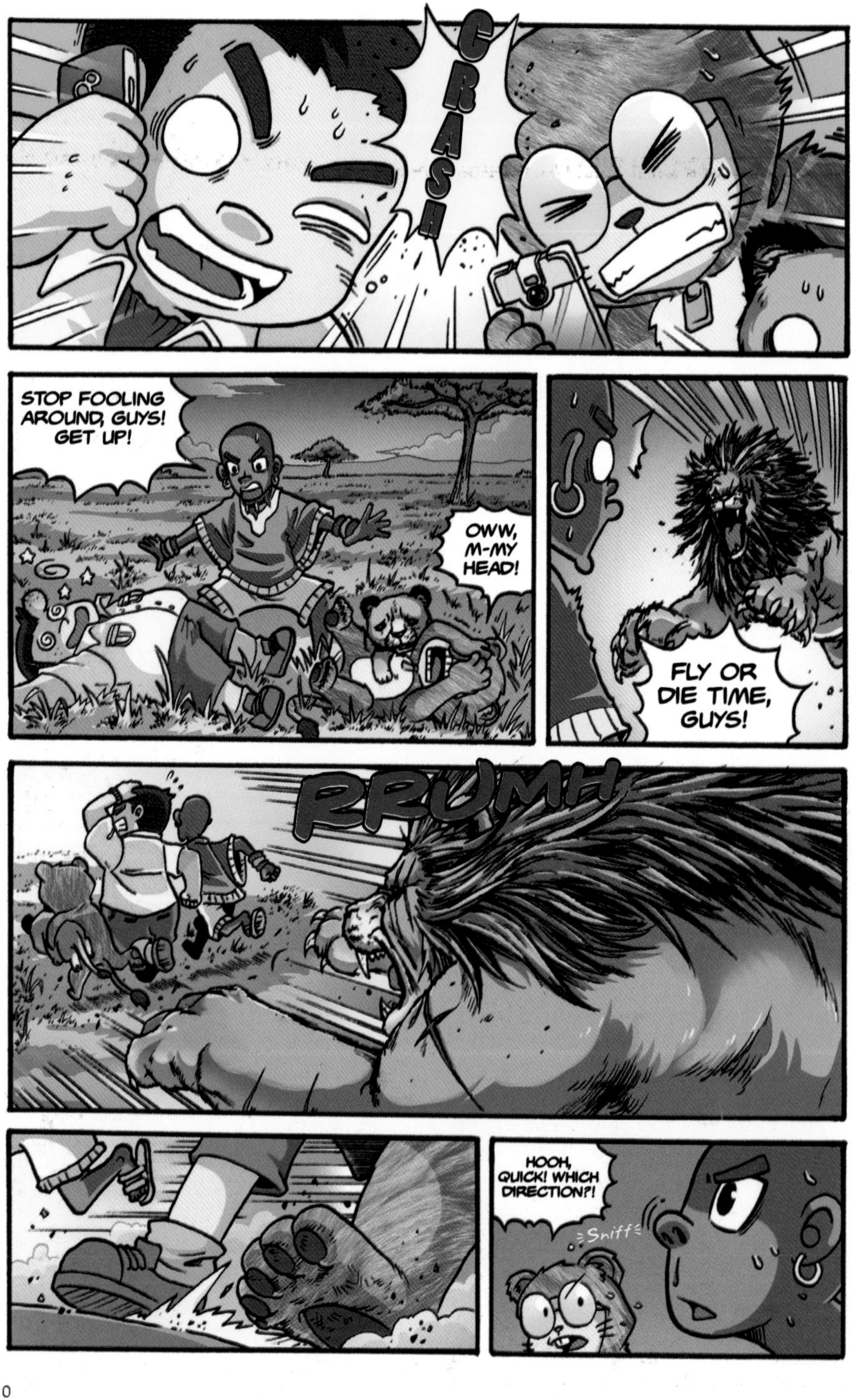
CRASH
STOP FOOLING AROUND, GUYS! GET UP!
OWW, M-MY HEAD!
FLY OR DIE TIME, GUYS!
RRUMH
HOOH, QUICK! WHICH DIRECTION?!
Sniff

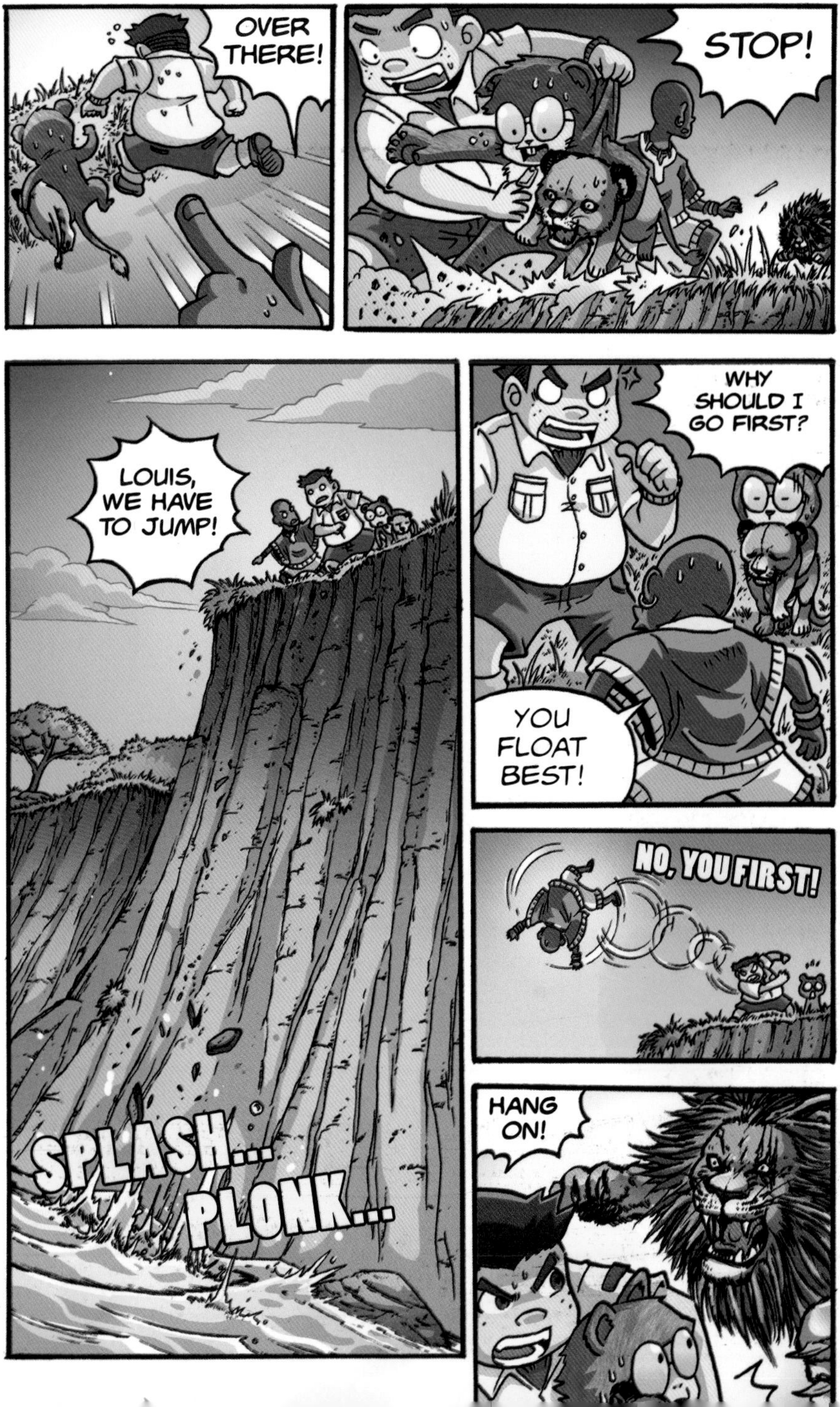
OVER THERE!
STOP!
LOUIS, WE HAVE TO JUMP!
SPLASH...
PLONK...
WHY SHOULD I GO FIRST?
YOU FLOAT BEST!
NO, YOU FIRST!
HANG ON!

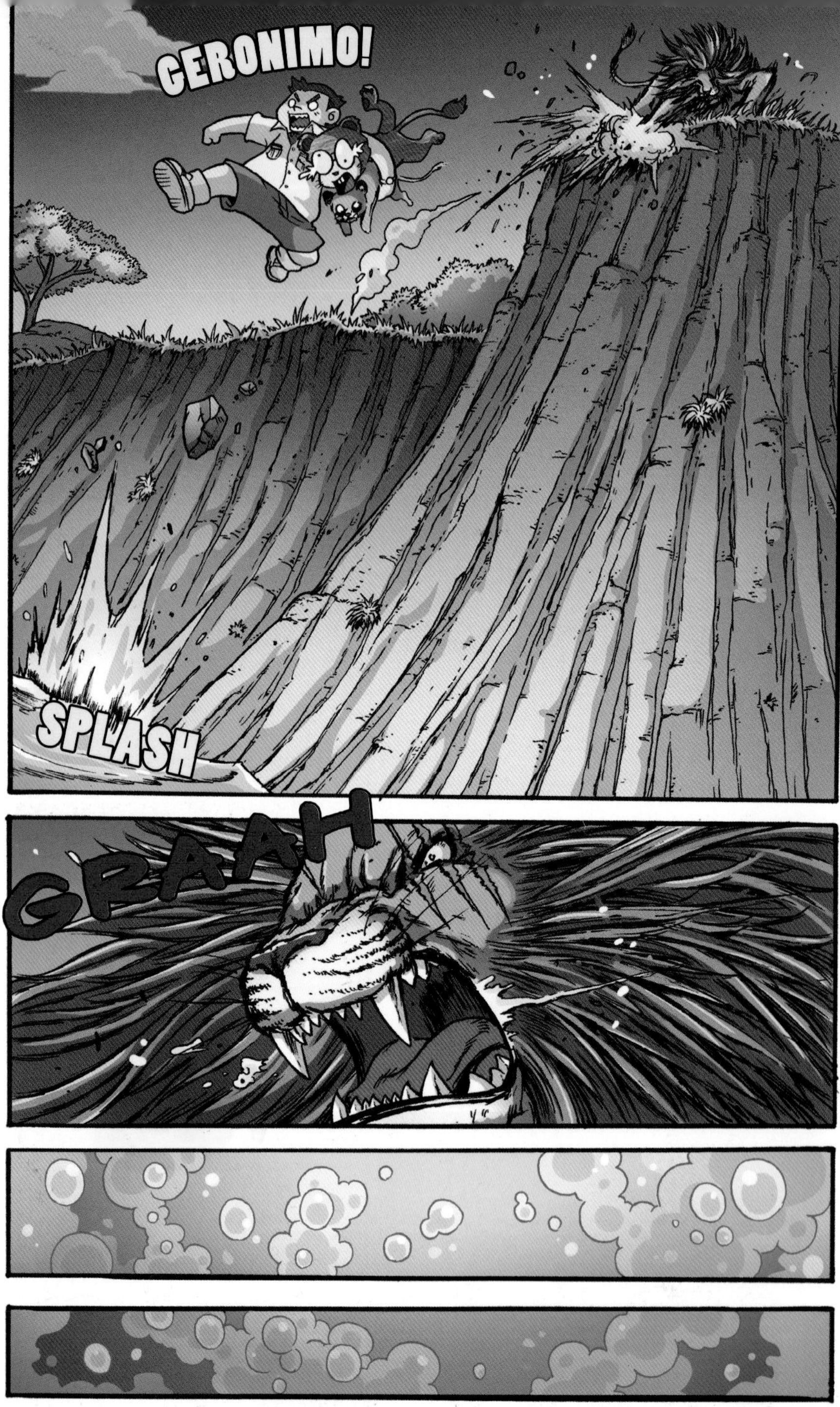
GERONIMO!
SPLASH
GRAAAH

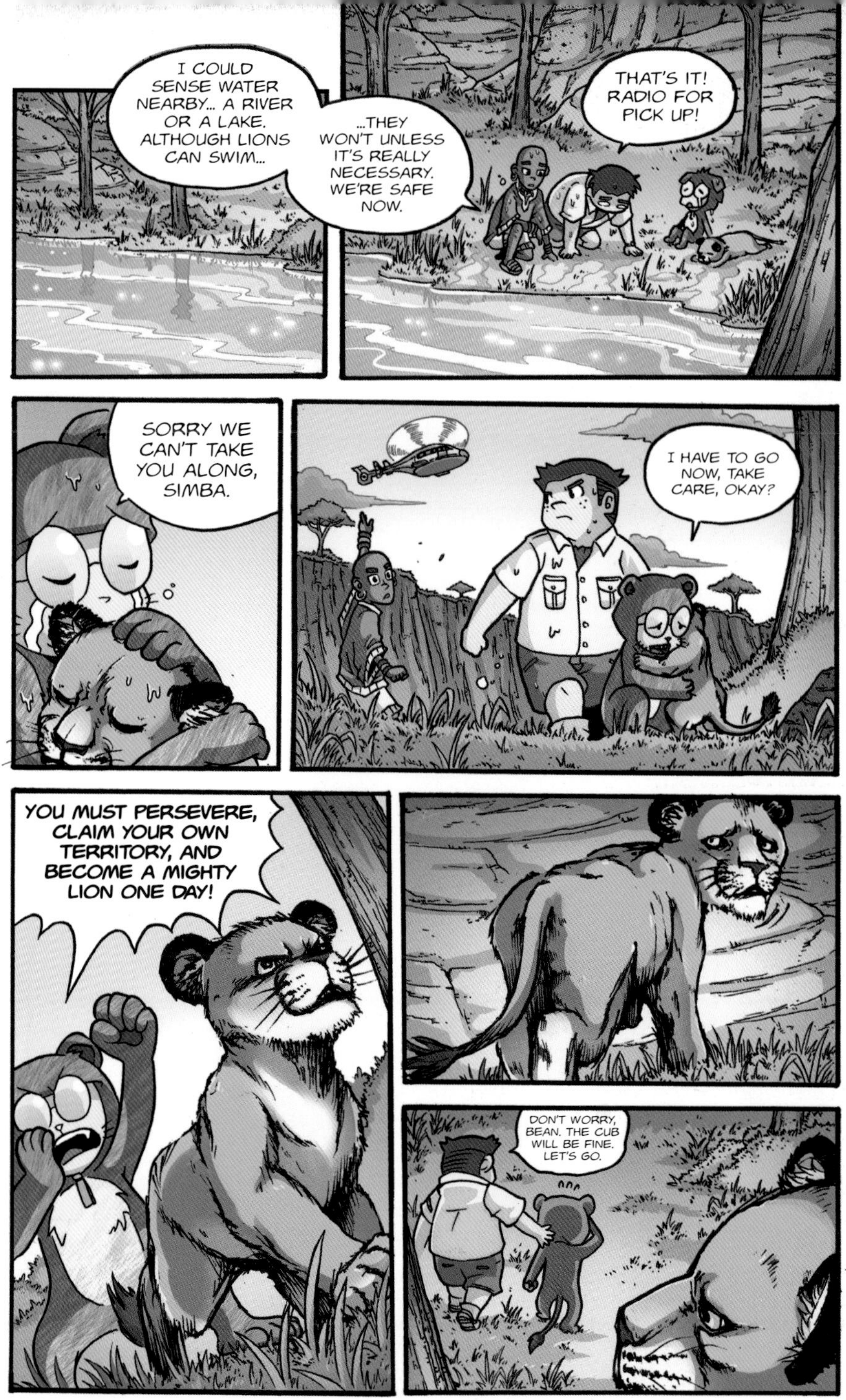

I COULD SENSE WATER NEARBY... A RIVER OR A LAKE. ALTHOUGH LIONS CAN SWIM...
...THEY WON'T UNLESS IT'S REALLY NECESSARY. WE'RE SAFE NOW.
THAT'S IT! RADIO FOR PICK UP!
SORRY WE CAN'T TAKE YOU ALONG, SIMBA.
I HAVE TO GO NOW, TAKE CARE, OKAY?
YOU MUST PERSEVERE, CLAIM YOUR OWN TERRITORY, AND BECOME A MIGHTY LION ONE DAY!
DON'T WORRY, BEAN. THE CUB WILL BE FINE. LET'S GO.

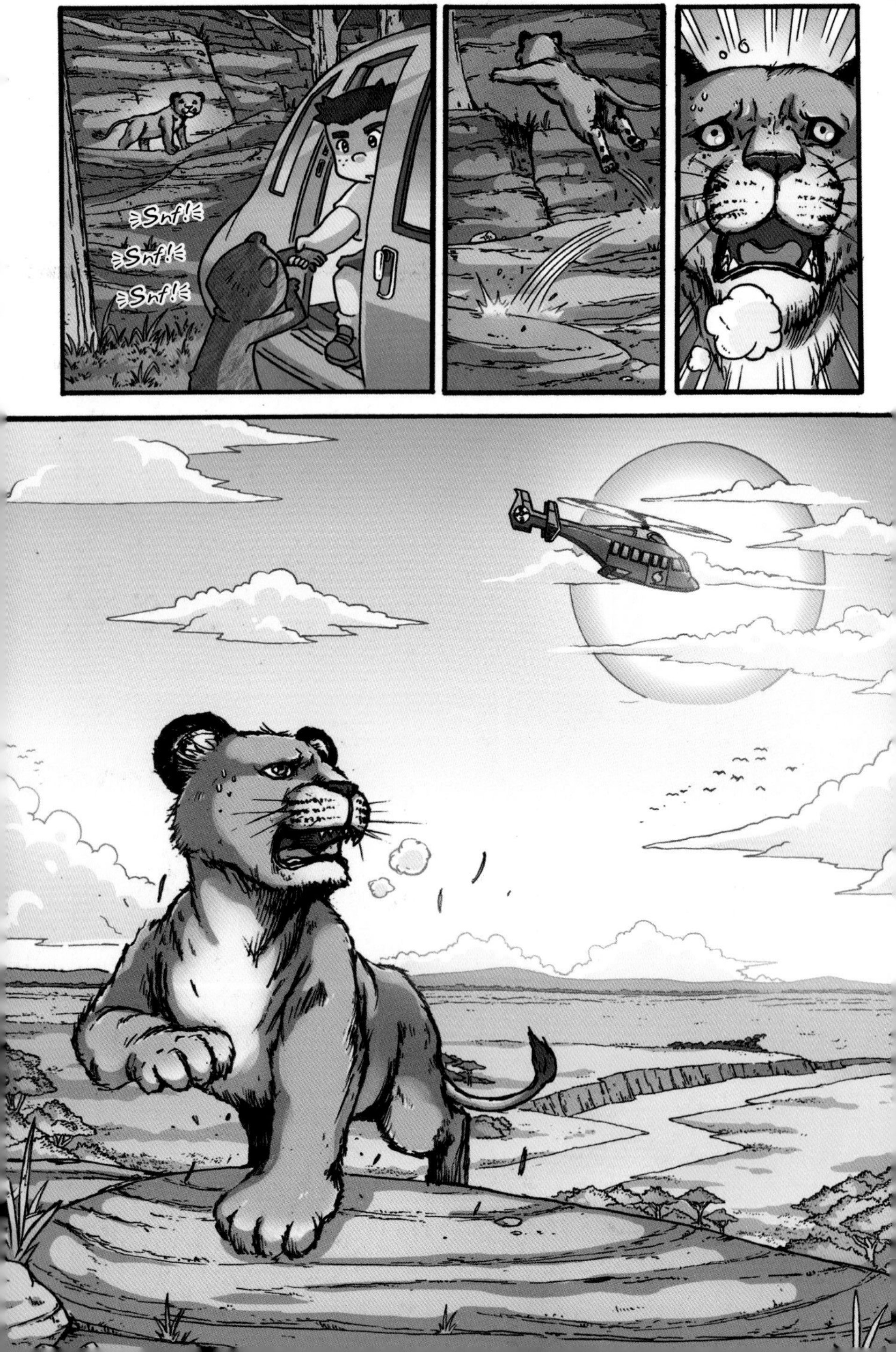
Snf!
Snf!
Snf!

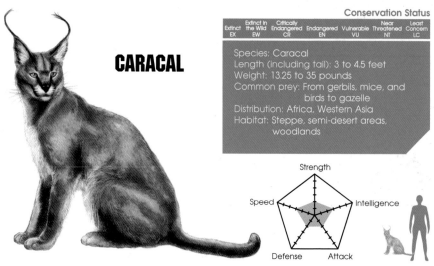

CARACAL

Conservation Status

Extinct EX	Extinct in the Wild EW	Critically Endangered CR	Endangered EN	Vulnerable VU	Near Threatened NT	Least Concern LC

Species: Caracal
Length (including tail): 3 to 4.5 feet
Weight: 13.25 to 35 pounds
Common prey: From gerbils, mice, and birds to gazelle
Distribution: Africa, Western Asia
Habitat: Steppe, semi-desert areas, woodlands

Strength
Speed
Intelligence
Defense
Attack

The distinctive tufted black ears and snub tail make the caracal closely resemble the lynx, hence its other name, desert lynx. As one of the largest of the small cats, it has impressive speed, climbing and jumping abilities, capable of springing to snatch birds in mid-flight. Quite easy to tame, it has been used in a domesticated hunting capacity in India and Iran. That said, it is rather elusive in its natural habitat.

Conservation Status

Extinct EX	Extinct in the Wild EW	Critically Endangered CR	Endangered EN	Vulnerable VU	Near Threatened NT	Least Concern LC

Scientific name: Uncia
Length (including tail): 5.25 to 7.5 feet
Weight: 55 to 165 pounds
Common prey: From carrion, livestock, and hares to Siberian ibex
Distribution: Central Asia
Habitat: Arctic highlands and mountainous areas

Strength
Speed
Intelligence
Defense
Attack

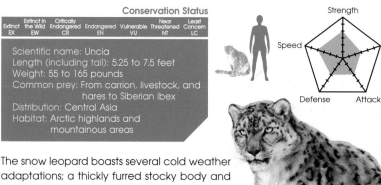

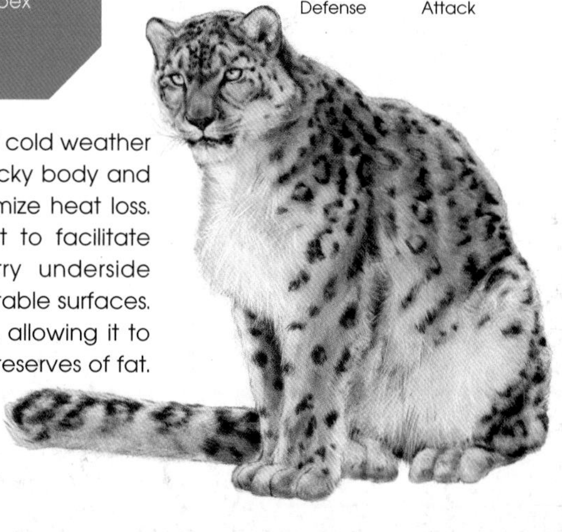

The snow leopard boasts several cold weather adaptations; a thickly furred stocky body and small, rounded ears which minimize heat loss. Wide paws distribute its weight to facilitate walking on snow, and a furry underside increases grip on steep and unstable surfaces. Its tail is long, thick and flexible, allowing it to maintain balance, and to store reserves of fat.

SNOW LEOPARD

BLACK PANTHER

Panthers are melanistic variations of the jaguar and cougar of the Americas, and the Asian/African leopard, and not a separate species at all. As such, panthers are essentially the same as their spotted siblings, just dark-furred.

The unique dark tint caused by a genetic quirk is called melanism, which is essentially the opposite of albinism, which produces white tigers, and if you get to observe closely, you will see that the distinctive markings are still present, meaning panthers are not completely black-furred.

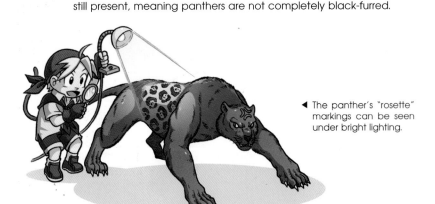

◀ The panther's "rosette" markings can be seen under bright lighting.

LEARN MORE

Do black panthers give birth to black cubs?
Yes. Since their black fur is caused by a dominant gene, female adults will give birth to black offspring if mated with a black male. But if its partner is a normal felid, its offspring may be a mixture of black and spotted cubs.

CHAPTER 7

READY TO RUMBLE!

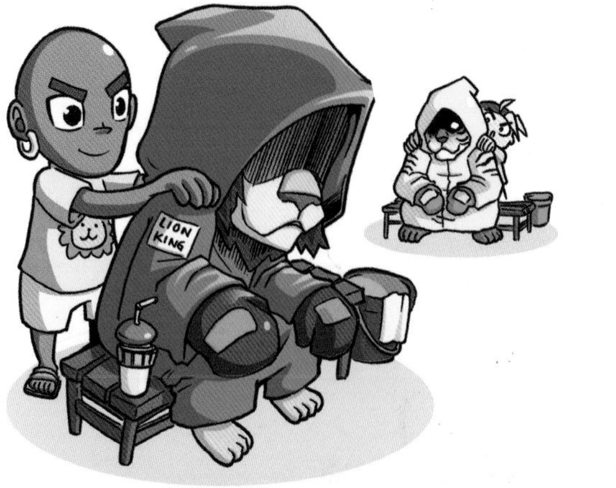
LION KING

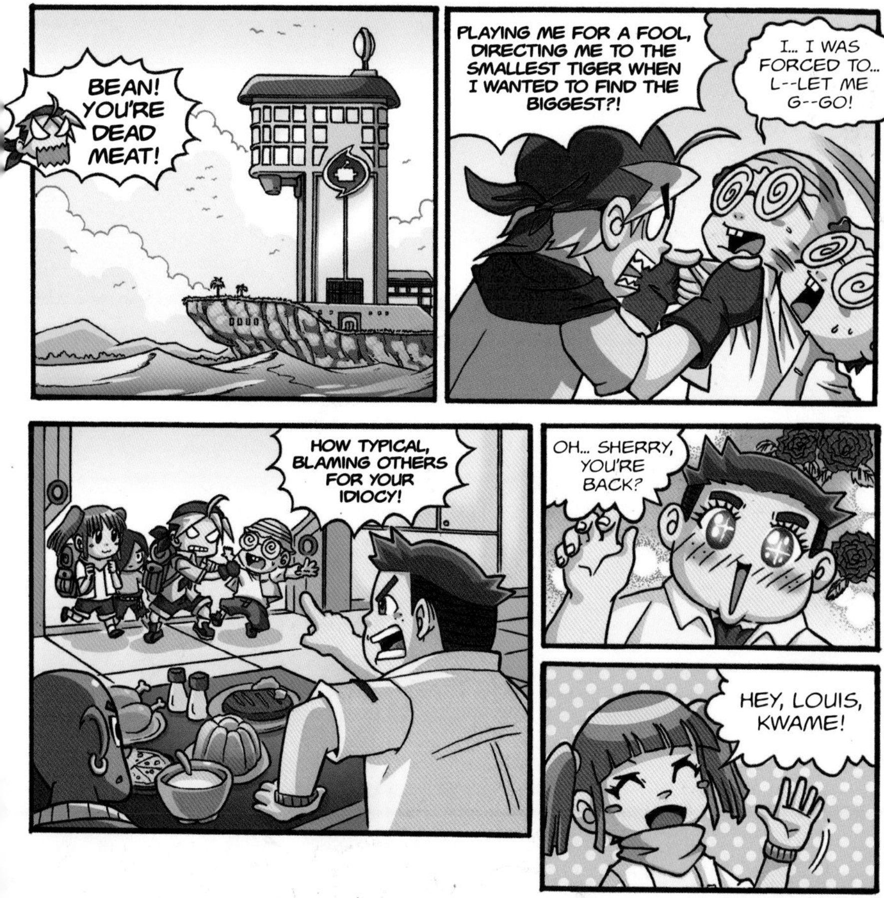
BEAN! YOU'RE DEAD MEAT!
PLAYING ME FOR A FOOL, DIRECTING ME TO THE SMALLEST TIGER WHEN I WANTED TO FIND THE BIGGEST?!
I... I WAS FORCED TO... L--LET ME G--GO!
HOW TYPICAL, BLAMING OTHERS FOR YOUR IDIOCY!
OH... SHERRY, YOU'RE BACK?
HEY, LOUIS, KWAME!

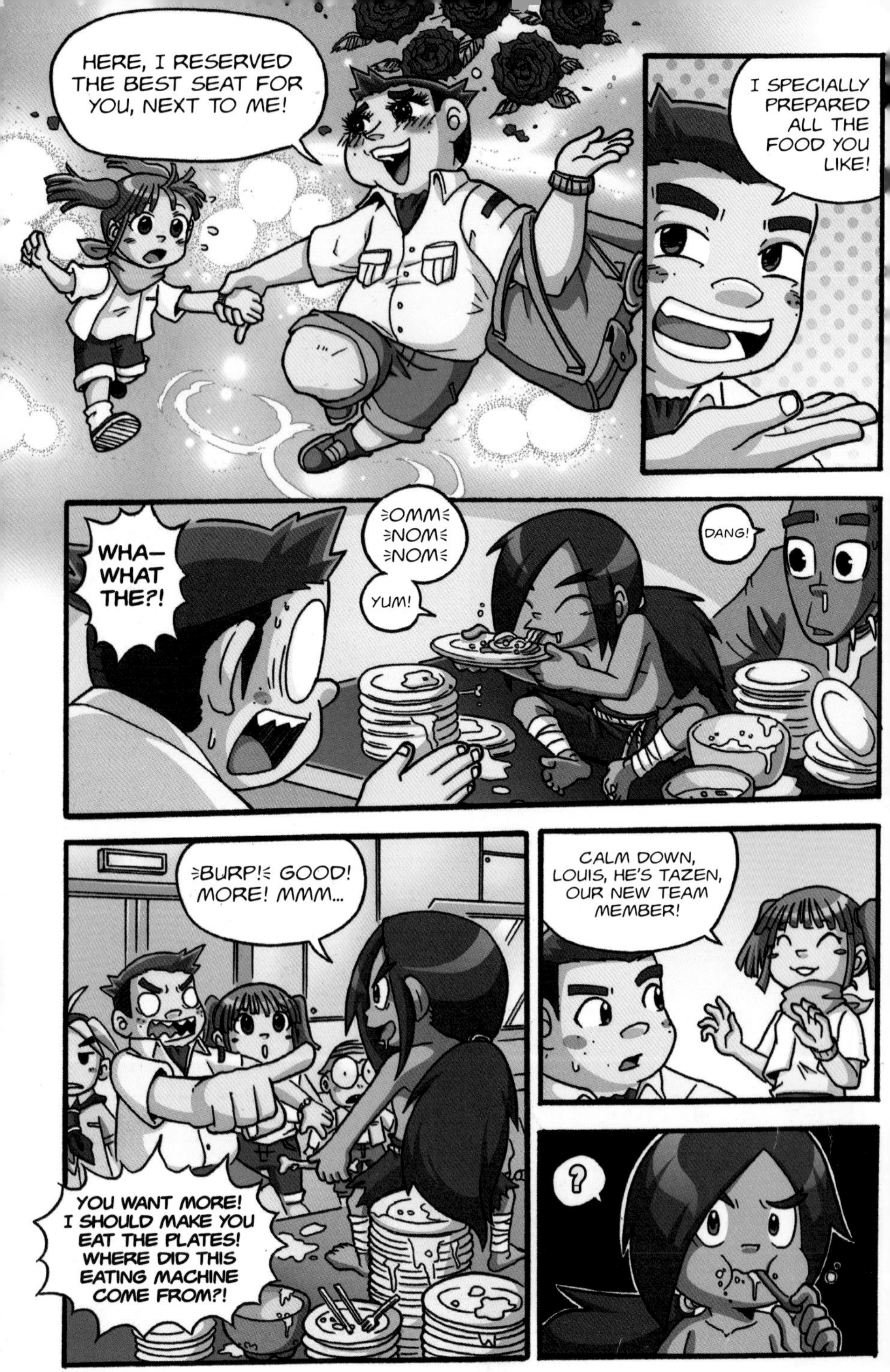

HERE, I RESERVED THE BEST SEAT FOR YOU, NEXT TO ME!
I SPECIALLY PREPARED ALL THE FOOD YOU LIKE!
WHA— WHAT THE?!
OMM NOM NOM
YUM!
DANG!
BURP! GOOD! MORE! MMM...
YOU WANT MORE! I SHOULD MAKE YOU EAT THE PLATES! WHERE DID THIS EATING MACHINE COME FROM?!
CALM DOWN, LOUIS, HE'S TAZEN, OUR NEW TEAM MEMBER!
?

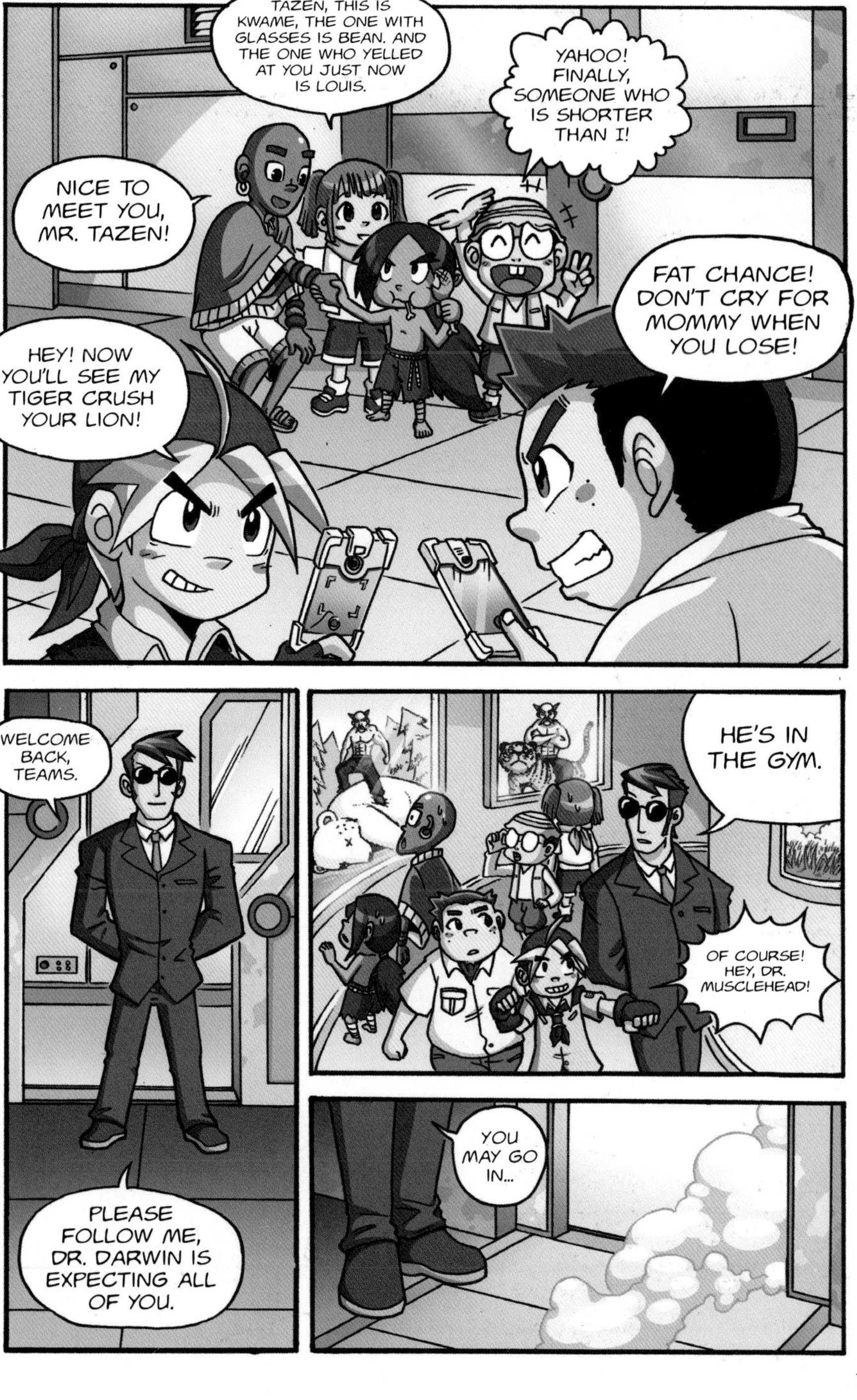
TAZEN, THIS IS KWAME, THE ONE WITH GLASSES IS BEAN. AND THE ONE WHO YELLED AT YOU JUST NOW IS LOUIS.
YAHOO! FINALLY, SOMEONE WHO IS SHORTER THAN I!
NICE TO MEET YOU, MR. TAZEN!
FAT CHANCE! DON'T CRY FOR MOMMY WHEN YOU LOSE!
HEY! NOW YOU'LL SEE MY TIGER CRUSH YOUR LION!
WELCOME BACK, TEAMS.
PLEASE FOLLOW ME, DR. DARWIN IS EXPECTING ALL OF YOU.
HE'S IN THE GYM.
OF COURSE! HEY, DR. MUSCLEHEAD!
YOU MAY GO IN...

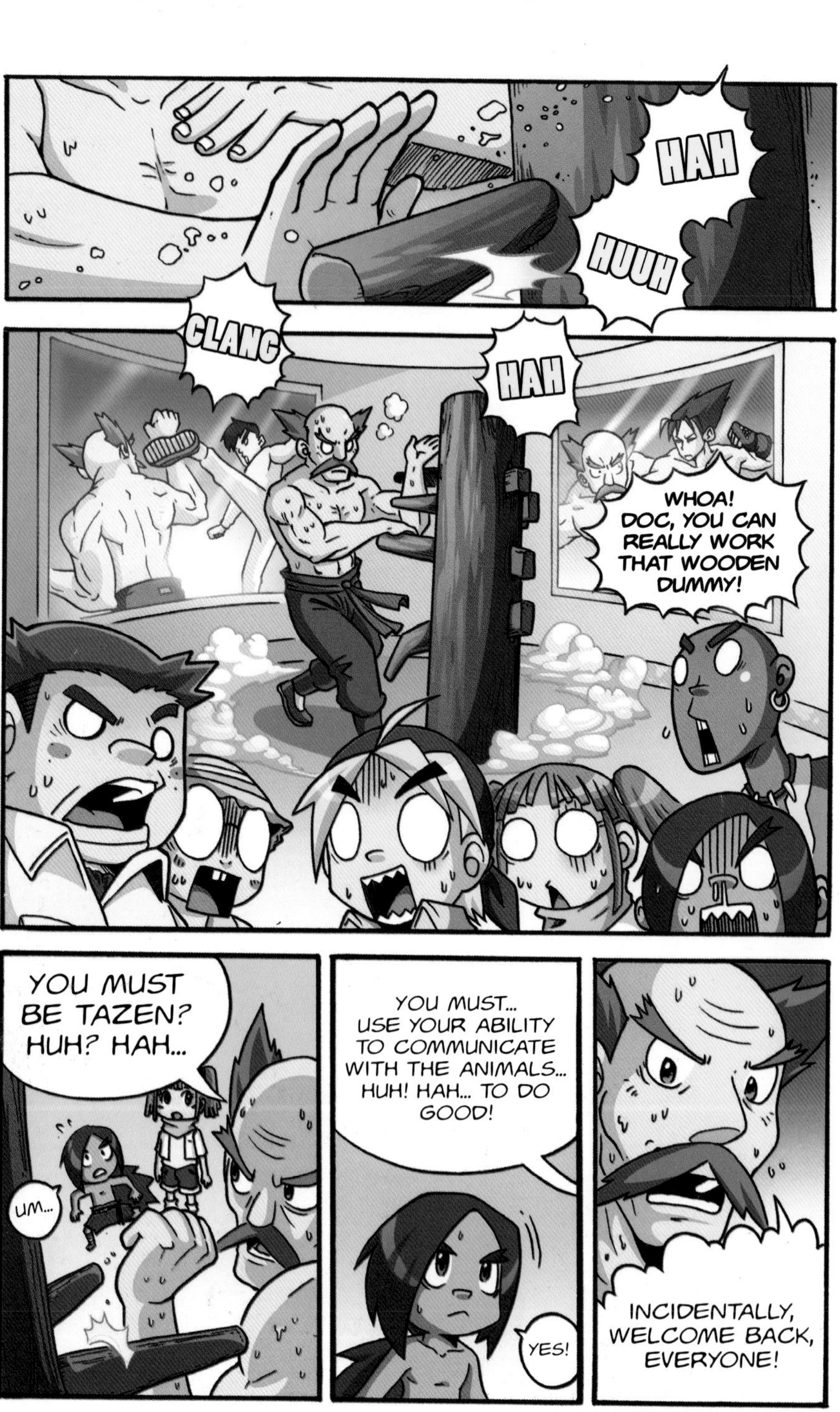

HAH
HUUH
CLANG
HAH
WHOA! DOC, YOU CAN REALLY WORK THAT WOODEN DUMMY!
YOU MUST BE TAZEN? HUH? HAH...
UM...
YOU MUST... USE YOUR ABILITY TO COMMUNICATE WITH THE ANIMALS... HUH! HAH... TO DO GOOD!
YES!
INCIDENTALLY, WELCOME BACK, EVERYONE!

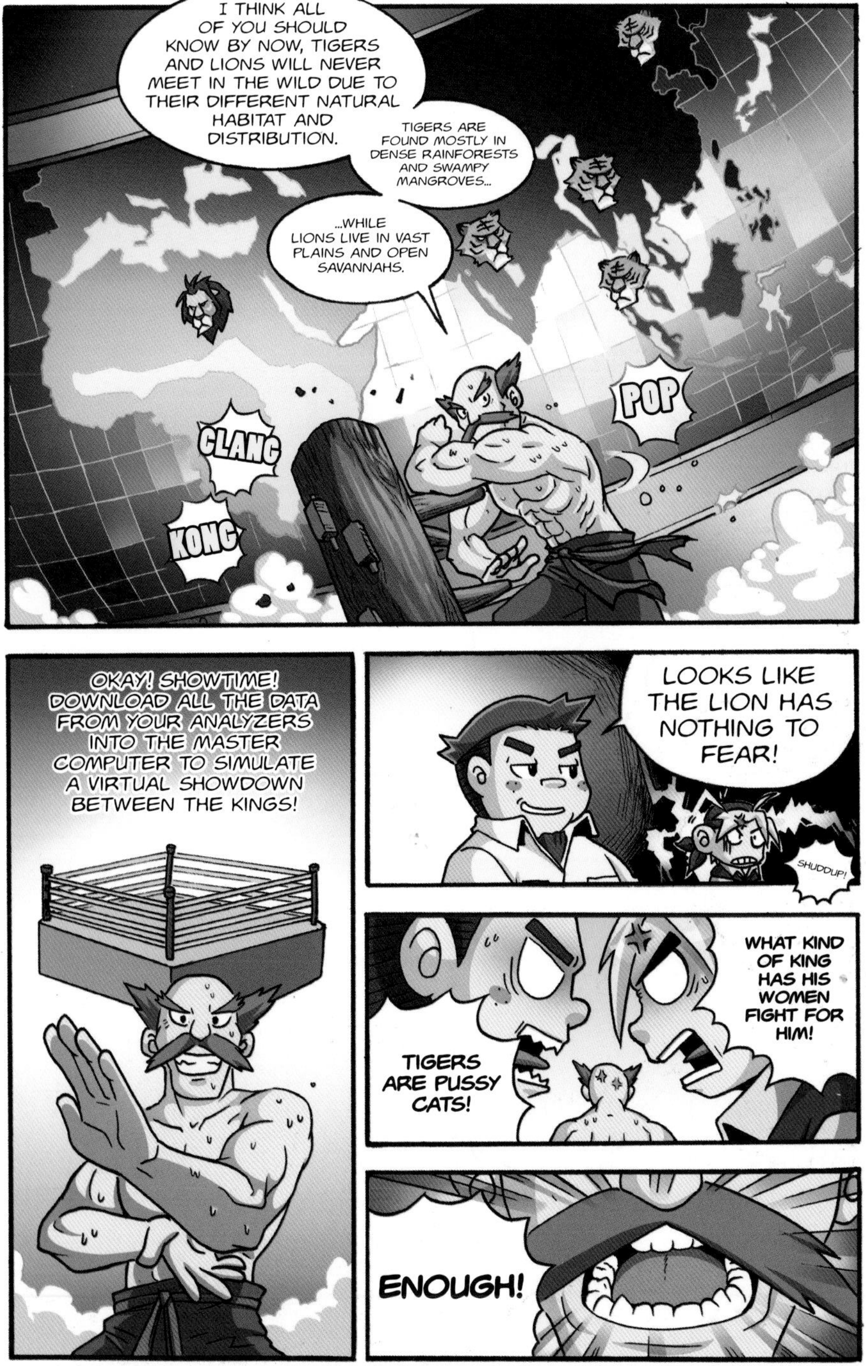
I THINK ALL OF YOU SHOULD KNOW BY NOW, TIGERS AND LIONS WILL NEVER MEET IN THE WILD DUE TO THEIR DIFFERENT NATURAL HABITAT AND DISTRIBUTION.
TIGERS ARE FOUND MOSTLY IN DENSE RAINFORESTS AND SWAMPY MANGROVES...
...WHILE LIONS LIVE IN VAST PLAINS AND OPEN SAVANNAHS.
POP
CLANG
KONG
OKAY! SHOWTIME! DOWNLOAD ALL THE DATA FROM YOUR ANALYZERS INTO THE MASTER COMPUTER TO SIMULATE A VIRTUAL SHOWDOWN BETWEEN THE KINGS!
LOOKS LIKE THE LION HAS NOTHING TO FEAR!
SHUDDUP!
WHAT KIND OF KING HAS HIS WOMEN FIGHT FOR HIM!
TIGERS ARE PUSSY CATS!
ENOUGH!

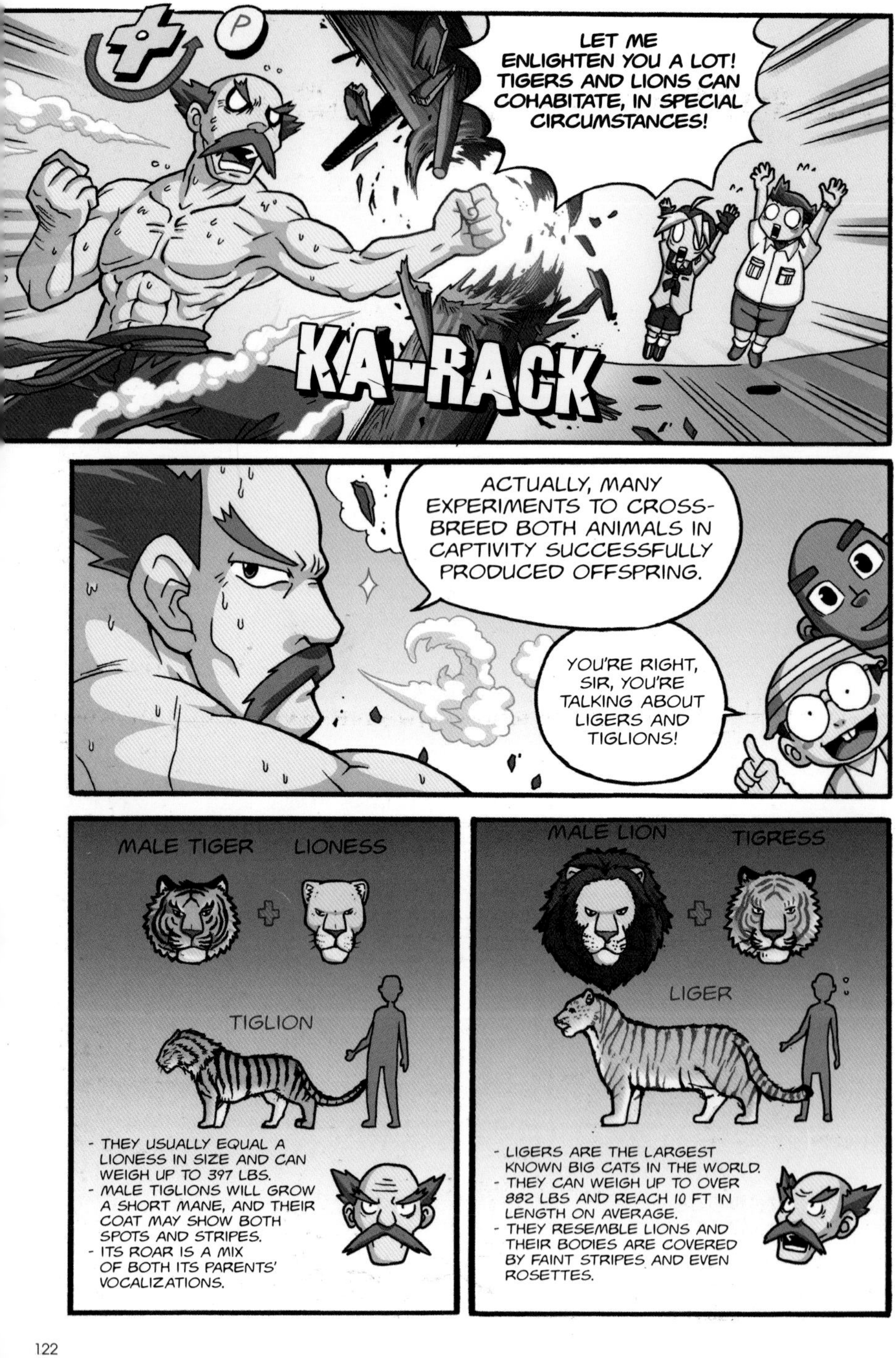
P
LET ME ENLIGHTEN YOU A LOT! TIGERS AND LIONS CAN COHABITATE, IN SPECIAL CIRCUMSTANCES!
KA-RACK
ACTUALLY, MANY EXPERIMENTS TO CROSS-BREED BOTH ANIMALS IN CAPTIVITY SUCCESSFULLY PRODUCED OFFSPRING.
YOU'RE RIGHT, SIR, YOU'RE TALKING ABOUT LIGERS AND TIGLIONS!
MALE TIGER
LIONESS
TIGLION
- THEY USUALLY EQUAL A LIONESS IN SIZE AND CAN WEIGH UP TO 397 LBS.
- MALE TIGLIONS WILL GROW A SHORT MANE, AND THEIR COAT MAY SHOW BOTH SPOTS AND STRIPES.
- ITS ROAR IS A MIX OF BOTH ITS PARENTS' VOCALIZATIONS.
MALE LION
TIGRESS
LIGER
- LIGERS ARE THE LARGEST KNOWN BIG CATS IN THE WORLD.
- THEY CAN WEIGH UP TO OVER 882 LBS AND REACH 10 FT IN LENGTH ON AVERAGE.
- THEY RESEMBLE LIONS AND THEIR BODIES ARE COVERED BY FAINT STRIPES AND EVEN ROSETTES.

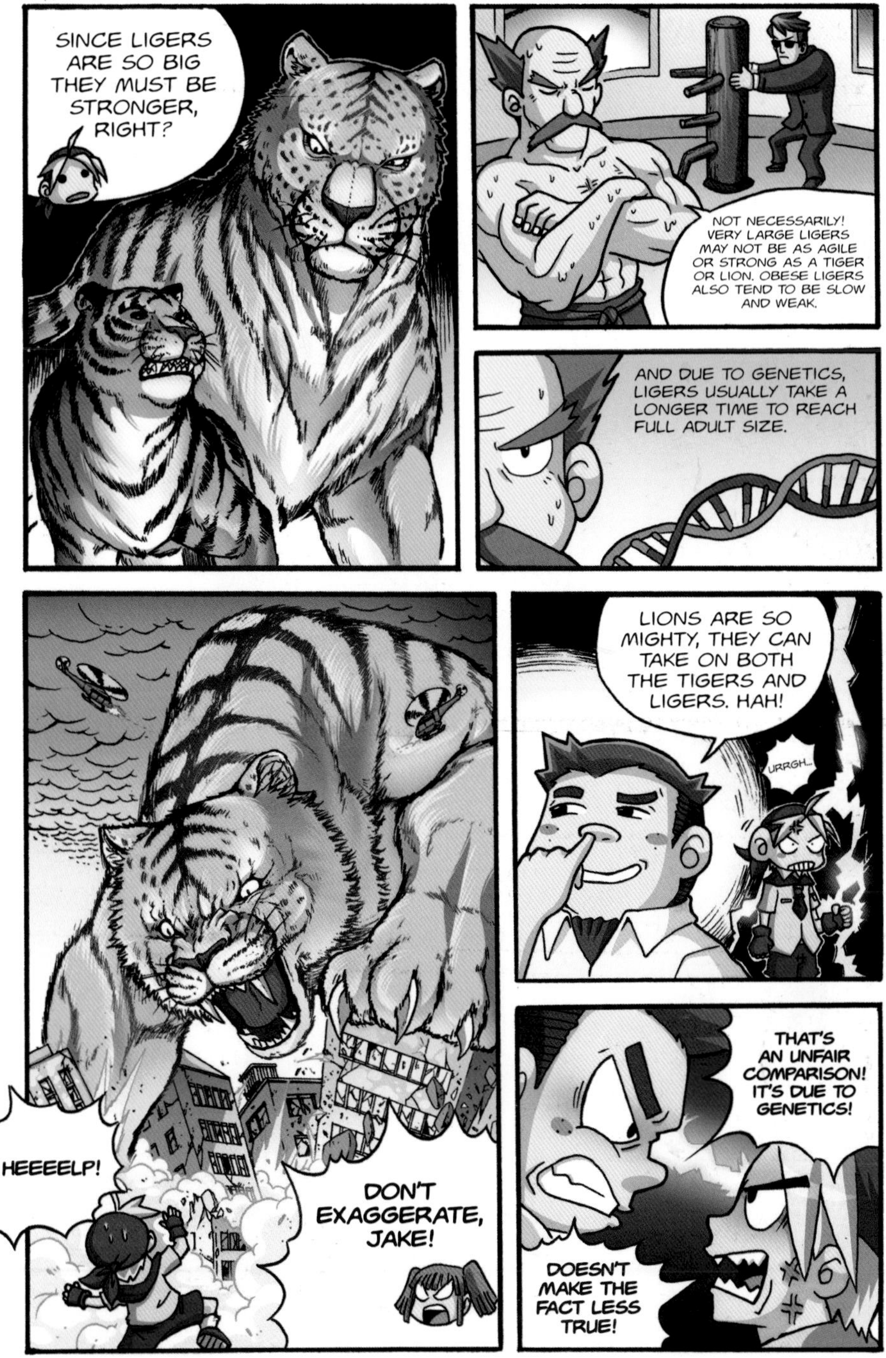
SINCE LIGERS ARE SO BIG THEY MUST BE STRONGER, RIGHT?
NOT NECESSARILY! VERY LARGE LIGERS MAY NOT BE AS AGILE OR STRONG AS A TIGER OR LION. OBESE LIGERS ALSO TEND TO BE SLOW AND WEAK.
AND DUE TO GENETICS, LIGERS USUALLY TAKE A LONGER TIME TO REACH FULL ADULT SIZE.
HEEEELP!
DON'T EXAGGERATE, JAKE!
LIONS ARE SO MIGHTY, THEY CAN TAKE ON BOTH THE TIGERS AND LIGERS. HAH!
URRGH...
THAT'S AN UNFAIR COMPARISON! IT'S DUE TO GENETICS!
DOESN'T MAKE THE FACT LESS TRUE!

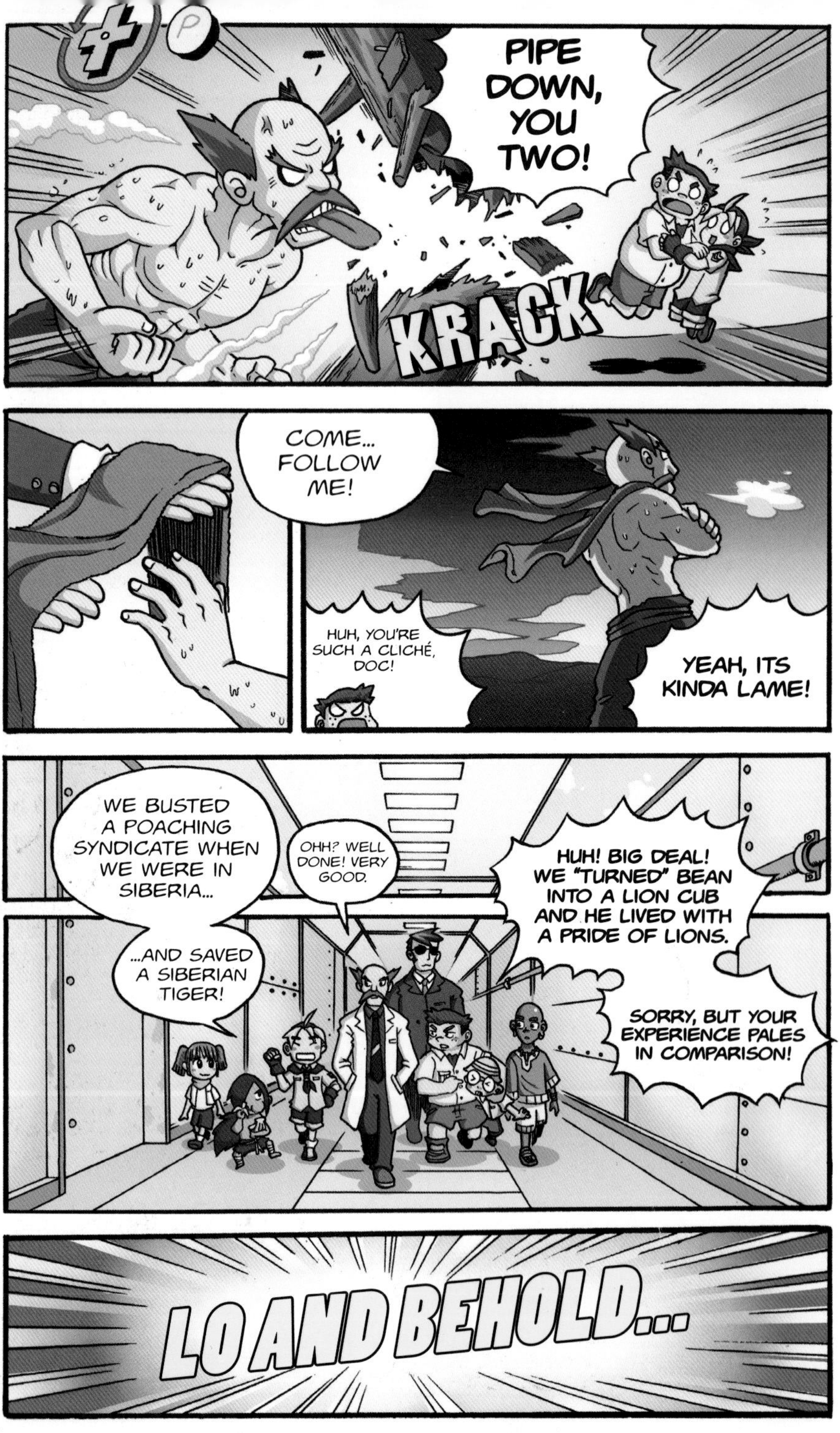
PIPE DOWN, YOU TWO!
KRACK
COME... FOLLOW ME!
HUH, YOU'RE SUCH A CLICHÉ, DOC!
YEAH, ITS KINDA LAME!
WE BUSTED A POACHING SYNDICATE WHEN WE WERE IN SIBERIA...
...AND SAVED A SIBERIAN TIGER!
OHH? WELL DONE! VERY GOOD.
HUH! BIG DEAL! WE "TURNED" BEAN INTO A LION CUB AND HE LIVED WITH A PRIDE OF LIONS.
SORRY, BUT YOUR EXPERIENCE PALES IN COMPARISON!
LO AND BEHOLD...

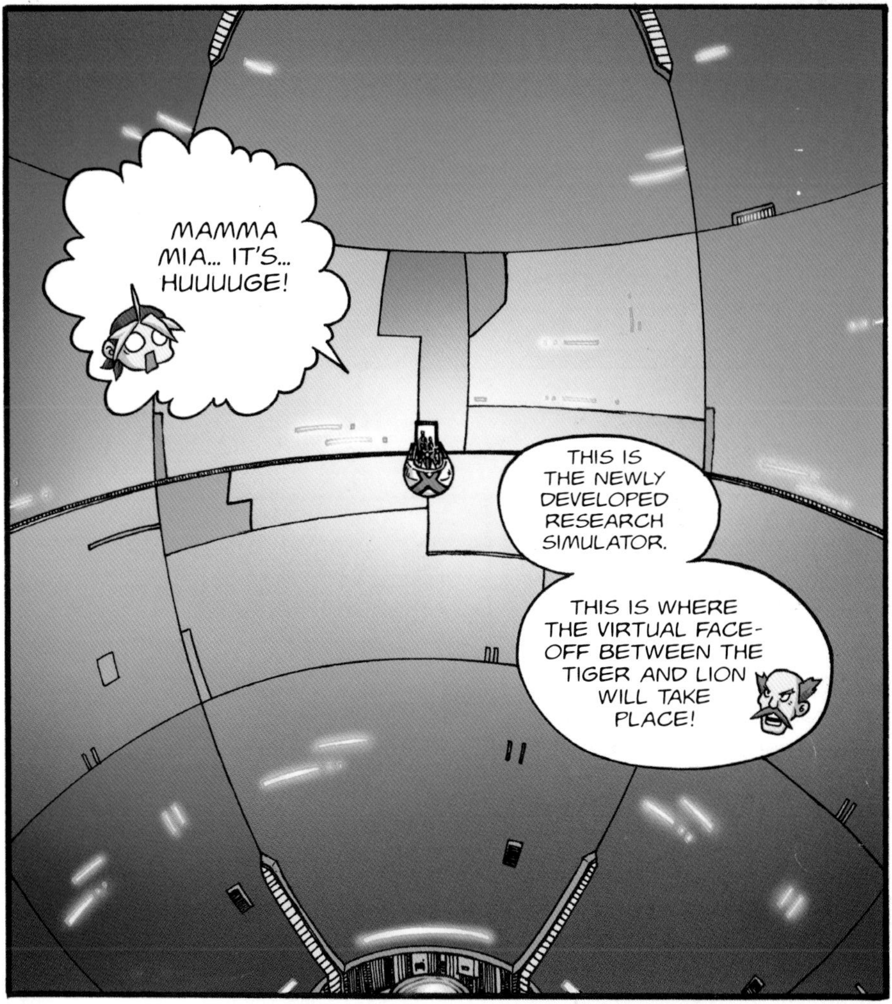
MAMMA MIA... IT'S... HUUUUGE!
THIS IS THE NEWLY DEVELOPED RESEARCH SIMULATOR.
THIS IS WHERE THE VIRTUAL FACE-OFF BETWEEN THE TIGER AND LION WILL TAKE PLACE!

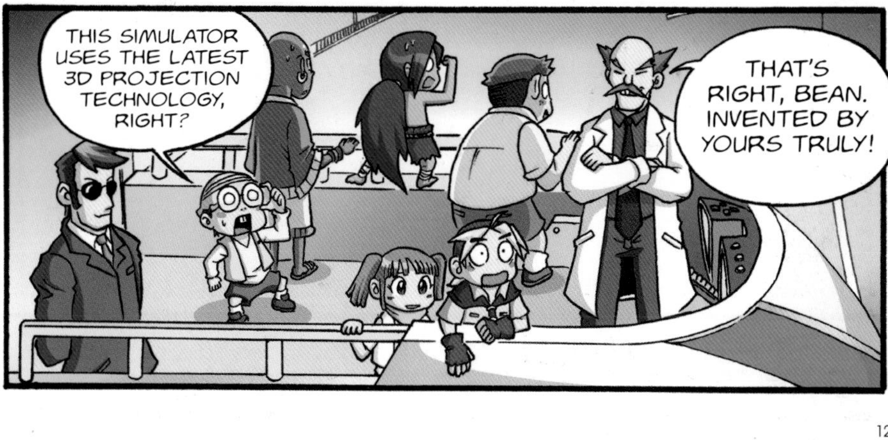
THIS SIMULATOR USES THE LATEST 3D PROJECTION TECHNOLOGY, RIGHT?
THAT'S RIGHT, BEAN. INVENTED BY YOURS TRULY!

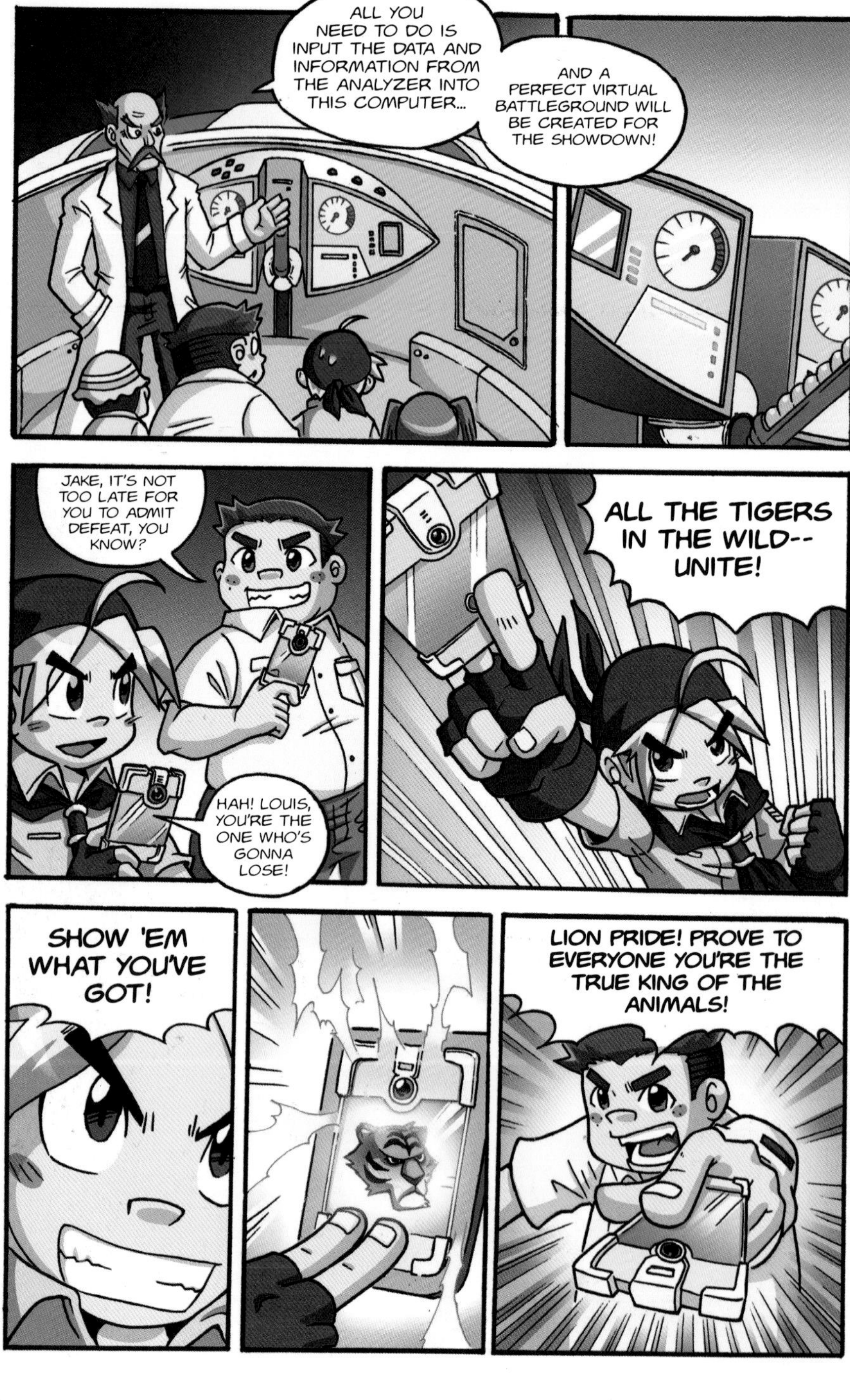

ALL YOU NEED TO DO IS INPUT THE DATA AND INFORMATION FROM THE ANALYZER INTO THIS COMPUTER...
AND A PERFECT VIRTUAL BATTLEGROUND WILL BE CREATED FOR THE SHOWDOWN!
JAKE, IT'S NOT TOO LATE FOR YOU TO ADMIT DEFEAT, YOU KNOW?
HAH! LOUIS, YOU'RE THE ONE WHO'S GONNA LOSE!
ALL THE TIGERS IN THE WILD-- UNITE!
SHOW 'EM WHAT YOU'VE GOT!
LION PRIDE! PROVE TO EVERYONE YOU'RE THE TRUE KING OF THE ANIMALS!

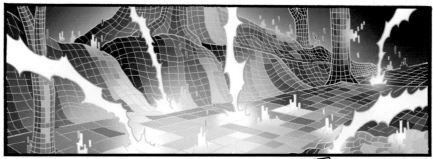

WOOOOOW!

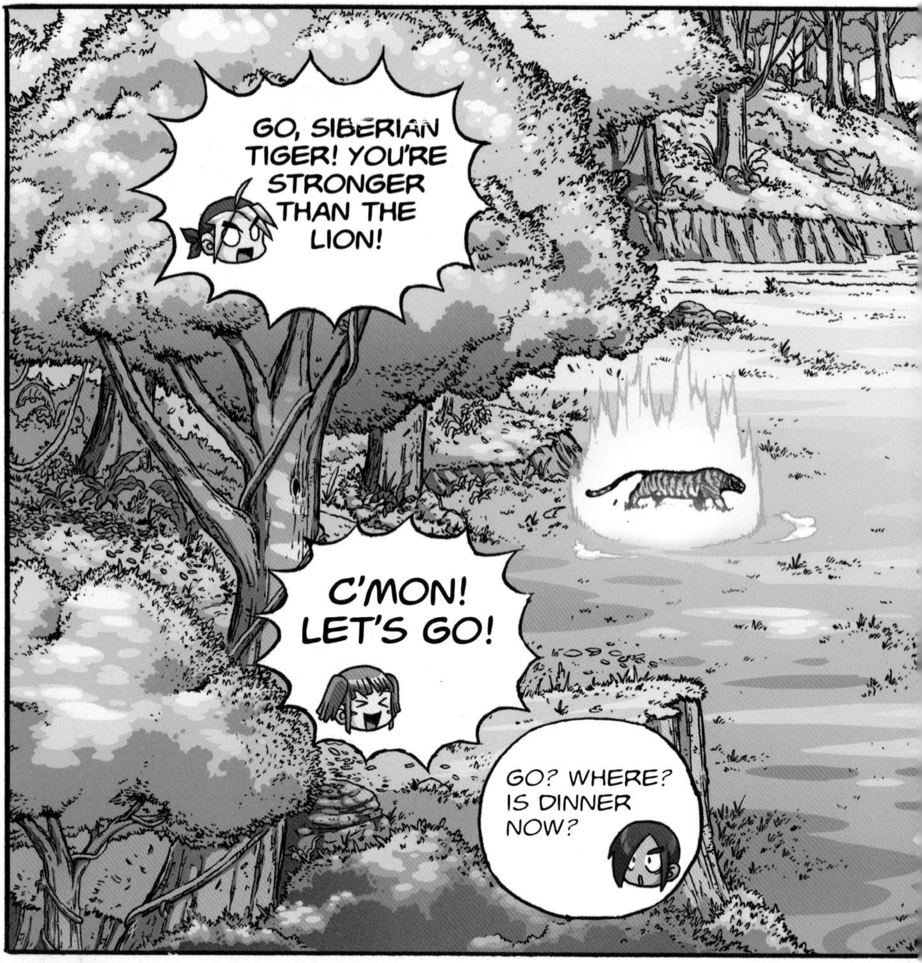
GO, SIBERIAN TIGER! YOU'RE STRONGER THAN THE LION!
C'MON! LET'S GO!
GO? WHERE? IS DINNER NOW?

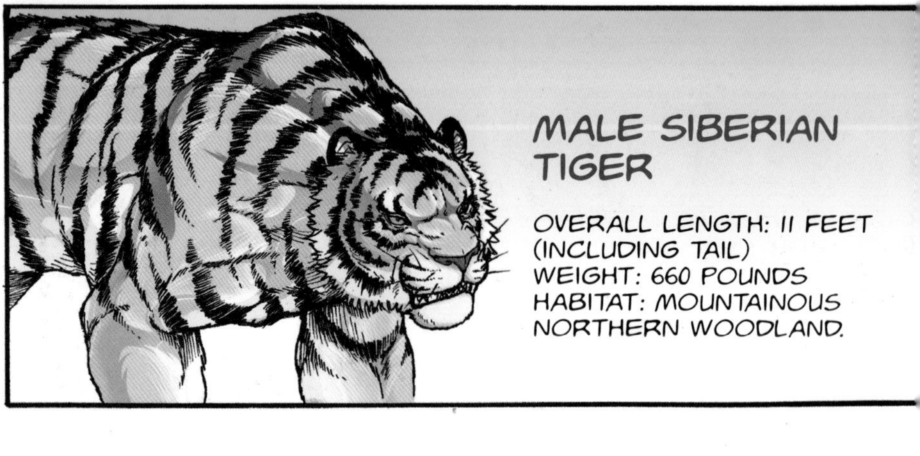
MALE SIBERIAN TIGER
OVERALL LENGTH: 11 FEET (INCLUDING TAIL)
WEIGHT: 660 POUNDS
HABITAT: MOUNTAINOUS NORTHERN WOODLAND.

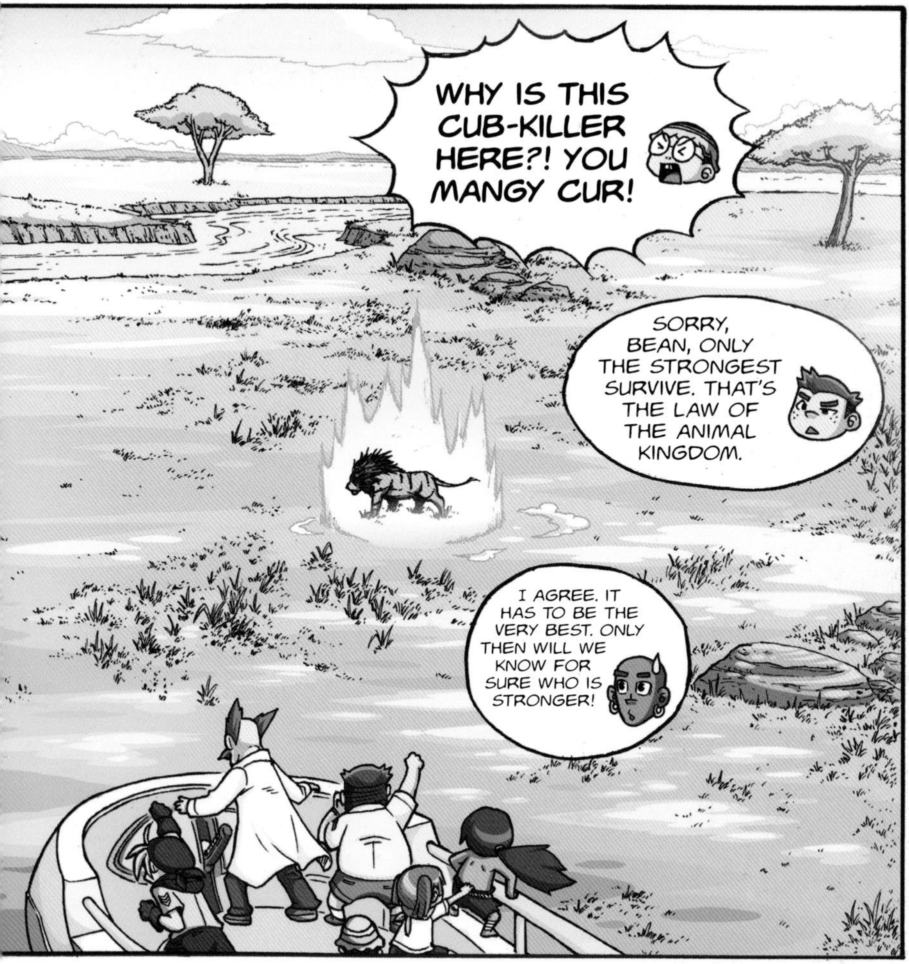
WHY IS THIS CUB-KILLER HERE?! YOU MANGY CUR!
SORRY, BEAN, ONLY THE STRONGEST SURVIVE. THAT'S THE LAW OF THE ANIMAL KINGDOM.
I AGREE. IT HAS TO BE THE VERY BEST. ONLY THEN WILL WE KNOW FOR SURE WHO IS STRONGER!

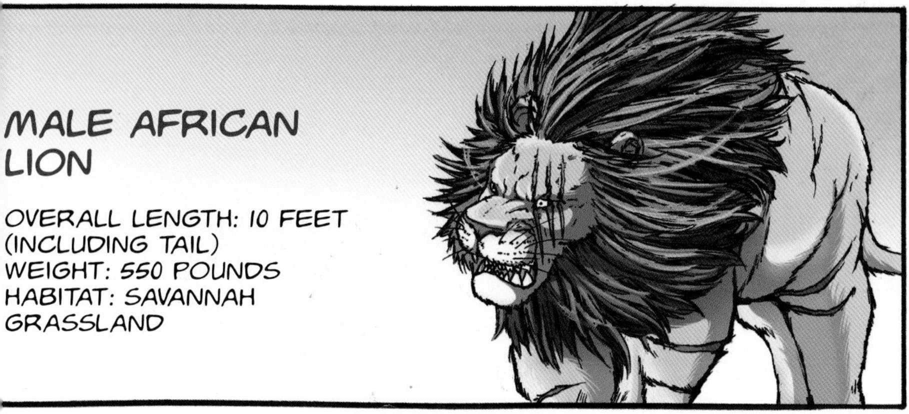
MALE AFRICAN LION
OVERALL LENGTH: 10 FEET (INCLUDING TAIL)
WEIGHT: 550 POUNDS
HABITAT: SAVANNAH GRASSLAND

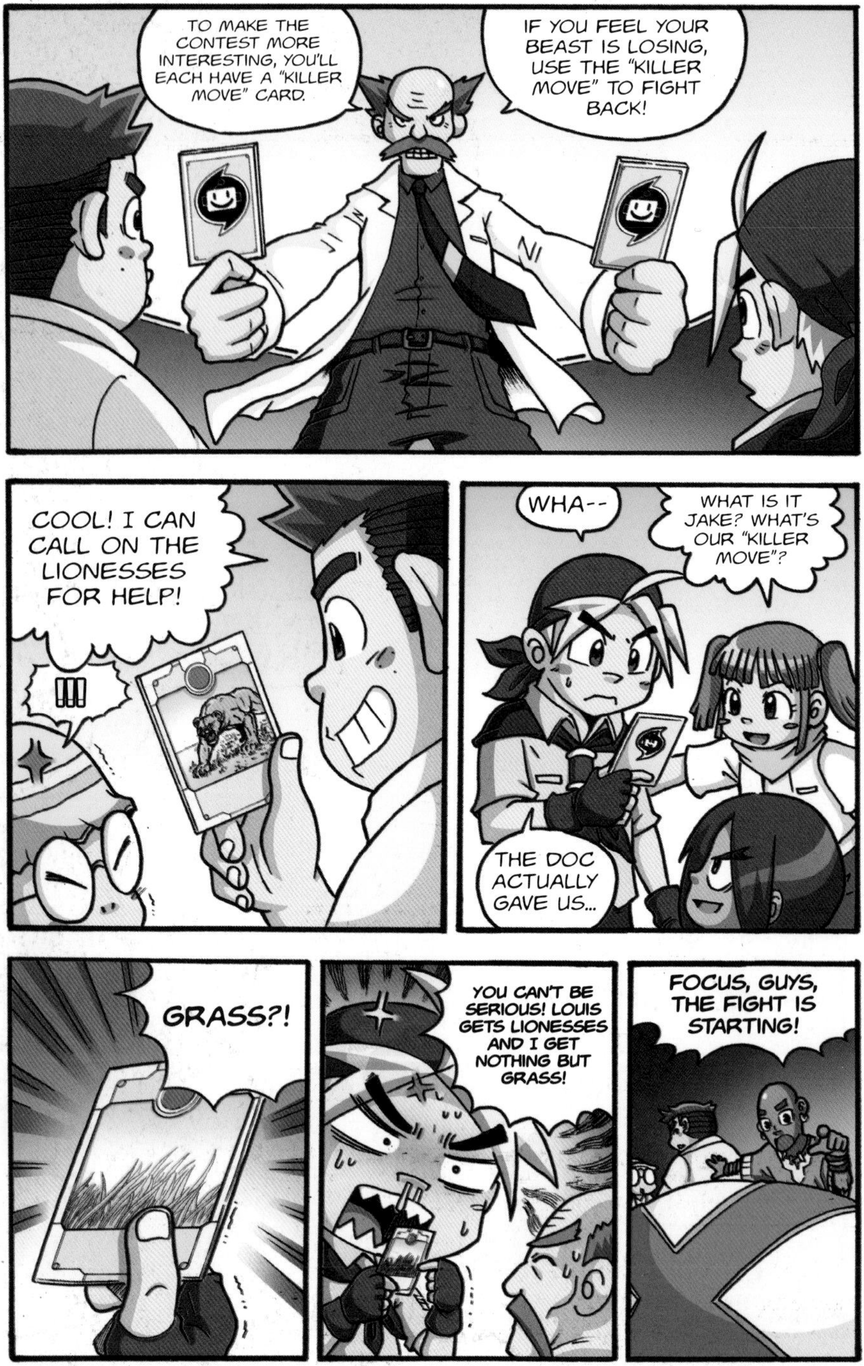
TO MAKE THE CONTEST MORE INTERESTING, YOU'LL EACH HAVE A "KILLER MOVE" CARD.
IF YOU FEEL YOUR BEAST IS LOSING, USE THE "KILLER MOVE" TO FIGHT BACK!
COOL! I CAN CALL ON THE LIONESSES FOR HELP!
!!!
WHA--
WHAT IS IT JAKE? WHAT'S OUR "KILLER MOVE"?
THE DOC ACTUALLY GAVE US...
GRASS?!
YOU CAN'T BE SERIOUS! LOUIS GETS LIONESSES AND I GET NOTHING BUT GRASS!
FOCUS, GUYS, THE FIGHT IS STARTING!

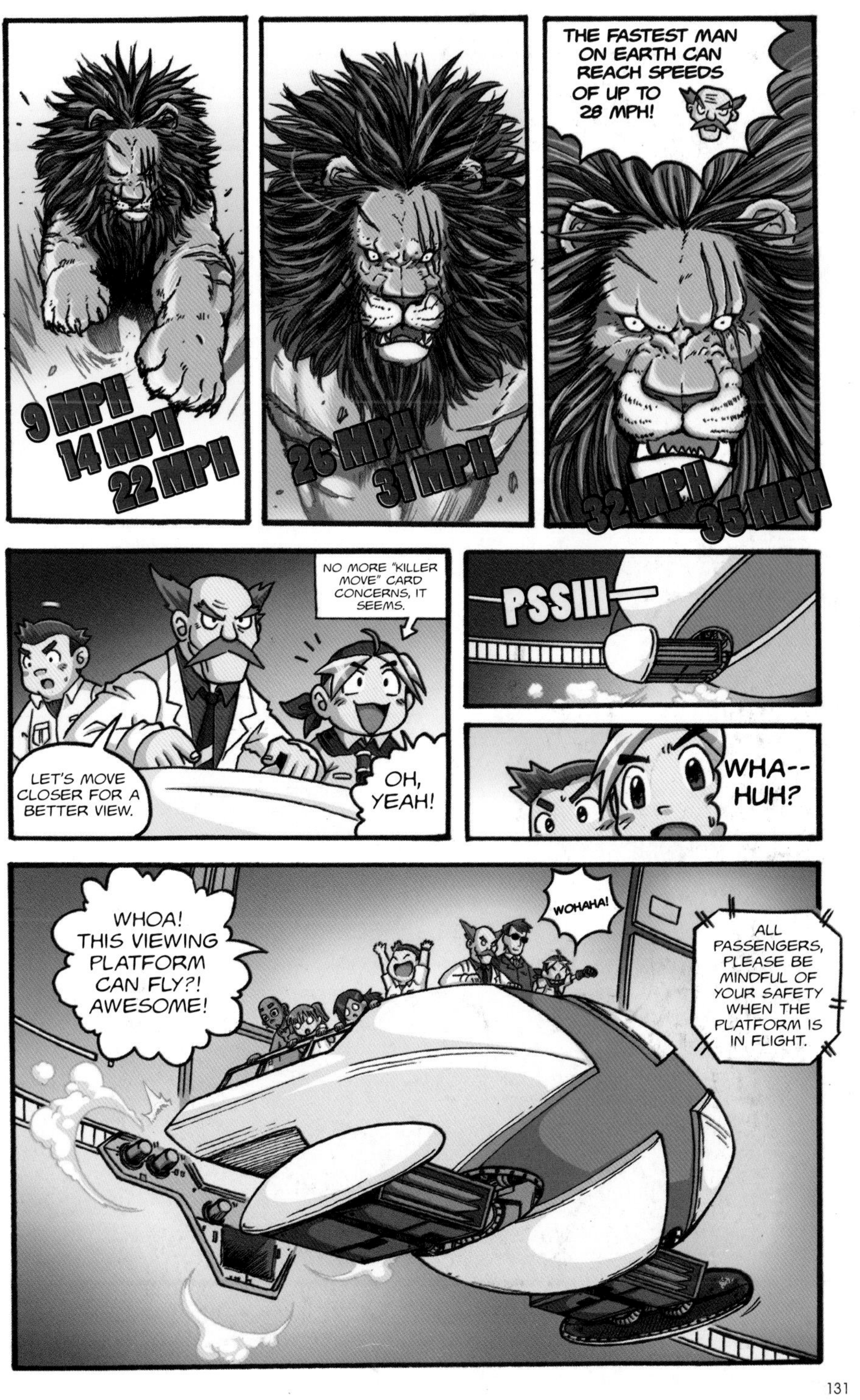
9 MPH
14 MPH
22 MPH
26 MPH
31 MPH
THE FASTEST MAN ON EARTH CAN REACH SPEEDS OF UP TO 28 MPH!
32 MPH
35 MPH
NO MORE "KILLER MOVE" CARD CONCERNS, IT SEEMS.
LET'S MOVE CLOSER FOR A BETTER VIEW.
OH, YEAH!
PSSIII
WHA-- HUH?
WHOA! THIS VIEWING PLATFORM CAN FLY?! AWESOME!
WOHAHA!
ALL PASSENGERS, PLEASE BE MINDFUL OF YOUR SAFETY WHEN THE PLATFORM IS IN FLIGHT.

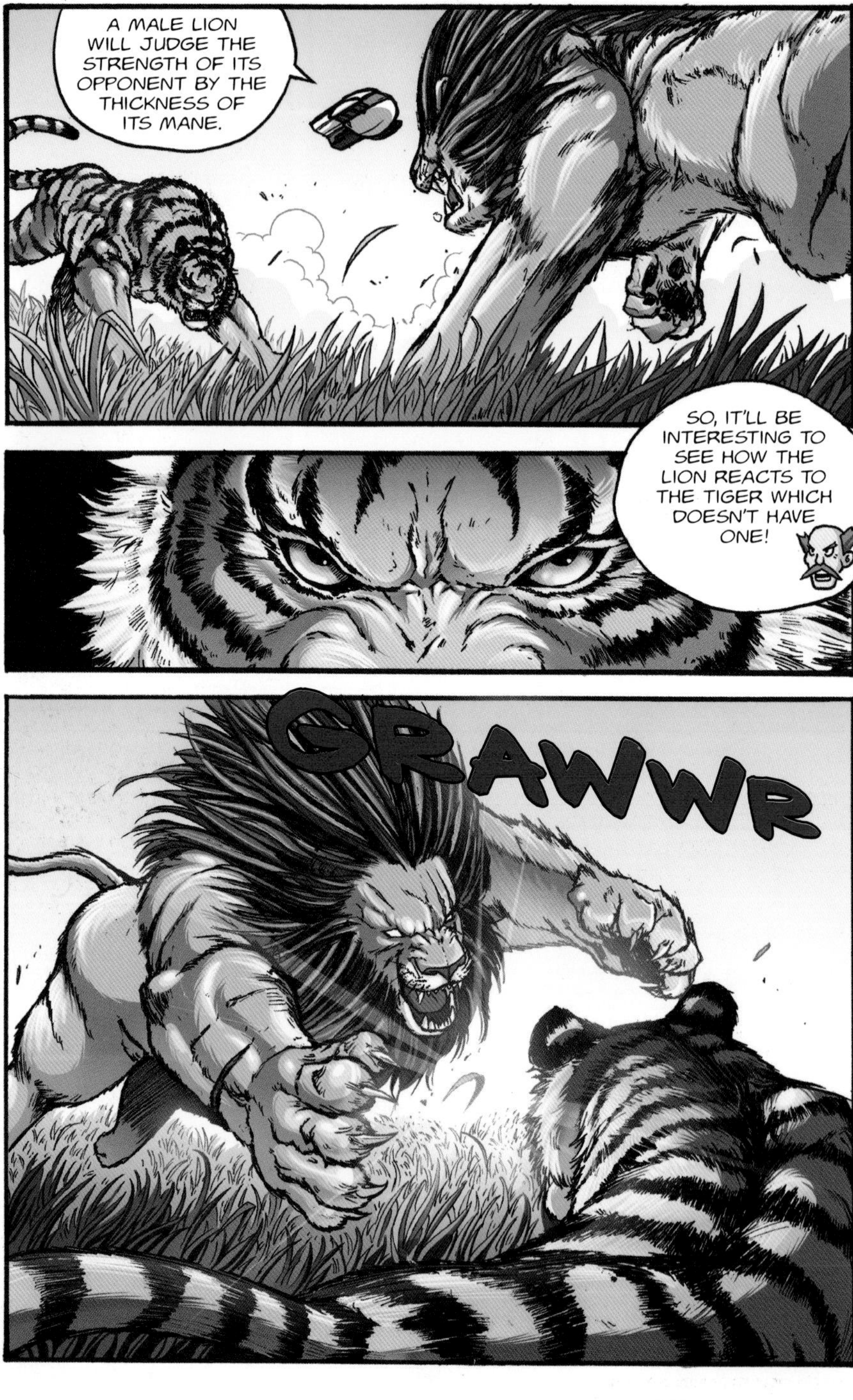
A MALE LION WILL JUDGE THE STRENGTH OF ITS OPPONENT BY THE THICKNESS OF ITS MANE.
SO, IT'LL BE INTERESTING TO SEE HOW THE LION REACTS TO THE TIGER WHICH DOESN'T HAVE ONE!
GRAWWR

Conservation Status

Extinct EX	Extinct in the Wild EW	Critically Endangered CR	Endangered EN	Vulnerable VU	Near Threatened NT	Least Concern LC

Species: Panthera onca
Length (including tail): 5.5 to 9 feet
Weight: 125 to 210 lbs (up to 350)
Common prey: From capybaras to anacondas
Distribution: North, Central, and South America
Habitat: Tropical rainforest, riverine locations

Strength
Speed
Intelligence
Defense
Attack

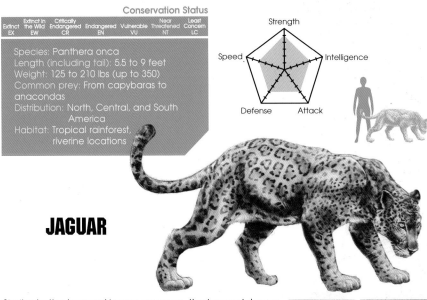

JAGUAR

Similar to the leopard in appearance, the jaguar is larger, bulkier, and more powerfully built than its Afro-Asian cousin. With more defined, wider-spaced rosettes, the jaguar's mannerisms and social habits mirror that of the tiger. The largest feline in the New World, fittingly, is the apex predator of the Amazonian rainforest, and its jaws can deliver the most powerful bite of all family Felidae, capable of crushing turtle shells. Unique among felids, the jaguar sometimes targets the head, puncturing the skull with its terrible jaws.

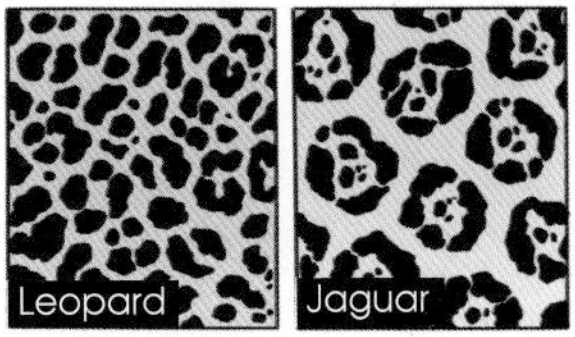

Leopard
Jaguar

▲ Jaguars typically have bigger spots (rosettes) on their coats compared to leopards, with small, central black dots.

BITE FORCE FACE OFF:

African lion
approximately 900 psi

Siberian tiger
approximately 1000 psi

Jaguar
approximately 2000 psi

The South American jaguar has been definitively measured as having the most powerful bite of all family Felidae.

※ psi = pounds per square inch

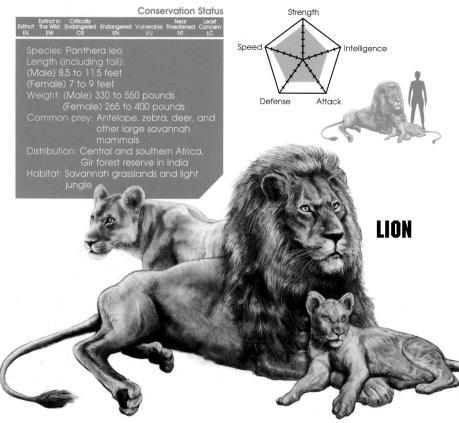

Conservation Status

	Extinct in the Wild	Critically Endangered	Endangered	Vulnerable	Near Threatened	Least Concern
Extinct EX	EW	CR	EN	VU	NT	LC

Species: Panthera leo
Length (including tail):
(Male) 8.5 to 11.5 feet
(Female) 7 to 9 feet
Weight: (Male) 330 to 550 pounds
(Female) 265 to 400 pounds
Common prey: Antelope, zebra, deer, and
other large savannah
mammals
Distribution: Central and southern Africa,
Gir forest reserve in India
Habitat: Savannah grasslands and light
jungle

Strength
Speed
Intelligence
Defense
Attack

LION

Second only in size to some tiger species, lions are the only member of family Felidae to display sexual dimorphism (when males and females look different). Adult males have a mane which makes them look larger, more regal and more attractive to lionesses during mating season. Lions are gregarious, eschewing the solitary behavior of other felids for the solidarity of a hierarchical pride which usually includes one or two adult males and five to six females and their offspring.

The pride allows lions to hunt, defend their territory, and raise their cubs more effectively. Upon maturity, male cubs are expelled from the pride while their female siblings usually remain. Lounging around lazily during daytime, the pride shapes up for the hunt come nightfall, and it is left to the lionesses to identify and take down prey, while the lead male gets first taste of the kill, before feeding opportunities are allocated according to position in the pride hierarchy. Occasionally, lions gang up and drive off other hunters, such as hyenas and cheetahs, stealing their kills.

Due to human encroachment, illegal hunting, and disease, the number of wild African lions continues to decline.

THE LIFE OF THE KING

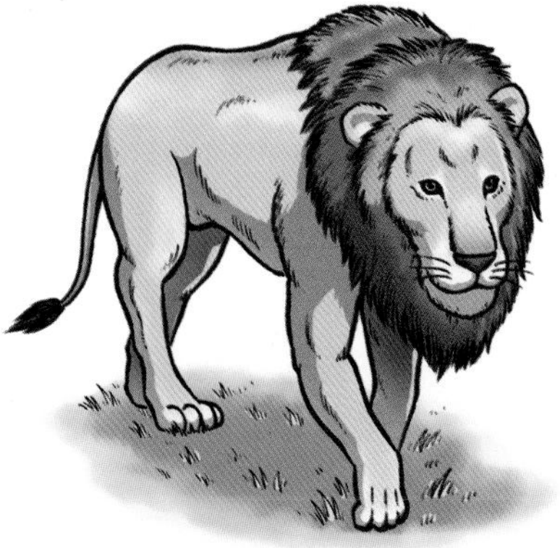

When male cubs reach maturity in two to three years, they will be expelled from the pride. These juveniles will usually form a temporary or permanent coalition and roam the plains for a few years until they reach adulthood.

Upon adulthood, they will most likely challenge an incumbent, an older lion, for dominance of a pride. If successful, the challenger takes over the pride and becomes the new leader, if defeated, depending on injuries sustained, the loser will either go on to further challenges, or perish.

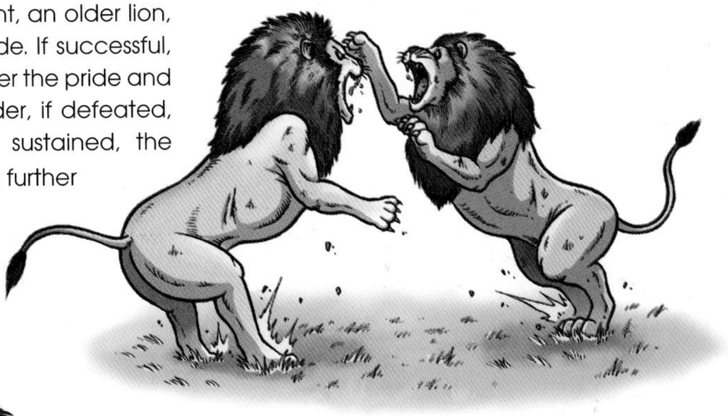

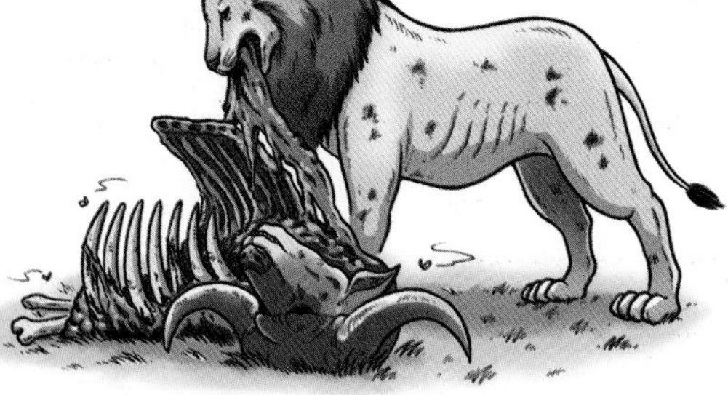

Dominant males tend to lose their powers between the ages of 10 to 15, making them vulnerable to challenges by younger lions, as well as diseases. If a dominant male is deposed, but survives, the fallen king will wander the plains as nomadic loners until they die.

DID YOU KNOW?

The roar of an adult male lion can be heard from a distance of up to 5 miles. It is used to announce its presence, ward off potential challengers or recall members back to the pride.

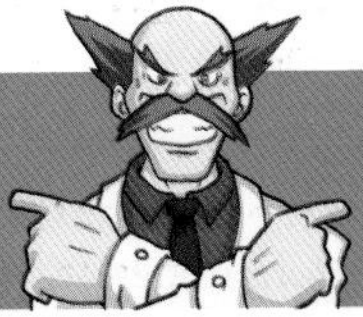

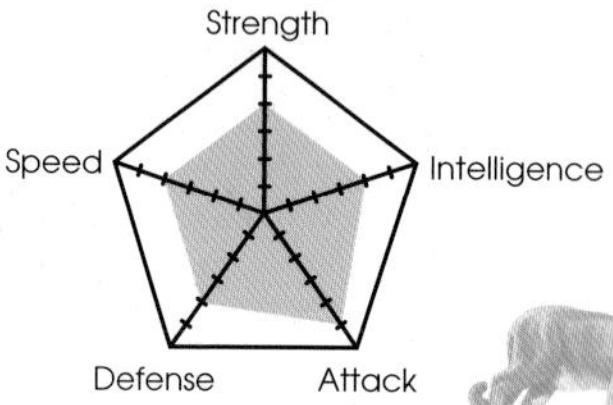
Strength
Speed
Intelligence
Defense
Attack

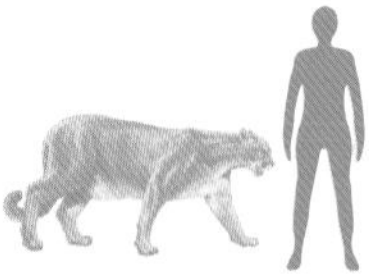

Conservation Status

Extinct EX	Extinct in the Wild EW	Critically Endangered CR	Endangered EN	Vulnerable VU	Near Threatened NT	Least Concern LC

Species: Puma concolor
Length (including tail): 5 to 9 feet
Weight: 64 to 220 pounds
Common prey: From domestic sheep to moose
Distribution: North and South America
Habitats: Forest, dense brush, and rocky terrain

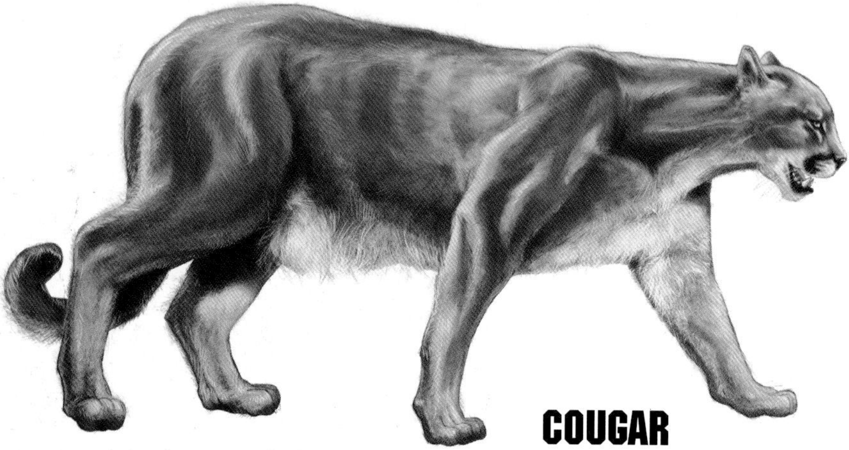

COUGAR

The cougar, also known as puma, mountain lion, panther or catamount, is the second largest New World felid after the jaguar. This elusive beast has the widest range of habitat of all land mammals in the western hemisphere. Solitary by nature, the nocturnal cougar is nearer genetically to the domestic cat than true lions. Superior ambush predators, cougars are not picky when it comes to prey.

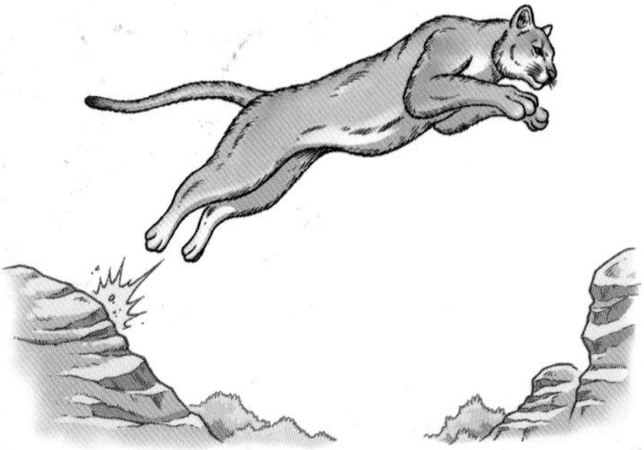

◀ Having large paws and proportionally the largest hind legs in the cat family, cougars are able to leap over 16 feet vertically and 151 feet horizontally in a single bound, and has a top speed of 50 miles per hour.

CHAPTER 8

THE FINAL SHOWDOWN

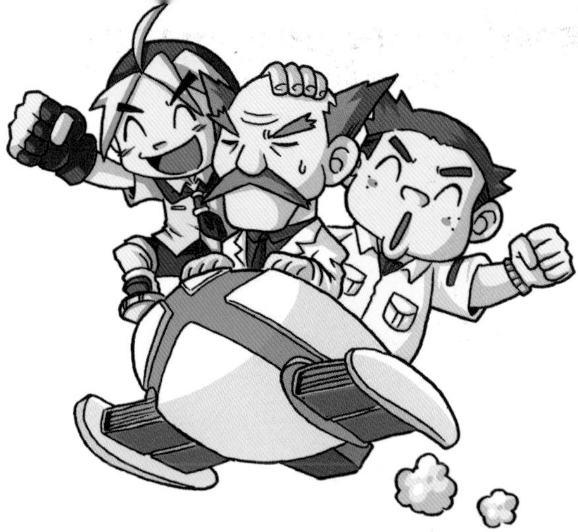

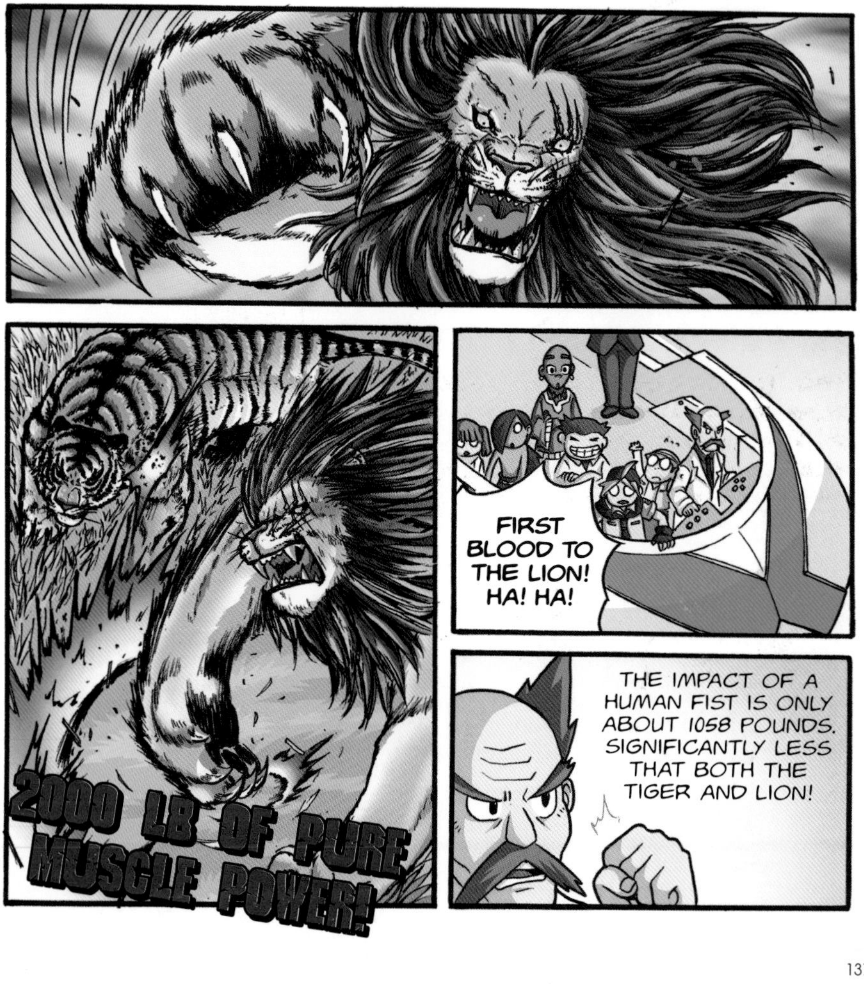
2000 LB OF PURE MUSCLE POWER!
FIRST BLOOD TO THE LION! HA! HA!
THE IMPACT OF A HUMAN FIST IS ONLY ABOUT 1058 POUNDS. SIGNIFICANTLY LESS THAT BOTH THE TIGER AND LION!

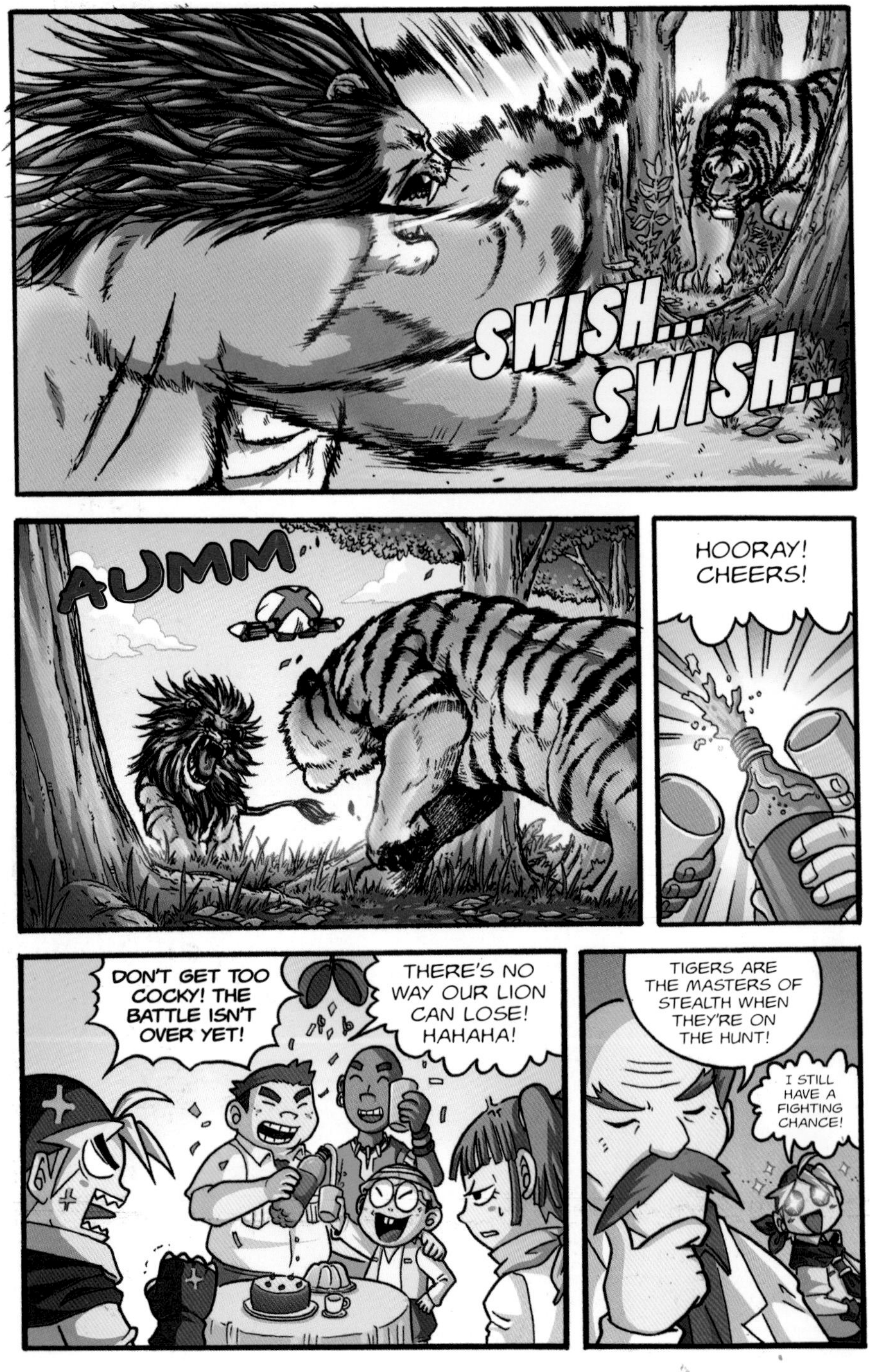
SWISH...
SWISH...
AUMM
HOORAY! CHEERS!
DON'T GET TOO COCKY! THE BATTLE ISN'T OVER YET!
THERE'S NO WAY OUR LION CAN LOSE! HAHAHA!
TIGERS ARE THE MASTERS OF STEALTH WHEN THEY'RE ON THE HUNT!
I STILL HAVE A FIGHTING CHANCE!

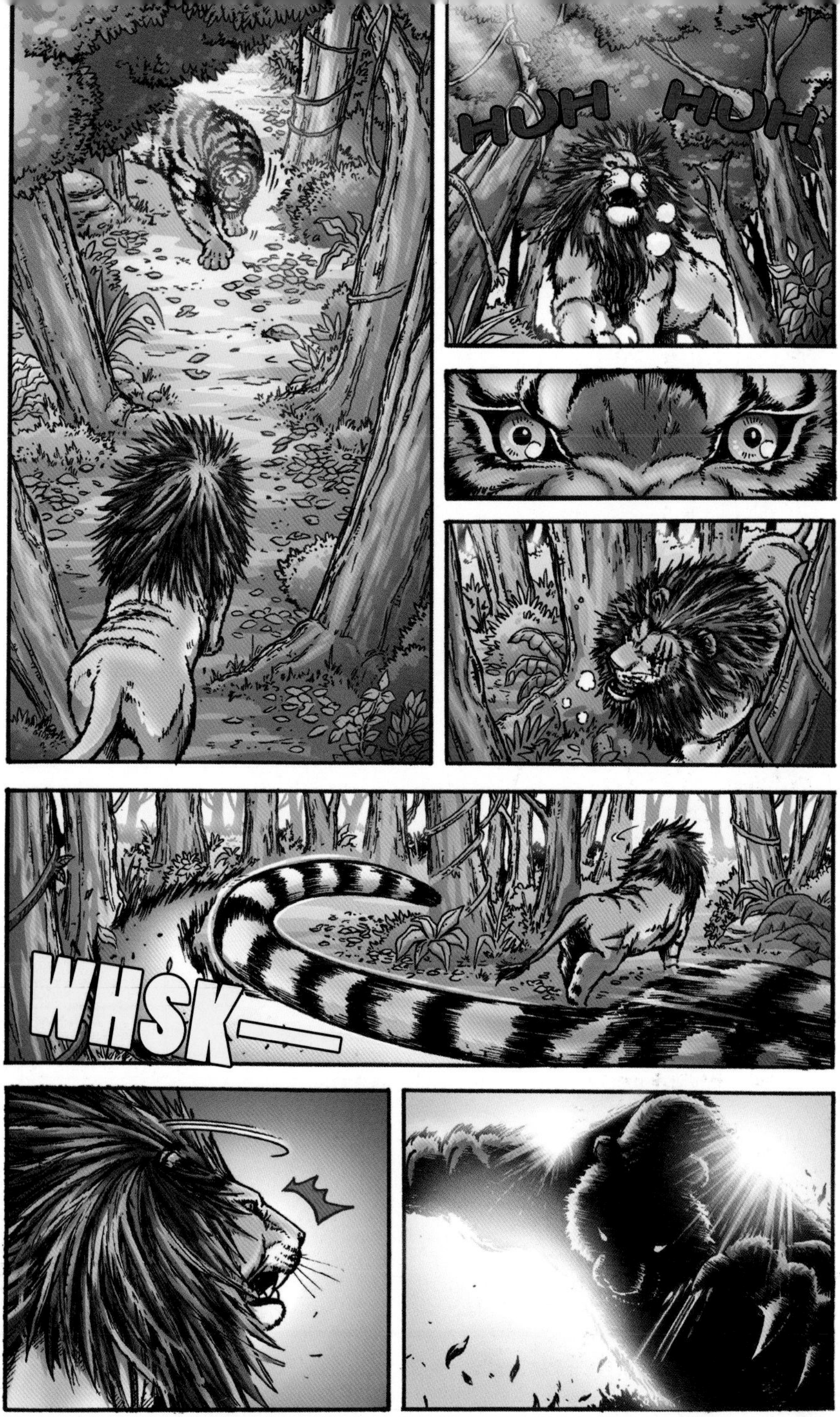
HUH HUH
WHSK—

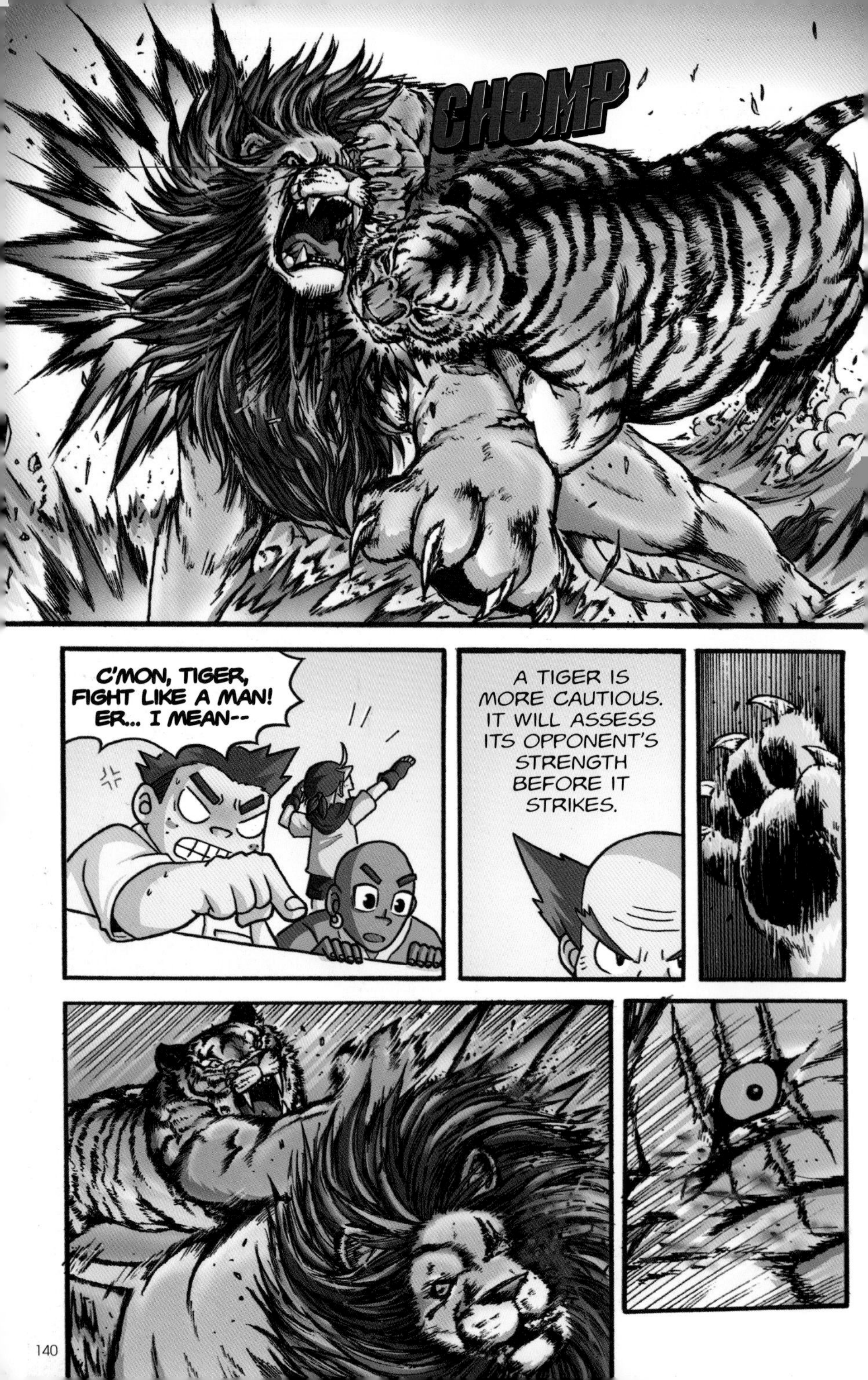
CHOMP
C'MON, TIGER, FIGHT LIKE A MAN! ER... I MEAN--
A TIGER IS MORE CAUTIOUS. IT WILL ASSESS ITS OPPONENT'S STRENGTH BEFORE IT STRIKES.

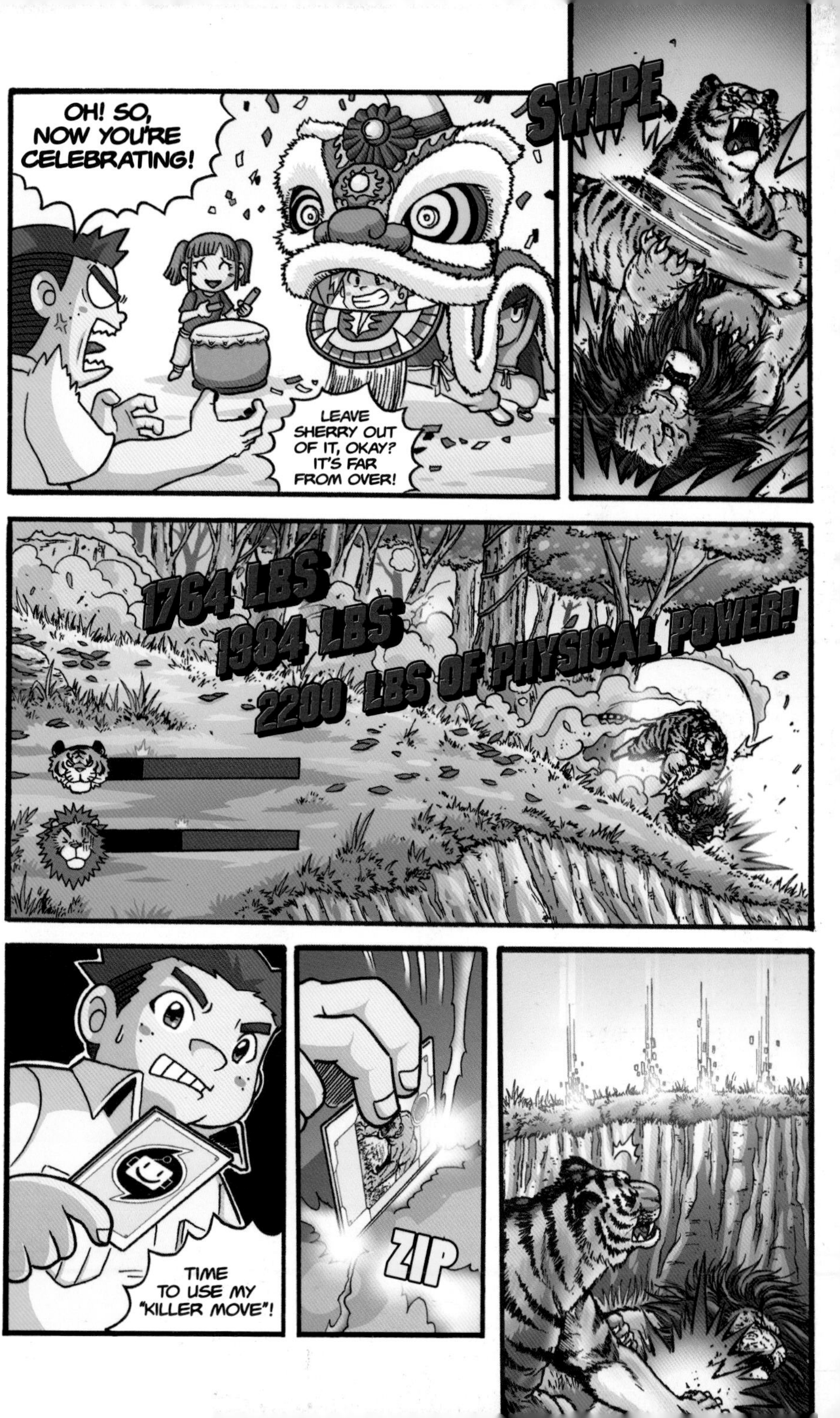
OH! SO, NOW YOU'RE CELEBRATING!
LEAVE SHERRY OUT OF IT, OKAY? IT'S FAR FROM OVER!
SWIPE
1764 LBS
1984 LBS
2200 LBS OF PHYSICAL POWER!
TIME TO USE MY "KILLER MOVE"!
ZIP

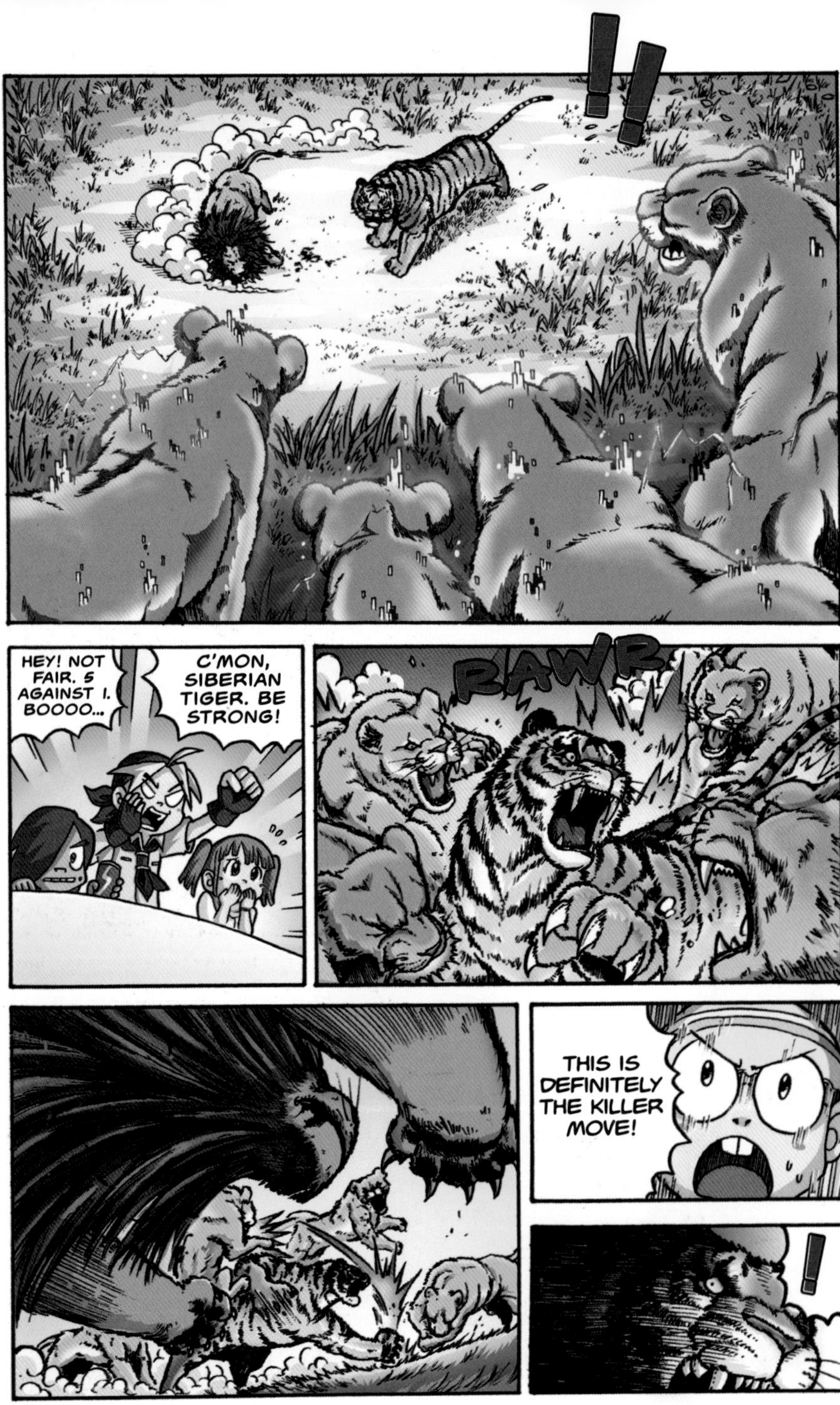
HEY! NOT FAIR. 5 AGAINST 1. BOOOO...
C'MON, SIBERIAN TIGER. BE STRONG!
RAWR
THIS IS DEFINITELY THE KILLER MOVE!

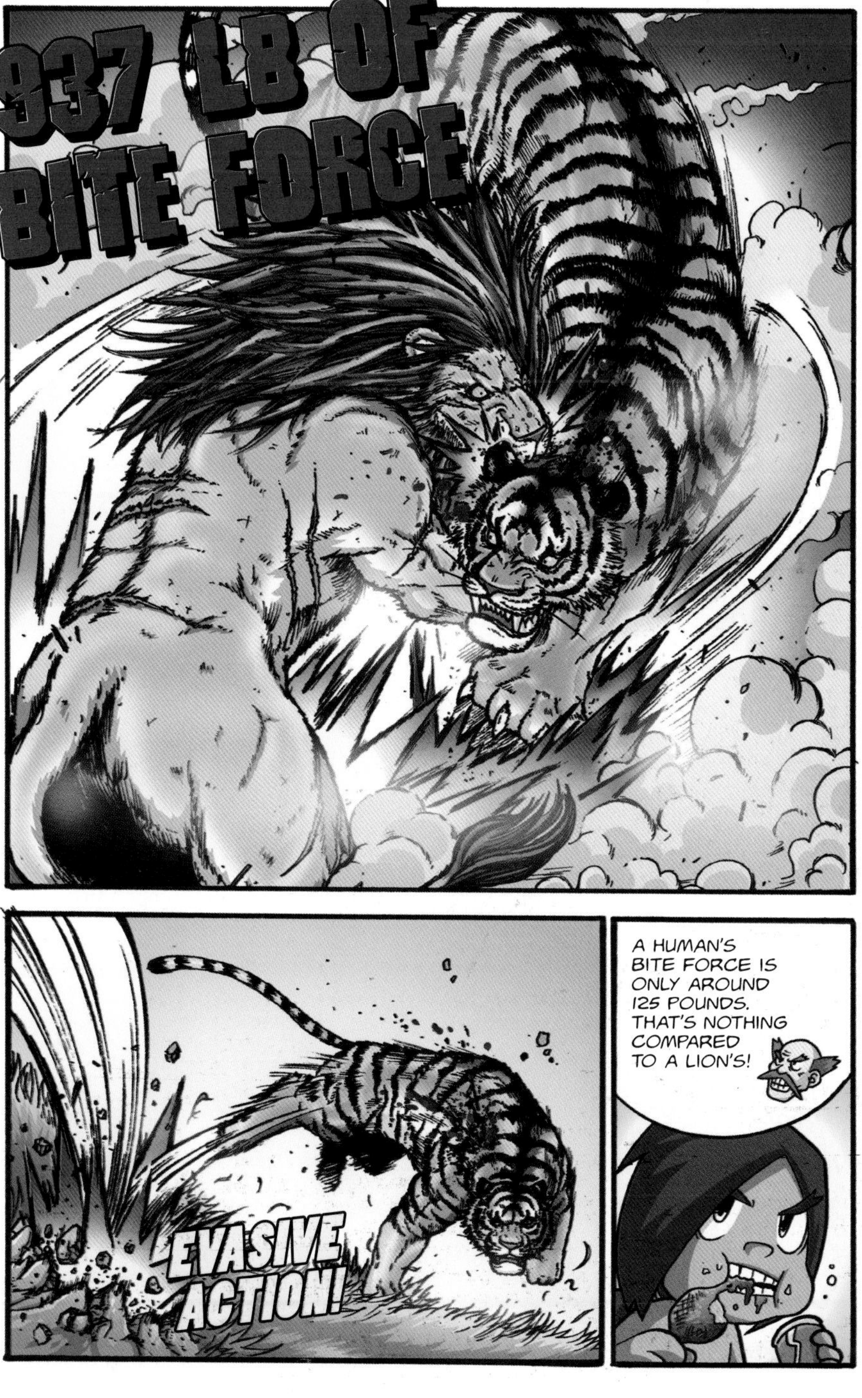
937 LB OF BITE FORCE
EVASIVE ACTION!
A HUMAN'S BITE FORCE IS ONLY AROUND 125 POUNDS. THAT'S NOTHING COMPARED TO A LION'S!

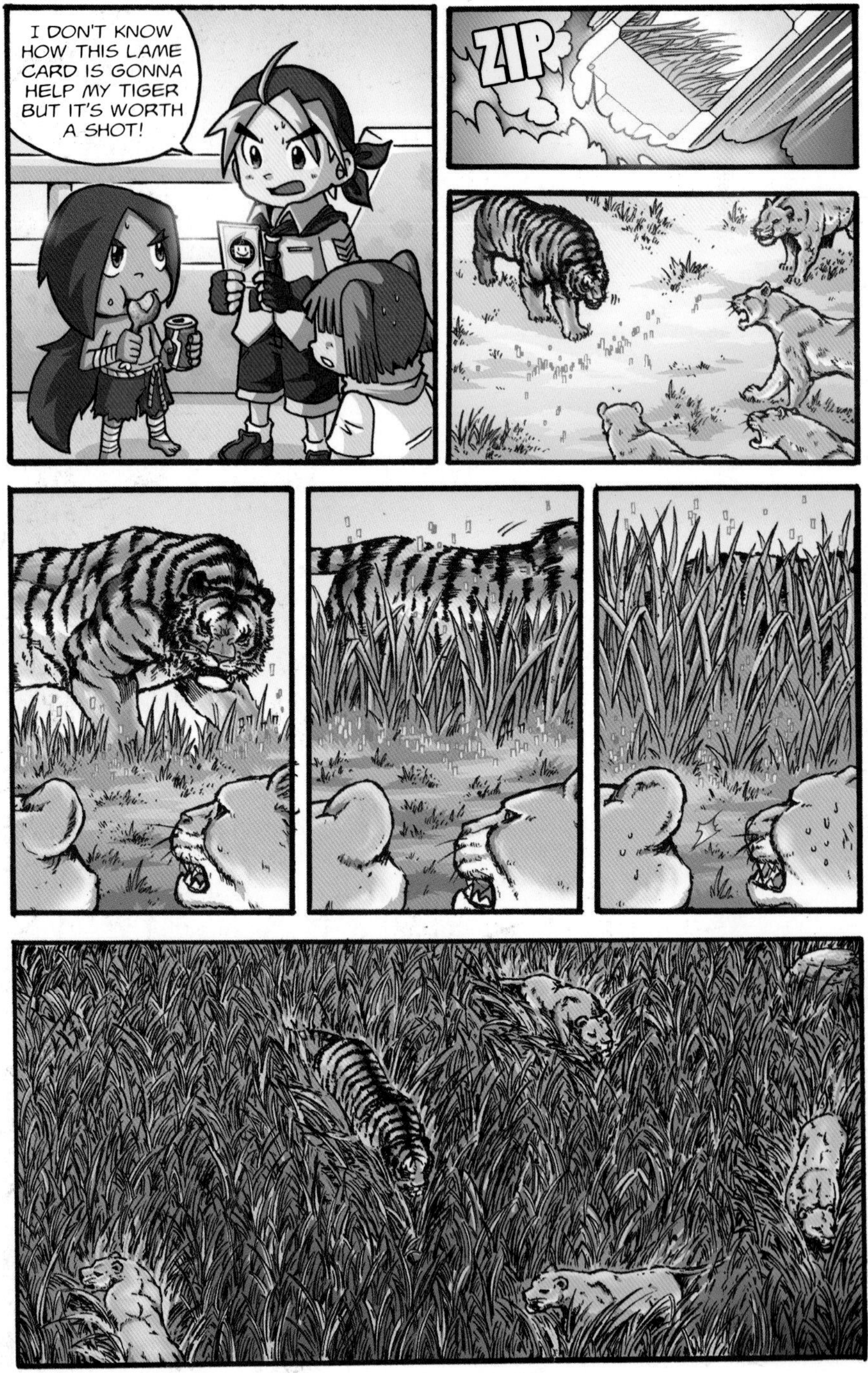
I DON'T KNOW HOW THIS LAME CARD IS GONNA HELP MY TIGER BUT IT'S WORTH A SHOT!
ZIP

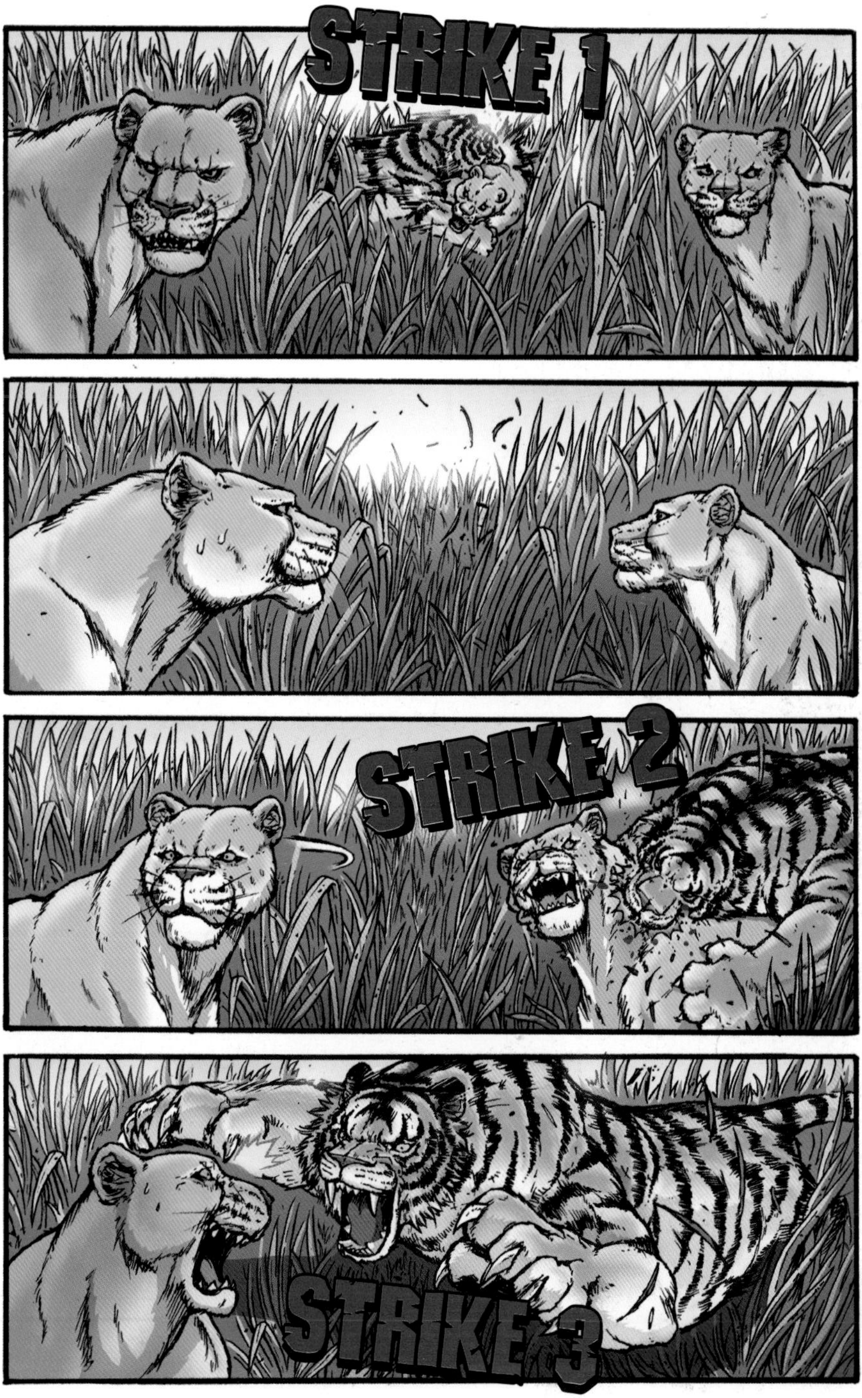
STRIKE 1
STRIKE 2
STRIKE 3

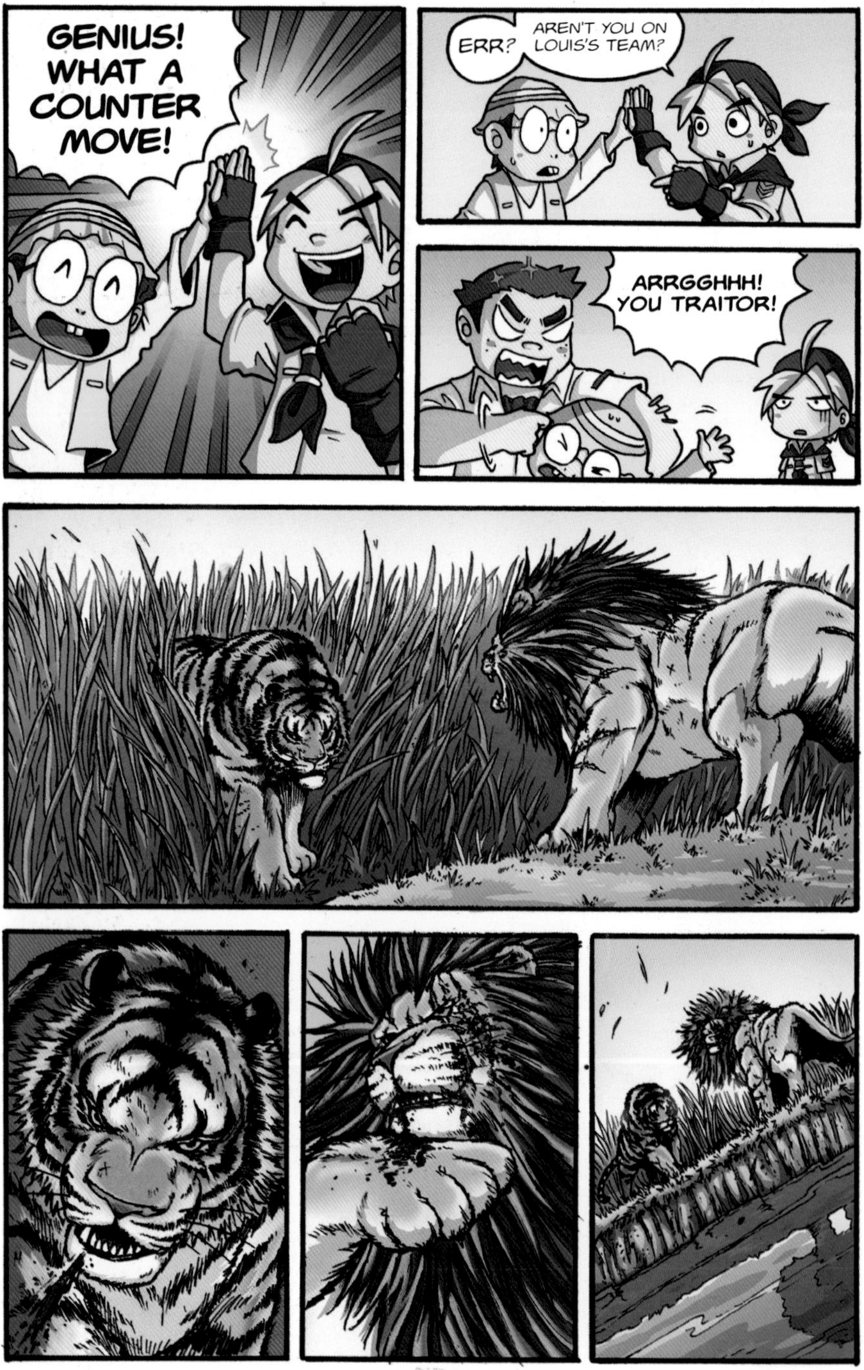
GENIUS! WHAT A COUNTER MOVE!
ERR?
AREN'T YOU ON LOUIS'S TEAM?
ARRGGHHH! YOU TRAITOR!

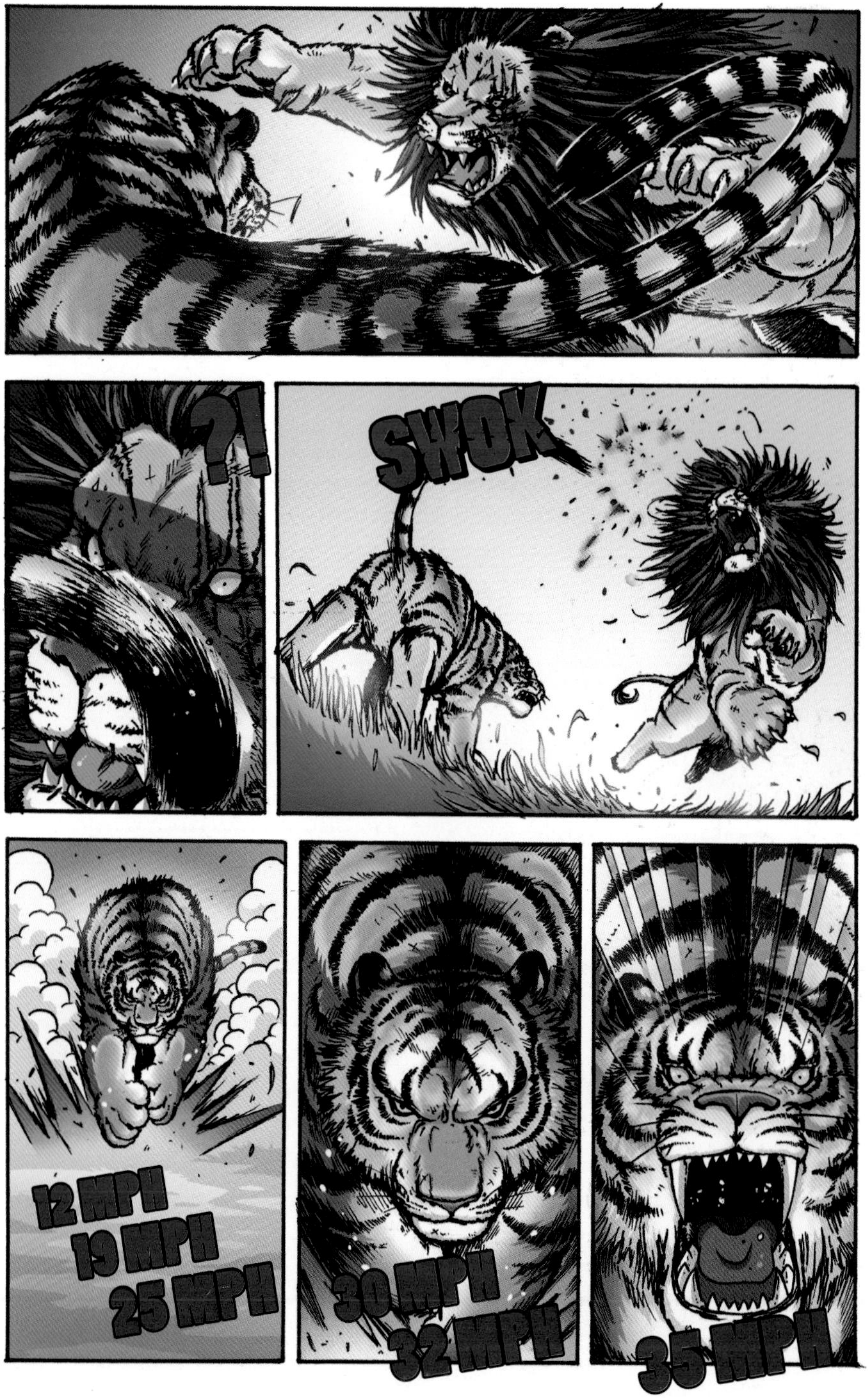
?!
SWOK
12 MPH
19 MPH
25 MPH
30 MPH
32 MPH
35 MPH

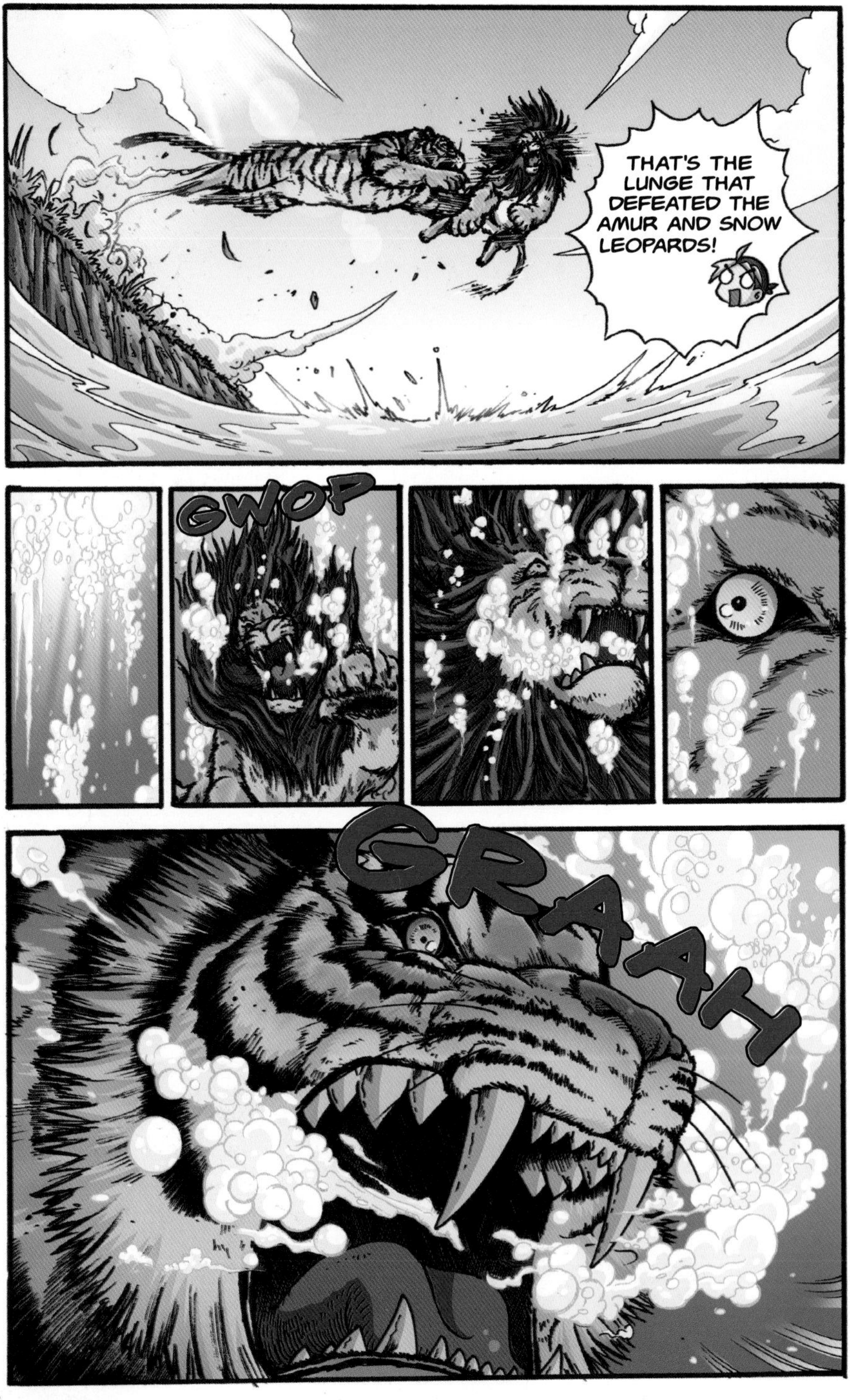
THAT'S THE LUNGE THAT DEFEATED THE AMUR AND SNOW LEOPARDS!
GWOP
GRAAAH

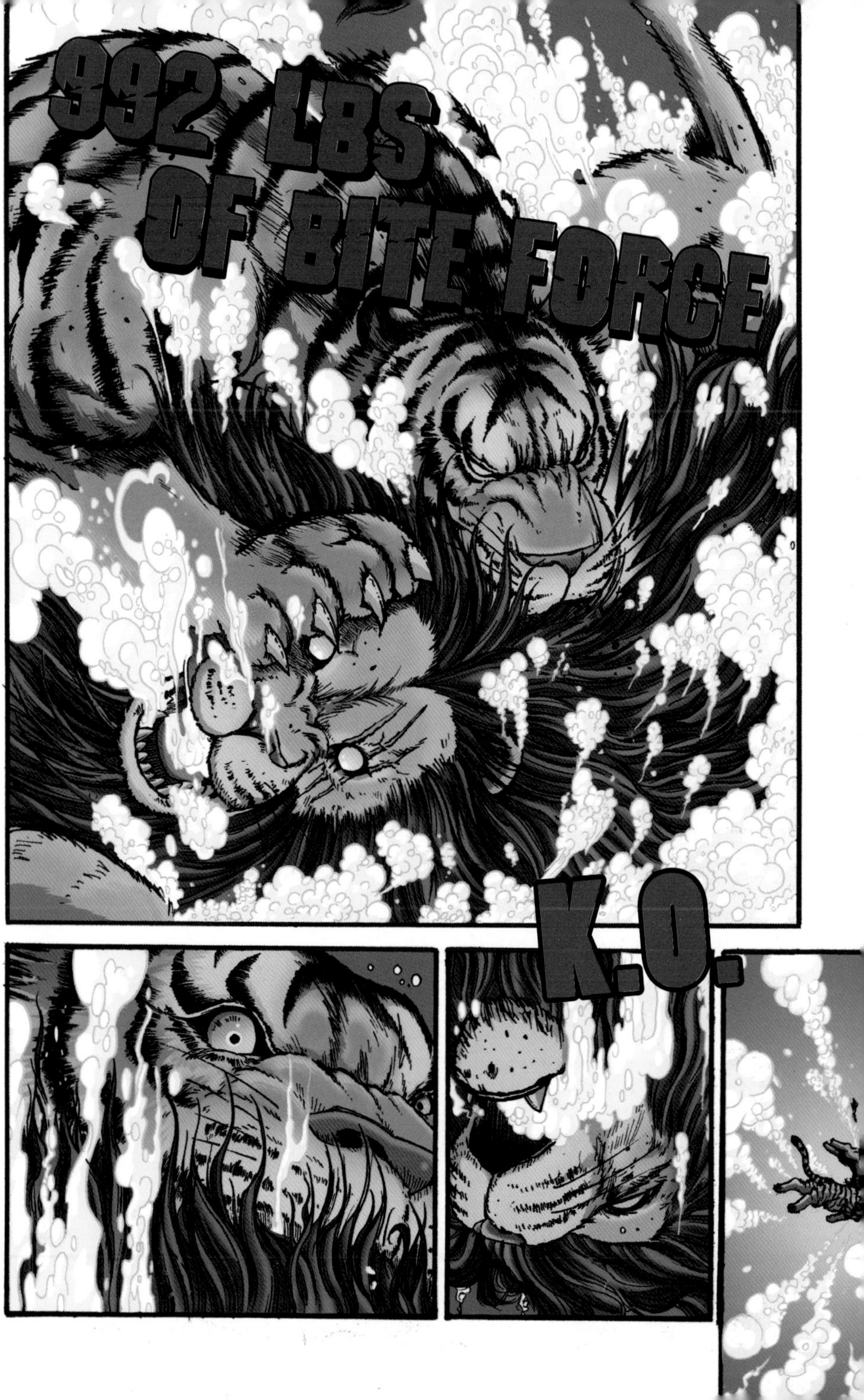
992 LBS
OF BITE FORCE
K.O.

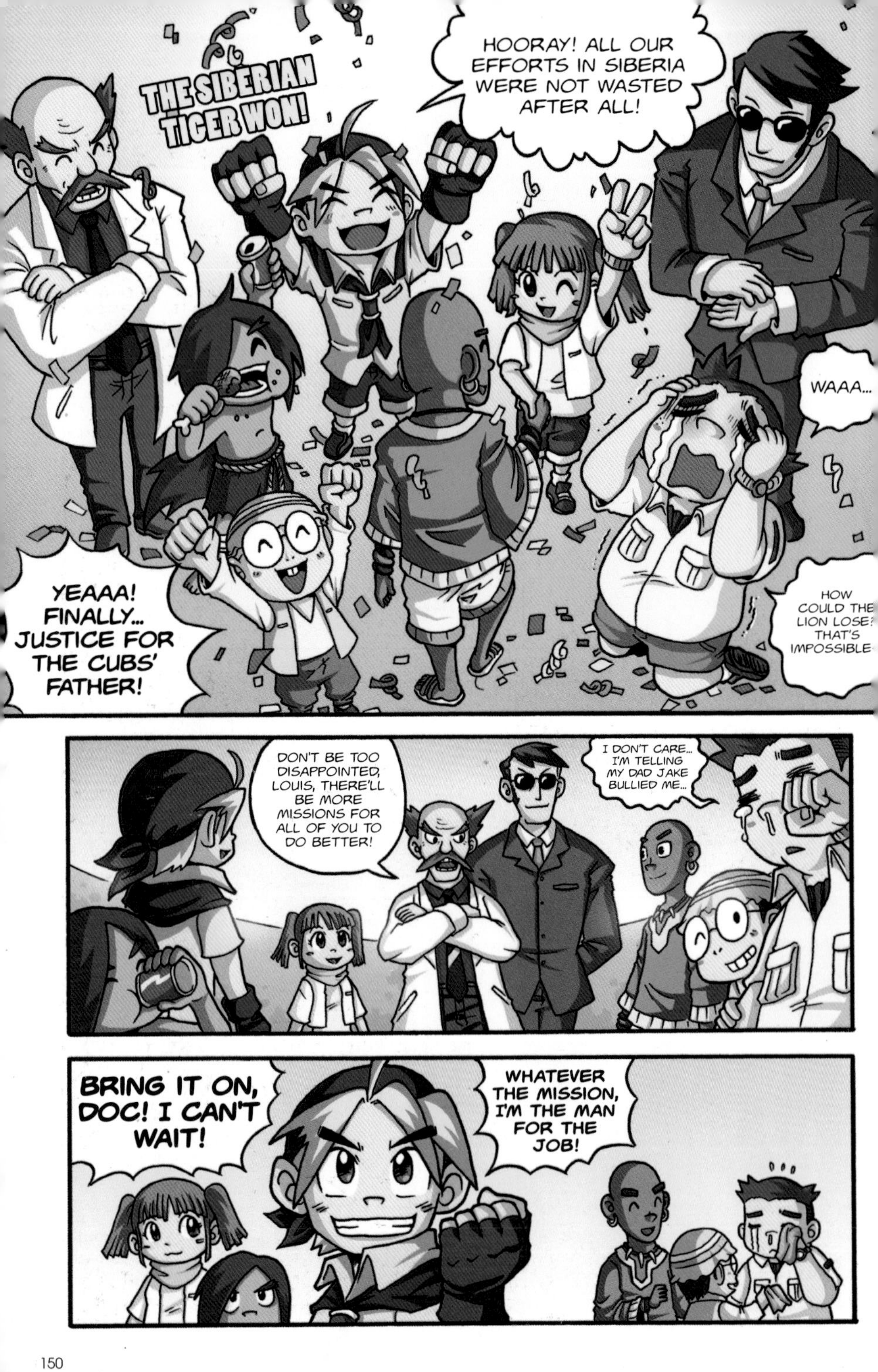
THE SIBERIAN TIGER WON!
HOORAY! ALL OUR EFFORTS IN SIBERIA WERE NOT WASTED AFTER ALL!
WAAA...
YEAAA! FINALLY... JUSTICE FOR THE CUBS' FATHER!
HOW COULD THE LION LOSE? THAT'S IMPOSSIBLE
DON'T BE TOO DISAPPOINTED, LOUIS, THERE'LL BE MORE MISSIONS FOR ALL OF YOU TO DO BETTER!
I DON'T CARE... I'M TELLING MY DAD JAKE BULLIED ME...
BRING IT ON, DOC! I CAN'T WAIT!
WHATEVER THE MISSION, I'M THE MAN FOR THE JOB!

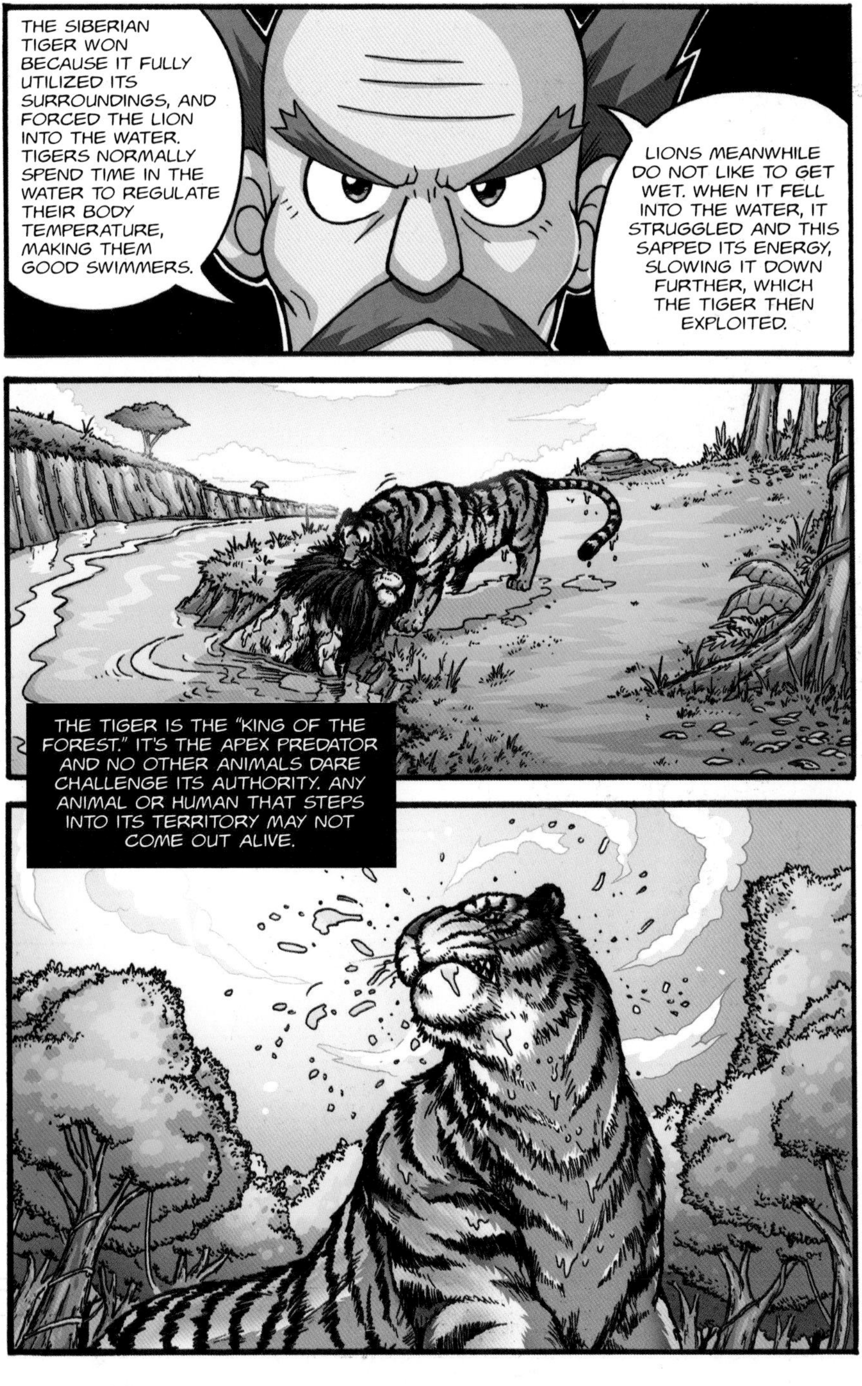
THE SIBERIAN TIGER WON BECAUSE IT FULLY UTILIZED ITS SURROUNDINGS, AND FORCED THE LION INTO THE WATER. TIGERS NORMALLY SPEND TIME IN THE WATER TO REGULATE THEIR BODY TEMPERATURE, MAKING THEM GOOD SWIMMERS.
LIONS MEANWHILE DO NOT LIKE TO GET WET. WHEN IT FELL INTO THE WATER, IT STRUGGLED AND THIS SAPPED ITS ENERGY, SLOWING IT DOWN FURTHER, WHICH THE TIGER THEN EXPLOITED.
THE TIGER IS THE "KING OF THE FOREST." IT'S THE APEX PREDATOR AND NO OTHER ANIMALS DARE CHALLENGE ITS AUTHORITY. ANY ANIMAL OR HUMAN THAT STEPS INTO ITS TERRITORY MAY NOT COME OUT ALIVE.

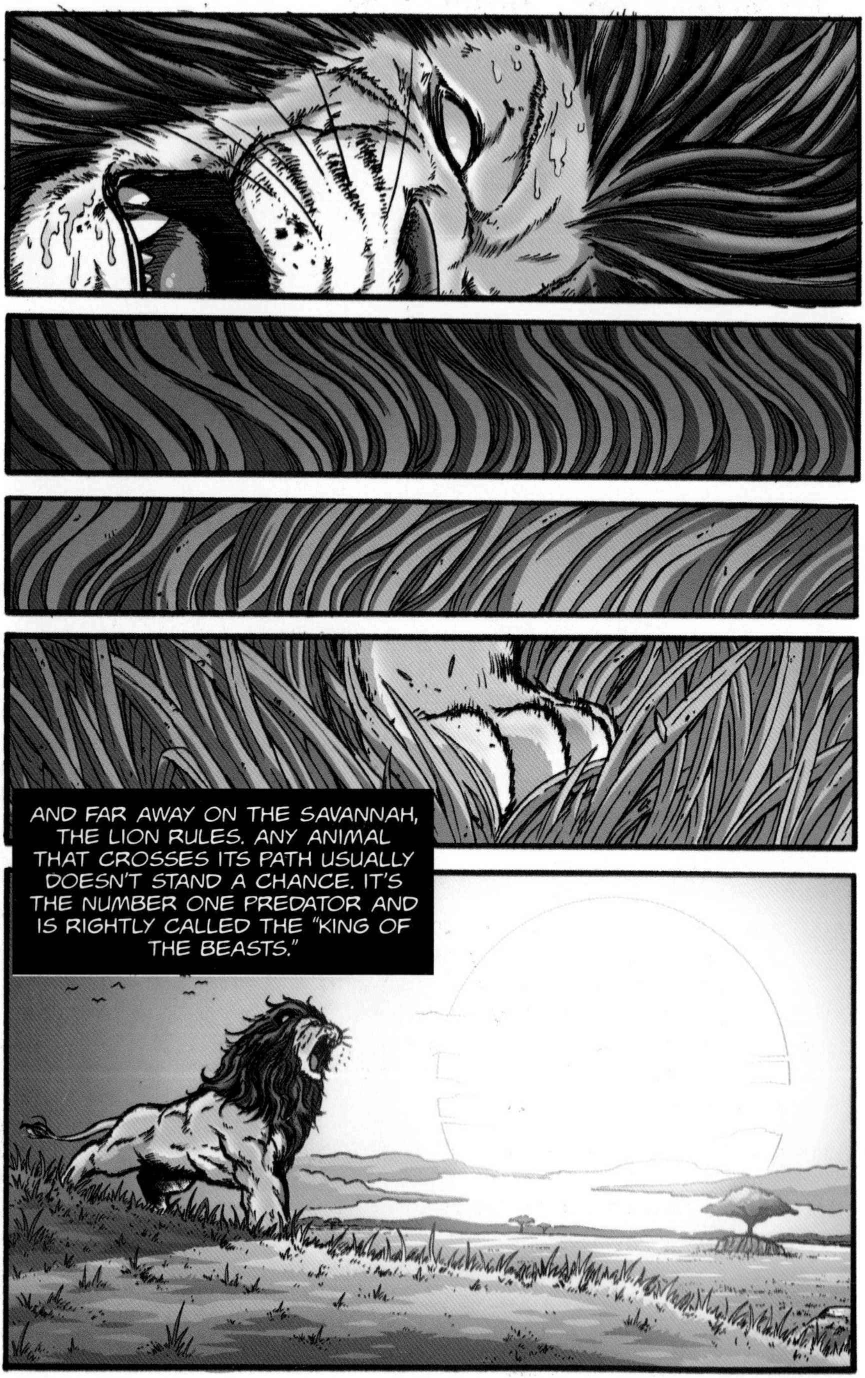
AND FAR AWAY ON THE SAVANNAH, THE LION RULES. ANY ANIMAL THAT CROSSES ITS PATH USUALLY DOESN'T STAND A CHANCE. IT'S THE NUMBER ONE PREDATOR AND IS RIGHTLY CALLED THE "KING OF THE BEASTS."

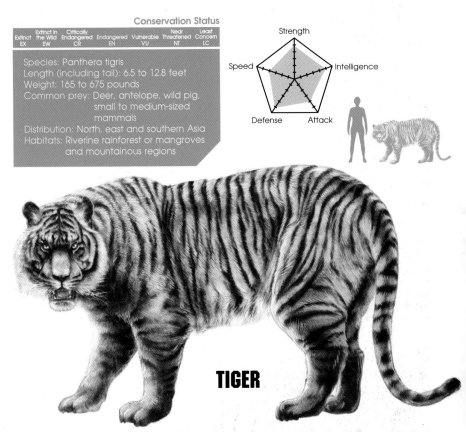

Conservation Status

Extinct EX	Extinct in the Wild EW	Critically Endangered CR	Endangered EN	Vulnerable VU	Near Threatened NT	Least Concern LC

Species: Panthera tigris
Length (including tail): 6.5 to 12.8 feet
Weight: 165 to 675 pounds
Common prey: Deer, antelope, wild pig, small to medium-sized mammals
Distribution: North, east and southern Asia
Habitats: Riverine rainforest or mangroves and mountainous regions

Strength
Speed — Intelligence
Defense — Attack

TIGER

The tiger is the largest felid in the cat family and displays the largest variation in extant species and size. From nine tiger subspecies, three (the Bali, Caspian and Javan tiger) are extinct. The remaining six are the Bengal or Indian, Indochinese, Malayan, Sumatran (smallest), Siberian (largest) and South China tiger. Adult tigers lead solitary lives, and use defecation as a means of marking their territories, which they jealously protect. Cubs are brought up by mature females, leaving to fend for themselves by the age 2 years.

Tigers are predominantly nocturnal. Despite their ability to run 31 to 37 miles per hour, they are more inclined to stalk than chase prey. Tigers knock their prey off balance before killing them with a bite to the neck. If the tiger cannot finish the kill in one sitting, it will be hidden, to be consumed over a period of days.

We are the tiger's only enemy. In the past 100 years, their habitat has shrunk by 93% due to deforestation, poaching, and social expansion. The illegal trade of tiger parts for purported medicinal value has added to the decline in tiger populations, leaving only several thousand in the wild today.

White tigers rarely occur in the wild and are the result of a recessive gene present most notably in Bengal tigers. The presence of dark stripes indicates it is not an albino, a common misconception. Fascination has caused the breeding of white tigers to increase in captivity, to the detriment of the creature, which experiences a greater likelihood of being born with physical defects, such as cleft palates and scoliosis (curvature of the spine).

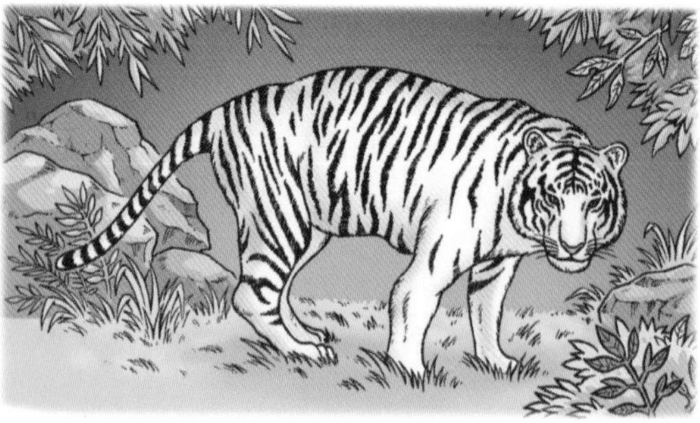

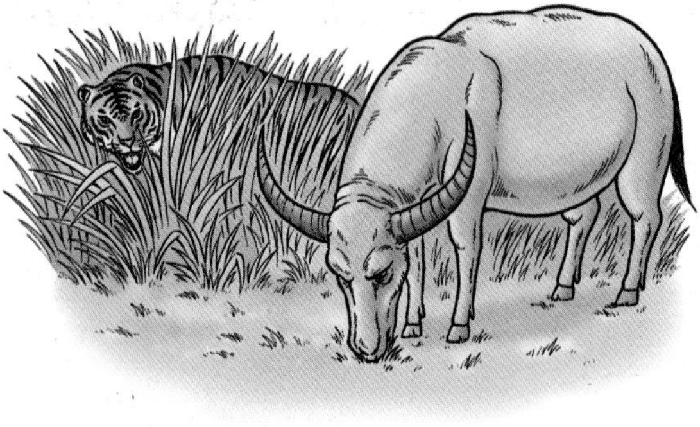

A tiger's stripes serve to identify them individually, much in the way our fingerprints make us unique. This alternating orange — black markings afford it great camouflage in the long grasses of its habitat, rendering them virtually invisible, until it is too late!

Like its South American cousin the jaguar, tigers are expert swimmers, capable of continuing the hunt in the water. Tigers, like all cats, cannot regulate body heat through sweat as they lack sweat glands, meaning swimming also serves to cool them down.

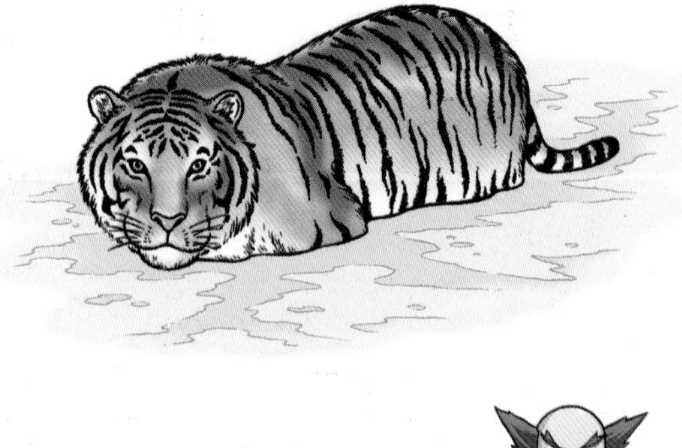

DID YOU KNOW?

Tigers living in temperate regions are lighter and bigger, while tigers in the tropical countries, on the other hand, are darker and smaller.

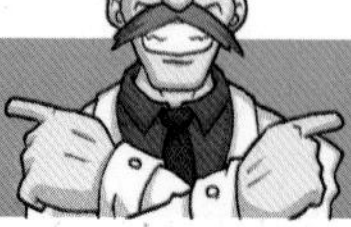

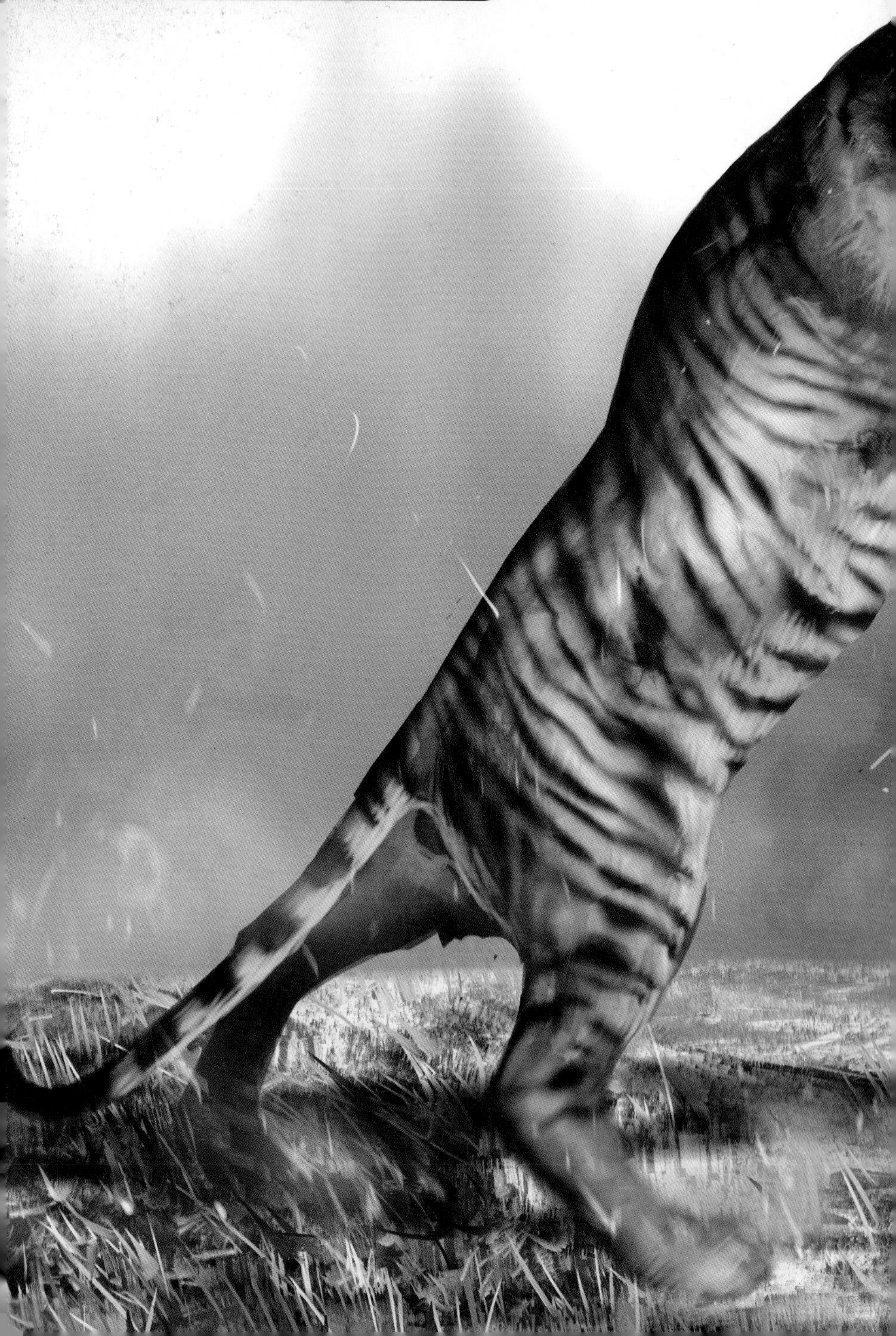

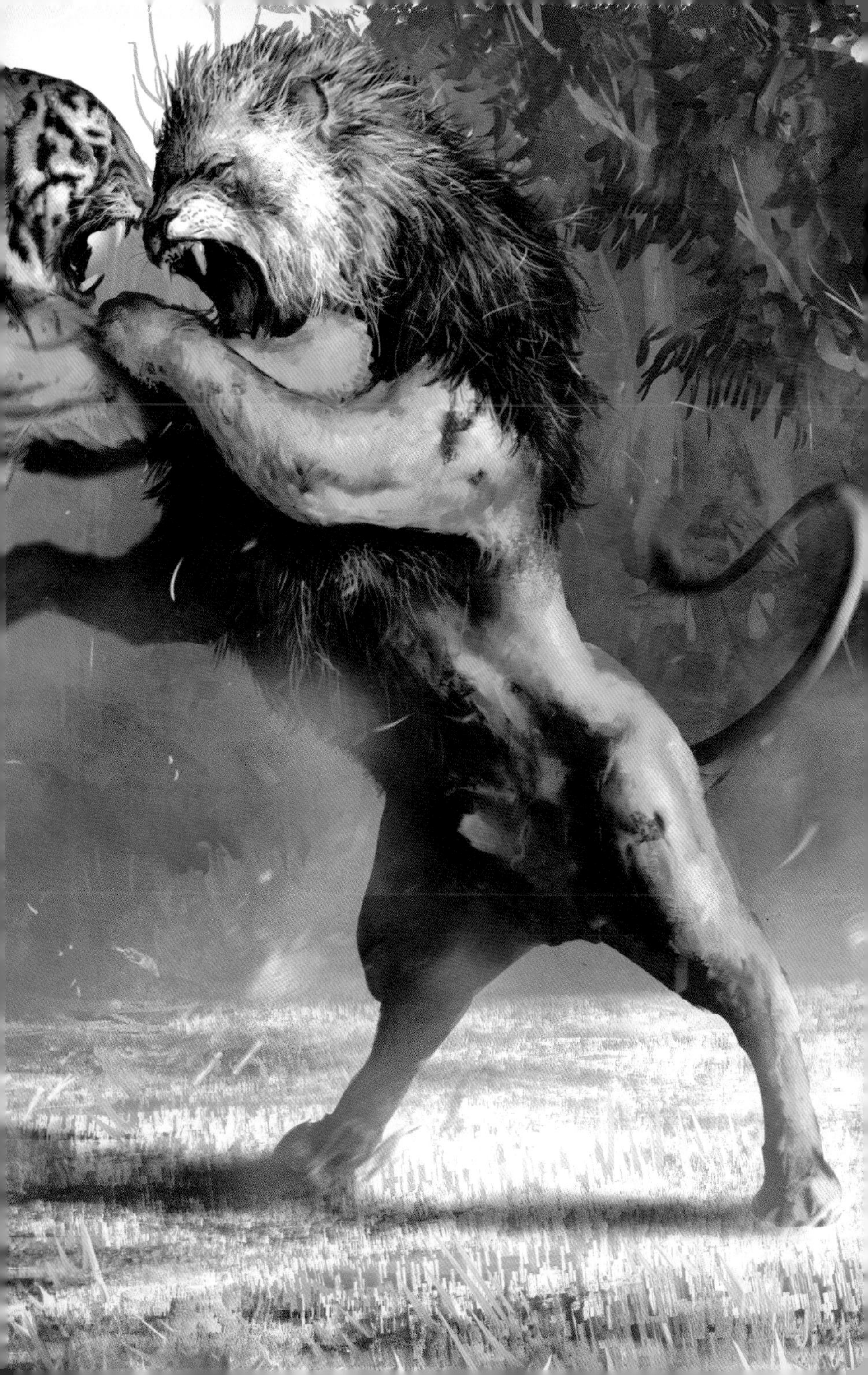

EXERCISE

01 **Which of the following animals is not a felid?**
   A. Lion   **B.** Elephant   **C.** Eurasian Lynx

02 Which is the originator of family Felidae?

A. Pseudaelurus   **B.** Smilodon   **C.** Proailurus

 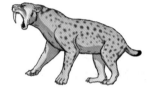 

03 **What is the main feature of the Sumatran tiger?**
   A. Light-colored fur
   B. Smallest tiger species
   C. Widely-spaced stripes

04 Which cat has its claws and the end of its limbs covered by thick hair?

   A. Sand cat   **B.** Serval   **C.** Fishing cat

05 **What is the function of the long hair on the tips of the ears of Eurasian lynx?**
   A. To observe its surroundings
   B. For decoration
   C. To enhance its hearing

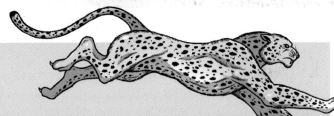

06 What is the cheetah's estimated top speed?

A. 31 mph   **B.** 43.5 mph   **C.** 62 mph

07 Which part of the snow leopard helps it to maintain balance while climbing and running?

A. Its long, thick tail

B. Its small rounded ears

C. Its thick insulating fur

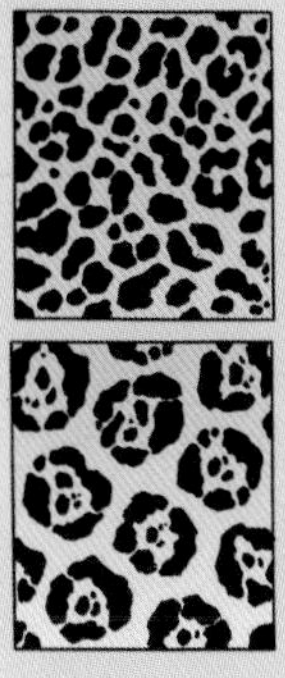

08 What is the difference between the cheetah and leopard's spots?

A. Cheetah spots appear three months after birth. Leopard cubs are born spotted.

B. Leopard spots are arranged in "rosettes," whereas cheetah spots are scattered loosely.

C. Cheetah spots aren't as dark as a leopard's spots.

09 Which family member of the lion pride gets priority to eat first?

A. Female lions

B. Male lions

C. Cubs

10 The white tiger is observed more in which subspecies?

A. Siberian tiger   **B.** Malayan tiger   **C.** Bengal tiger

HERE YOU GO...

01B 02C 03B 04A 05C
06C 07A 08B 09B 10C

PERFECT 10!

I'm not a born genius, it's just that I do a lot of reading in my free time!

SCORED 8 TO 9

To achieve my ambition, I must try harder!

SCORED 6 TO 7

Seeing animals in action in their natural habitat is much more interesting than researching sterile facts!

SCORED 4 TO 5

Sometimes I.... find difficult... to speak what... I know, but... I will not give up!

SCORED 2 TO 3

Huh? B-but I love observing animals! This must change!

SCORED 0 TO 1

What?! Jake is smarter than me? No way!